THE
LIGHTNING
STENOGRAPHY
DEVICE

THE LIGHTNING STENOGRAPHY DEVICE

M. F. SULLIVAN

The Lightning Stenography Device
© 2018 M. F. Sullivan
ISBN: 978-0-9965395-3-1

Text: M. F. Sullivan
Editing: Michelle Hope
Cover Design: Nuno Moreira
Typesetting: Jennifer Cant

Web: www.paintedblindpublishing.com
Email: m.frances.sullivan@gmail.com

Printed in the United States of America

SECOND EDITION

*A king's secret it is prudent to keep, but the works of God
are to be declared and made known.
Praise them with due honor.*

—Tobit 12:7

*This is a work of fiction. Names, characters, businesses, places,
events and incidents are either products of the author's imagination
or used in a fictitious manner. Any resemblance to actual persons,
living or dead, is purely coincidental.*

—Minerva Reinholdt

Mount Ida

I

The dissent of Hermes began, not with the creation of their Device, but with the morning his brother dropped the first printout beside breakfast's hash browns. This, at the time, engendered disinterest. "Are you branching into fiction, Enoch?"

"I fell asleep with the Device on my head and woke up to this."

For a man who claimed to have slept, Hermes's sibling had the bloodshot eyes and three-day beard of a man on a bender. High with inspiration, Enoch tapped the printout. "This is incredible. Revelatory."

Skeptical, Hermes squinted at the page which presaged their conversation. He wiped his mouth with his lavender napkin (one of the good ones he'd taken out for Easter, whatever that was worth); he sipped his water; he read his actions on the page; then, he said to his brother, "This is a most disturbing discovery, my dear."

"'Disturbing'? It's amazing! Who wrote this story? It wasn't me, and it surely wasn't you."

"I assure you: while you worked long into the night, I was asleep."

"Working all night was the plan, but coffee wasn't enough. And good thing, too. If it wasn't you or me who wrote this story, don't you see who it must have been? Whose narrative voice it's written in?"

Arching a pale brow, Hermes studied the page again, slid the wire-framed glasses from his nose, and said, "Surely you don't suppose it's the work of God."

"Why not?" With another, brighter laugh, Enoch snatched up the page and mimicked his brother's permanently preoccupied tone as he read, "'I just don't think that sounds like a feasible proposition.' This, Hermes caught himself saying only once he had said it. With a humorless mien for his brother's growing amusement, he rose to clear the table. 'Nor do I agree with the characterization of my attitude as "humorless."'"

"That is sufficient," said Hermes, briskly smoothing the sleeves of his white silk shirt. "At any rate, I am not so certain that the presence of this—story," he said with audible disdain for the offending page, "indicates anything more than the nature of your very active imagination, which, evidently, cannot allow itself to rest even in sleep."

"So God, then."

"Your imagination—your sleeping right brain—produced, while you slept, a story." His left hand momentarily refused to cooperate in buttoning his right sleeve. "A model of the universe, perhaps, and no doubt an influence on the conversation we are having by way of a kind of unconscious suggestion, but to say that this is the work of God..." Hermes laughed and patted the hand of his still-smiling younger brother. "I just don't think that sounds like a feasible proposition."

This, Hermes caught himself saying only once he had said it. With a humorless mien for his brother's growing amusement, he rose to clear the table. "Nor do I agree with the characterization of my attitude as 'humorless'. If this is indeed the work of the Lord, perhaps He might do with a good editor. Someone to declutter those adverbs."

"Well, the page is running out, so from here I'm as blind to our conversation as you. Happier?"

"We shall see; though how am I to know if I do not have a page to tell me?" Batting blond lashes and making no effort to hide his small smirk at the roll of his brother's eyes, Hermes busied himself with the dishes, feeling haloed by a sensation most uncanny. They had been working their whole lives to produce the Device, all things having, in retrospect, led to the production of the prototype which was still so new it seemed unreal. Had it not been their choice? Inspired, perhaps, by the plight of an arthritic writer-mother, but—

"It's not so much that anybody needs this sort of thing," said Enoch, then adding with some consideration, "in fact, it's probably not healthy for the average person to experience something like this." A frown crossed beneath his stubble while he pushed himself from the table. As Enoch watched the pasture, horses ambled beyond the window. "I'm still processing all of it." Again, in as merry and strange a mood as he was, Enoch laughed, then seemed stirred by his laughter and, a hand over his mouth, gazed out among the horses. "I really didn't write that, Hermes."

"I know you didn't consciously write it."

"Unconsciously, sure, but if something is done unconsciously, who's doing it? Especially something like this, a prescient story. I mean, my God, Hermes. That little band of metal and wires upstairs: we made that. Sure, you made a genius algorithm to clarify the low-resolution data recorded through the skull, but it's still just a computer program. Just a Device. All it does is replace the act of typing on a keyboard: thought to text. You can't have the text if you're not thinking, right? But who's doing the thinking if the sleeping brain is the entity producing it?"

Lips compressed, Hermes focused out his own window, on the rams which idled to gnaw a few spots of wet grass near the distant edge of the fence. "Why would God be interested in writing a story about us, if that is indeed what you are getting at? Further, why would God be interested in writing a story at all, when He has created a whole world, and the act of story writing—indeed, all creative acts—are a paltry parody of the ultimate act of so-called deific creation?"

Rocking back on his heels, then forward to brace himself against the edge of the window, Enoch pressed his face so close to the glass that both his reflection and breath were rendered visible to the brother who came to his side. "What if this story is the reason why anything exists at all? What if the act of writing the story brings the world into being? To create a human being who can write a story, you make a whole world, but maybe the inverse is true. Maybe you need a story for the world to exist."

"Perhaps were we characters in a book, that would be true, but we are far more than all that! We have existed our whole lives, after all. A whole train of memories lies behind us, running down the track. That is the narrative you mean. You mean our memories."

With a once-over for his brother, Enoch asked, "Have we really existed all that time? What evidence do you have of our thirty-five, thirty-three years against the eternity of the universe? The past is intangible. It could just be a setup put into our heads right this very moment, and you and I have just begun to exist now, or now, or now. Or do we really exist at all?"

"One has tangible evidence of memories. You made this table, dear man." Hermes patted the oak dining table. "It was just after mother died, remember?"

"Of course I remember. I'm not really trying to say the past didn't happen. It did. Or, we perceive it as having happened; we have mementos of it and everything to indicate that it did happen. But really, the past is just as real as the future. All we have is this single moment, this tiny"—his eyes drifted to the knots of the hardwood floor, then, reverently, toward the ceiling—"thread of cognition. This single moment in time. Without any interface by which to experience it, by which to make something real, something can't be experienced and can't be said to be real; but this reality, this artifice, is held by so tenuous a thing as a thread. As a story, presaging a conversation between two brothers. To write that story, you'd have to build a whole world of people, things, physical and chemical laws, shapes, colors, technology—everything. Just to write a single story. To paint a single painting. To relate to somebody a story about some brothers."

But Hermes had the distinct feeling that the story would prove more than just that. Outwardly, he maintained skepticism. Inwardly, he trembled with wonder for the mystery unfurling before him, for, of course, his brother was quite right. There was a kind of logic puzzle at work here: an experience waiting to be had by way of the Device. Placing a hand upon his brother's forearm, Hermes said, "I should like very much to observe this phenomenon. If it would not be too troublesome for you, perhaps tonight we will try to replicate the experiment."

Nodding, Enoch told him, "I was going to ask you, actually, if you could make sure I'm not just crazy and sleep-writing." With a grin, the younger brother watched over the horses. "There's no real way to prove this thing that's happening. That's the weird part, the scary part. From the outside, once all this is said and done, anybody who reads the final story will think it's written after the fact. That it's me, dabbling in fiction, like you said. But it's not me. It's really not me."

"I know you don't think it is you," insisted Hermes with another, gentler pat, his tone of voice softening. "We shall see what it is and get the matter sorted out, one way or another."

2

Neither seemed reassured by the notion, nor convinced that a completed story produced by Enoch's sleeping brain would answer more questions than it raised. Each man went about his day in eerie unease, half focused on work around their ranch at the base of Mount Ida, a Colorado mountain overlooking the historic home left them by their late mother. The manual labor filled much time and was good for a thinking man: Enoch was always a proponent of physical activities as a method of rousing the brain in the morning, and though Hermes was less inclined to spend time out of doors unless it was to photograph cemeteries for his genealogical hobby, he had a certain appreciation for the care of livestock which he could not deny. Once he'd fed the animals, however, he shut himself inside again, comfortable in the office where he was free to read or write or tinker with the code of the Device's word processor to further improve its efficiency. As important as was the hardware's functioning, so too was the speed and accuracy of the processor; the entire point was that it transmit information at the speed of thought. Until that day, Hermes had only been interested in maintaining the highest speed and resolution. Now, he scanned the code for something else. Some explanation for the result Enoch had discovered. But, of course, Hermes knew the secret to this could not be found in the code, the mere delivery system for whatever functions occurred in the sleep-bound brain; any explanation for this dreaming story was hidden within the human mind and its sleep cycles. For all the years he and his brother had spent endeavoring to create this device, they, or at least Hermes, had never considered the very basic question of what might happen to the sleeping mind while wearing it. But the question now screamed at him, and behind it arose a host of other, far more disturbing concerns.

Jaw set, Hermes shut off his computer and sat back in his seat, much as, that night, he would make himself as comfortable as possible in a chair beside his brother's bed. The younger man wore upon his head the crown of wires that was the fruit of their long labor, and slept in a way so peaceful Hermes might only envy. The actual process of dreaming, of course, would not begin for some time; until then, Hermes, with *Finnegans Wake* in his lap, waited for something to happen.

The idea of anything happening was still, to Hermes, rather absurd. This was because the very nature of the Device required one's intention to write. It was, at its heart, the same as holding a pen, after all, and if one fell asleep holding a pen, one did not awaken to Rimbaud! At least, Hermes did not; he had not asked the same of his younger brother before his going to sleep. It was a strange and absurd idea, that there was something so very sentient lodged within the human mind that it could presage the entirety of a breakfast conversation. Surely it was some vastly impractical and lucky prank; surely there was an explanation which did not call into question anything untoward. Hermes had long since settled his mind on the idea of God, after all. God, and any truth about the idea, was unknowable. Priests were deluded egoists and new-age cultists were acidheads who had taken the whole thing too far. Atheists who worshiped science were the same thing as the religious who confused their model of reality with the be-all-end-all of explanations. When it came to what man knew or didn't, there was no winner, and Hermes was sure there never could be.

It was an hour and a half before anything happened, and two hours before the writing began. Though Enoch was the neurotechnologist, more thoroughly acquainted with the operation of the brain, Hermes was aware of the pre-REM nature of sleep's delta waves and found himself intrigued to note that the Device interpreted these as the letter *D*. He would have to adjust the programming, he mused, to print delta waves with the Greek letter. A funny thing, that letter: the fourth letter of the Greek alphabet, and yet, delineated by a triangle. A square was a more sensible shape, was it not? But then, Hermes supposed there was dual meaning to the shape. After all, a triangle was made up of three sides *and* the whole, creating, then, a separate figure which was the culmination of the triumvirate: the "true" triangle. A sort of independent entity. One had "Triangle A," made up of three sides, and "Triangle B," the triangle as a seamless unit; and though they were the same, they were just subtle enough in distinction that it seemed more akin to a kind of transposition, of one state upon another: of the completed state upon the in-progress state.

The arrival of the words which broke the scroll of delta placeholders required a few seconds to draw Hermes from his musing on the fourth letter of the Greeks. In the outset muddled by delta noise, the text soon organized itself into a conversation so eerily familiar that Hermes, a rational man, lowered his book to sit forward just as the narrative resumed:

DDDmiDDDghtDdoDDwiDth DDDa good editor. Someone to declutter those adverbs."

"Well, the page is running out, so from here I'm blind to our conversation as you. Happier?"

"We shall see; though how am I to know if I do not have a page to tell me?"

Hermes watched the unfurling of the text with a silence thicker than that of a cathedral in its off hours. The page recalled the conversation with his brother exactly as it had happened: their movements, all their ways of being were catalogued as if by some additional observer, some alien, inward or outward, beyond perception, beyond knowing, thinking, reasoning. Something which knew everything about everything. Something which dwelt in the dreaming mind of his brother, yet which knew Hermes's thoughts not moments before: thoughts displayed in a way which raced his heart. As he reread his musing on the nature of the letter "delta," lips parted, glasses long removed, Hermes's eyes filled with tears. Hand to his mouth, he rose from the chair and crept from what had once been their mother's bedroom to lower himself to the floor of the hallway where, kissing the wood floor, he wept.

"Oh, God! My God! My God—" A breath sharper than a knife pierced the depths of his lungs and welled his eyes with another wave of tears. "My Lord, my God, all this time I have denied what I thought I could not know!"

Lips trembling, the elder brother rose to stumble through the dark of their house, unfamiliar, as if he had not been raised there. Indeed, with a shock of nausea for Hermes, the very corner of the stairs leapt out to assault his knee with a force so sharp he could not help but fall away with a cry. Recovering himself against that house which attacked him, that house which ushered him out lest he wake his sleeping brother, Hermes stumbled down the final flight of stairs to sprint into the starry dark, where half the swirling cosmos was veiled by an overhang of pregnant clouds behind a mountain which dwarfed the very sky. Falling to his knees, hands alternately clasping and gripping the collar of his own shirt, Hermes could naught but say, "Please, please," and, "Oh, I am sorry. Oh, I see you!"

His brother, like all humans Hermes had ever known or read about, was not a telepath. Why, his brother could not even be said to have been present at the time of the strange story's creation, being as he was in the depths of a thick sleep! For the sleeping man, or the machine, to guess with such detail the nature of Hermes's thoughts there in the room, still and alone, would require an act of preternatural prescience. At the very least, it implied that his brother's dreaming brain was being used as an antenna, perhaps, or that the right brain was linked to the cosmic unconscious, maybe, or that, at the very least, there existed some nontemporal figure which seemed as though to drive the course of human events: to know them, start to finish, inward and outward, as their author.

As rain fell, at first a slow drip, the elder brother tore open the buttons of his shirt and fell back upon the blades of grass. Around him spun the cosmos. His mother, of all things, possessed him: how she had been a stern but kind woman; how she had been generous and maintained high expectations for both her sons. He recalled all the times he had disappointed her in some petty way, and all the times she had in turn disappointed him. Amazed, Hermes felt it all melt into meaninglessness. She was not his true mother, at any rate; both his parents seemed inside his heart, which he touched as he jolted up and said, "My Lord, my Lord! What would you have me do! What I would do for you, only to better know you. Ah," he smiled rapturously at the stars and cried, "tomorrow I shall take my turn with the Device! That's just the thing. Perhaps I can serve you in the manner of my brother."

Stumbling to his feet and blowing kisses to the rain, Hermes laughed and said, "There is no explanation for this. No, no explanation at all."

That night, as, in the room next door, Enoch's sleeping brain produced a story line by line, Hermes dreamt a strange symbol of what happened after death: He imagined being in a laboratory, either the fourth and newest in a group of scientists, or some invisible observer who lurked along the sidelines. In the center of the lab was a square pool raised from the floor, and into this pool was placed a tiny man no more than a few centimeters tall. While in this pool, the fellow seemed to struggle to remember what he was, and the scientists took notation on how long it would take him to remember. "Maybe I'm a rat," said the man, and, briefly, he was a rat. "A worm, perhaps," and like that, then, he was a worm. But at last, after all of these transformations in the strange plasmic pool, the being which had once been a small man said at last, "Aha! I remember. I remember what I am!" And, transforming into a golden thread, he wiggled from the pool and drifted off into the aether, into which he disappeared. Pleased, evidently, by this progress, the scientists murmured among themselves, took a few notes on their clipboards, and then Hermes awoke, strangely reassured.

The rain which had begun the night before seemed disinterested in letting up. As Hermes grated potatoes, Enoch rubbed eyes shadowed despite eight hours of rest.

"Did you sleep well?" asked Hermes, his encouraging tone doing a poor job of hiding his excitement. "I noticed you didn't bring a printout of last night's efforts. Was it that disappointing an experiment?"

His brother snorted, a man trying to laugh but not quite able. "It was fine. Ended up being, uh, about four thousand words, so far."

"An incredible length!" Unable to restrain his delight, Hermes jerked from his cooking. "May I see it?"

Enoch focused on the fog between himself and the muddy pasture. "I still have to print it. Poor horses, having to tromp around in the rain to get any exercise."

"A little rain is good for the soul." Pausing, hip leaning against the counter, Hermes tilted his head and assessed the increasingly haggard appearance of his little brother. "You're beginning to concern me. Did you discover something disturbing hidden in those pages? Some troubling implications, perhaps bleak foreshadowing?"

"I couldn't say." Rubbing the bridge of his nose, Enoch amended, "It was mostly about you, as it happens. Mostly stuff that had already happened, and some of this conversation. How you're going to ask me if you can use the Device tonight."

"May I?" asked Hermes with a winsome bat of black eyes, which made his blue-eyed brother laugh for the first that dreary morning.

"You can. I'm just worried what we'll find."

The noise of displeasure which followed was for himself as much for his brother, for no sooner had Hermes begun to open his mouth than the hand with the potato slipped and skinned the knuckle of his left index finger. Lifting it to his mouth and then turning to wash it, he said, "Only yesterday you awoke so excited you could hardly express your thoughts, and today, for no reason at all, you seem to be developing some tedious sense of dread."

"Yeah, this all has me thinking. Magritte. *The Treachery of Images.*"

"*Ceci n'est pas une pipe,*" recalled the older brother, frowning at the blood welling in the folds of his flesh. "Yes, Enoch, I can see from my own early vantage in this thought experiment how easy it is to arrive at the piece."

"Neither is the image a pipe, nor is the word 'pipe' actually the thing which it defines." His broad fingers extended toward the same table so studied yesterday. "But what about the thing itself? Like this 'table.'" He stopped short of touching it at the last second and faced the brother, who watched Enoch the way Enoch watched everything else. "This table is just a word. A word and a perception. Sensum organized into a physical representation of the memories and places and things and relations all attached to this table. And it's all the words that organize the memory. The real treachery of images," he said, at last easing with reluctance into his seat at the head of the table, "is that we think we're observing three-dimensional space. We think we're observing a world which is...independent of us."

"And what are we observing," asked Hermes, sliding the potatoes into a bowl of ice water before flipping on the burner, "if not images? If not time, if not space?"

"Words," was all that Enoch said.

3

The day dragged on, each second of work around the house or with the program of their Device intended by Hermes to bridge the gap between himself and his opportunity to fall asleep with the band around his head. Why, if his brother's mind had been so able to probe into his own, or at least act as the outlet of something which could probe into his own, then Hermes had a duty to see what might come of his! Excitement filled him as he reread that morning's printout. Though he confessed that the growing storm seemed to be setting a troubling tone when he read it on paper, it was a matter of perspective. Hermes loved the rain, himself: a good thunderstorm was welcome, even if thunderstorms worried his brother with the prospect of fires. Calamity could not deter a man's passion for that most sublime show of nature. The performance forecast no omens of profound abatement as night further blackened the already black day and their Internet connection was lost, a minor inconvenience like the gap between "now" and "later." Every passing moment reeled him closer to that which he longed to experience: firsthand evidence of God, interacting with him. What an extraordinary thing that would be! Such a queer thing. A terrifying thing; a sublime thing. That night, with the laptop arranged upon his nightstand, Hermes slipped the crown of wires upon his head with all the reverence he might a genuine diadem, activated the word processor, and went to bed.

Every Western child knows how difficult a thing it is to fall asleep awaiting Santa. No one could ever know this anticipation, or how it was made more difficult by the way the headband clutched his skull, its wires digging into his scalp to prevent any semblance of comfortable contact with the pillow. It was only with much shifting and turning and focus on breathing that Hermes slept, and then, only by midnight, when the storm hushed for him; but after a thick and dreamless sleep from which he awoke as though he had been unconscious ten minutes, Hermes confirmed the storm's respite was temporary. Outside the bedroom window, it had become a downright tempest, and he thought not of the animals, but of his brother, who, he was certain, ensured the beasts were comforted amid the raging storm. There he was, going stall to stall in the stable of the mind's eye, whispering to each horse and kissing their noses and stroking their faces, then stopping over to coo and pat the horns of the rams. Hermes slid the Device from his head and rose, trembling.

The author of the Device's software gazed out the window, the headband clutched to his chest, then up at the ceiling. He crossed himself with his right hand as his mother had tried to teach him, and as had only interested Enoch. What had once been a hollow gesture was beginning to become imbued with meaning for reasons he could not articulate. There was a significance in it, this gesture of the cross, not because some man was hung on it, but for some reason more profound. Quivering to predict how precious a thing would be this achievement of the Lord through him, the elder of the brothers came around his bed, sank to his knees, and smiled as he scrolled through the field of triangles with which he had augmented the program the day prior. Page after page, he scrolled, his pace hurrying as they began to seem without end until, with a nauseous disappointment which began as a lump in his throat, Hermes reached the top of the document and found not a single cogent phrase recorded.

"Did I not sleep?" he asked himself, the computer, the Device. "Did I not wear it through the night? Perhaps it sat askew upon my head."

But no: he knew in his heart such a thing was not the least bit true. Lips parted, eyes scanning fruitlessly through unbroken pages of triangles, Hermes gazed at the ceiling, then back down at what he had hoped to contain some religious work, or some assurance of his future, or some gift of knowledge or understanding. But this was not even words! Just delta waves. Perhaps he had not entered REM sleep. Surely that was it. He had not dreamed, and dreaming was a requirement to channel a story in one's sleep! Yes, that was it.

He had just reached this conclusion when, downstairs, the front door slammed open, polluting the house with the roar of the gale as Enoch, having comforted the animals as much as he could without bringing them into the house, reentered. Sitting up, Hermes straightened his bedclothes and smoothed back his hair, and by the time he was striding down the stairs still in pajamas, his brother had extricated himself from his sopping raincoat and was bent untying his boots.

The creak of a stair beneath the older brother's bare foot merited a lift of the younger's wary eyes. Hermes felt obliged to speak first. "You ought to have awoken me. Here I am in my pajamas, and you have been working since...well, one cannot rightly call it 'dawn' outside."

That got half a chuckle from his brother, who was, for whatever reason, becoming drained of humor as the days went by. Hermes decided it was the lack of sunshine as Enoch unlaced his right boot. "I just didn't want to wake you up. Don't worry about it. Besides, you had your experiment up and running. How'd it go?"

"Poorly. I do not recall any dreams last night, and when I awoke, the Device had recorded fifty pages of delta waves. Nothing at all like what I observed with you. Tell me, when you dream while you wear the Device—"

"I don't remember having dreams while wearing the Device," said Enoch, straightening as he kicked off his left boot and unpeeled soaked socks from wet feet. "Though, that's not entirely true. I think I remember something about Mom, maybe. Selling us eggs or something. But I don't know. I'm hazy on the details. That was just the first night I got writing out of it. The second night, when you were there as I fell asleep, I didn't dream."

"I see," said Hermes, still not wholly convinced that this was not an issue of REM sleep. "May I try again tonight?"

"Be my guest," said Enoch, ascending the stairs past his older brother. "Do whatever you want with it."

How unlike his brother to say such a thing! Hermes opened his mouth, but too soon the man was at the landing, around the corner, and gone, upstairs. The older sibling could not help but feel that probing too deeply into the subject would be ill-advised, Enoch having just come in out of the rain. Rolling up his sleeves, Hermes went, as usual, to make breakfast, and one of the soft-boiled eggs cracked in the pan, which irritated him because they had not kept chickens for a year. Not since Enoch had decided he wanted them to go into town more often. Eggs were a commodity most precious. Did his brother's dream portend this, or did his spoon slip as he lowered the egg because he had heard the dream? It didn't matter. They would have to leave the property soon, whatever the answer. It was undeniable that Hermes detested venturing out, and though he was reluctant to consider himself a shut-in, it was increasingly true that he was, say, "an eccentric and reclusive scholar," of sorts. That was a far better label, and how he would ensure himself depicted when the Device brought them money. It would be one of the gifts they had given themselves through their work, and, in a way most curious, one of the gifts God had given them, for there was an exquisite perfection in every moment. Even last night's failed experiment he regarded with good cheer as he ate breakfast with his sullen brother and, in a strange reversal of roles, endeavored to play the cheerful one by suggesting, "I thought perhaps we'd play a bit of chess today, what with the rain. And then why not a film or two? Take a day off and relax ourselves, since we're housebound."

"I'm going to have to check on the animals," said Enoch toward the window, and Hermes went on, "Well, of course, but between the movies! Why not a Kubrick marathon—say, *The Shining* and *Barry Lyndon,* a double feature. That shall be a splendid pair with the rain."

With a slight snort from beneath a fallen curl, that black shock against the white of his face, Enoch said, "I suppose that sounds reasonable, but they're a little...heavy."

"You would prefer something lighter? Perhaps *Dr. Strangelove*?"

"No." His brother laughed out toward the pasture, toward the barn and the stables. "The first two are fine."

"And what of you?" Staring into his empty glass, then up at Enoch, Hermes arched a pale brow. "Are you fine?"

"I'm just...concerned."

"About?"

Enoch grimaced as, in the distance, a blade of lightning cleaved the sky. "It's serious out there," he said, thunder barking behind. "What did the weather report say before the connection was lost? Forty days and forty nights?"

"More like four more days and five more nights," said the older brother, which made the younger run his hands over his untrimmed whiskers and moan sadly.

"The horses," he said, "my poor horses."

"They shall be perfectly content to spend time in the barn. You'll see them frolicking in the jade of the field soon enough, I promise." When that earned no response, Hermes tried again. "You never told me your concern."

"My concern is that I've done everything I've set out to do, and I have nothing else."

Scoffing, Hermes began, "What an absurd notion," but Enoch went on, focused out the window, brother half-forgotten amid the rage of nature against their land.

"I have studied my entire life to create something grand. We've only really been serious since Leda died," he said to the portrait of the mother who stared out from above the kitchen doorway like an ascetic Madonna. "It seems like everything in our lives has led up to this point, and now..."

"It is the start of our grand career," finished joyful Hermes as he swept away the dishes. "Why not celebrate! Why not make a good time of it!"

"Because, what if this is it? What if this is what I do? I mean, this *is* what I do. What I'll be known for." Enoch laughed at himself, then at the ceiling. "'Enoch Anatida, cocreator of the of the first consumer thought to text Device...'"

"I would much prefer if you were to take full credit for it."

"I didn't create all of it, though. If it weren't for you, it never would have gotten anywhere. I mean, my God—you've done more than half."

"The software," admitted Hermes, pleased when his brother rebuffed. "If I didn't have you to rely on, I would have been at a desk, then sitting here alone when Mom died. You and I both know it—at least, I know it. And God knows it, too."

"We have no way of knowing what God knows," said Hermes, falling back into his default habit of assumption. "If God is anything, the fact that it is an entity sentient enough to produce an actual word through the human mind is stupendous. Would the Lord be able to speak at all, I wonder, if not for the existence of humans? Would there be a God at all, then?"

His brother stood. "I'm sort of surprised you haven't accepted it yet."

"Accepted what?" asked Hermes, as Enoch paused en route to the den to place a hand on his brother's shoulder.

"We have every way of knowing what God knows. God knows whatever we know. God knows everything that everybody knows. Everything everybody thinks. Everybody's potential, everybody's endgame. And I can't help but feel swamped by this. By what we've made. Because this is the thing the whole world will remember us for. Whatever I do, all of it after this will be nothing."

"Nonsense," said Hermes, though he had to admit that the man had a point. "There is a long and glorious road ahead. I should think you of all people would be able to see it."

4

That night, as before, Hermes felt aflutter with anticipation as he settled down to sleep. He had asked his brother to sit with him and ensure he did not toss and turn. This proved unnecessary; with the soft breathing of his brother as he read their mother's Bible (a book neither man had touched in twenty years, even with Enoch's professed half-faith), Hermes was soon to drift into a very sound slumber. It was only a matter of time before he was at a retail outlet in town with his brother, and an old man was trying very insistently to sell them a box of newsboy caps. The caps, the old man was saying, were just example caps—for what was wonderful about this box was that it was a hat-making kit, containing materials and instructions for many more hats like the twelve which came free in the box. Hermes was intrigued, even if uncertain he needed so many hats; though, he had to confess they were quite fine hats, and it was an unbeatable deal to receive such a great number of hats with the potential for so many more, at so small a cost as $12.99. When he awoke in a groggy malaise with no dream but that one on his mind, and his brother again out tending to the animals in the harrowing fury of the storm, Hermes slipped off the Device, leapt from his place, and, despite how low he kept his expectations when checking the laptop, was nevertheless crushed by the sight of ceaseless delta waves, a sight as bad (or worse) than corrupted data in a traditional word processor.

Why was this! Why, he had dreamed last night, hadn't he? Hadn't he entered REM sleep? He had, for he had dreamed. And if the Device had gone askew on his head, his brother would have been there to help him set it right, at least at the outset. Yet, there was nothing! Nothing at all. Not a thing reflected on the page but a load of nonsense which so blackened Hermes's heart that, as Enoch returned from the storm, the older sibling called from the top of the stairs, "I am afraid I am feeling rather ill this morning, my brother. Rather more tired than usual. Would you forgive me if I did not cook?"

"I'd be happy to do it," said Enoch, but Hermes insisted, "That isn't necessary; you do so much. Only let me rest, and I'll be fine." As his younger brother appeared at the bottom of the stairs, still damp from the storm but not quite so soggy as yesterday, Hermes asked, "How are the animals?"

"Restless."

"You should have woken me," he said just as he had the day before. At this ritual chiding, if nothing else, Enoch smiled.

Upstairs, Hermes removed the Device and the laptop from his room and replaced them both in his brother's office before returning to bed, where, surrounded by books, he alternately read and sulked like an indignant child. What did it mean? Why was it that his mind created nothing but delta waves? What was it that caused this wall of non-output when his brother seemed capable of channeling an entity which was, to some degree or another, omniscient? Or so it would seem, at any rate. It struck Hermes sometime midmorning that he had simply taken at face value the events of before, and had leapt to the conclusion that they indicated some sort of God. Really there was nothing to prove that Enoch was not making it up. For all Hermes knew, his brother was lying there, a more skilled writer than the man had ever expected, and a more skilled reader of body language. At least, a skilled predictor of Hermes's thought processes. After all, the output of the Device at work with Enoch's sleeping mind had probed so thoroughly into Hermes's internal monologue that it had been downright startling—but who was to say it was not just a good guess? A good guess of what Hermes might think, observing a screen filling up with *D*s, for "delta waves," and how triangles would be better suited, and how triangles were an odd fourth letter, and on, and on. This was not so unnatural a stream of consciousness, was it? This was not something which was impossible to predict or follow, surely?

It was not in his brother's nature to be deceptive, but as Hermes reclined in the leather couch while Enoch, wrapped in their mother's muddy afghan, played a game of solitaire, he considered this might be some demented ploy on the part of the younger man to convince the older to believe in God. It had been something of a minor sticking point between them, and each had mostly condescended to ignore the other's belief or nonbelief because each was so lackadaisical about his own opinion that, in the end, it didn't seem to matter: Enoch had belief in God but was not passionate about it, and Hermes had no belief in God but was not sure enough any one way to dissuade his younger brother into more rational thinking. Now Hermes was desperate to dissuade himself into more rational thinking, for the implications of anything else were far too vast and much too crushing. What all of this was beginning to imply, after all, was the idea of a God who played favorites: a God who favored Enoch, and not Hermes. At least, this was how it seemed to Hermes, who, as his brother slipped the king of diamonds from the second stack to the newly opened slot of the first, suggested, "Perhaps you had ought to take your turn with the Device tonight, Enoch. I cannot seem to replicate your result."

As he slapped upright a new trio of cards and contemplated the two of spades, the younger brother said, "Sure, I'll wear it. But I don't think it's going to help us prove anything."

"I am interested in exploring the issue. We have before us an opportunity to prove or disprove the existence of a possible God—or, at least, to come closer to comprehending the issue. Don't you suppose it is our duty to shoulder the problem?"

"It's the Device," he said, shifting the two atop a three and leaving himself with a seven, which did nothing but make him flip three more cards and produce the likewise-useless queen of diamonds. "The Device is our duty: the creation and propagation of the Device. Or my duty, anyway. You're liberated, Hermes. You can do whatever you want." Laughing, Enoch said, "You're not bound by some book being created by your sleeping mind."

"I was under the impression it was only a few pages long. Four thousand words, that was what you had me read. Hardly a book."

"It doesn't matter how many words it is," evaded his brother as he slapped over more cards, ran out the deck, and was forced to start again with the discards. "I feel hyperaware of the track to which my life is bound. I can feel it...rumbling. Feel the train off in the distance, getting closer all the time."

"And what is that train?"

"I hate to make predictions," said Enoch with a bitter smile, then turning down the cards and sighing. "I don't think it's happening."

"Do you remember what mother used to say when losing at solitaire?" When Enoch's eyes fell away, the older brother smiled. "'The Devil beat me.'"

5

That night, as they had three nights ago, the brothers arranged them-selves with Enoch as the sleeper and Hermes, the observer. This time, Hermes studied whether his brother truly slept. It certainly seemed for all the world that this was indeed the case, both based on the way he breathed and the way his brain produced delta waves. It was not, then, a matter of deception. What was it about Enoch which made his brain pick up where the four thousand words had left off, story rambling along as if it had never stopped, visibly picking up steam as the REM cycle drew on? As he observed the text beginning to emerge, his jaw tensed. Enoch talked about feeling as though his life were bound to a rail because of this story, but it was not even about him! Clearly, it was about Hermes. He was, after all, the viewpoint character, through which all perceptions were filtered, even though it came from Enoch's brain. Perhaps that was the source of the younger brother's foreboding; perhaps that was the source of Hermes's bitterness. For, if it was truly a story in which he was the main character, should he not have been the one producing it? Yet he had the feeling this story was one of those deceptive ones, where the viewpoint narrator is mostly there to allow the audience to get to know another person, or to experience and react to an event, or to explain the reasons behind a horrific tragedy. Yes, that was what this piece was shaping up to be: a tragedy.

But more than the hovering tragedy, intangible and yet unavoidable, Hermes felt only the toxic force of his umbrage. The Lord thought nothing of plumbing his mind to share with his brother, but could not do him the dignity of a miraculous feat of his own! What a thing his brother could do, after all. To channel a story in one's sleep was an accomplishment, a magic trick in the most genuine of senses. And Enoch did not appreciate it! Why, if Hermes were given such a skill, he would kiss every day the ground of the Earth, and praise every night the glow of the stars, and burn incense in offering, or pray, or meditate, or whatever else the Lord could ask.

Perhaps it was an issue of something that Hermes was not doing; this, he decided as the screen recounted his brother's card game. Perhaps it was something God wanted. Perhaps there was something obvious. Some expectation which required fulfillment, the way Enoch seemed so convinced that the Lord expected nothing from his life but the creation of the Device. It was easy to say all this was because Hermes was a nonbeliever, or because he did not pray, but Enoch was at best a semi-believer and did not pray either, so those explanations were out. The more Hermes thought about it, the more he considered this was the major problem of all religions: figuring out what God wanted. Did God want His people to love one another? To hate undesirables? Did God want His people to achieve their highest potential, or subjugate themselves to His wrath and tyranny? Did God want something pre-determined? Something out of the brothers' control? Could anything be said to be the result of free will, if that was the case? Or was he naught but a most convincing artificial intelligence, a lively character in the mind of some writer?

That might have been the sin, though: his questioning. He had been converted by the revelation, yet still sought to explain it. Was not the basis of faith the chalice of the heart, rather than the trap of the mind? It was not a subject with which Hermes had much personal familiarity, but it seemed to him true enough, just as it was true that since he had been forced to acknowledge the presence of God, he could never again deny it. He could only further descend into the tumultuous sea of belief, for it already seemed to him as if he had never not believed in God. It was as if all his life had been but preparation for belief, just as their whole working lives until this point seemed in preparation for the creation of the Device. This sense that he had until this point been, to some degree, guided, bolstered him onward, for if Hermes did something to prove to the Lord his faith not just in word but in action, then perhaps he might be forgiven his doubts! Perhaps he, too, might be given God's favor and awaken one morning to a story produced by the cycles of his dreams! But what was there to do? What was there he could possibly do? He had nothing to give, no way to repent, and a priest seemed an unnecessary interference between himself and this thing in him, which quite possibly was him in so many ways, and not him in so many ways—something above and beyond him, beyond all time and space and yet the ground for all time and space, which vibrated the very molecules of his body, or perhaps was proven by the vibrations of the molecules within his body. Vibrations which ever increased as he sat alone with his brother.

What was it about Enoch which made him special? What was it about him which picked up the signal of God, the signal his brother could only observe? *Was* it God? Was that the way to describe it? It was not right, necessarily, to call it "God." Not right to call it anything. Such a thing was powered by, yet stood beyond, that which one called "language." It was a thing which expressed itself in metaphors every-where, in everything, in the interactions of men with their fellows, of women with their lovers, of sons with parents, of brothers with sisters. There was one beautiful, singular thing which reached through all things, all works of poetry and music and writing and painting and song and dance and cooking and engineering and architecture and every blossom on every tree, and him, thought Hermes, thinking of his brother, and me: I, also, am a part of this one, beautiful, singular thing, and my anger is a part of this beautiful, singular thing. I have a right to be angry, he told himself, rising, feeling in his chest the beating of a lion's heart. My wrath, he decided while admiring the storm, is God's wrath: God is furious at me, and I am furious at myself, and so I will repent fury with fury.

Silent as his shadow in the dim light of the laptop, Hermes slipped from his sleeping brother's room and crept through the dark of the house. The house cooperated, every lacquered maple surface swelling for his passage down the stairs, each step imbued with confidence. All things in his life, after all, had driven him to this point, so this dark disappointment that he was not the favored brother in the eye of God was somehow also liberating. For what was said of the favored brother? More tragic things than favorable ones. Epimetheus, or the death of Castor, he recalled while drawing the boning knife from the kitchen block, and the fate of the Lamb went without mention!

In the storm, Hermes pulled his coat around him and clutched tight the blade of the kitchen knife, head lifted as the rain faded but the wind rose. Wading through the grass, he started for the sheepcotes where slept his treasured rams, for he thought to put one to the slaughter to repent for what he had done by disbelief of God. But he stopped himself, fell back upon his heel with the squelch of mud, and eyed the other structure on their land, dark stables he knew to be the color of raspberries, or his coat, or the barn. Two buildings: his rams, in the barn; Enoch's horses, in the stables. It was then that Hermes grasped a kind of magic. Haunted by his own intentions, he contemplated the knife in his hand as the storm began once more to rise.

When Enoch awoke the next morning, it was with a start so violent it also awoke Hermes, who had returned to his post in time to see the eight thousandth word lain on the page before falling asleep upright. Another thousand had appeared since, and Enoch slipped the headband from his temples, then read the night's product without acknowledging his brother. Hermes made a show of rubbing his face and yawning as he asked, "How did you sleep?"

"Did you hear them last night, or did I dream? I couldn't tell; it was all so vivid."

"What did you hear?"

"My horses. I thought I dreamed them crying last night."

"I wouldn't put much credence in a dream," chided Hermes, but Enoch was already stumbling for his trousers and yanking on socks.

"There's something wrong. I feel it. They might be sick."

"Perhaps," said Hermes, shadowing the younger man as he yanked on his shirt and charged downstairs. The older brother adjusted the cuff of his own crimson sleeve and smoothed wrinkles from arms crossed in sleep. "Perhaps the storm has sickened you. Perhaps you're hearing things."

Perhaps, but soon as Enoch's boots were on, he charged into the storm, which just that morning was starting to subside—for once the sky was, rather than the black of coal, the gray of drying chalkboard slate. That did not mean the rain had ceased, so Hermes tarried to slide on his coat. Shoes, too, of course. Could not forget those. And his gloves were just on around the time his brother's stable-borne cry lacerated that blissful post-deluge silence. By the time the older man reached the younger, his beloved baby sibling was hysterical with tears, lying on the floor of the stables with his arms around his favorite, a chestnut mare, who, like the rest of the horses, lay slaughtered in a massacre of equine horror. Hands covered in coagulated blood sticky like pancake syrup (which made Hermes think he had not made pancakes for breakfast for quite some time), Enoch stared up at his older brother. "What happened? Oh, God, oh, God!"

Adjusting his gloves, Hermes lifted his right hand to shield his nose from the putrid-sweet scent of animal death. "God, indeed. A force of nature worked here last night." As his black eyes fell upon his brother, he suggested, "A wolf blundered in, I should wager. A cougar, perhaps. Or a bear."

A stillness rising in his tears, Enoch rasped, "What did you do while I slept, Hermes? While the story was being recorded."

"I was sleeping. Why, I never even had an opportunity to get in my pajamas."

"You were wearing a green shirt yesterday," said Enoch, and Hermes did not emote while his brother went on, "and today you're wearing a red shirt, and you're telling me you didn't change."

"I said I had no opportunity to get in my pajamas."

"Why would you do this?" Enoch's breast heaved with a gasp which possessed the qualities of a sob. "Why would you do this to my horses?"

"I still think it was a wolf, got in," repeated the older brother, turning away and assessing the dead animals. "I'm so very sorry, Enoch. I know how much you loved your horses. Perhaps, in the forthcoming spring, after the Device has brought us success, we shall buy you some more. Come." With a fond pat for his brother's head, Hermes made his way back to the house. "Let's have breakfast, and we shall worry about the bodies in due time."

Hermes was not surprised when Enoch did not immediately come; what was surprising was that Enoch came to breakfast at all. He seemed quite calm, though still bloody-handed when he appeared in the kitchen. He stood across from his brother, who unveiled no emotion while flipping pancakes. Enoch shrugged his coat from his shoulders and hung it upon the peg beneath the calendar of Magritte artwork. This month was, appropriately, *Golconda*. His silence, it seemed, extended to the water, which Hermes did not hear run—nor did he see it run, for he turned his back to his brother, who then moved past him to set the table, as he did most every morning unless Hermes got to it first.

Ah, to know his little brother's thoughts! If the Device produced a story with the brain of the elder brother, perhaps it would be about the mind of the younger brother. Perhaps something else entirely. Hermes might have paid any price to know at that moment what his brother thought—better, to know at that moment what God thought, assuming of course God thought anything at all. Sitting across from his brother, who avoided acknowledging the raspberry-syrup pancakes before taking his first bite, Hermes found the man's face devoid of all light, but also all stress, all pain. There was an eerie calm to him, and so, halfway through breakfast, after sipping his coffee, Hermes spoke the first words since the barn. "Will the wolf return to our home, one should wonder, and next come to eat of my rams?"

"I don't think so," said the younger brother with a small, grim smile, one devoid of all humor. "I think your rams will be safe."

"Are you so certain? It seems to me, after all, that you are quite beloved of God. If I am somehow to blame for the horses, as you seemed to believe, surely the Lord will see to it that I am punished. My rams are the most obvious recompense."

"I don't think anybody wants to punish you," said Enoch to his plate. "And I don't think I'm beloved of anybody."

"I would not be so sure. You are capable of an extraordinary feat! You are a channel for God. Like a Sybil of Apollo, you channel things exactly as they happen. And so, dear Enoch"—with a smile and spread hands—"you must admit that if I am to blame for the deaths of the horses, you will see that reflected in the words of God! You, of all people, my pythius, will see such a thing."

"I'm not a prophet."

"No, not a prophet, perhaps, but you are indeed an extraordinary man. You are a man who can tap into God, or into whom God has chosen to tap. Aren't you lucky!"

The younger brother cast a sharp glare at the older. "Am I?" When Hermes did not even blink, Enoch sliced off another pancake triangle. "I don't know if I would call it 'luck,' so much as a sign of a condition."

"Is there anyone else in the world capable of such a thing?" asked Hermes of himself, of his brother, of the God he was convinced he would come to know quite well. "Is there anyone else, I wonder, who has so captured the attention of the Lord that they, in their sleep, might channel stories?"

"Surely there is someone," said Enoch, engaged in the conversation through no will of his own. "I can't be the only one capable of this. A whole planet full of people."

"Imagine the opportunities we have to study. All the things we could try! It raises so many questions." Coming to terms as he was with the fact that there were those who could and could not channel a REM Novel, Hermes pondered, "What, for instance, happens when someone capable of producing a story in their sleep—let us call them a 'Receiver'—has a seizure while wearing the Device? What happens when a Receiver is under the influence of psychedelic drugs?"

"Sort of a psychedelic experience, this whole thing. This feedback loop of reading reality." With a snort, Enoch suggested, "Maybe we call it the Lightning Stenography Device, the LSD."

Delighted by his brother's good humor in light of his pain, Hermes cried, "Why, yes, of course! What a clever man you are. One must wonder what happens when Receivers takes psychedelics—better yet, propofol, or other anesthesia. What then?" Stirred by an idea which roosted in both himself and his brother at once, for their eyes met in the same second, in the same way, the older brother offered a wren-like tilt of his head. "What happens, I wonder, when a Receiver dies while wearing the LSD?"

A chill rippled across the air between them, the two brothers, each at his separate end of the table, Hermes at the head, Enoch at the foot. Neither said anything; neither moved nor broke eye contact, until Hermes lifted his coffee mug. "We are out of eggs, but I am in the mood for an excursion into town for once, since the storm has lifted. Would you care to join me?"

"No," said Enoch, "I wouldn't."

6

The nearest town, Estes Park, was enough of a resort and full enough of people that the two men from twenty miles away made little local impact. Sometimes they came together; sometimes, separate. Hermes had the feeling they went completely unremembered, anonymous in the town where they had never truly lived, from which they had been sheltered by home tutors, and which, in adulthood, they had never visited more than twice before the death of their mother. Gentrified and meant for skiers, it was not a town where shop-going regulars had memorable faces unless that was what they sought, and Hermes was an infrequent-enough visitor that he moved like a ghost through his errands, invisible, liberated, yet somehow more exposed than ever in his life.

The strange thing was, during all the last night's business, Hermes never once questioned whether he had been meant to slaughter the horses. It had come to him as a whim, and once the whim was upon him, he had no choice but obey it. Of course he had been meant to slaughter the horses. If he had not been meant to, something would have prevented it. That force which experienced his innermost thoughts from the depths of his brother's brain, or somewhere beyond; that force which had orchestrated all things in their life through this point, which had educated them both in exactly the ways they needed, which had led them both through an elaborate tapestry of causal and synchronistic happenings required to bring them exactly thus; that force could have, at any point, prevented the deaths of the horses. One might have bashed in his skull; he might have been struck by lightning on his way to the barn; his brother might have awoken, not taken it for dream, and come in time to save a few. But none of that had happened. The horses were dead, and they were dead because Hermes had made the choice to kill them. Because Hermes willed that they should die and, so too, evidently, had God. So, then, the possible thing was made manifest, and Hermes had been the method by which it had manifested. There was a kind of strength in that, as there had been when he had smeared his face with the blood of the horses, had licked it from his fingers and breathed in their terror and bitten the heart of one raw like a wild animal, this secret bloody sacrifice between him and whatever compelled him.

Feeling so at ease as he did with what had happened, Hermes made his way through the farmers' market slowly, and even suffered himself to speak somewhat about the deluge which had saturated the mountain, the town, and the roads to make them treacherous as they might have been for pioneers. He purchased eggs and milk and some lovely peppers, and then thought that he had better find a way to apologize to his brother, so he bought him a bouquet of roses which he paid the florist to adorn with a peacock's feather. Then he purchased some almond croissants, loaded it all up in the car, and went home wondering why he didn't leave the house more often. It was perfectly pleasant, and not at all a bad drive. A bit treacherous with the rain, but that was beginning to clear, and as their ranch came into sight, Hermes smiled to see the clouds part for sunlight to pour upon their home. Humming as he parked, he retrieved the purchases, adjusted the roses in his left arm, mounted the steps of their dead mother's house, shifted one of the bags to his right hand, and then extricated from his left pocket the key he fit into the lock of a door which swung open in time for Hermes to see his brother's neck snap as the younger man hanged himself over the edge of the staircase, the long cord of the LSD jerking the laptop forward upon the stool upstairs far enough to rattle it, but not far enough to force the computer to share the fate of its owner.

Everything in Hermes's arms dropped to the floor. The eggs were crushed by the impact, but he could not really hear them because all he was really hearing, again and again, was the celery snap of his dead brother's neck: his brother who swung, staring through bulging eyes and a purpled face crowned by wire branches and screw thorns, with his mouth opened in the shock which Hermes reflected as he cried, "My God! Enoch—Enoch, my God!" because he could think of nothing else to say.

Trembling, Hermes stumbled forward and, damp-eyed, reached toward Enoch, but took better stock, then, of the Device around his brother's head. He withdrew, hands folding to his breast as he recalled their conversation. Why, yes. Hermes's eyes rose the length of the wire which connected the Device to the laptop. As the stairs protested every step, he left behind his brother to investigate the screen, and stilled. There were no delta waves. The computer was frozen as if struggling to process and print a massive input with which it was forced to catch up. As, after grinding, it hit its stride, Hermes could read parts of, first a paragraph, and then, gradually, an entire book about a stranger. With a swell of horror, Hermes realized he was reading the chronicle of a dead man—but not his brother. Not the brother hanging, head still wreathed in wires, from the staircase down which their mother had slipped while high on pain medication.

Desperate to have space between himself and the corpse, Hermes escaped to his brother's study in search of a suicide note. There, he discovered stuffed beneath paperwork something which Enoch had hidden: the remainder of a story which Hermes had thought to have tapered off around word nine thousand. He laughed right up to its end, then left the study near tears. Papers in his hand, he tossed them over the rail to watch them fall like snow around his brother's head.

"You should have warned me," he chided, still half laughing. "No wonder you've been in such a mood! Any God can deliver the text in any order desired, but it takes a very cruel one to give you the deaths of the horses and your own suicide, does it not?"

Hermes's heart sank at the finality of silence's response, but the full text of the story had bolstered him. Sacrifices had to be made—even if great. Even if painful. As the laptop stuttered, shuddered, then continued to unfurl the massive backlog of text outpoured at death, the surviving brother found he could not bear to touch either the dead man or the Device, lest the process be disturbed. Leaving everything—the roses and peacock's feather smeared in milk and broken eggs, his brother so still as to seem a plastic prop—Hermes found their mother's Bible where his brother had left it upon the hallway table of photographs, and he retreated to the depths of his dead brother's study to wait.

Cassius

I

People hoped for more gossip about Katherine before the Device and the seizure and this book, but I never intended to revisit the subject after 2030's *The Fields, The Flowers*. The number-one question Minerva has gotten since its publication is why she kept me as her client after the divorce, and I'm not sure she knows the answer. I do, though: I'm too valuable. Lest we forget, the last book was a fictionalized version of my affair, and that lined her bachelorette pad with dollar bills. It was so successful that I couldn't fathom fulfilling the expectations of a follow-up. Explaining my trouble to Minerva via video call had me sweating, and the summer heat baking Arizona wasn't helping. Five minutes into the conversation, I had already been reduced to pointing out, "I gave you a book last year. It topped every best-seller list; we had headlines for weeks. A guy from *TIME* magazine called me the greatest living writer."

"Because people were speculating you'd died. Do you know how many inquiries I've fended off in the past three years because it took you *seven* to squeeze out your last book? It's good, Cassius, but give me a break." She retrieved from off camera a desk calendar which filled the frame as she tapped the bold "9." "It's been eleven months, Cassius. Eleven months since your last book was published, and what do I have from you?"

"I'm working on it," I insisted as the calendar gave way to her hostile face. "Minnie—"

"Don't you 'Minnie' me." She swept the sunglasses from atop her auburn hair and used them to point at the camera. "You were greatest living writer *last* year, Cassius. You can only be greatest living writer if you write, right? I keep hearing all this bullshit about how far along you are, how you're definitely onto something here; then, when I pry, it's perpetually fifteen thousand words, and something to do with this Lazarus character you've been talking about since we were married."

"I think he might be a writer, actually, or in some way related to one." I'd hoped to slip that in somewhere below the threshold of her ranting consciousness, which meant she latched right on to it, blue eyes a theatrical width.

"Cassius, no! Writing about writers is self-indulgent masturbation." Though behind her lurked the shut blinds of her office window and the edge of a ficus she'd somehow kept alive since I'd last seen her in person three years before, she was not deterred from snatching up her bourbon. "Nobody wants to read that. Writers write for readers, not for other writers."

I reconsidered the arguments I'd made to myself in justifying that very problem. "This wouldn't really be a book about writers, though. No more than *The Master and Margarita*, say. The main character happens to be a writer because that's the vehicle for—"

"You're telling me you want to jerk off all over the page. Why don't you just call the book *Katherine?*"

My problem with video calls, and modern technology in general, has never been the requirement to fully shave, shower, and dress before a simple conversation. It's more my terrible poker face, and my inability to hold it together in front of Minerva. A normal phone call would have hidden the way I threw my hands in the air and left only the phantom of my sigh as I said, "You're really never going to get over this."

"I will never get over the affair you had with a seventeen-year-old you met at a funeral, Cassius, no."

"We were hardly even friends for the first five years we knew each other! You always act like we screwed on the casket." The swamp cooler clicked on to soften the edge of the late-afternoon heat with a spritz of humidity. Elbow resting on the desk's edge, I pointed at the camera. "Do you really want to rehash the past? Open the door of your office, see if you can get some fresh gossip going. Call up some of your tabloid friends. You act like you've done me some big favor keeping me as your client, but I'm the one doing you the favor. I'm the author."

"And you wouldn't be shit," hissed Minerva, teeth bared, "if I didn't say. Want to rehash the past, do I? Do you know how bad your first five books were?" Frothing at the mouth, Minerva brandished the tattered navy cover of *The Crows' Cries at Dawn*, the first of the Jason Eagle trilogy, which had put me on bookshelves to start with. I grimaced. "You couldn't have picked a worse title! What does that mean, Cassius?" A few more hairs loosed from her bun as she slammed down the paperback. "It means I went out of my way to see that you were successful, anyway, because you had all the potential in the world. And you're good! Your last book was top-notch. I love the new direction, content aside. But, seven years? And now you tell me you don't even know this character, and you 'think' he 'might' be a writer, or related to one? You're joking."

"That's who the character is, all right? It's our foundation. It has little to do with the actual story."

"Just what is the actual story, then, my deeply defensive friend?"

"It's—about God, I think."

Minerva steeled her expression against an eye roll like a hotel concierge faced with customer attitude. "Let me ask you again: What is the actual story?"

Tongue planted against my teeth, I stared through the sliding door of the clay-tiled kitchenette cluttered with dishes I resolutely ignored. Beyond them rested my barren patio, moated by gravel and enclosed by an even more depressing adobe wall. I needed a garden. As I started saying, "I think he's in love with a younger woman," my agent leapt from her seat with such force the camera shook while her chair rolled into the ficus with an audible slam.

"The last book was your therapy story. You should be over your guilt by now. You don't get to write that again! You can't just sit on this without deciding something better. I'll be dead in another seven years!"

"Seven years," I repeated, queasy in the face of the number. As Minerva slapped her desk, one thick lock of hair came out of place to reveal a glint of Baba Yaga gray at her scalp.

"That's right, you clod: seven years of conversations like this! Do you think I want to go through that again? You think I want to spend my time holding your hand to make sure you're writing?"

"You think I want that, either? If I could wave a magic wand to solve the problem, I would."

"You can," she said, reclaiming her seat, now far enough from the camera to reveal the rear wall of her office had been repainted pale salmon. Stuck to the metal cabinet formerly behind her head was a twenty-year-old picture of our Thomas, which held my attention as she went on, "It's called 'writing.' Why don't you go out and get one of those Lightning Stenography Devices?"

"The headband? I don't know. Sounds like people want something to do their writing for them."

"Is that not literally what you just lamented to me that you didn't have? Whoever's doing the writing, *how* ever, thought-to-text headband, speech-to-text microphone, carved in a clay tablet in cuneiform, I don't care." After throwing back her bourbon, she slammed the empty glass back into place near the edge of her desk. "So long as it gets done before we're both too old to read it."

"You have never been this impatient for a book in all my life. You owe somebody money?"

Using her legs to propel the rolling chair toward the screen in a way I normally would have found hilarious, she snapped, "Yeah, it just so happens I owe my future self a big, fat retirement check for carrying you for forty thankless years. Next time we talk, you had better come back with a more thorough idea than another book about writers and God and a man who loves a younger woman."

"It might be kind of science fiction, too. But fantasy?"

About to choke on her own tongue, my agent leaned forward until her face ballooned the entirety of the screen. I leaned away amid her verbal onslaught, "I will ruin you. I will drop you as a client and smear your reputation all over town, this town and all others."

"So it's threats."

"Ultimatums, more like. Use it as inspiration! Just write me a book. And soon."

"Do you think it'll happen overnight?" I asked, helpless as she reached for her computer mouse.

"Kiddo," she said, though we were only one year apart, fifty-nine and fifty-eight, "ideas are like lightning. They hit you all at once, and, if you're lucky, they might leave you alive."

With a bubble-popping sound effect, Minerva disappeared, and I was left sighing at a list of our call history in my empty Tucson apartment tucked in the city's west side. If only I'd stuck to thrillers. I could piss those out in a week's worth of work. Maybe two weeks if I was having a hard time getting my head right. But those days were already long gone. Katherine had groomed cheap fiction out of me, because she had seen from the start of our relationship as writer and editrix that my stories were worth more than the scaffolding presenting them. That professional relationship had been, in and of itself, quite a surprise. At seventeen, she had just been a kid, a surprise heiress rewarded against all expectation by a dead aunt she'd met but once, but by the time she came to stay with Minerva and I to have a base from which she found one of her own, her writing shined so bright I hired her to help me finish my last thriller. I just hadn't counted on the way things would spiral out of control, both in our relationship and my own writing style, which was never the same after we started working and, eventually, loving together. She encouraged me to pour all my time and energy into the true heart of the craft in a way nobody else had. My literary work had blossomed in my love with her, but that was a double-edged sword because some of these more serious books required serious consideration. (So I thought back then, when I was still under the impression I was responsible for anything I wrote.) That kind of pressure on your shoulders, I'll tell you, it's killer. After getting off a call with his agent, sometimes all a man wants is a drink and a warm body, and I'd given up heavy drinking, so I thought I'd go over to Katherine's, which usually happened around two or three in the afternoon. That day, because of the meeting with Minerva, the watch pinching my sweat-sticky wrist informed me it was already four.

None of this would have been a concern if she had, anytime in the past ten years, agreed to live together again, but women have their reasons. Her presence in the Wagner home was only ever intended as a temporary setup. She had meant to get a place of her own, and found and fell in love with one around the time my divorce came to completion. I wasn't ready to move, she wasn't ready to settle down and live with someone, blah, blah…and it happened a lot quicker than I made it seem in *The Fields*, and a lot more decisively, too, but that's what poetic license and William Wordsworth references do to a man's fiction. We're still together, the both of us having sworn off marriage and cohabitation forever, though I admit I've softened on the issue in my years. But, it's like I said: women have their reasons. Katherine, especially, has reasons for everything. There wasn't much point in complaining. It wasn't like I was spending money on gas for my electric car, or driving the damn thing, since it, like about 60 percent of cars on the road, was auto-driving. Still, it might have been nice to have the warm body to sleep up against all night, without having to leave it or feel it, eventually, leave me.

She didn't answer her phone, but that was nothing new, so, sunglasses atop my grayed noggin, I paused in my bookcase-cluttered living room, sure I had forgotten something nagging; I patted my wallet and touched my sunglasses, became conscious of the keys in my hand, and said to myself, Fine, suppose it's all in my head. At last, I emerged from my apartment with a wince for the blast of heat. Going outside always felt more like opening an oven than an exterior door. The sun still exhibited its needling edge from the furious meteorological climax of the standard Tucson August, that bringer of life rendered igneous orb of loathsome rays which sought to penetrate the flesh of a helpless man hurrying to his car, the silver Mercury which, at the proximity of its key, awakened with the engine's croon. Inside, as it pumped itself full of the cool air which would prevent its rider from suffocating, it asked where I wanted to go, and I told it, "Kitty's."

The primary computer screen set over the radio rotated through options before settling on the address of her Winterhaven home, "Winterhaven" being possibly the most inappropriately named neighborhood in the United States. It received its moniker from its HOA requirement to put up Christmas lights, which Katherine detested but obeyed despite resenting more every year the doe-eyed looky-loos who drove through the neighborhood to admire the displays and made it impossible to live. Every summer, the heat inspired her to talk about moving, and so did winter gawkers. I lived in perpetual fear that someday she would really do it, and without me. Even so, despite her passionate hatred, she'd lived there for over ten years, having once told me it reminded her of her childhood home—though it was better than anything a Chicago suburb could have had. The place was a fairy-tale village transplanted in the middle of one of America's most hellish cities, and even at the end of the summer season it possessed a dreamy cheer which ended as soon as you left the boundary for the squat mishmash of commerce and residences which was Tucson's arid skeleton. Winterhaven was an oasis, and I think she really liked it because it made her forget she lived in Tucson. Thinking about how much she hated that place made me feel badly, because she had come, in part, out of secret love of me. She had met me once, in a painful and confusing time, and hung her star on me just a little bit so that, by the time she reached out to us to say she was thinking of moving out West, we both knew, deep down, exactly what would unfurl between us. In hindsight, I admit I can't imagine it any other way.

Of all the houses along the winding roads, Katherine's was the most beautiful, but that might be personal bias: it was small, really, and plain, featuring none of the sundials, stone benches, or other yard accoutrements cluttering neighbors' facades, so it was easy for the eye to skip in favor of more garish displays. But the little two-story, timbered in soft mocha against frondescent plaster, seemed the guardhouse of an enchanted forest—so much so that, when I let myself in to take a deep breath of blessed air conditioner, I was readier than ever for a talking animal. Coming in was like coming home in the way that visiting your old friend's house was coming home, or the way visiting the house of parents who no longer had a room for you was coming home. That was what Katherine was like, even if she was so much younger than me. The perpetually divorced mom, seeing her kid on alternate weekends and using the rest of her time to drink too heavily. In Katherine's case, it was more pot than booze, but that never mattered to me. What mattered to me was that she was always more interested in spending time by herself than with me. To a limited extent, I understood why, because it was time spent doing the same thing I was doing: writing. Most of the time, my visits interrupted her. That was why, as I slid from my oxfords in the gray stone entry of the cottage living room to pad across the wooden floor, I grew haunted by a quietude, as if going for a nature walk, then noticing the eerie absence of birds. The missing element was distant typing.

I hurried my step, half-triumphant, half-angry. This was why I wanted us to live together: if something happened to her or to me, the other would be there to help. But there was no corpse in the unswept kitchen, and she hadn't fractured her skull on the edge of the bathroom sink (at least, not the downstairs one). It was upstairs that I found her like usual, alive and well and in her office, but it seemed she wasn't writing. In retrospect, I guess she wasn't, but that's sort of an existential argument. It seemed she wasn't doing anything, her pristine body sunken in the leather embrace of her chair, glazed green eyes unfixed but moving, sometimes, from screen to something invisible. I knew that glaze because it was the one I got while pounding at the keyboard. Seeing the expression without the accompanying motion of her hands bothered me, but not as much as the text unfurling across the screen, collected from the silver band around her forehead instead of moving fingers. Katherine, of all people, had bought into the latest consumerist scheme being pushed down our Capitalist throats.

Minerva had cursed me. I was going to use the Device whether I wanted to or not. I hovered on the edge of Katherine's office, the one room which she had bothered to update with modern amenities, and which was cold in that slick way of modern things. A feeling of humanity was something I noticed in other people's houses less and less, and there was almost none of it in Kitty's office, which deceived the eye with seamless planes so perfect they formed, by illusion, the smooth curve of a sphere designed to minimize distraction. It gave me the sense of being enclosed within an egg, or maybe something more nonlinear, like the infinite perception of whatever being grew within that egg. In fact, before stepping in, I was clutched by the fancy that this was no room at all, but a two-dimensional plane suspended within a pocket dimension provided by this doorway. If I entered, I wouldn't be able to leave because I would only be able to move across the x-axis, but my exit would have to be reached from the "y," and I, constrained in two dimensions, might not even remember I was supposed to return to the third. I would be hypnotized by this, this space, this false plane. But this false plane was where Katherine, unseeing, was crowned in silver, so I penetrated it, and at my footsteps, she jumped from reverie with an avian "Ah!" of surprise.

"You scared me," she said, lifting her chin to pout for a kiss. "I was in the middle of a good part."

"Sorry to startle you." The corner of her satin mouth tasted like powder. Makeup? My utilitarian Calypso saved that for special occasions, so I faltered, but I had no chance to inquire.

"It's fine. I figured you'd be here soon. I was wrapping up."

Her guilty eyes darted toward the screen as I, laughing, lifted the silver band from her head to turn it in my hands. "I suppose you wanted to squirrel away your works before I got here, techno junkie. Ruining laptop chargers is passé: time to get a new Device on the charger treadmill."

"I knew you were going to tease me about it! You probably haven't even tried the LSD."

"Only in college." I pinched her cheek so she, with a sour sigh for my pun, spun in her seat to dispel her current work in progress with a click of her mouse. While she continued clicking through the program, I rolled the silver circlet between my matching apish hands. "You know what somebody told me at dinner last week?"

"What?"

"The LSD will destroy writing as we know it. Said, with the creation of this Device, there's no way anyone will be able to write a whole work of fiction to completion. With the LSD, we'll start to work and...wander off, say. Lose focus, start daydreaming."

Kitty laughed at that. "Are the people you hang out with these days so afraid they've got nothing to write about? So afraid of what they'll find in their imaginations?"

"Aren't you? Who knows what's in there."

Scoffing, she snatched back the band to slip it around the cap of her skull. "What do you mean, who knows what's in there? You do. It's your mind, isn't it?"

"Is it?" I asked her, because I really wasn't sure I knew. She who had known everything since seventeen rolled her eyes and reclined again in her chair.

"Watch." Arms crossed, my djinni closed her eyes. Words sprang upon the screen like drops of water pooling on the earth:

Do you see all the potential you have when unfiltered thought pours right from the mind? No keyboard. No typos. No wrong keystrokes or indecision. The mind creates and pours it out on the page. Think of this like a faucet. Just sit down, never agonize what word to type next: only think. It's the same as it ever was, right? People who are going to agonize over their writing are going to agonize over it. People who are going to get it done are still going to get it done. They're just going to get it done faster.

"Not that it isn't weird," she admitted aloud, and I jolted to hear her because I'd been reading the words in her voice. "But you should try it."

"I don't know, baby," I said as she rose and removed her crown.

"Turn on, tune in, drop out, daddy-o," she insisted, guiding me to her vacated seat. "We'll get you hooked up, and you'll never go back."

"It's not exactly writing, though, is it?"

"People were saying that about typewriters before you were even born, old man."

As she resized the Device several notches larger to accommodate my head, I tried, "It's not writing. 'The Lightning Stenography Device.' All it does is transcribe your thoughts."

"That's writing," she said, crossing her eyes at me. "What is it, if it isn't writing?"

Her cherry desk featured simple monitor, keyboard, mouse, and black strip of a processing tower built partially into the wall behind, yet my eyes stuck to the one piece of technology I perceived as an alien menace. "Writing implies a sort of act. A verb."

"This doesn't?"

"I haven't tried it, so I don't know."

She compared the Device to my head as she laughed, then added another centimeter of diameter. "Then you're not allowed to have an opinion yet, are you! We're going to calibrate it."

Though at first she leaned over my shoulder to navigate the screen, soon she slipped into my lap to more easily minimize document after document. One of my drafts blinked past, a short story, the basis of my next work—those fifteen thousand words Minerva was on me about. "Hey," I chimed, pleased, and Katherine smiled as she minimized it.

"I'm almost done with it."

"Do you like it?"

"I think it's excellent," she said, and I didn't trust her because I knew she'd lost sight of the vision the way I had after all this time. "A little purple here and there, but let's worry about it later."

Sighing, I nodded as she stood again and opened the program whose representation was visible on the desktop of her computer as an icon shaped like a diamond, gleaming amid her digital clutter. A default version of the word processor opened, this one sleek and futuristic, a frame of silver and black enclosing the classic blank page where blinked the solemn "I" of the cursor, that which portends the whole universe. From the menu in the upper-left-hand corner, Katherine selected the command "Calibration," and a pleasant blue window popped up.

"Hello," began a measured, feminine voice, "and thank you for buying the Lightning Stenography Device, or LSD. My name is LEDA, and I am your Learning Engineered Device Administrator. To maximize the potential of the LSD, some initial calibration is required. You will be instructed to think of specific words and phrases. Please follow these directions to the best of your abilities, as cooperation during calibration is imperative to accurate functioning of your Device. To continue, think the word 'Yes.'"

The thought was barely formed, having blossomed from both hearing and seeing the request, when the screen flipped over to a video of a misty sea lapping along a shore. "Thank you," said the voice, her script fading in at blissful pace over the water, "next, please think of the word 'Sea.'"

Again, in the instant I became aware of my thinking the word "Sea," a green circle swept around the word to wipe it all away. "Thank you," repeated the voice, showing me a goblet, suggesting next, "the word 'Cup.'"

It went on for a minute, moving on to full sentences, among them, "The quick brown fox jumps over the lazy dog" and many other elementary-school favorites. At last, with a pleasant beep, the screen indicated that the calibration was complete, the voice thanked me again, and I was left with only the word processor.

"Okay," I said as the cursor blinked, "now what?"

"Well write, won't you?"

"That's pretty easy to say to an old guy like me confronted with a thing like this." I hunched to assume a helpless-old-man posture to make her laugh, but, of course, she didn't so much as crack a smile. Just arched her brow at the screen so I snapped, "I can't do it with you watching me."

"What is this, a sperm sample? You love when I watch you give those." But, tittering, she left me to grumble to myself and confront the white screen alone. It gazed back, null and dull, as I searched inside myself for a spark of something and thought instead of my unfinished work. How, even though Katherine loved it, and even though I loved it, it was a thinly fleshed-out mess of a story. The problem was, I didn't know all its characters as well as I should have. But how much better could I get to know everybody, and how much could they really affect the story? And what story were they supposed to affect? That was the real problem: the over-arching problem, along with the characters, was left underdeveloped. That's why the verb "to develop" is used in characters the way it is in film. The best picture isn't instant; it focuses in with time and sweat and a lot of prodding in the chemical dark. How much could that process improve with a dissolution of the boundaries between thought and writing?

This Device might help me plunge that much deeper into the flow of my work, and the heads of my characters, but, my God, what did it mean for mankind? A thing like that, laying words right out onto the computer screen. Didn't it herald uncanny implications about the nature of writing? Of thought? For years I'd declared no drug was as good as writing, but I was frightened, because they'd finally gone and done it: they'd really made writing a drug, just like convenience, like cars, like money, like the Internet. Soon people wouldn't be able to function without the shortcuts of technology. What would happen when the power went out? What would happen, centuries in the future, when the grid crashed and generations of people raised by technology were facing the world on their own? Sublingual, having been granted the privilege of machines which communicated for them, of computers which wrote for them and toilets which wiped their asses, the people of the future would regress very quickly to something more primeval. Terrified of the corpse of technology left behind in the wake of electricity, Man would move from the depths of cities to the comforts of caves, to the safety, to the warmth, where they would paint and hunt in the serenity of nature. And then, with time, one advanced ape might intuit the concept of "I," might uncover the secret of language, a burden once taken on by loving computers so future Man could go without the pains of awareness, and the whole thing would start all over again.

"And you call me 'cynical,'" Katherine said, jarring me.

Startled, I discovered upon the screen all my thoughts, arranged, two paragraphs like inert blocks in the masonry of a story, while, at the end, the cursor blinked in petulant impatience, waiting, always, for more.

"I didn't realize I was writing. I thought I was just thinking."

"Well, as you yourself just articulated, is there a difference with a thing like this?"

Frowning, I slipped the band from my forehead and examined it with the reverence she had used to lift it from its place upon her desk. I forgot all about the stress from Minerva which had guided me there, forgot, indeed, all earthly qualms, like the nagging, intangible gap in my memory. There was only the opportunity for limitless writing so consuming and immersive that I feared as much as hoped I would get lost in it. After all, what other reason could there be for writing, in the end?

"I thought I told you not to watch me write," I said, turning to pinch her butt.

"According to you, I wasn't," she said, pinching mine. "I was watching you think." She brushed a few hairs of bobbed sable behind her ear, where they were pinned with the sunglasses she'd snatched from a desk otherwise immaculate but for her two published novels: *Burning Lilies*, which made me fall in love with her mind, and *Romulus*, which made Minerva's nearest rival, Drake Wolfram, fall in love with her work. I was in the middle of wondering whether Drake berated his clients in public when, lingering by the door, Katherine asked, "So, are we still going to Chase's house for dinner, or..."

It was as though the question dislodged some crumb from my teeth. I had been forgetting something, after all! I knew I wasn't demented yet. Of course, the price for vindication was the overbearing shadow of my brother, already looming across me, though we hadn't even left the house. I grimaced at the hexagonal clock which seemed to float against the falsely curved surface of the wall, then scrambled up to adjust the collar of my shirt. "I almost forgot. You know how he'll be if we're late."

"Maybe he'll do the thing where he lies on the floor in protest while everybody else eats," she said with a laugh, though I didn't find the idea as hilarious.

"We'll see," I said before a recollection arose apropos of nothing. "Writing about writers isn't masturbatory, is it?"

"It depends whether we're talking, say, Charles Bukowski's *Post Office*, or Stephen King's literal cameo appearance in his own novel."

"I don't know. Bukowski was writing about himself, wasn't he?"

"Well, sure, but writing has nothing to do with it. *Post Office*, *Factotum*, all he does is talk about writing, drinking, and screwing, but those books mean more than just that. They're about the human condition, right? The everyday man with an unexpressed artistic side. Like you, when you used to drink."

"And Stephen King? What's the difference between him and Vonnegut? *Breakfast of Champions*, right?"

Katherine sucked her tooth in the way of a lost argument. "You'll make us later," she said, shaking her head as she left her office behind, leaving me time enough for one glimpse over my shoulder at the silver band which gleamed until the pale lights shut off.

2

Now, I'm man enough to admit that most of the reason why I got my Device was because my older brother so derided it during dinner. But who could blame me? He's the sort of guy with an opinion on everything, even things he has nothing to do with. Ask him the last thing he wrote, and he'll tell you about an angry letter to a department store, but as soon as Kitty's response to his question, "What's new?" was an almost eager, "I've just forced Cassius to try the LSD," Chase was rolling his eyes in a way that so mirrored our father I could have punched him out in his own pueblo-style living room.

"Tell me you two aren't going to get sucked into this trend," he begged, leading us through the living room and into the asada-scented kitchen, where Naomi, a few blonde hairs falling across her eyes, perked up from chopping cabbage at the tiled island.

"Cassie! Kitty!"

"Please tell your uncle," said calm Chase to his daughter, "that he's too good a writer to try something like a thought to text Device. Honestly, Cassius"—he wheeled on me, snatching up a Tempranillo, a diamond-shaped label adorning the thing he waved like a cudgel—"imagine your hero Nabokov trying to dictate *Lolita* with a microphone and speech to text."

"But thought is different from speech," insisted Naomi. While Katherine nodded, Chase snorted and opened the wine.

"That doesn't mean it won't make mistakes."

"You clearly don't know what my job description is, yet, do you?" asked Katherine of Chase in a wry way, getting glasses down from sleek flat panel cabinets she'd been in a thousand times, for a thousand dinners, because she was a part of the family even if she wasn't. "Cassius makes plenty of mistakes on his own, let me tell you. And the LSD limits mistakes, because the program knows how to spell. It knows what you mean. What you intend to mean, anyway."

"It allows for sloppy work. Nobody needs to know how to spell anything, anymore!"

"They said that about spell-check, once," I said, wincing from a safe distance away as my brother jerked the cork from the bottle. At the stone table, I could sit and watch the unsetting sun glare across the face of Arizona, free of potential projectiles. "The same way independent publishing on the Internet was going to destroy publishing."

"Wasn't I just making that same sort of argument to you?" murmured Kitty under her breath as she dropped off my wine. As I struggled to hide my smirk, my brother went on to ask, "Didn't it? The online bookstores are pumped full of trash because everybody with a keyboard got it into their head that they could write and publish a book, and everybody has. And now they don't even need a keyboard to pump out their trash!"

"But you've still got good writers writing good things," Naomi said, gesturing toward me with the knife, and as I waved a hand and Katherine swallowed hard her wine, she went on, "and they're still being recognized, so what's the problem? Maybe this is just how the good writers will get their work out faster."

"Easy for someone like Cassius to say atop of Mount Success. How about we ask somebody like Katherine how easy it is to get attention with the industry drowning in novella mills." Of course, he didn't ask Katherine, and instead went on without missing a breath: "I can see it's three on one, but let's be realistic. This Device is a flash-in-the-pan trend." My brother sipped his wine and set it at the head of the table, across from where I had already made myself comfortable. "It'll be the fun new thing, really explode around Christmas, turn into a fashion statement, and then everybody will have forgotten about it by this time next year."

"I think you're wrong about that." My brother shooed his daughter away from the island and then turned away to lift the lid on the barbecued flank steak, and all the while I carried on. "I just tried the thing, Chase. It's a marvel! I've never written so smoothly in my life. All of you people arguing against this Device...the problem is none of you have tried it; nobody's even written a book with it, yet everybody's reaction is to outright dismiss it."

As Naomi, bearing a plate of tortillas, hurried to set the table, Chase shook his head with a sigh for my ignorance. "Writing will lose its soul," he lamented, and I felt as though his comment struck me blind. Katherine, who had taken her place at my right hand, leaned forward to suggest, "Surely more efficient methods of transmitting thoughts to page only bode well for the future of writing."

Chase scoffed again, his favorite sound, like a vacuum cleaner sputtering with a wad of malamute hair caught in its hose. "It's primitive. Uncensored. With all the fuss about self-publishing that's been the tizzy of the past thirty years, the quality of writing has declined, declined, declined. There's nothing out there today which isn't derivative to an aggressive degree."

"Jesus, Chase," I said at last, "reality is derivative. Can you expect more from writing?"

"Not with this ridiculous headband on the market. The effort of writing is all invalidated. Sit down on Friday, tune in, turn on, drop out, and by the time you're off to work on Monday morning, you've finished a novel."

"Wonderful," I cried into my wine, and Chase seemed insulted by the very notion that someone, let alone his brother, could take joy in such a thing.

"*No*," he said, "*not* wonderful, Cassius. What's going to happen when those novels are finished, hm?"

"The same thing that always happens to novels. They'll sit in a drawer, get reworked and rewritten, and one day, if they're good, they'll get read one way or another."

"Wrong." With a pompous twinkle in his eye, Chase crossed his arms before the half-shredded steak and said, "These weekend writers are going to have their crap on the market by Tuesday. You'll go to Amazon and see a hundred thousand different covers, MS Paint–style stick figures."

"Feel free to correct me, but isn't it like that already? Didn't you just say a few minutes ago that the publishing industry has already been inundated with crap?"

"Of course it is, but it's going to get worse!"

I laughed, and said, "So? Let it get worse. The great work—the really great work—will always rise to the top eventually."

Sneering, Chase resumed his work on the steak and suggested, "There have been many incredible writers whose works were never read despite their profuse efforts."

"Oh, yeah? Name them."

"Well—"

An answer for everything! The man was incredible. "Let me stop you: you can't. By literal definition, you can't name them. And you can't name them, because their work wasn't good enough. Tons of writers have been undiscovered until they were dead. Kafka is only the immediate example that comes to mind. He was discovered days after he died, and there have been plenty of others like him. Dickinson, Pessoa. After their deaths, their work was so transcendent that it compelled survivors to publish it. That is some powerful work. Yeah, some families may have been after a quick buck, but most seriously believed in the message of the work."

I leaned forward to snatch up a few tortillas and slam back the rest of my wine, my last bastion of booze, before saying, "Great work is great work. That's just it. Great work will always find its way to the public independent of the writer, because once the writer puts it on the page, that's it. It's its own entity, existent unto itself, consisting of its own laws and mechanics and purpose. Just like a person. And so, just like a person, great work, truly great work, won't rot in a drawer."

"Say there's a shut-in who perished in a house fire," barked Chase, snatching up his cutting board and steak and bringing it all to the table. "He's well-known among friends and family for being a writer. Say he was poised to be successful, then died in this terrible accident, and his work went with him. It could have been world shattering. Could have been tremendous."

There was no argument he put forth to which I could not rise. Somehow, my brother thought I liked to argue, when the problem was that he was always wrong. "But it wasn't world shattering or tremendous. It might as well have never existed at all. You say he was poised to be a successful writer, but from the sounds of his whole story, he was really poised to be a struggling writer who burned to death in his own study. Let's talk about his work. Say it was going to be bigger than the Bible, his book. Didn't I just tell you reality is derivative? You complained about the derivative writing of today, but there's a reason for that: it's so the ideas that must get out are able to get out. Calling memetic ideas derivative is like calling genetic codes derivative. Of course they are; they have to be to ensure perpetuation."

As my brother at last sat across from me, I leaned for the tongs and loaded up my tortillas with a few strips of steak. "If our man in a house fire lives in America, well, it's possible that there's a man in Japan writing almost the same story. Or a very different story which says the same thing. It doesn't matter the form, so much as the message transmitted. But think of all the times two inventors hit on the same discovery: the telephone, the Tesla/Edison feud, hell, probably even the wheel. Since the invention of inventing, there's always been some schmuck off to the side, burned because he didn't get it out there fast enough. That's the truth of the writing, too. It's a risk you take as a writer when you reach out and touch that live wire: you'll either get it out fast enough and well enough, get it read enough, that the idea will become associated with you; or it and the world will reject you because you were too slow, were not quite right, were doing it at the wrong time or for the wrong reasons. It's natural selection of the psychic variety. The strongest ideas blossom here, and here, and here, so that even if one strand is lost to the vicissitudes of existence, there are all these others that can grow and get their message spread."

Chase huffed and puffed, and, after a swig of wine, suggested, "And what about all those struggling writers out there, with great work and bad timing? Should they just stop?"

"Well," I began, not discompassionately, "I think it's important for those writers to write. But every writer asks who he's serving: the writing or himself. Do you want to write for the sake of creating worlds? For producing a self-contained act of existence, an eternal lesson? For that moment of just..." I couldn't find a word for it, the experience of what it was to be in the flow of writing, and so waved my hand before me and said, "being there? If so, and if you see another writer more successful than you, doing the same or a similar thing as you, or even a different thing, well, then you just smile and move on and go back to the keyboard, to the laptop, to the LSD, to the work. I mean, what do you want with your recognition? What's the point? Isn't the point of writing to leave yourself, your ego? To feel what it's like to make a new world, to be God, infinite, omnipotent?"

At last I was the one scoffing as I snatched up my first taco to signal I was through with the conversation. "People who get upset about everybody writing and sharing all their work in an instant...those writers are just worried that people will realize they really have nothing to say, like Katherine said to me earlier."

With a dark cast to his arctic eyes, Chase stared me down as though considering a response, but instead he turned his attention to his innocent-eyed daughter. "Did you try the wine yet, sweetheart?" he asked in that too-gentle tone he assumed when trying to strong-arm somebody into doing something. "It's fantastic stuff, a genealogy friend from Oregon just sent it to me."

Naomi, who had, through the course of my diatribe, listened and eaten and made eye contact with Katherine as though trying to telegraph via blink her amusement with the family drama, sat straighter. "Oh, I haven't. You were so busy talking to Uncle Cassie before, I didn't want to bother you, but I can't have wine tonight. Do you want it, Kitty?"

"Sure," glittered her oscine voice as Chase, stricken, said, "Half the fun of coming to dinner is trying the wine."

"Not when you're pregnant," interrupted my niece, her grin unfurling as her eyes jumped from her father, to me, to her pseudo aunt, whose mouth opened as Chase gasped, "What!"

Of all the people at the table, I might have been most excited. A baby in the family! "Oh, honey!" Thomas was the last Wagner to be born, way back in 2007, a date which seemed too high to be considered "way back." Had it really been so long? All petty squabbles with her father entirely forgotten, I rose to embrace my niece, stealing the inaugural hug while my brother, having been shown up, blustered into his wine-glass. "Congratulations, sweetheart! How far along are you?"

"Three months," she informed us with a pat of her tummy beneath the batiste of her cornflower shirt. Her proud smile was directed to me, much to the certain relief of Katherine, who had strong feelings about the presence of children. I could already see her struggling to form a truly genuine smile at the thought of future babysitting as Naomi went on to explain that her husband, "Alex, wanted to come tonight, but somebody called in sick at the casino, and blackjack doesn't deal itself."

"You think he would have put his foot down for a thing like a pregnancy announcement," said Chase, unable to breathe, I think, without criticizing, and unable to find fault at that moment in his pregnant daughter. His fault, then, turned upon first his absent son-in-law, and then upon me. "Here we've been squabbling like a couple of children, Cassius running his mouth, and you've been waiting to tell me I'm going to be a grandfather!" There was a mist in his eye which left Katherine and I identically wry before she, lowering her emptied glass, smiled for Naomi.

"I'm really happy you're so excited, congratulations. Do you want a boy or a girl?"

"I don't know, I don't know! It's all so crazy!" One hand still on her stomach and the other on her forehead, Naomi laughed, flush-faced without need of wine. "We're having someone come to paint the den next week, but we're just going to do soft green, something neutral. I don't want to influence the baby one way or another. I feel like if I set my hopes on one thing, I'll get the other." While she laughed, Chase rolled his eyes.

"That's ridiculous, honey, that's just not how probability works. Anyway..." More accepting of her previous idea, Chase whisked away his daughter's glass to deposit before Katherine. "Let's have a toast to the new mother!"

"Not yet," she insisted, waving her hands while we lifted our glasses. "I'm not a mother yet."

"You will be soon enough," said Chase, crying, "Cheers!"

On the auto road home beneath the kaleidoscope of Tucson stars, Katherine leaned her head against the glass of her window, her soft breaths fogging to obscure the pensive statue of her image. I cradled her hand and said, "I'm sorry nobody asked how your work is going, sweetheart."

"That doesn't bother me. I'm used to it. I wouldn't have known what to say if they'd asked." She laughed in a terse way.

I considered asking her about her work in progress, but found myself stuck on the queer vibration of her mood, and probed a little more. "We don't have to babysit if you don't want to, honey."

"It's not that," said Katherine, frowning as the operator of the vehicle next to us did a double take and turned to tell his passenger who we were. A sigh rattled from her. "This is the problem with autos. You can't hurry them up to escape conversation without abusing emergency functions. I really wish you wouldn't put your picture on dust jackets. It affects me, too."

I sidestepped her nagging, at least this time around. "For somebody who loves the LSD so much, you sure hate self-driving cars."

"It's a coffin on wheels. If something goes wrong, I'm trapped and dead. Worse than a plane."

"That's not necessarily true. There are always ways to survive. And, anyway, all cars are coffins on wheels. Manual cars most of all, since operator error comes into play."

"I'd just much rather be in control of my own ability to kill myself or keep myself alive, thank you." Rolling down her passenger window, Katherine fished a joint from her pocketbook and bent her head to light her cannabis cigarette as the strangers called across the whipping highway.

"Rock on! Cassius Wagner, right? You should write more Jason Eagle books so they'll make another season of the show." I thought the voice was a girl's because of its pitch as it thought to add, "I love your work," which at least elicited a gracious smile and a blind wave and a "Thank you," from me, because it was what I was used to. People sometimes recognized me and loved to talk to me about my work and, by and large, about the show, a thing with which I'd had very little to do in any capacity other than as a viewer. Katherine, likewise, was used to what she heard, and I knew that she would have given anything for someone to talk to her about her work, instead.

"Mrs. Beauvoir, Mrs. Beauvoir!" A boy's voice rose over the whipping wind, and I realized the kids were probably teenagers—the edgy types, with black fingernail polish and a pretty big collection of Ozzy Osbourne CDs, assuming they knew what CDs were. "I learned about you on this documentary I saw on your uncle. It seemed like nobody can figure anything out, and your family won't let them! Is it true that your real father was your grandfather? Do you know? Are you going to write a book about it? I'm your uncle's biggest fan. Of his paintings, I mean, ha-ha. I love his paintings."

"It's 'Ms.' Beauvoir," she said around a drag as sizzling as her tone.

"Roll up your window, honey," I suggested, but she continued smoking.

"I hate hot-boxing. Pigeon noises, traffic noises." She ashed her joint violently, maybe hoping a spark would meteor into their window. "Anyway, I think it's nice. About Naomi. She'll be a wonderful mom."

"I'm sure she will," I said, and I wasn't sure whether to pat her hand. There were times when Katherine would reject affection while too deep in thought. She'd had, not necessarily a bad life, but a strange life. We had talked about it a lot in our first year or so together, but after a certain point she resented having to acknowledge the details of her family issues, either to herself or to me. The remains of her family were almost entirely female, so it wasn't fair to use "clammed up" to describe the women in her family when it just described her family as a unit. It was what they had to resort to psychologically after all that happened, though the repression manifested in a way unique, like differently expressed genes, in each member of the family. She hadn't talked to her mother, Vera, in about six months by then, but in the almost-eighteen years since the news broke, she'd faded in and out with her, and with her Aunt Ada, too, and her grandmother, Bernadette, who had finally died in 2023 neglected by her family members. All of them, like Katherine, went out of their way to avoid the grisly-if-artistically-sublime paintings their relative had created with the blood of his victims, the last one, being the one I had incidentally seen in a crime documentary about the case. Katherine didn't know that I'd seen it; it was painful enough for her to talk about her overbearing surviving relatives, let alone the evil, dead ones. There were a lot of things none of the Vasko women knew about Katherine—maybe because they had her stuck as Katie, or because they held presumptions based on her inheritance from her Aunt Susan and the path she had taken to end up with me. Whatever the problem was, it seemed Katherine's family had different expectations of her than what she was doing at any given moment. But wasn't that always the problem with family? That reminded me, I needed to call my son. I was always doing that, needing to call him without doing it. But I'd get to it tomorrow, I decided as I dropped Katherine off at her house with a kiss and an embrace that seemed deeply needed by her. There was a lot I'd have to do tomorrow, and wasn't there always? Yet, I would find some time.

I'd do it right after I bought my LSD.

3

Chase was right about one thing: the Lightning Stenography Device was a fashion statement. Mine had a nice, brassy sheen that contrasted Katherine's well, since I expected we would use them together often enough I might otherwise mix them up. Other than color, it was just the same as hers: a strange circlet of metal with a few wires drooping like Christmas lights around its circumference and a wireless plug which connected to the computer once the software was installed.

My father was an engineer. It wasn't my calling, but I grew up around PCs before they were common and even helped him build one or two. I was no stranger to technology—certainly less fearful of it than Chase—and the little headband was as innocuous as it got those days. Yet it wasn't the technology that was the problem, I told myself. It was the software. The mere idea of using a new word processor somehow repelled me. Was I getting old? What was the cause of this resistance? Any such resistance was a surefire path to ending up like Chase. That couldn't happen. I slipped the circlet on, calibrated it with LEDA's help, and relearned how to write.

The thing about writers is that some people (writers and would-be writers, especially) act like we're foreign entities; the root of the writing experience is the same as any form of art, or athleticism, or way of living, really: the flow. You sit at your keyboard if you're a writer, or pick up your racket if you're tennis player, or clamber into your car if you're a driver, and your brain just kicks off. Consciousness falls away along with all worries, all sense of being, and you're invested in the activity. You *become* the activity. The activity is all that there is, or ever was, and then, boom: you've got a finished book, or a game won, or a record-setting race. You come out of it, and you feel like you've been dreaming. Or fucking. The finest drug there is, the flow, and it's something that takes practice to initiate, but after a while, you feel it every time. As soon as you engage in your activity, there it is: what used to take twenty minutes to initiate takes ten, then five, then you feel it every time you need it. Every time you want it. And it doesn't matter what you're doing within the parameters of your activity, so much as that you're doing your activity; it doesn't matter what sort of game you're playing, so long as you're playing at all.

That's the attitude I've always had toward writing: it didn't matter what I was writing if I was writing, and I worked to avoid thinking too hard about what I would write next. But the LSD brought it to a new level—it was disorienting to sit there without moving my hands, to think of the words in a way I never had. It's hard to explain, but when I'm in the flow, it feels like the words are coming from somewhere behind me, like they dance around the outside of my brain and appear in my fingers without my having consciously thought them. In art, the subjective mechanics of creative thought are veiled by the mechanics of typing or painting or sculpting, like a sleight of hand magician relying on the misdirection of the pretty assistant to keep the audience from seeing the real trick. But with the LSD, without any typing to distract, there was only a deep and powerful form of meditation, of creating something by observation. And that's a powerful feeling, but also unnerving, because it feels too powerful. Like it brings the conscious mind too close to the gate of the unconscious. Words seemed fresher, more alien somehow, the first time I consciously used it for fiction, and descended faster as they realized they weren't hampered by slow fingers. It was really like watching a story write itself, writing something with the LSD.

But it reinforced what I'd said: something like this couldn't be called "writing." "Writing" seemed to imply a mechanical act. This was a kind of entelechy, as described by Aristotle. The form of story realized into matter with minimal entropy. Enteleking, maybe. I was enteleking fiction.

In the end, when I was done, I recognized I had been sitting in place for three hours. It was as if I had dozed off, from the feeling in my mouth and in my body; a full bladder, in fact, was all that had disturbed my reverie, and there I found an almost finished short story, one I had barely been conscious of writing, about the two brothers who were the main characters of my work in progress. There have been many times when, upon reading something I'd written, it felt I hadn't written it at all, had never seen the text before, or seen it, maybe, in a dream. But this was like reading something new. Sure, it was my story. But the process had been so different. It was thrilling. So thrilling, in fact, that I found I could suffer only a five-or-so-minute break of walking around the house and drinking some water before getting back to it. No, the LSD didn't do your writing for you. It just seemed like it, if you had enough practice with a keyboard.

I must have spent hours before that monitor, throwing myself down all the byways of story that crossed my mind. It was as fun as discovering writing as a boy, and more powerful because, without body movement to distract me, I could really become lost in my imagination. Though my eyes might flitter around the room, drift past a picture of Katherine or her tiger lilies brought to beautify my house, I was hardly aware of my surroundings. There was only the world of my character. My perception didn't matter, because the image in my mind's eye was more powerful than that in my physical one.

And then, at some point, as happens when you're sitting still and intensely dreaming, I fell asleep. No dreams came to me. Nothing noteworthy happened as far as I was aware. I'm the sort of man who falls asleep in his chair if he's doing nothing but thinking, so when I stirred awake at my desk, I hardly thought about it; I just slid the headband from my head and smacked my lips. The clock proclaimed it ten at night. A guilty spasm twisted my stomach to think of how I had left Katherine in the lurch, but maybe she wanted me to leave her alone with no phone call now and then since she was so resistant to living with me. Still, maybe I would send her a text with my excuse, and that was what I was thinking as I realized there were words on the screen which had not been there when I had fallen asleep. Oh, yes, the tail end of the scene I'd been writing about Lazarus was still there at the top of the page, but then for a few lines after, it seemed I'd passed out on the keyboard. The page-long paragraph which followed consisted of a confusion of letters and numbers and pound signs before it relinquished control to the Greek letter "delta," which the machine's tutorial had explained to be normal interference in the case of loss of user focus or a problem with the hardware. What was not normal was that the white noise was followed by cogent, yet unfamiliar, paragraphs, and the first one looked like this:

> *People hoped for more gossip about Katherine before the Device and the seizure and this book, but I never intended to revisit the subject after 2030's* The Fields, The Flowers. *The number-one question Minerva has gotten since its publication is why she kept me as her client after the divorce, and I'm not sure she knows the answer. I do, though: I'm too valuable. Lest we forget, the last book was a fictionalized version of my affair, and that lined her bachelorette pad with dollar bills. It was so successful that I couldn't fathom fulfilling the expectations of a follow-up. Explaining my trouble to Minerva via video call had me sweating, and the summer heat baking Arizona wasn't helping. Five minutes into the conversation I had already been reduced to pointing out, "I gave you a book last year. It topped every best-seller list; we had headlines for weeks. A guy from* TIME *magazine called me the greatest living writer."*

I don't know if I can properly articulate what it is to wake up to something like this on your computer screen, as if you yourself had typed it out. I was baffled, at first. Reading the lines over, I slid into my seat and leaned forward to squint at one word at a time. It was most assuredly written in my voice. Not the voice of a character, but my own voice, which I only used for private, unpublished short stories. This was something I had not written, because it was nothing I would think to write; if I was going to write about myself, I was going to write about something which had happened, which was worth writing about, and not about a seizure I hadn't experienced. If I were writing a fictional story, I'd use a fictional character, not myself. Based on that alone, these paragraphs were bizarre. But then sank in the implication. As I read the paragraphs recounting my meeting with Minerva before their abrupt end on my awakening, I felt the buzz of paranoia, as though eyes were on the back of my head. I just kept reading, over and over, wondering where the words had come from and what they meant. Whether they were true.

I was never a religious man. Not the type to believe in God or any other superstitious entity; I thought people who claimed to divine the future were crazy. There was always a logical explanation for things. But, after minimizing the offending, disturbing paragraphs, a cursory search on the Internet confirmed what made sense: that people who used the LSD and tried it in their sleep awoke to nothing but visual noise. There were reports of people noting the occasional scattered phrase, "carrot" or "lawn mower" or something plausible floating around in all the static without meaning or reason. All seemed to think the appearances of such words were due more to the human nature of pattern recognition rather than to the LSD's potential as some gateway into the future. Of course, I agreed. But, as I minimized the browser and again summoned the offending paragraphs, I thought to myself that there was pattern recognition, and then there was waking up to something like the start of this story you're reading right now.

I want to emphasize again how crazy I know everything sounds, and how crazy I felt the first time I read those lines. The disturbing idea was not that I might be potentially facing a seizure, or that I predicted such a thing in my sleep, but rather that something was writing this story through me. That was the feeling I had from the outset about the REM Novel, because even though this thing was written in my voice, ostensibly about me, I clearly had not written it. If, as discussed before, one component of the verb "to write" is the implication of mechanical action, the second, even more important component of the verb is *intent*. If you don't intend to write something, if you aren't consciously aware of the desire to produce something, is it still writing? Sitting with the LSD on my head transmitting words to the screen was one thing, but thinking about nothing and instead, say, picturing the flame of a candle, or going off on a meandering stream-of-consciousness thought about what I wanted for dinner shouldn't produce writing, should it? The LSD might still interpret the text as a stream of consciousness, but the operator wouldn't be writing, just thinking. Any on-screen appearance of thoughts as text would be circumstantial. Yet, circumstance could not explain away the appearance of the text. It couldn't have appeared from nowhere, yet somebody must have written it. If I'm sleeping or thinking, or doing anything else, for that matter, what's doing the writing that appears on the screen? LEDA? The LSD? They were like women carrying water. But whence came the water they carried? From the well of my brain, I supposed. But could a well be said to be the source of the water it contained?

It was a question that bothered me with increasing depth the more I absorbed those paragraphs. The whole room altered, and I leapt up in search of signs of entry, though nothing anywhere in the room had been disturbed. The apartment was small—two bedrooms, two bathrooms, sparsely decorated but for book and manuscript clutter and a few Jason Eagle posters along with family photos, nothing of any real value—so anybody who tried to break in while I was asleep was just as likely to disturb me as anything else. Breaking and entering didn't seem reasonable, nor did it seem reasonable that anybody would break in to plant evidence of writing. The only person with the key to my apartment was Katherine, and she wouldn't gaslight me so much as wake me up and climb on top of me, and not necessarily in that order. Nobody else would have any way into the apartment, and if somebody broke into it, they were probably breaking in to steal something, not write something on my word processor.

On heated overdrive, my brain conjured a thousand wild ideas, each making less sense than its forebear. Perhaps computer hackers got into my device and somehow put text on the screen; maybe the device had malfunctioned and had gotten a wire crossed somewhere that produced a random but unnerving string of text, like a thousand monkeys and a thousand typewriters getting lucky with a few lines of *Midsummer.* Could be it was some sort of sleep-talking, and maybe I had, in fact, sleep-talked, and the Device interpreted that as conscious enough to put on the screen. But, of course, it was all ludicrous, and as the hollow sun rose in the pale window above my computer, I shuffled upstairs to shower, wash my face, shave, touch the right temple of my forehead five or six unnecessary times, wander back downstairs in a spectral haze to make oatmeal, then sulk in the window seat of my dining nook. A fat raven in my neighbor's mimosa produced the cooing chirrup of a toad's love song. Who'd hear it if I choked and died? The raspberries were going sour, and I had to buy more milk, and there was a problem with the wall in Katherine's garage. Nobody could be stricken with an ailment; there was too much to do around here. What was this thing talking about, a seizure!

It wasn't even seven in the morning before I was at Katherine's. When we lived together, we spent every morning together, but if we spent too much time together now, she got anxious and started to talk about how she was sacrificing her liberty, how she'd end up like Shirley Jackson, dying depressed and famous for being a funny housewife rather than her superb horror. Letting her do what she wanted resulted in a sort of a terrible, lonely feeling, even though I understood her polite refusals to marry me arose from independence and not a lack of love. But I needed her often, and needed her more that morning than I ever had since Minerva left. It was terrible to see the possibility of a kind of mortality with no one around to help, and the thought of dying alone because I'd swallowed my tongue drove me to a profusion of tears at least once on the ride over. At her house, I paused by the front door with the manuscript in one hand and the keys in the other, feeling ridiculous. From the telephone stand near the first busy bookshelf of the living room, the seven faces of her pink orchids gazed placidly upon me, and I basked in their sympathy until Katherine called from several rooms away, "Cassius? Is everything okay?"

She emerged in the living room amid the swaying silk of her silver robe and the peppermint scent of fresh soap, her nose and cheeks and neck still flushed from her shower, which brought back the days we would sit at the breakfast table and she would sweep toast crumbs from her fingers before pointing out whatever offending sentence sat on the manuscript between us, and, "Oh, honey," she said with a furrowing brow to draw me from my thoughts, "are you crying?"

My free hand flew to shield my face, because even though she had told me many times she thought it was lovely to see a man cry, I couldn't bear for her to see my weakness. Everything was so overwhelming, though, that I couldn't help it, and I let her draw my head to her shoulder where it could rest, where I admitted, "I'm scared, Kitty."

"What is it?" she asked me, hushed, and I lifted the page and started to give it to her, but paused and cleared my throat and blustered away to wipe my face with the back of my fist.

"I promise you I'm not making things up. I fell asleep wearing the LSD last night." I didn't know how to continue but to give her the page. "I woke up to this." She studied me curiously from behind those verdant eyes, then lowered them. She skimmed past the visual noise before the start of REM sleep. As she came to the words, her pupils constricted to pinpoints.

"So you can see it, at least," I said with a half a sigh. "I'm not just crazy."

But Katherine didn't respond for a few seconds, and I started to get nervous until her lips parted enough to allow a jagged inhalation. Then she was saying, "It's garbage."

"What!"

"It's trash, Cassius," she said, tearing the printout in half while I gaped. "Delete the original."

"I bring this to you and tell you I'm afraid, and you just tell me it's trash? You don't have anything to say beyond that?"

"It's ridiculous. Seiz—" She stopped with a sort of hiccup at the tatters, which she yanked to further pieces. "I wish you hadn't shown me this."

"I wish I hadn't woken up to this!" Agitated, I followed her over the threshold of the kitchen with its big chessboard tiles, where she began slamming away dishes while I continued, "Why are you getting mad at me? It's not like I wrote this. You don't think I'm putting you on, do you?"

"I'm not mad at you, Cassius," she snapped, and I fell back a step, unfairly castigated. "It's scary, okay? I'm scared."

"Join the club!"

I only realized my voice was raising at the tension in her face, and we shared a deep breath. "I'm sorry," I said, and she turned away, picking a dry bluebird towel from the drawer near the sink.

"I'm sorry, too. I just don't think this is good, Cassius."

She buffed a cereal bowl while I put away glasses. "It's obviously not good, Kitty, but what am I supposed to do? I'm terrified. Have you experienced anything like this?"

Jaw set, she zeroed in on a spot on the bowl's orange rim. "If I woke up to the LSD writing a novel for me, I'd probably start going crazy."

"That's comforting."

"That's why you can't think about this, Cassius." She lowered the bowl to squeeze my hand. "I'm begging you. Thinking about this isn't going to do you or me or anybody any good. It's just going to stress us out. Think about how many prophecies never would have come to fruition if the stupid prophets had just kept their mouths shut." I stood back as she wiped the counter. After a few strokes, she leaned forward and, forearms poised against the linoleum, said, "Whatever this is, paying it attention is only going to end badly."

"But, Kitty," I said, feeling like a helpless boy, "I can't help but pay it attention."

"Don't say that." Her hand landed flat on the counter, and we both jumped in surprise at its force, mutually displeased until her head ducked. "I'm really not mad at you, I promise."

As I nodded, the kitchen doorway seemed to shrink to hide the small cyan wastebasket in the living room. What if I died? She said my name across a distant desert, but all I really heard was the ticking of the kitchen clock and the sweeping of a vast and endless wind, and upon the other side of the desert stood, I knew, the source of the wind: Lazarus. An incomplete work, haunting me.

"Cassius," she said again, her hand upon my chest.

"I have to finish it," I told her, drawing her against my heart. "It's too important, Katherine."

"I've been waiting for this book for almost twenty years," she said with a petulant sniff. "You can't pay this thing attention, because if it comes true and something happens— I'm scared."

"I know," I said, my cheek against the top of her head. "I'm scared, too."

But we lapsed into silence, because we both knew I was going to chase this thing, and we both knew I didn't want to lie to her about it, so we didn't talk about it again that day. We went to her Aegean bedroom and made love, and spent all day together, got ice cream and went to my apartment where neither of us neared my darkened computer whose singular eye scrutinized the living room. Instead, we watched *2001: A Space Odyssey*, and I held her while she cried for HAL's electric death, and then made love again like we were thirteen years younger. In a quiet voice, she asked if she could stay the night with me, just this once, and of course I told her "of course." Nonetheless, she left around four in the morning as she always did on those miraculous occasions when she stayed at my house like she wanted to see me.

I knew she wanted to see me and was just scared, but sometimes it was hard to avoid bitterness. I lay awake with my head aching, Katherine relegated to a tiny heap I cradled now and then to the sound of sleepy coos. We had sacrificed so much to be together. Was it possible to tell the greater loss? Katherine had damaged her connection with her religious family by engaging in a relationship with a married man and choosing a career path which kept the public ever vaguely conscious of her relatives' crimes. And I, of course, had destroyed my relationship with my own family, and with the person I had thought I was. But I had been so alone, and she had been so beautiful and so young and so much like me, and things had just developed. We wrote about once a year, and when her first novel was finished, I loved it. What developed between us was never just lust; it had been from the start a very real and powerful thing which recalled love's aged blossoming between myself and Minerva. That bud had withered before Katherine had arrived, but let's just say that Kitty's blossom made all the other flora seem like weeds. It was a pure, adoring love between us. First I was enchanted, then my wife was gone with my son, and after a year of living with me to make sure I wasn't going to kill myself, Kitty bought the Winterhaven house and said I could visit anytime I wanted.

Of course, I didn't want to visit her. I wanted to live with her. But that was beside the point, what I wanted, wasn't it? It didn't matter. I was glad just to hold her. I was glad to have these moments with her when we were both getting older by the second. Me, especially. As the minutes passed, I grew more grateful to turn over and kiss the soft curve of her neck, to smell her, to fall asleep against her as though nothing at all were wrong—and all to lose her as she absconded with the break of dawn, saying, as she kissed me, "Have a good morning. Don't think about that manuscript."

4

Avoiding the manuscript was easier said than done. I hadn't been alone an hour before I unlocked my computer to confront the mystery pages. Their foretelling of the seizure conjured the word "ominous" in its most literal sense. That the start of my conversation with Minerva was reprinted with such rank deliberation was disturbing enough, but my forehead misted at my obsession over what might happen if I had the seizure while alone. Worse than biting off my tongue, maybe my consciousness would float off forever and never return, leaving me a vegetable. Say the seizure turned into a brain aneurism; say I felled a bookshelf during the ordeal and awoke paraplegic, remembered forever as one of those crippled success stories who overcame the odds and wrote or acted or whatever despite their physical handicap. Of course, I realized with a snort that the Lightning Stenography Device rendered that kind of success a lot less of an achievement.

Never had I wished so fervently, nor with such bitter resonance, that Katherine deigned to live with me. At last, late afternoon, alone in the car, I asked the unresponsive machine what solitude was doing for her that I wasn't. For that matter, Minerva hadn't remarried after leaving me. Was I so bad that women would rather be alone than live out their lives with me? Was she hung up? Was it me? Normally I could only sacrifice so much energy to being around other, non-Katherine people; anything over my allotted amount and my whole workday would be shot, and the next day, too, as I recovered. Even the time I spent around my own son was that way. Maybe especially that way, sad to say, but I was never cut out to be a father. The operation had been daunting before it even began. It wasn't that I was a terrible dad, it was just that when you've got a passion, you'd might as well already have triplets. You don't have time for your son until you're almost sixty and sweating a seizure; then you're on the other side of his metal security door, straightening the lapel of your jacket and hoping he doesn't turn you away, breathing a sigh of relief when he greets you, after all, with, "Dad!"

"Hey, kid," I said, taking off my jacket as he opened the door. The swamp cooler inside didn't touch the heat, made sticky by the lingering clouds of monsoon season. "I hope you don't mind, but I thought I'd drop by and see if you're home. No work today?"

"No," said Thomas, who, as I had at his age, worked as a glazier for a window company, and was thus paid by the window and not for the twelve grueling hours spent installing them under Sol's blistering scrutiny. "I think most people are afraid to open their doors, let alone expose their house to the sun for the time it takes to install a window. Make yourself at home."

I decided to leave my shoes on, compromising by leaving my sports coat over the arm of a couch cluttered by beer cans and work shirts ruined by hardened beads of caulk. "I remember living like this back before your mom. Boy, did she straighten my ass out." I averted my face as I laughed because I knew Thomas hated when I talked about his mother as though I still loved her, which, of course, I did in little ways. I would always love what we were. What I loved about her then and what we shared when it was good would never change, and Thomas was walking proof of it. Crossing my arms as though against this notion, I asked, "How's she been?"

With a shrug that revealed sweat stains under the pits of his T-shirt, Thomas stooped to collect cans which he stuffed in the crook of his right elbow while his left hand grabbed an abandoned Kleenex or moved an errant video-game controller. "You probably know better than I do. I haven't called her enough, I guess."

"You'd ought to, kiddo, or else she's liable to show up uninvited. She won't be half as blasé about the way you're keeping your place. Not that it's her business, or mine." As I edged from his way to allow him access to the kitchen, with its overflowing trash can and sink full of dishes (mostly mugs and bowls and not a single pan or cooking implement, so who knows what he'd been eating), I focused on the screen of his paused racing game to avoid acknowledging on a conscious level the conditions in which my son lived. "What are you going to do when you get a girlfriend?"

That merited another shrug, and I, half realizing I criticized the boy to whom I'd come for comfort, stared into the weed-filled patio, and lied that, "Kitty's been asking after you."

"Tell her," he began at last, his voice edged for the steely defense, "that if I decide to go back to school, and if I decide to accept her help, then I'll call her. I just don't know what I want to do, okay?"

"Son, I wasn't trying to get into that. Katherine just loves you. She's trying to help you."

"She's only trying to help me because she feels guilty about— It doesn't matter." Laughing irritably, the boy jerked open the fridge, retrieved a new beer can which gleamed in the sun pouring through the thin patio curtains, and said, "I get it. Everybody wants me to go back to school. It's nice, I feel supported. I just don't think it's right for me."

We'd had the discussion about twenty times in the past five years, and I was so tired of it that I was in danger of forgetting why I'd come by. Tommy had moved back to Tucson to escape his mother in New York and go to journalism school at the University of Arizona, when he was still under the impression that writing was what it took to make me proud. That delusion lasted all of one semester, and by the second he'd dropped out and borrowed money from Katherine to buy a share of the co-op where he had since lived. He was right: she gave him money because she felt guilty, knowing there was no chance she'd ever see it again, and I had advised her against it, just like I advised her against trying to be a good influence by bribing him back to school. I knew he'd be weird about it. It would have been better to get him going of his own volition, on his own dime or scholarships, and then offer to pay once he was already in. Once Katherine gets an idea, though, she acts on it before anyone can change her mind. It's that kind of bull-headedness that she has in common with Thomas, and it's a trait that makes me want to choke them both, a little, sometimes.

"I didn't come here to badger you about school." He slunk past me to drop again into his futon seat and open his beer with a hiss I'd long since stopped missing. "Or girls, or your room. I'm sorry."

"Why did you come, then?"

My mouth opened, hovered that way, then shut itself as I realized I didn't have a coherent answer. "Could you help me with something?"

Thumb poised a millimeter from the "Start" button of the controller, that question, seldom asked of anyone, let alone my son, snatched his attention. "With what, new windows?"

Nudging an abandoned sock to perch beside him, I settled on, "It's that Lightning Stenography Device. I'm thinking of writing a story about it. Do you know much about them, these things?"

"Oh, yeah. I was thinking about getting one next paycheck. But who wants to read a story about one? It'd be like reading a story about a keyboard."

"I don't know, seems like something that could be interesting. Not a story unto itself, but the start of one, anyway. A good premise. Say a guy falls asleep with the thing on his head"—I felt more hopelessly inadequate in my storytelling skills at that moment than ever in my life—"and wakes up to a story, about himself."

"Sounds as creepy as it does implausible. How's his brain going to write a story in his sleep?"

"That's what I'm trying to figure out, hey? I thought you might know more about it, the way it works." In the corner of my eye, askew between the coffee table and futon, sat a plastic milk crate overfull with electronic ephemera. "You're more up to date on technology than I am these days."

Let it be said that I may have never been close to my son, but I knew his ego, and I knew his grandfather, and I knew that they both took pride in their breadth of knowledge about every and any technical subject under the sun. Puffing up, the boy offered a sage nod. "The algorithm associates speech sounds with various ways neurons fire, I think, and it's designed to 'learn' over time, become more precise for its individual user. I guess maybe it depends on whether the neurons are firing in the same way during sleep, and the software's sensitivity. Like, maybe this could be a result of the same phenomenon that causes night terrors, or sleep-talking, or sleepwalking."

"But how would you account for all the detail? All of the lucidity you find in a finished work of fiction, or projections forward into the future?"

"What, so, you're writing about a character reading the story you're writing?" I nodded once, and, rubbing jaw stubble sandy the way mine had once been, the boy suggested, "I mean, in-universe, you could justify it by referencing the idea of the impersonal unconscious, and the way the subconscious is distinct from it. That is, there's a personal subconscious, like the data on the hard drive of your computer—local storage—and then there's the impersonal unconscious. That's like the Internet and all the data on it, right? If you want to go for the reasonable, in-universe explanation, you would use a metaphor like the idea that the human brain is a computer. That everything you've ever seen or done or thought is stored locally, in your subconscious. When the brain is going back over the day in its sleep, maybe the LSD is recording those recollections, or accepting the dumped information."

I didn't want the in-universe explanation, of course. I wanted the real explanation. "Right. But what about things like foreshadowing, for instance, or predictions, or…" I reached for my heart, for my pocket square, and realized that I had removed my jacket. As my eyes traced across the room, I was forced to see its contents: chicken bones left on a plate on the coffee table; stacks of huge books about programming languages, psychology, medical dictionaries, and more; a pretty fair assortment of magazines, along with paperwork and abandoned mail forming a depressing trail of bread crumbs into the hallway, toward the bedroom and bathroom. I tried to focus as I lumbered across the obstacle course and slammed my shin on the edge of the coffee table. It and I jumped opposite directions, it squeaking, me swearing, my tongue bitten with the boy asking in the background, "Are you all right?" while I, hissing, snatched up my coat, snapped out the white handkerchief, and insisted, "I'm fine, I'm fine."

As I mopped my brow, realizing I'd no idea where I'd left off, the boy resumed for me without lingering on the mess of the apartment and the injury it had caused. "I guess, to justify things like motifs and imagery"— the boy lifted the nearby remote control, until that point invisible to my eye amid the rest of the clutter—"that's probably where the impersonal unconscious would come in, right? Jungian archetypes, and all. The unconscious contains not only all formations of past and present data, but also future data which we yet lack the context to experience. From the character's perspective, maybe they're just tapping deeply into the unconscious. Or maybe something more."

"Where did you learn so much about this?" I asked him, navigating my slow way back, eyeing the odd piece of open mail to make sure he wasn't behind on bills. "About consciousness, I mean."

"I got interested in it at U of A, when I was taking psychology. I don't want to go into the psychiatric field, though," he added brusquely, cutting me off at the pass as he changed the television input and swapped the video-game controller in his lap for a laptop, which, connected already to the television, manifested from beneath the boy's seat. I resettled beside him.

"If there's an impersonal unconscious, and it's adding some kind of 'literary flair' to the whole thing, let's say—some spice to the narrative to get across not just the facts of the thing, but the feeling of the thing— doesn't that imply some awareness? Some motivation?"

"I guess, but that's just you, isn't it? The author?" He turned a bright eye upon me as I remembered with a start we were supposed to be talking about some novel I was producing. Lamely, I said, "I guess," and he asked with the same hushed curiosity I got at dentist's offices, coffee shops, bookstores, and signings, "Does this thing you're working on have to do with your Lazarus character?"

I fumbled at the thought that this would inevitably work its way back to Minerva. "Maybe. I think he's sort of an abstract figure." I folded my hands between my knees. "Like a psychopomp, or a hero who's absent for most of the story. A symbol, a guide, a, uh..."

"An unconscious archetype made conscious, maybe?"

"Yeah, maybe."

"Then the important thing is to find out what he symbolizes, right? Hey"—the boy grinned in a cheeky way that made my heart hurt for a thousand opportunities wasted for the tapping of my keyboard—"maybe your guy in this story can have a talk with Lazarus, figure what he's all about."

I laughed dryly and fell back in my seat, all sense of humor sapped. "I'm not sure I know enough about all of this to write a story about it," I said at last, still probing, still trying to find some evidence one way or another of the accuracy of the Device, of its history of predictions, of anything. "I'm not sure it even sounds reasonable, or if I could make it sound reasonable. I mean, what could justify having a character have this experience, have the LSD create a cogent story in their sleep?"

"Well, again, I mean, it's not the LSD creating a cogent story, or even the character. It's you."

Feeling weaker by the moment, I crossed my arms. "I guess, asking that question, I might as well ask why any character is picked to be the main character of a particular work."

And my boy, unwillingly literary through his parents and would-be stepmother, shrugged. "Because they're just the character for it, that's all. Edison was just the guy to steal the credit for the light bulb, Ford was just the guy to work out assembly lines. People are just who they'll be in the end."

I felt like asking him whether or not he'd been doing stronger drugs than cannabis, but he was in a browser whose double appeared on the television while he searched, as I more or less had, for "LSD Lightning Stenography sleep writing." The search engine, scouring all the information it could find, conjured limitless pages organized as website links.

Scanning results without selecting one, he was shaking his head around the third page until, at the bottom, he found something that made him say, "Oh," and made me refocus back on the present rather than on my compulsive questions about why I was the person to whom this was happening. The link he clicked was a forum about something called "lucid dreaming."

"It's when you're in a dream and you realize you're dreaming so you have control of it. It's a thing you can practice. There's a huge subculture of people who do it on the Internet. Guides and stuff."

The boy's disturbing breadth of knowledge on Internet subcultures and (apparently useless) hobbies like lucid dreaming had me pondering how many days of work he was getting off due to the summer heat. Was a job that allowed so much downtime good for him? I almost wasn't listening as he said, "Okay, so, this thread, Dad, see?"

The title of the thread, in bold mauve letters against the cotton-candy background of the site, read, "USING THE LSD FOR DREAM JOURNALING?"

The original poster asked, *I was thinking about getting an LSD for the school year but was also wondering if it could be used for lucid dreaming. Does anybody know if it's possible to record dreams?*

To this, the resounding answer was an emphatic "No," occasionally a, "No, you moron." *If you fell asleep with your face on your keyboard,* chided one user, *would you wake up to Tolstoy?*

"I suppose not," I muttered aloud, but the boy scrolled one more page and revealed a longer-than-average post which made me touch his wrist. A new user with the cumbersome handle "HermesTetramegistus," had answered without nearly the derision of the rest of the board:

There is certainly nothing wrong with attempting to record dreams using the Lightning Stenography Device, although success is by no means guaranteed. I personally have heard of some new users on tech boards falling asleep and coming awake to fully formed words amid lines of gibberish. Who knows what an advanced lucid dreamer might find on their screen in the morning? If nothing else, the Device serves as a ready method to record one's dreams right upon waking, without worry for pen or pencil. True, the sensation of writing something longhand helps one to remember what is written, but haste is often necessary with dream recall, is it not?

"Dude sounds kind of pompous. What is with that name?" The boy laughed, and so did I. Through the patio glass, the late fire of the sky was dying, cooling from coral to violet, soon to be black. Yeah. What was it about that name? It bothered me. Everything about the response, in fact, bothered me, and as the boy backed out of the site, I carved its title into my mind. No way could I afford to let go of a lead like that one.

When I was home alone, the first thing I did was summon the site, reread the thread, and notice, then, that Hermes Tetramegistus was not just a new user. As it happened, he had made only that one post in his short career on the forum.

The second thing I did was scour the Internet for more mentions of that same Hermes Tetramegistus, and that proved a tall order. It turned out that he took his handle from another guy, Hermes Trismegistus, or Thrice-Greatest Hermes, whose teachings allegedly founded an obscure and, well, hermetic religious cult. Or philosophy, maybe? I couldn't tell and felt increasingly like I didn't have the time to find out. Instead I sifted through the results to the best of my ability, trying to keep the search engine from helpfully correcting "Tetramegistus" to the more commonly searched "Trismegistus" until it at last decided I was a hopeless know-nothing beyond its assistance. Of course, I knew nothing except a potential seizure, and possible insanity.

But, through incredible luck, I found it. First, I dropped the "megistus" and searched for "Hermes Tetra." Then, through some strange synchronicity, some quirk of the search engine, I found a *TIME* magazine article about the creator of the Lightning Stenography Device. Sitting in my boxers at one in the morning, haggard for want of sleep and the ceaseless churning of my mind, I realized belatedly that this was an odd thing to see amid the search results for Hermes Tetramegistus. Most of the results had been due to typos and various links to one person's blog of reposted animations, which did not strike me as the work of the guy I sought. There were also pages upon pages about crazy things like sacred geometry, and one site was just an abandoned username on a music forum, all its posts deleted. Having waded through all that garbage, seeing something relating to the LSD startled me, and I skimmed the article to find it a disappointing profile on the eccentric recluse, Enoch Azarias, who lived in Oregon and, very sensibly, didn't want to be bothered by reporters, or anybody else. He was shrouded in mystery because of the nature of the Device. There was a lot of speculation about how he had potentially stolen components of the headband from some engineering firm, because the remarkable thing about the LSD wasn't really *what* it did. Rudimentary thought-to-text technology was as many years old as Katherine's Aunt Susan was dead, so the real achievement of the thing was the sensitivity of the Device and the discerning nature of its algorithm. According to the article, most early thought-to-text technology was researched on epilepsy patients whose brains were exposed for surgery. Electrode grids placed upon the brain did the reading, since getting a reading through the scalp was a lot more imprecise. That wasn't practical for your average consumer, so it was never a matter of developing the technology to perform the function successfully. It was a matter of developing the technology to monetize the function without requiring some sort of surgical implant. This Enoch guy claimed to have discovered and produced by himself the means to focus the metaphorical image, and people were divided as to whether such a thing was possible to achieve alone. Azarias wasn't the least bit interested in defending himself, and he was happy to let the speculation run rampant. But at the page's bottom, amid all the inane Internet chatter and slander, I found a comment from the poster HermesTetra, who had been forced to give an e-mail to post, I knew, because I myself had been lured into one or two anonymous wars in the comment section of that online magazine.

I am personally rather surprised at the journalist's implication that Mr. Azarias is anything but what he claims to be. Having met the man in person, I can say for certain he is of high ethical character and would never dare steal the work of another. If he did indeed work with contributors, the most likely explanation is that those contributors wished equal or greater anonymity than that of the Device's figurehead.

And while poster after poster thought his claim of having met the creator of the Device was ludicrous and lacking in evidence, I felt an eerie certainty. My hands moving on their own, I clicked his username and sent him a private message I wasn't sure he would get.

Dear Hermes,

My name is Cassius Wagner. I'm a fiction author, not a journalist. I don't know if you've heard of me, but I'd like to talk to you about the Lightning Stenography Device. You've posted about it a couple of times on a couple of different Internet boards, which I know is a weird thing for me to have noticed, but I'm in a weird situation, and I would like some help.

How much do you know about the Device? Have you ever heard of people waking up to a story they didn't write? Do you think it's physically possible? I might be going crazy. Nobody else on the Internet has mentioned anything, and you'd think they would have by now if this was a noted capability. Maybe it really is like falling asleep with your face on the keyboard, or maybe I'm sleep-writing, or maybe I'm crazy, but if I'm crazy, I really shouldn't be going around telling everybody this, right? That's why I'm telling you. I get the feeling you might know. It's an emergency; it's saying I'm going to have a seizure, and I'd rather not.

Thanks for your time,
Cassius Wagner

I sent it off before I could second-guess myself, collapsed into sleep with the Device on my head, and the next morning awoke to the first two chapters of this book, completed, there, on my screen, with an alert blinking on my phone. Incredibly, as though he had been waiting for it, Hermes responded overnight, and I imagined a pimple-faced man with nothing better to do locked up in the basement of his mother's home, spinning outrageous lies about knowing entrepreneurs. The Cassius of ten in the morning asked the Cassius of one in the morning just why he had believed this random guy on the Internet would know anything at all. All the same, I read the note I'd been sent, shadowed by a vague feeling of cotton-mouthed dread.

Mister Wagner:

Forgive my brevity. I think perhaps you should speak personally with Mr. Azarias. He is an extremely private man, but if you are who you say you are, have experienced what you say you have, and tell him that Hermes sent you, I am sure he will be thrilled to make your acquaintance and discuss your situation. Please do not share his address with anyone you know, except perhaps vouchsafed to one or two individuals if you are concerned for safety. One never knows, after all, to whom one is talking on the Internet.

What followed was the address of a house (located on B Street of Ashland, Oregon) and the feeling that I had no choice but to follow the instructions of an anonymous stranger I had no reason to trust. I had no choice because, in the word processor running in the background lurked nearly fifteen thousand words of disturbingly accurate narrative describing everything significant in my life since being introduced to the LSD. Granted, there was plenty left out—meals eaten, trips to the bathroom, joints smoked, showers taken. That was why Kitty had thrown the first page into the trash, why I had been so uneasy about the conversation with Thomas. This whole thing implied some intelligence at work—something which knew what to put in and what to leave out—and my sleeping brain didn't seem intelligent enough to write a book no matter how often or well it wrote in waking. Yet the narrative was going to follow me all the way up to the seizure, and probably beyond—and my writer's sense could perceive the outline of something emerging in the narrative, some Magic Eye shape growing clearer by the minute as though I were in the process of not living so much as remembering, or seeing what was already there.

5

Even with my worldview thrown off-kilter by the manuscript, a more pressing anxiety clutched my attention. Didn't my discovery of the address seem too easy? If I were writing this thing as some investigatory thriller, somebody would only get an address this easily if it weren't as important as it seemed, or if it were some sort of trap. Since I was getting the surreal feeling of being a character in one of my own books, I had to start thinking like a character in one of my own books. This was why I waited until after sex to tell Katherine about Ashland.

"Oregon!" She pushed herself up amid her wrinkled silver sheets. "You want to go on one of your trips, honey? Right now? I thought you had a novel to write."

Feeling it unnecessary to mention that I was technically writing a novel every night (or a novel was writing me), I pushed a fan of hair from her scrutinizing eyes. "A change of environment will be good. There's tons of excellent restaurants, and the Shakespeare Festival is still going on. They're doing, uh, *Timon of Athens*, I think, and *Titus Andronicus*. Lots of *T*'s this year, I guess."

"Do you remember seeing *Twelfth Night* when we were first dating?" she asked, her face relaxing and then disappearing against my palm. "I wished you'd been happier, then."

"Minerva had just left. What was I supposed to do?"

"I know," she said. "I know, I know." This seemed to get her thinking, and it was like I could feel the emotions swell in her skin until, at last, she tilted her head. "Okay, honey. A trip would be fine. Nice. It would be nice."

"I think so." My thumb fit to the outer corner of her eye like one spoon stacked perfectly upon its forebear, rubbing there so that she blinked once, smiled. "Are you all right, Kitty? You love trips, I thought. It's not like we'll be flying. We'll drive, just like always." In fact, she'd never called it that before, distinguishing my trip from hers as if I were dragging her along for the ride. I was being too sensitive, but a writer gets hung up on words, and there was audible regret in her voice as she said, "Yes, of course," in one breath, then added with an evasive eye dart, "I guess I'm just bothered by that page."

"It's not easy for me either, Kitten. Probably worse. I might have a *seizure*! At this rate, the way the manuscript is going, I'm going to walk right into it."

I realized my mistake only when her face stiffened again, when her eyes darkened and her lips hardened as she bolted upright. "Cassius! You're not still writing that thing, are you? You need to stop!"

"But maybe if I read it closely enough, I'll find some way to stop it." My annoyed lover flounced from bed to whisk on her shimmering kimono and shield her nudity, then pushed her sleeves to her elbows while I carried on. "I feel like I should be able to read this thing, to see some foreshadowing. See where I'm going to go wrong in the future, based on the past. That's all of life, though, right?" Weakly, I laughed, and Kitty stormed into the bathroom whence her shadow poured along with the erupting, angry light. "Right, Kitty, baby?"

"I really don't know, daddy." This was something she only called me when extremely affectionate or extremely annoyed, and even if I were stupid, I could tell it was the latter from the growl of the electric toothbrush and the rattle of the toothpaste tube rammed back into its customary lilac cup. "I guess so, I guess you're right. We've got to learn from our mistakes. From other people's mistakes."

"You're pissed at me because of this novel."

A sigh rattled from her foaming mouth as her face appeared in the doorway. "I'm not—" With a gargle of fury, she disappeared to the expulsive sound of spit, then wiped her face as she stormed back in. "I'm not pissed at you. I'm scared, Cassius, and I'm annoyed, and I don't think you should be writing or reading that thing. You should be working on the Lazarus story."

My tongue itched against my canine as she shut butterscotch curtains which should have been closed hours before. At last she came into my arms as I said, "Maybe to write this Lazarus story, I have to be able to finish this."

"You're taking it for granted that you're going to be able to finish it at all."

By that point I had become an expert on consoling myself with the thinnest rationalizations possible. "The novel's written in my voice, in past tense. I'm pretty sure I'll survive. Seizures don't kill people, generally. Julius Caesar was probably epileptic, I read once."

"But you're not an epileptic; you have no history of seizures. Why would you have one? If you had a seizure at your age, it would be the sign of something very wrong internally, or externally."

"What do you mean, 'externally'?" I asked, but her lips pressed shut.

"I don't know what I mean. I don't know, it's not like you're photo-sensitive or anything. So if you are going to have a seizure, don't you think that's the sign of something wrong? Maybe instead of going to Ashland for vacation, we should scan your brain for tumors."

"A couple of days isn't going to make a difference, honey," I said, displeasure blooming in her face until I consented, "I'll make an appointment, but it'll be at least a week or two out, so we'd might as well go to Ashland tomorrow."

"You want to go to *morrow*," she clarified in surprise. I smiled, weakly, about to excuse my impulsivity as a flight of fancy when her face again narrowed, and she asked with tightening jaw, "What's in Ashland, Cassius? Just tell me why, please."

"Because"—I hovered on the threshold of explanation—"I have an opportunity to meet someone who might know about this story, and why it's happening."

Urgency possessed her. She turned herself in my arms to see me. "What's his name, Cassius."

"He's a very private person," I said, guilty to find myself truly evasive with Katherine for the first time in all the years we'd known each other. Luckily, she relieved the burden of that guilt with her voice a warbling pitch: "Is it someone named 'Enoch,' Cassius?"

A chill dashed through me as I jerked my head back, yanked her away from me, laughed at the absurdity, and said, "It is, but—"

"I don't think you should go." She wiggled away to flip out her light, then untie her robe.

"But how—"

"I don't want to talk about it. I won't talk about it. But I don't think you should go," she said again, taking up my hand. "You probably feel you have to, don't you? But you don't have to, Cassius. You don't have to go anywhere. The story you're writing in your sleep, is it all in the past? All except the narration?" When I nodded, she said, with a hopeful light in her eye, "Then it's not set in stone, is it? And even if it did predict the future, of course that wouldn't be set in stone then, either! It's just a story. Only a story," she emphasized, more to herself than to me, frowning in the dark as she slipped her naked frame beneath the blankets. "You can't let it take control of you, Cassius."

My head spun as I wet my lips and took her once more in my arms, her body small and hot against mine, the humidity of sex still perfuming the air around her skin. "I know it's just a story, but when a man discovers a thing like this is possible, he has a duty, doesn't he? To see through his discovery?"

"Let someone else make the discovery, take credit for the discovery." Her face turned away as I moved mute lips against the curve of her neck. "Let somebody else have it, please."

"How did you know, Kitty"—I lifted my head—"that I'm seeing a man named 'Enoch'?"

The question weighed in the air, leaden, until at last, she said, "That's the creator of the LSD, right? I read something the other day, about how he lives there. In Ashland. It came back to me when we were talking."

There was a peculiarity to her voice, like she guarded some secret: an old lover she hadn't told me about, or an affair it was impossible for her to have had. I was baffled, lying there, holding her as her breathing slowed. As I sensed her on the cusp of sleep, I murmured, "If I went to Ashland, anyway, even though you warned me, would you still come along?"

With a quiet sigh more patient than the sum of both our ages, she said, "Yes, of course. Go home, then, and pack."

That kind of acceptance is all you can ask in a lover, isn't it?

Because Katherine was so used to my impulsive decisions to go for trips local, state, country, or international, she was ready to go by the time I returned with the sunrise at six, the light a slap in her squinting face as she opened the door to meet me. "I packed for six days," she said groggily, already holding the briefcase containing, I knew, her laptop. "I wasn't sure how long you wanted to stay. You made reservations and everything, right?"

"We'll make them on the way," I said, snatching the handle of her rolling suitcase before she changed her mind. "There'll be plenty of places to stay, I'm sure."

"Cassius," she said, her voice dropping to that low maternal warning note, so funny to hear from she who had never been a mother and never wanted the title. "Is this going to end up like that time we tried to go to Vegas and got halfway there before you realized it was Labor Day and there wasn't a single room left in the city?"

"I promise, Kitty"—I closed the trunk of the car with a button's tap and, with another, slid Kitty's door open at cybernetic behest—"this trip is going to be nothing like that. It'll be fine. I just want to have a talk with this guy, see what he knows about the Device. Then you and I can go see *Titus*."

Less than pleased, Katherine, all the same, climbed into the Mercury and let me kiss her cheek before I shut the door. Minutes later, we were on the road, crawling through the mess of a half-planned map to the highway, chased all the while by crackling sunlight which roasted the desert beneath its bitter glare. The highway stretched without end across the desert, winding past fields of cacti which ended, inevitably, in the looming Arizona mountains and mesas that had long since lost their charm for both of us but which had somehow, like the edges of a bowl, kept us held in Tucson, maybe because we were content enough with traveling to excuse our hatred of the place we lived. After all, we were writers, and successful ones by any measure. There were signings, conferences, interviews. That didn't leave much time for lingering in Arizona, so we were able to convince ourselves it was fine living in a boiling pot which inspired in neither of us anything but complaints. Even as we left it behind, Katherine, sliding her sunglasses on, frowned and said, "The sunlight just pierces right into your skull."

But soon enough we settled into the rhythm of the ride—as much as I could be settled. Or she, for that matter. I could tell she was tense with displeasure and didn't like me following through with this story now any more than she had the night before. For my part, I was overwhelmed by the shadow of this thing growing every morning like some tumor made of ink and paper, its digital ghost ensuring it could never be entirely killed. That morning, in fact, I'd discovered after fitful sleep a recounting of my conversation with Thomas, and felt with distress that the narrative was beginning to push toward a kind of crescendo. I had so many questions (Was it a novel, a novella, a short story? Was I retelling it from beyond the grave?) and couldn't voice any because each which emerged would upset Katherine more than the last. All I could do was watch the scenery whip past, watch the wheel of the car drive itself just in case I needed to get involved in an emergency capacity, and hope that I wouldn't end up dead at the end of this story, whatever its length, because it would be a damn shame if I died before I wrote the book about Lazarus. Maybe, I decided as we emerged in California, it would be a road novel, in part. An odyssey, like Homer's. Maybe I would make the character drive himself, instead of using an auto. Or, not cars, but horses. Suits the era better.

I admit I love the convenience they provide—autos, that is, not horses—but nothing beats the feeling of driving a car, especially cruising that luscious California expanse on a sunny September day. Oh, it's true, we made a straight quick shot with the Mercury, but with less control there was somehow less leisure; I was less inclined to appreciate little things like cows grazing in rolling pastures or the rapid-fire flicker of sunlight through passing redwoods sputtering like the bulb of an old projector clicking through a loose film strip. As we drew farther north, the car carried us through what should have been our sleep but proved only many hours of silent contemplation with eyes not quite half-shut. Plenty of novels have been written extolling the American landscape, I suppose, but that's because it's an easy thing to extoll, and so different end to end. You can start in the spire mountains of West Virginia and end up in the extraterrestrial desert of Albuquerque, amazed to find yourself still in the same country. Driving through California specifically is a queer little microcosmic edition of America, claimed and tamed into farmland and industry by man until, at last, far north, man begins to lose his grip and give it up to nature—where the rising sun, after a stop for a few hours at an auto charging station, revealed clouds hanging low in bassinet mountains, their cotton wisps tangled around the too-perfect forests littering every visible incline.

Only once did we speak, and that was because I awoke from my uncomfortable doze to the typing of her laptop keyboard. In some drowsy surprise, unsure of the time, the place, as the car drove us easily through the mountains and Katherine's fingers fired away, I smacked my lips. "Thought you were all about the LSD."

She shook her head, her fingers pausing as I waded into her stream of consciousness. "I'm past it. Chase was right, it's a fad. I prefer the keyboard."

Snorting, I cleaned my eyes in time to see the theatrical appearance of Mount Shasta in the distance, more a painting of a mountain than an actual mountain—too perfect, too archetypal, to be a mountain. "This whole thing has me thinking about swearing off the Device, too."

Katherine said nothing to that, but she closed her laptop and, at the sight of the mountain, parted her lips in a sigh so sweet it refreshed me the way the restless night hadn't. But when, at last, the word "Ashland" appeared on the car's computer screen, the juniper background of GPS mountains interrupted by a sapphire orb, the air between us echoed with the visceral stiffening of Katherine's body. Her hand landed on mine, and she studied my face, but when I asked her if something was wrong, she shook her head and withdrew from me, and said, "It doesn't matter."

It only doesn't matter if you don't say it out loud, I thought to myself, to her, as if she might hear me. Maybe because I knew she would be able to read the words someday, when my thoughts, exposed like anatomical drawings, would appear on the page without my reckoning. Of course, even that wasn't true. Readers know nothing in a good story is included without reason. Katherine, her decision to not say what she was thinking—I should have realized the problem, shouldn't I? I should have puzzled it together. But hindsight is so clear, and all the clearer when you have a narrative you can read, full of artistic decisions designed to prepare your mind for the ultimate (and only) conclusion toward which the story can head. At the time, Ashland felt like that conclusion, but it was barely the beginning, and it was barely my story. Not mine alone, anyway.

There's something about Ashland: as soon as you cruise around the mountainside and see the first green sign, you feel yourself enter another dimension. This whole time you've been ascending and descending, then ascending again without end, so when you see the town, you feel you've broken into something half real at best. I admired it off in the distance, a model town tucked in a valley it seemed we'd never reach until our car exited the highway and slowed to a residential-appropriate crawl. Its slowed pace showed off countless oaks, maples, sycamores, pines, willows, more trees than I'd ever seen, and as Katherine touched my hand with a gasp she couldn't help, it was like coming home. We laughed at Mary Jane Avenue to the left and noted on the map with a shock of recognition a blue vein labeled "Wagner Creek," as if this place had waited all my life to be found in that moment, with Katherine's body warm against mine and her eyes full of a light she didn't want to acknowledge lest she admit being here gave her pleasure. Lest she be proved not entirely right about it being a bad place.

Nothing abominable would happen here, I was sure. Surrounded by immaculate houses and Florentine stores, I absorbed the surreality of this paradise bright with local industry to find that the town's penchant for theater had spilled out of the Oregon Shakespeare Festival; poured across its streets and stores; and involved all its citizens, to varying degrees of willingness, in the biggest theatrical production devised by God or Man or both. Whatever happened here would be, for lack of a better metaphor, a kind of play. At the end of the show, the dead and dying and wounded would rise, smiling, and take a bow. Everything would be perfectly fine. In that instant came the phantom kiss of divine grace, ferrying with it this idea that the day would be all right no matter how everything seemed to go. The meaning of grace struck me so profoundly I didn't bring it up to Katherine, mostly because she allowed herself to enjoy the town once we'd passed the university.

"Everything here is so cute. And *clean*. It's nothing like Tucson, my God. I haven't seen a single person smoking this whole time. Oh, Cassius, look at that, is this their downtown?"

I knew why she was excited. Most of the small towns in America were plagued by a run-down vibration as though covered in a sizable layer of grit, a price of existence from which they could never recover. They had fallen into disrepair, and their squalid downtowns were wretched hellholes. But Ashland, maybe through gentrification in the face of such a booming theater industry, glowed. As we passed the local post office and then a bank within a block of a baker, I found myself saying, "Bet you twenty bucks if I got out of the car I could find a butcher and a candlestick maker."

Tapping my arm, Katherine jested, "A butcher, this place? Too vegan, look at that busker's dreadlocks," then turned her face toward the white tower of our hotel, leaning out the window with a squint to see past it. "Is that the theater up there?"

"I think so, all three of them. They have a tour." I checked my watch, acutely aware of the note folded in my pocket, containing both the original communication from Hermes (who had, for the record, offered no response to my thank-you note and follow-up inquiry about the nature of his relationship to Azarias) and the address. "Maybe you could check it out while I take care of my business."

As though just remembering that detail of our trip, Katherine fell limp against her seat and said with a low sigh, "I wouldn't want to go without you."

"I won't be long." Kissing the cupid's-bow corner of her pouting mouth, I said, "Don't be worried, okay, baby?"

"Of course I'm worried! You don't know anything about this guy. You don't even know if this is his real address. Maybe this Hermes guy is luring you here to kidnap you. Maybe it's going to end up like *Misery*, where Stephen King's writer is kidnapped by his crazy fan."

"Look at you, Miss Stephen King. You were just trashing him the other day. That story was about cocaine addiction, you know. Anyway, does this seem like a place a crazy person would live?"

"I don't know," she said, a wry little smirk appearing at the corner of her mouth. "I'm thinking how nice it would be to live in a place like this, after all."

It always seemed to me that Katherine was saner than I was, but I supposed it was the influence of her family that made her question her own rationality. Sympathetic, I patted her hand, and thought better than to try to argue or console her. "You have to have a rational mind to be an editor," I said at last, then insisting as the car pulled in front of the hotel, "Why don't you check in for us? I made the reservation under both our names."

"You're going to go meet him? Did you even sleep last night?" When my only response was a pathetic smile, her sighing expression resurrected for a fraction of a second the dead woman I had known a lot better than Kitty ever had, her aunt, my friend. They couldn't have been more different, but there were little familiarities in her eyes and her petulant reactions to annoying men. "Honey, I really feel like you need to sleep if you're going to talk to this man. You need to be ready for anything."

"He's just some entrepreneur," I said, opening the car door and leaning over to kiss her, to encourage her to leave. "It'll be fine, okay? If anything goes wrong, at least this town has a hospital."

Then again emanated that Vasko scoff from the mouth of my Beauvoir, but she tolerated my kiss—returned it, even—before she left the car, fetched her bag, and nodded once to the bellhop who got the door. I, waiting until she was safe inside of the hotel, removed the address from my pocket and typed it into the dashboard.

Mere minutes later (much too soon, by my reckoning) I stood before a towering cerulean house located on B Street, its property enclosed by a wrought-iron fence which inspired the foreboding intuition that a witch, of all juvenile things, lived there. This suspicion wasn't helped by the trees swaying before it: one was an old willow set on the corner by some previous privacy-conscious owner; the other, a camphor, lifted bushy branches toward the eaves of the second floor, having been planted, I suspected, by the present owner, because it was just old enough to shield what the willow tree couldn't and blend this witch's house into the urban forest of the town. The feeling followed me as I confirmed the street was deserted, then put my hand on the gate just as a curtain in that high, camphor-obscured window shifted. I, mouth dry, chided myself for boyish hesitance, and knocked once, boldly, upon the building's dark door beneath the belligerent eye of a white-eye-browed blue bird, which, laughing, rocketed from the camphor tree as I was finally answered.

6

When last I checked, there were a handful of Enoch Azarias photographs floating around the Internet, but none did justice to his peculiarity. It was hard to pin down what it was about the guy that gave him such an unnatural aura; he had a plain but beautiful sort of face arranged in the permanently impassive expression of an Old Netherlandish painting. Maybe it was the hint of androgyny. There was, to be certain, a kind of femininity to the inquisitive light of his dark eyes as, with languid, swaying limbs, he opened the door to reveal a living room fireplace-warmed in September. Rain, I figured.

"Mr. Azarias?" I asked, holding the note like a student brandishing their excuse for yesterday's absence. "My name is Cassius Wagner. I'm very sorry to bother you. I know you value your privacy, but I need help. You might help me decide whether I'm crazy." I laughed, praying those crammed-full bookshelves behind him contained at least one of my books, or that he was aware of my work, and that such familiarity would be enough to get me in. After scanning the note handed to him, his black eyes focused on my face.

"Have you brought the manuscript in question, Mr. Wagner?"

Surprised by his response, measured as though not to betray over-eagerness, I fell back one more step, off his stoop, and managed a laughing, "Yes, actually. Were you expecting me?"

"Please, Cassius, if you would be so kind as to hurry, one never knows when Oregon rain will begin this time of year. I prefer the inside of my house dry to wet. Worse, the cat may get out."

"Of course, so sorry," I said, sufficiently distracted to dart back down the path and collect from the car my laptop, along with the case containing my LSD. Was I a bumbling fool wasting the time of a genius who wanted peace and solitude? When I shut the trunk and faced his house, I caught him watching me with utmost caution. I felt under such scrutiny that I fancied whether there wasn't a receiver embedded in the LSD, some means by which it could receive text written by someone else. Say, someone in control of the operation. That seemed so paranoid I dismissed it outright; it would imply a vast network of cameras or a broad conspiracy of spies. Lunacy. Occam's razor, and all. But did Occam's razor really apply to a situation like this?

Just inside the front door, slipping off my shoes, I discovered I had been allowed entrance into not so much a house as a library. My stomach tightened with a giddy flutter of envy to see such a vast collection. As a writer you read, but even my shelves were barren next to those in Enoch's living room. Space not crammed with books was painted goldenrod, except the ceiling. That was frescoed (and, I mean, genuinely frescoed), with an image I shamelessly admired as the shutting door sealed me in with the warm scent of the fire and whatever cinnamon-sweet thing was baking in the kitchen.

"Castor and Pollux," said my host. The two men, positioned at opposite corners of the ceiling, had both their eyes fixed upon the gentle face of a woman who held the darker-haired figure in her arms. As Enoch lifted brows as pale blond as those of Pollux, he explained, "I do so love the motifs of classical mythology. May I bring you coffee, Cassius? You look quite tired."

"God, yes, please." I sank into the antique cabriole sofa as, with an approving smile, my host disappeared into the bright light of the adjoining kitchen. "We drove all day and most of the night to get here. I've never been in this area before, it's beautiful. I mean, I've visited Oregon before, but never this area. What was that bird? Did you see it, that big blue bird with the brown stripe and white breast?"

"The scrub jay? A Western bird, hilariously bad-tempered. Unrepentant thieves who chase away doves and harass the chickadees. One finds them in California, as well."

"I can't believe I've never noticed one before. They sure do have some pipes on them, huh? The most interesting bird we get in Tucson is quail."

As I spoke, I found *The Fields, The Flowers* on a shelf beside the couch, which was flatteringly devoted to some of the old literary powerhouses: there was Hemmingway, and Joyce, with poetry by William Blake and the lesser-known Leda Anatida faced out, on display. The Anatida was an original printing. I was reaching for it when my host called from the kitchen, "I hope you take sugar in your coffee, Cassius. I am sorry to say that since the death of my brother I have been in the unbroken habit of sugaring whatever second cup I make. When I've occasion to make a second cup, that is."

"I'm sorry to hear about your brother. Was it recent?"

"Several years ago, shortly after we completed production of the Device. But"—a rattle announced the approaching tea service, and Enoch appeared in the doorway bearing a tray stacked with cinnamon buns and two mugs of coffee—"lifelong habits are difficult to shake, even after something as definite as death."

Nodding once, I took up the mug he didn't. "I know the feeling. Before my mother died, I called her every Saturday. I had the impulse for months after she was gone. Hey, speaking of Castor and Pollux: Leda Anatida! I love her poetry."

Pleased behind his mug, Enoch remarked, "Not many people have heard of her. She died in some obscurity."

"Well, when you're a writer, you have to read. I love the lesser-known geniuses, they're treasure troves. But, speaking of reading..." I took a sip of my coffee and found its smoky sweetness exotic, evoking the pilgrimage made to Tangier with Katherine a few years prior. With my free hand, I opened my briefcase.

"This is a very interesting conversation you had," said Enoch as he, like a street magician, rolled the sleeves of his silver shirt to his elbows, then produced from his breast pocket the note given him on my arrival.

"This phenomenon of awakening to a story one has not written...yes, I am familiar with this being an occasional side effect of the LSD. So far as I know, it is exceedingly rare."

"Who is that Hermes guy? Another person like me?"

With a small smirk, my host leaned forward, his eyes closing as he spoke. "Hermes is a man who values his privacy even more than I. He was a tremendous inspiration for the LSD, but he is not, I should say, capable of channeling metafiction in his sleep. May I?"

The papers I handed over brought a glitter to Enoch's eyes. By then, it was worth thirty pages and had caught up to the start of our trip. My literary double, once days behind, was now apart from me by a few hours. As I wiped sweaty palms on my knees, he examined the stack.

"This is shaping up to be a rather long one, is it not, Cassius."

"Read the first paragraph," I said in grim response to his delight, staring toward the flower-laden lunette above the bookshelf. On my way to grab a cinnamon bun I saw the second Enoch's eyes reached the word "seizure." Their barely perceptible movements paused. They soon restarted, moving slower, until at the bottom of the first page, he lowered the manuscript, expression tranquil.

"Yes," he admitted, tapping upon his right knee the glasses he'd removed to read, "yes, I can see why that would be disturbing."

"But you've seen this sort of thing before?" My heart rate rose as I set down the half-eaten roll, licked clean my fingers, and all but begged, "People waking up to find a novel."

"Yes. Once. May I keep this copy to read, Cassius?"

"By all means. Getting an objective eye on it will make me feel more...I don't know, grounded." Polishing off my coffee, I cleared my throat, set the mug aside, and asked, "But what causes this? What does it mean when this happens? What's doing this?"

"It would be the epitome of hubris for me to presume I knew the true mechanism by which this occurs, my good man, but suffice to say the realization that such a thing is possible has, as it were, brought me home to God. That is not how I would put it, myself, but that is the broad, general understanding of what conclusions I draw as a result of such a discovery."

"You mean, you don't know what causes it."

"One has one's theories. I personally suspect it is similar to the mechanism of dreaming, a means by which we access the impersonal unconscious. Or it may be a kind of aggressive takeover of the 'left brain' by the mute 'right brain' once it realizes it has been given an outlet. Or perhaps something is using the brain as a kind of transmitter." Glasses back upon his nose, Enoch let the manuscript droop upon his left thigh while, between the arms of the chair, he tented his fingers. "Near as I have been able to tell in my personal experience with the Device, there are two kinds of people: those who are capable of this, and those who are not capable of this. In the broad overview, most people fall into the latter category. I have termed the elite few in the former category 'Receivers,' though it is, of course, not a term I have occasion to use."

Cold fingers clutched the back of my stomach, up toward my throat, and I attributed it to dread and a full cup of coffee on a mostly empty gut after a long car trip. In response, I snatched up the rest of my roll. "Do you think there are many others out there?"

"I have no way of knowing yet. I have only just released the Device for mass consumption, but my supposition would be that, if there are other Receivers, we will become aware of them in due time."

"What makes you so sure?"

"Because they, too, will be clutched by panic on discovering a story they did not write. You said before that 'we' were driving all night. With whom did you come?"

"Well, Katherine," I said, swallowing the last of my roll in hopes it would settle my stomach. "My editor, my, uh— girlfriend."

That light rose in his eyes again, and I attributed it to the reflection of the fire as they widened, but it still seemed unnatural. "So, K. P. Beauvoir has also come to town with you. Has she produced a story of this sort?"

My lips formed the word "no," but I couldn't bring myself to vocalize it because, posed the question, I realized I didn't know. How abruptly, after all, had she stopped using the LSD; how had she reacted to the manuscript? What had she wanted to say that fleeting instant before we arrived at Ashland, but stopped herself from saying?

He was waiting for me. My lips and throat were dry, and I tried to clear the latter and dampen the former. "I don't really know. I would have thought she'd tell me if she discovered something like that. I mean, we've been together a pretty long time."

"Even those we have known for years may seem enemies when we make such a sinister discovery. Perhaps it is of a deeply personal nature. I understand she has many issues with her family."

After years of shutting down any conversation about the Vaskos for the sake of Katherine's privacy, I nodded once. "Katherine doesn't like to talk about that situation."

"And who could blame her? The crimes of Richard Vasko were as repugnant as the works of any killer. When one finds oneself related to such a person, one can hardly be blamed for wishing to turn one's face away. The struggle to escape the shadows of our ancestors can be an intense and lifelong personal battle. If she is indeed producing—call it a 'REM Story'—it may possess some disturbing recollection she would prefer to keep private. Perhaps you had ought to ask Miss Beauvoir if she has experienced this phenomenon. It is only too bad that she is not here."

Ready to excuse her absence with something polite, I was all at once back in bed with her as she guessed I would be meeting Enoch. She had insisted I shouldn't. Enoch's fire made me aware of the sweat beading my brow, of how the heat of the house was too high for my tie. I loosened it with my left hand and admitted at last, "I don't know why she's not here."

"Perhaps something in her REM Story prevented her," suggested Enoch. I, laughing, rose from my seat as my stomach clenched at, I believed, the thought of there being something in Katherine's story so terrifying she was paralyzed by it. I needed a minute. Just a minute to breathe.

"I'm sorry, is there a washroom around? My hand is just coated in frosting."

"Of course, down the hall." He gestured to his left, to a juncture which turned just before the kitchen, leading beneath the stairs. My stomach feeling fuller than possible, I hurried around the corner to shut myself in the cramped powder room. The light found me face-to-face with my reflection, older and paler and more glistening than normal. I washed my hand, then started to wash my face, but as the cool water touched my forehead, something climbed my esophagus. Grimacing, I turned on the fan to keep my host from hearing me, removed my tie, and fell to my knees to vomit. It happened just once, but painfully, the roll and most of the coffee coming up in a few sharp, knifepoint gags which filled the toilet. I averted my eyes. It was the altitude, I decided, and the length of the trip, and we hadn't really been eating much. I would deal with it in the hotel room, whatever it was. Katherine would be in fits. But I had come here for a reason. I rinsed my mouth, flushed the toilet, washed my face, and tried to convince myself that I felt better, that my stomach wasn't cramping up and the muscles of my neck weren't tight. Then, with as congenial a smile as any produced under the duress of a reading, I emerged from the bathroom, saying, "Sorry, I—" only to freeze before a painting once hidden by the door. It was a painting I had seen before, once, in a crime documentary never mentioned to Katherine; it made me gag again, like I was going to let go of the rest of the coffee there in the center of the floor.

"Is that a print?"

"No," said Enoch without looking up from the manuscript, already on the third page, "that is an original Vasko."

"Why do you have this?" I was almost shrieking. "Susan Vasko was my *friend*." Rage I hadn't felt in years so dizzied me that I had to clutch the nearest bookshelf, my fingers bumping Rilke's *Book of Hours* out of place as I waved my free hand to the repugnant piece of "art" that had filled the papers to give that little rat a kind of posthumous fame most better artists would never have. All because he killed women, and his mother, and his wife, and himself, the coward. No amount of technical sublimity could take away what he had done to create his works. I hadn't been consciously angry about the subject in years, but to see the real painting before me had my mouth hypersalivating. Swallowing back the urge to vomit up bile, I snapped, "Owning a thing like that. What kind of person are you?"

"Susan Vasko, I am certain, would approve of its ownership."

That was probably true, but, outraged, I could only bark, "What would you know about Susan?"

As though I had fallen into a trap, Enoch smiled, set aside the manuscript, and unfurled from his seat. "Would you allow me to show you something? One of the first REM Stories."

"I thought you said you'd only seen a REM Story happen once before." Visions of Chase's aggressive demeanor through the years (our tire change fistfight in '94, near Cincinnati; the cab driver political argument when meeting Kitty and I in Morocco; the Thanksgiving with the hapless pumpkin pie, which, sugarless through Chase's oversight and not its own, was nonetheless pitched through the patio door in a fit of pique to produce a high-tipping installation for Thomas) flickered through my mind. My nostrils flared to see him in myself in that sickened and sleep-deprived moment before a painting produced with the blood of my dead friend, the blood of Katherine's dead aunt.

Unruffled, he led me up the creaking stairs. "I have only known one Receiver, but that person produced two stories."

"So you're not a Receiver?" I asked, clutching the handrail as I trailed behind.

"I am not." Though I couldn't see his face, I could imagine his smirk, dry enough to compliment his tone. He felt it a misfortune! By the minute, I felt less myself and shorter of temper, and I wasn't sure whether it was for my stomach or my company.

"Don't sound disappointed. You said it yourself. It's a nightmare, waking up to that."

"To some. But, much as the mystic and schizophrenic draw from the same source, so, too, does the artist, and certainly the Receiver. Even without Receiving, who can be said to create his own artwork? A writer who has been writing as long as yourself, I am certain, understands the phenomenon of being guided by the work. What, then, is the harm, the difference, in being a Receiver?"

"The harm is that I presumably wouldn't be having a seizure if I weren't a Receiver."

"A bold presumption to make, though possibly correct." My host led me into his study, whose window was protected by the branches of the camphor tree. The narrow space was further whittled by bookshelves lining each wall, volumes far more esoteric than the collection downstairs: books on theology and philosophy, Sufism, various Bibles in Latin and English, Torahs, Korans, volumes on Hermeticism and Kabbalah and magic, thick books on alchemy, textbooks about psychiatric hypnotism, old editions of books like *Finnegans Wake* and *Paradise Lost* and Goethe's *Faust*, and a set of black-bound volumes which resolved for my blurring eyes (the lack of sleep, I insisted) as the collected works of Carl Jung, which culminated in a single red book. My attention was drawn to all these and more until a thump upon the desk at the end of the room jolted me from my scrutiny: Enoch had placed a crocodile-skin briefcase upon the cluttered stacks of paperwork. As I came to his side, he unlocked it. Opened it. I, hands in my pockets, read the first page. My jaw tightened, and I flipped to the second, and paused there, and said, "I see."

"Yes."

"Who was the other Receiver?" I asked, and Enoch explained, "My brother."

I thumbed through the pages, and as I did, my host mimicked my body language, slipping a hand into the pocket of his trousers. "You appear," he said, "for all of a page."

"I'll bet I know when, too. Was it a party?" With the twinkle in his black eye unable to be explained away by the fireplace, the man gave a delicate nod, which I avoided. "Yeah. I remember. Remembered, that is, after the news came out, that I'd met him the last night I saw Susan." I hadn't told Katherine about that, either. I hadn't told anybody about that. It was a few weeks before Suze's disappearance, and it just didn't seem worth mentioning to the police. Doubly so, after she and he and the girl in the paintings were all found dead. What was the point of bringing it up? Easier to pretend it didn't happen, that meeting. But it would be there, hidden in those pages. Those impossible pages.

"Your final conversation with her was not recorded in the REM Novel. It was pleasant, I hope?"

"Always," I said, frowning. "It was always good to talk to Susan. She seemed happy, or as happy as she could ever be, anyway. She was the saddest woman I've ever known, even sadder than Katherine. Better at hiding it, though." I half heard my host ask if I would like to see the scene in question. At that, I shook my head and fell back a step, from the case, from the desk, from the man. "No, please. Thank you."

With a single nod, Enoch removed his hand from his pocket and turned his eyes upon the relic. "I hover at all times between releasing this thing, and burning it. You see why I was compelled to acquire the painting? There is something intangibly significant about all this. I suspect there are some stories which had ought to be left well enough alone. This story is far too crass a thing to exist in this world, but yet, it exists all the same, and not because someone here chose to write it. Why, one must wonder? Why this story, and why did you appear so briefly near its end, in a seemingly meaningless exchange which did little more than bolster the ego of the murderous protagonist with enough confidence to commit his climactic crime?"

I shook my head, feeling pale, wretched, saying, "I didn't bolster anything," but the words came out deflated, so I tried again. "The REM Story I'm writing doesn't have anything to do with this guy."

The room swayed in a way I didn't like as Enoch tilted his head. "Are you so sure? Perhaps this manuscript found its way here so as to ready me to meet you."

I wasn't sure about anything, but it didn't seem worth getting into with the room an amusement-park Tilt-A-Whirl. Finally, I broke. "I don't know, but I'll tell you, Enoch, I'm not feeling so well. This trip has really kicked my ass, if you'll pardon my French."

"Of course. I won't draw out this meeting much further, but perhaps you would humor me with something? I would like to see you operate the LSD, if you have a moment."

"Sure, but nothing's different about my using it while I'm awake."

All the same, Enoch gave another gesture, this one wordless, and so it was I who led the way this time, back down the stairs to the living room, speed-walking to get this over with as I reached for my briefcase still on the sofa. With a heavy hand, I dumped my laptop and LSD upon the coffee table. As, upstairs, my delayed host made a deal of noise in getting something from his office, I booted up my machine only to have trouble picking up the headband. As a curse for my fumbling hands muttered from my lips, Enoch descended the stairs with a laptop under his arm and a small disk drive in his hand. The operation of getting the Device on my head proved harder than ever, and had me praying that what he wanted would be fast so I could get back to the hotel, with Katherine and a bed to sleep in.

"Is the Device up and running?"

I nodded once as I opened the word processor. On the sofa beside me, Enoch opened his own laptop and connected it to mine as I asked, "Do you want me to...what, just write anything?"

"Whatsoever you like," he said, and there erupted a stream of consciousness about how exhausted the ride had made me and how raw my stomach felt, how my head was pounding and how the sickly cinnamon bittersweet smell of the house was nice but nagging on me, on my mouth and lungs and stomach. I regretted not forcing Katherine to come with me because I needed to know whether she had a REM Story of her own. What was my story, after all? Not a whole story. It seemed a mere part of something. Enoch was right. If there were other Receivers living in the world (somewhere around this time, Enoch got up to sit across from me, his fingers tented) we would all probably find one another. But the most sensible thing, from a writing standpoint, from a meta-reality standpoint, would be for the Receivers to know each other already. Anyway, if my life and what was going on with the LSD and everything really was fiction, and I had been the one writing it, that would be how I'd write it. Maybe connect them all to Enoch. Like his brother.

"How did your brother die?" I asked, derailed by the question, my impulse control delirium-deadened.

"He killed himself," said my unmoving host. I leaned back to stare toward the ceiling; toward Castor and Pollux; toward the sky of supple clouds craving to be touched; toward the soft arms of the woman who held the dark-haired twin. Then, at once, my nausea lifted, and a bang from the front door, far off behind my right ear, shocked me into blinking.

7

The funny thing about the seizure was that, after all that fuss, it really was just a blink. You'll never convince me it wasn't a blink. Though I may well have had some mystical experience, it wasn't conscious. I was sitting there, feeling wretched and miserable, the Device on my head in the house of a stranger whose residence I had violated with my vomit; I closed my eyes to blink; and when I opened them, a new stranger's face was poised too close to mine, and I became aware I was on my back as the face chanted, "Cassius, can you hear me? Cassius—"

"Of course I can hear you," I told him, baffled, the words thick in my mouth. "I'm right here."

Relief passed through the unfamiliar steel eyes, shared with a nearby man in like uniform. I was just, with speeding heartbeat, realizing they were paramedics as the nearest man said, "Cassius, I need you to stay calm, and still. You've had a seizure."

"What?" I laughed between the half-focused faces to where Enoch hovered in the background, expression inscrutable. "No, I didn't."

"Yes, you did."

"No, I didn't," I insisted again, agitated by what seemed in that instant some condemnation of my character. "I was just talking to Enoch."

"Do you know who the president is, Cassius?" asked the man, the picture of patience. My mind raced. Jesus, uh— Carter and Reagan,

Clinton, and the Bushes, it wasn't any of those, and not Obama anymore, nor Trump, for that matter, and Nixon was my parents' problem—

"I don't remember," I admitted at last, my throat tight as I tried to maintain some semblance of composure while on my back amid accusatory strangers, "but that doesn't mean I've had a seizure."

More patience flitted between the faces of Enoch and the paramedics. The one whose voice brought me back to consciousness said, sympathetically, "I know it's disorienting, Cassius, but I need you to think. Have you taken any drugs? Have you been drinking today, or stopped drinking after a long period of alcohol use?"

"No, no, I haven't done anything. I don't even drink anymore, anything but wine! I smoke pot sometimes, but not today. I just had"— I frowned, trying to remember—"coffee and a cinnamon roll."

The paramedic I'd find to be the driver studied my host. "The smell of his vomit is very distinct," said the man, and only then did I realize I had at some point been ill on myself, my shirt ruined. At last, in the face of this undeniable evidence, I burst into little-boy tears of embarrassment. I tried to cover my eyes but received a gentle reprimand from the nearest paramedic, who held my hand while the driver carried on to Enoch, "You don't use camphor as a sweetener, do you?"

"I certainly do when I am using variants of Middle Eastern flavor profiles," Enoch coolly confessed to the driver, then the man holding my hand. "I'm rather shocked to see such a reaction. I have been eating my cinnamon rolls all morning and suffered no issue. Frankly, I thought I had better lay off them for the sake of my trousers, not my frontal lobe."

The chiding drive sucked a tooth. "In high amounts, camphor can be seriously toxic."

"I had no idea," said Enoch, his tone so careless it all but declared his intimacy with the poison. I gaped as the paramedic got out of my way.

"You gave me camphor to give me a seizure?"

"You're saying he did this on purpose?" asked the driver, dark brow arched. Enoch watched, impassive. My laptop and Lightning Stenography Device and his laptop, too, were all gone from the table near his hip. The REM Story returned to me with its warnings of the seizure, and my tears cleared in the ringing of my amazed laughter to find myself just where I knew I'd end up. Katherine had said I would make the prophecy come true by acknowledging it, and she had been right. I'd have to tell her she was right. I inhaled. "Oh, I have to call Kitty."

Enoch's expression was angelic. "I have already taken the liberty of calling Miss Beauvoir from your cell phone, Cassius, after calling the paramedics. I expect she is already on her way to the hospital by one means or another."

"I wish I'd left her the car," I lamented, crying again, helpless on the floor in front of all these strangers. "Oh, Kitty, Katherine! I want to see Katherine."

"Then it sounds like we need to get you to the hospital," said the paramedic, while the driver continued to press, "Is this something that's going to have to be investigated, Cassius?"

Dry mouth rank from vomit, I shook my head for the pressing men and said, "No, I'm sorry, I'm just confused. I've never had a seizure before. Or camphor, either. I might be sensitive to it. Jesus, I don't know what's happened. I just want to see Katherine."

"You will," soothed the paramedic, whose name tag read "Roy." "We'll have you with her soon, Cassius. I'm just going to need you to relax so we can get you onto this stretcher, all right? Count of three." They were shifting me over, then elevating the stretcher to wheel me from the house, Enoch following, saying, "I will be at the hospital, Cassius, with your personal effects. Shoes, and all."

The word "shoes" was like a trigger, and, for reasons I couldn't articulate, I became enormously concerned with not just their location, but with the location of my wallet. "Wait a minute, wait." I tried to lift my head, but at some point in the blurring process I had been strapped down, and as I was loaded into the ambulance, I babbled to Roy and his driver, "My shoes."

"I think that was one of the things Mr. Azarias said he'd bring to you."

"And my wallet? My wallet, it's—"

"Is this it, sir, in your jacket?" Roy barely flinched as his gloved finger nudged my once-fine coat, now sticky with vomit, to probe the leather square within.

Frowning, I found it impossible to place why I was concerned with the state of my wallet. Of course I had my wallet. Enoch wouldn't have touched it, I was sure. "I'm just confused, I guess."

"We'll get you sorted out soon, Cassius," said Roy as his driver shut the door. Seconds later, we were rolling to the hospital, and I think I must have cried the whole way. For Christ's sake, I was nearly sixty, and had been warned the seizure would be coming. I was so disoriented, though. Who could blame me? Minutes before I had been feeling out of sorts, sure—but that complete displacement of space, and loss of time, was the fuse on a bomb of panic and loneliness and terror. Terror that something might happen to Katherine on the way to the hospital, or that she might not want to be with me now that I'd had a moment of weakness, even though I knew that was a ridiculous fear. But what if it took them a long time to do everything that needed doing, and what if I didn't have a chance to see her for hours? I'd barely been to the doctor for more than an annual physical in my life, yet there I was, with Dr. Benjamin Whey acquiring vitals from a nurse and asking things I couldn't remember or didn't seem to know, like how long ago I'd vomited or how much camphor I'd ingested. Then came the hustle of the tube crawling up my nose and down my throat, a sensation that still makes my skin crawl to think about, numbing or no numbing, benzodiazepine they pumped me with for the procedure, or no; then there was blood-taking, and of course they couldn't have been bothered to ask what arm I wrote with, so my left was the one that was pricked; and at one point the whitecoat had the nerve to, without diverting from the keyboard of the laptop at which he took furious notation, tell me, "I really loved your last book. Gotta keep you alive to write us the next one!"

It's the closest I've ever come to telling a professional of any sort to fuck off, let alone a medical professional with my life in his hands. Lucky for him (and for me), I was fairly loopy. The benzo, whatever it was, disassociated me from time and worry. Floating, carefree, in that white-paneled room of gleaming silver instruments and beeping machines, I realized it was the most relaxed I'd felt in weeks. When the fluid had been sucked out along with, hopefully, what was left of the undigested camphor, the doctor gave in to my begging and sent a peach-colored nurse off to fetch my visitor from the waiting room. Five minutes later she returned, and I was surprised to find with her not one person, but two: Katherine flew into the room, red-ringed eyes fixed on mine, and my heart swelled with relief like I'd never felt as she cried and laughed, said, "Oh, God, honey, you look horrible"; then slithered into the room the reason I'd had the seizure in the first place. My face fell, but his didn't. Shifting his cradled bouquet of lilies and roses from left arm to right, Enoch smiled in a placid way and lifted my briefcase.

"Cassius. You truly must accept my apologies." In retrospect, I think this was a sort of demand, based on how swiftly his black-eyed attention diverted to Katherine. "So this is Miss Beauvoir. A pleasure to make your acquaintance."

"Enoch," she pronounced with caution. The doctor at last turned his attention from his notations.

"Wait, now, Katherine Beauvoir, hey? Oh my God." There was a starstruck little sparkle in his eyes that made me realize how young he was—when did my doctors get younger than me?—and, flushed with thrill, he spread his hands. "I thought *Romulus* was one of the best contemporary works of literature I've read in years. Are you working on something new? You are, right? I thought I read something about a book called *On Orange Grove Road.*"

If she looked startled, it was because most people tended to recognize me over her. "Well, thank you," she said with a little smile, the kind I loved to see, which I wanted to put in a box and cherish, which made me reach out and take her hand as she flicked a grin back at me, then the doctor. "That's very nice of you to say. It's sort of a love story, about a girl and the devil. Kind of intended as a response to the romantic images society intends for women. Men, too."

"Sounds interesting. Not what I'd normally read, but, after *Romulus,*

I'll read anything you've got. Grocery lists," he said, and when that made her laugh, I felt another fleeting urge to clock him. "Forget whats-his-name from *TIME* magazine. You ask me, you're the greatest living writer. American, anyway." He rose, laptop under his arm. "I'll leave you folks alone, but is this the Enoch who was experimenting with Middle Eastern cinnamon rolls?"

"And coffee," admitted the unflappable man, arms still full as I noticed the bag in his elbow which I hoped contained my shoes. "There was not much. Perhaps not more than a teaspoon in the coffee, though I cannot possibly account for how much made it into his individual pastry."

With skeptical scrutiny for the mysterious entrepreneur who was a stranger even in the town where he resided; then for Katherine, who studied our hands to avoid eye contact; and then for me, too pumped full of benzos and too glad to have my shoes back to be confrontational, Dr. Whey shook his head. "I advise you cut out the kitchen experimentation. Mr. Wagner doesn't seem interested in pressing charges, but if somebody else is poisoned by your sweets, you might not be so lucky. And if you're the Enoch Azarias I'm thinking of, you have a lot to lose in a lawsuit."

"Of course, Doctor." Enoch adopted an ingénue's obedient moue. "No such thing shall happen again. Certainly not in my kitchen."

Nodding once, the doctor said, "I'll be back soon with the results of your blood test, so hang tight," and shut the door after him. He was approximately three steps down the hall before Katherine's face changed and she whirled toward Enoch.

"Camphor! You gave him *camphor*! Why the hell—"

"Honey," I tried.

"—would you even think of— Camphor is a *poison*, you tool bag, do you understand that? Camphor oil is for *topical* use—"

"Actually," replied patient Enoch, "camphor was widely used as a sweetener during the Middle Ages and was particularly popular—and still is—in many forms of Eastern cuisine."

"That doesn't excuse it. You could have killed him. I knew we shouldn't have come here."

"Ashland is the most beautiful town in America," I said cheerily, feeling very certain this was true, even though I had only driven around it the once and hadn't done anything but have a seizure and see its hospital. Enoch was happy to pick up the conversational ball.

"Isn't it just! My mother brought us here each year as small boys. She did so love the Shakespeare."

"Doesn't it feel like, I don't know, a parody of a town? It's so cute."

Katherine looked more impatient of our banter by the second. "Now's not the time to sell me the town, sweetie," said my lover, who turned back to face Enoch as he set the bag and LSD carrying case upon the chair, then lay the flowers and my briefcase upon the bedside table. "I'm not sure why you wouldn't sue, Cassius, or at least see to it that he's prosecuted so he doesn't do it to anyone else." She said all that like Enoch wasn't in the room, but that was Kitty when she was angry. I felt it was my job to calm her down, and so I said to Enoch, "You didn't want to hurt me, did you? I mean, you wouldn't be here, right?"

"Of course not. I only intended to be hospitable to you. But you know, Cassius, the circumstances of the seizure were most fortunate."

Bitter Katherine asked, "Fortunate? Yeah, real fortunate, a seizure."

"What was fortunate, dear woman, was not the seizure." Opening my briefcase as though it were his own, Enoch explained, "You see, while your husband—"

"*Boyfriend*," corrected my aggrieved lover, and her need to make the distinction in that way, at that moment, shot me through the heart, but I managed a smile and squeezed her hand.

"While your boyfriend," he carried on, unruffled, "was seizing upon my couch, he just so happened to be wearing the LSD."

A chill rippled through the hospital room, and from the top folder of my briefcase, Enoch removed a manuscript: crisp, new-printed, short. Katherine sweated against my palm, and when I lifted my hand away to accept the pages, she recoiled as though they were coated in anthrax.

"The results are most intriguing," said the man, as I, breathless, held this thing in my hands, skimmed the first few paragraphs, and leafed through its pages. "It appears to be a chronicle of the experience your, ego, let us call it, underwent during the seizure: when consciousness had left you, but your perception continued."

"How can you perceive something if you're not conscious?" asked Katherine, and Enoch, with a smile up at the ceiling, crossed himself in the swift way of a serious Catholic who did it often and took it more to heart than your average Jesus freak.

"That is the exquisite mystery of existence, Miss Beauvoir: that consciousness and the ego and the body are all intertwined and yet separate. Why, the very act of reading is enough to hearken such a revelation, consisting, as it does, of the parts of the author, the character, and the reader. Would you tell me, Katherine," he ventured at last, a certain eager edge hidden in the depths of his voice, "the REM story that you have channeled, is it about your uncle? Your aunt, perhaps, or grandfather?"

"'REM Story'?" asked Katherine, her face paling at mere mention of her family. As she turned scrambling eyes toward me, I remembered one of the things that had been bothering me so much in Enoch's house: her odd behavior, the little things she'd said or done. Lowering the manuscript, I asked, gently, "Did you write a story in your sleep, too, honey?"

As pallid as her face had grown, so, too, did her eyes darken. With a tremor to her lip, she said, "I don't know what that has to do with anything."

Now it was Enoch and I exchanging a glance. I, my brow furrowed, was quick to refocus on her. "You didn't tell me?"

She said nothing, and the heart wound caused earlier reopened at the notion that she didn't trust me enough to share something like this. I turned my pain outward on her, snapping, "All this time I thought I was crazy. I've thought there was something wrong with me, that I was writing in my sleep or the victim of some prank. Here you were going through the same thing. We could have been supporting each other all this time."

"I don't think it's good to acknowledge," she cautioned, avoiding my eyes in a way I hated. "You read your story, Cassius. You were compelled to follow it through, and now you're in the hospital."

The tip of Enoch's tongue wet his lower lip. "And he is holding in his hands an account from which many could potentially benefit. What treasures are held in your manuscript, Miss Beauvoir?"

"I haven't read it," said Katherine, shaking her head. "I don't know."

"Is it about your family," he pressed. "Your childhood?"

"It hasn't happened yet," she snapped. "None of it. It isn't like Cassius's story."

Marvel filled his voice as he surmised, "An entirely prophetic story. And what is it about?"

"I don't know. I just told you I haven't read it, and it's all out of order, anyway. I just...kept producing it until I stopped waking up to text, because I thought maybe I had to purge it. I don't know. When it was finished, I put my LSD away and didn't look back."

I reached for her, and she, with some reluctance, came into the embrace of my arm, blowing a few black strands out of her face as I asked, "What did you see?"

"It's a scene. There's a scene that's bothering me. I'm sitting on the ground with a human skull. I sort of...stopped reading after that. I don't know whose skull it is, or why it's there, or what. For all I know"—she laughed darkly, batting her eyes—"I could have been the one to make it. Or it could belong to you. Someone else I love. I don't know. I couldn't read it."

That same putrid silence from before reemerged, blooming like a corpse flower in its impossibly long cycle. Katherine still avoided eye contact by studying the window. Enoch focused on the manuscript. My mouth dry, I was trying to think of how to pose the suggestion I read her REM Story for her when I realized she was trembling, and I said, "Oh, honey."

"I want to move back in with you," she said at last, wiping a few tears from her eyes, and I thought my heart might stop. "I'm so scared, Cassius. I've been so scared. And then when I got the call from"—her eyes darted to the solemn man who waited—"I was so afraid. All the time I've wasted. What if you had died?"

"Do you mean it?" I asked, delirious. She nodded, and I laughed. "Are you sure I didn't die?"

"No, you didn't, don't say that." Sweeping her palm against her cheeks, Katherine gasped all the sharper. "If I lost you, I don't know what I'd do."

"You're going to lose me someday," I murmured, caressing the soft skin of her cheek, still so perfect and smooth, the way I felt it would be forever. Though the idea of my mortality normally bothered me as much as it bothered her then, I found, after my seizure, that I was carefree. Death and life seemed so abstract there in the hospital room, as she sorted herself with a breath.

"Please don't remind me. That's all the more reason to spend the time I can with you. Every scrap of time we can have together. Before, I was afraid for my career, but you're more important to me."

"I promise you, Kitty, I'll bend over backward to make sure everybody knows you're the giant you are. You want we should get Dr. Whey back in here and ask him again which of us is the best writer?" That made her laugh, and I turned my head to kiss her arm, trying to tamp down the butterflies of delight in my stomach. "It'll be okay. But would it make you feel better, or worse, if I read your REM Story for you? What if I read it over and was able to reassure you that everything was okay?"

Again, she stilled, and it was like I could hear her pulse drop out. "And if everything's not okay in the end?"

"Then we'll figure out a way to solve it. If everything's not okay in the end, that's more reason for us to meet the problem head-on, right?"

"And cause it to happen," she said, snorting.

Focused on the manuscript in my lap, Enoch suggested, "Depending on the way in which Cassius's REM Story ends, we may hardly be given a choice but to read it."

"How do you mean?" I asked, and the man waved a hand.

"You have not finished the REM Story quite yet, I suspect, and the text resulting from the seizure seems to be a kind of asynchronous addendum. It could, in theory, be placed in several ways with regards to the rest of the REM Story, but the most logical place would be either directly before or directly after Cassius's trip to the hospital, which, if I am not mistaken, has yet to be Received."

"That's true," I realized, laughing as the nefarious seizure resolved into a tool to acquire the document in my lap. "If I were writing this story, I'd probably set the denouement post seizure. That means I've got a whole section still to Receive."

Nodding once, Enoch suggested, "So depending, then, on how the denouement ends, we may not—in fact, likely will not—be presented with a full story. There is a broader arc at work here, a climactic goal to be had. Or am I alone in feeling this?"

"I promise, Kitty"—I kissed the smooth skin at the crease of her elbow—"if there's something wrong in it, something weird, I'll tell you, and help you. Whatever it is, we'll figure it out. But let me decipher it. All this time you've been editing my stuff, I've never edited any of yours. What do you say you let me take a crack at getting this thing into shape for you?"

Caught between Enoch and I, her fingers sinking into my arm, Katherine blinked at the ceiling, and, at last, said, "Okay, Cassius. You can read it. You can do whatever you want with it."

"I am quite certain that Cassius only wants the same thing you do, Katherine: to understand."

With a sea-salt gaze directed out the window, Katherine made no response, only lingered there with her arms crossed and her body warm against mine. It was this same window to which Enoch walked, this same window through which he admired the world, saying, "How beautiful it always is after the rain. You can hear the scrub jays even through all the hospital equipment."

8

The knock which broke our solitude frightened my attention toward the running yolk of its sound, while a matchstick-colored veil shielded the upper half of my vision in a way akin to the fluttering of eyelids. The front door of Enoch's house opened before my host could get it. This was strange, this door opening by itself, because I was certain it had been locked behind me, and because I had the most profound certainty, while the door was closed, that what lurked on the other side was nothing but a dog; yet, there stood a man whom Enoch thrilled to see.

"Ah," he said with delight, smiling, straightening, standing, "my brother! My brother has come to visit, Cassius, and at what a fortuitous time."

The new guest shut the door and took down the hood of his coat wet with rain; I knew his face in a thrilling, heart-wrenching instant. I knew him better than any old friend, better than Katherine, better than my own face, although I could not quite see his features, which seemed at times the vision I had seen in dreams, at others a sliding figment akin to the depiction of the dark-haired man on the ceiling of the room in which we all stood. I knew, of course, the guest's name before Enoch said it while coming to take his cloak: "My brother has many names, Herr Wagner, good man. Abel, Castor, and Esau, and sometimes Epimetheus. And when I am called the Devil, then he is called Christ, but when I am called Christ, he is called Lazarus, for he is that, too, and more."

There was no chance to ask him to narrow that down to one true name. Lazarus was rushing toward me, laughing, taking up my hand like the old friend he was to shake it with an almost parodic vigor which was yet the most genuine touch I've ever experienced from another human being—though my heart burned to be embraced by him, because he was, within, much more than human.

"Cassius! I've waited so long to meet you. Can you imagine this?" He fell back as though he were the amazed one, and I ran my hand over my face and laughed.

"What do you mean, can I imagine this! I always thought I'd have to die to meet you in the flesh. I thought," I added with a less-than-lucid laugh, "that you were a dog, out there in the rain. Do you remember that time, that Halloween, where Katherine and I had a knock at the door and thought it would be a trick-or-treater, but when we opened it up, it turned out to be the stray cat she'd been feeding?" I laughed harder, like I was high, and Lazarus laughed along with me.

"I remember! Your face was priceless. And hers, too. Say, Cassius." As his arm dropped around my shoulder, guiding me to the door, I realized Enoch had deserted us, disappeared from the coatrack in the corner as though he had never been. It seemed like him to scurry off, though I'd just met the guy. "I'd like to have a talk with you, and I'm not going to be in town for a very long time. You want to go get some food with me?"

"I'll go anywhere for a chance to figure you out."

With a wry laugh and a twinkle in his eye, acid blue and bright as the sunshine to which he opened the door, Lazarus teased, "If you want to find out about me, you're going to have to write."

At my withering expression, he giggled in delight, and behind us Enoch called, "Good day, Mr. Wagner, I shall see you soon," over the slam of the door. Waving my hands in frustration, I trailed along behind my character and insisted, "You know what you're about better than I do."

"Yeah, but it's one thing to *know* and another thing to *experience*, right?" Brow cocked, sometimes-bearded face stern over his shoulder, he emphasized, "You can impart knowledge, but you can't impart the experience of understanding knowledge. In order to understand me, you have to feel me. Feel me? And how does a writer feel his characters?" he asked in a way that was brotherly, fatherly, chiding, playful, as he opened the gate of Enoch's house and held it wide for me.

"By writing." I said with a guilty sigh. He nodded sagely, shutting his brother safe in solitude behind us.

"That's exactly right. I'm not here to help you understand me—well, I am. That's sort of a by-product, though, of what I'm trying to do here, to you, and for...let's say 'God.'"

My heart raced with excitement as I bounded along with him. There were plenty of people up and down the sidewalks now, smiling and nodding as we passed one another in the drying beauty of the day. "I know you're a religious man, right?"

"'Spiritual,' maybe," said Lazarus with a squint toward the sun. "I don't care for religion. Religions cause problems. My brother runs a cult."

"Yeah, and your brother keeps trying to steal the spotlight of the story."

"So, let him. It will all work itself out, or I'll work it out for you. I know what I'm doing better than you do," he said with a grin. "You need me to exist to know what I'll do, just the way the so-called God of this world needs you to exist to know what you'll do."

Laughing, I asked, "Why does the God of this world need to know what I'll do?"

As we made our way down the street, a cat mewled from the depths of an elderberry bush to our right, and Lazarus stooped to greet the animal which emerged, black and white, one-eyed. Its stretch seemed more bow for my friend than all that. "Well, for one thing, God needs to know what you'll do because it's inevitable that God knows what you'll do, since you exist. Your existence implies many logical conclusions: the existence of every human being, every animal," he said as he scratched the purring cat beneath its jaw, and just as I reached down to pet the animal, too, it resumed its business with little more than a polite bump for my shin. It even looked both ways before it crossed the street. "And every person and animal in turn implies the existence of you. Come here, let's get some coffee."

"No more coffee for me today, thanks. Maybe some water." I waved a hand as he opened the door of the coffee shop situated beyond the bush, its parking lot overcrowded but the shop itself mostly empty. It had more a restaurant's interior than that of a cafe, with long rows of booths rather than tables, and a jukebox arranged in the corner. I headed for one of the isolated seats, but Lazarus pulled me to the booth situated across from one of the only other sets of customers. He flashed a winning smile at the family there, then at the waitress who came by to take our orders of coffee and water. When she was gone, my animated friend was back in eager dialogue. "It's like the story God is sending you, Cassius, you see? It's a stone, a stone in a tower."

"A tower to what?"

With a more secretive smile, he lowered his head, his electric eyes twinkling. "You know why I love reading, Cassius? It's because you're there without being there at all. You forget for however long you're pulled into the story that you're an ego in a chair with a body and a book in your hand. Instead, you're just the story you're experiencing. When you go back and read this section, when you experience it consciously for the first time, you'll feel what I mean. You can sit there, feeling the character below you and feeling yourself animating the character with your consciousness, but that's never a—"

"Can I stop you for a second," I said as the waitress returned with the mug and the glass. Patient Lazarus stopped himself and picked up the coffee as I leaned my forearm against the edge of the table. "You said 'when I go back and read this section,' and 'when I experience it consciously,' but I'm experiencing it, right? I'm here."

"Oh, sure," said my friend, playing up the visage of a guilty man pretending to be innocent with a sly sip of coffee, "but I mean, who are we to say what 'now' really is? At any minute, we could find ourselves in a nontemporal state without ever having realized it. If the ego and consciousness were related but separate entities, and one absented from the other or consciousness differentiated itself to a bodily degree, that would cause the ego's perception of time to alter, like in dreams. Time is a method of organizing entropy in a manner comprehensible to consciousness as perceived by the human mind through the lens of the ego," he said between sips, as if I understood a quarter of that without stopping to think. By the time I'd caught on, he was already back at it. "When you wake up, you're not going to remember we had this conversation. You won't even remember the gap. It's for the best. It can be sort of terrifying to experience the things you're going to experience firsthand, but it has to happen so it can be recorded, because that's the way the story goes."

Although I wanted more than anything to interrupt him and leap on some of what he was saying about a gap and my waking up, trying to hold the thought was like trying to hold water in my hands. I found myself latching on to the last thing he'd said, about the story.

"If the universe were a novel, don't you suppose there'd be things missing? A lot fewer people."

"Of course not! Not from our perspective. Come on, Cassius. When you write a novel, do you name every person on the street? Or, when you say your character is walking in a crowded street, do you take it for granted that the street is crowded with people and not, say, crocodiles."

Snorting, I said, "They're obviously people, Lazarus, and you would know. But that doesn't mean I'm creating a universe."

"See them over there?"

On Lazarus's soft words, I acknowledged the family chattering to my left, a nice-enough soccer mom sort with her hair in a headband sitting across from her beefy husband while their children, laughing, threw ice at once another. Quietly, I sucked a tooth.

"What's wrong?" asked Lazarus.

"Acting like that in a restaurant," I muttered, while my dining companion picked ice from my glass and slipped it down my shirt. I yelped in surprise, and the children laughed while Lazarus, with a too-big grin, folded his hands.

"I couldn't resist! You were being such a curmudgeon. They're just kids, Cassius. See how much fun they're having? Ah, that's pure! And you know what's even more incredible?" he asked, eyebrows lifted. "Those people exist so we can see them." At that, I laughed because it seemed such a solipsistic thing to say, but he was undeterred. "The entity who orchestrates this universe, who operates it, who positions everything together, created them—or at least accounted for their existence and unconsciously shepherded them here—so that you and I could have a conversation about them."

"Doesn't that seem ludicrous to you?"

"It's true! I mean, God didn't consciously create those people. God didn't say, 'All right, I'm going to branch off this ancestral line here, and through this point, these specific things have to happen to get this family to this restaurant on this date.' Remember our 'crowded street' metaphor from before. You don't do that as an author, do you? There's an unconscious, material function which takes care of that so consciousness doesn't have to: the forward movement of genetic evolution instead of the upward, memetic one. There are a lot of layers to this operation. And that's why the whole thing is so incredible, so intricate. I mean, think about it: if a tree falls in a forest and no one is around to hear it, does it make a noise?"

"Oh, come on."

"Something has to be observed to be real," insisted Lazarus, tapping the Formica table.

"Those people would observe themselves, then."

"Not necessarily. I will refer you to a one-panel comic by the Sunday-morning strip artist, Gary Larson." He pulled from the lining of his robe a phone and began tapping away. "Two microbes are married, and the husband microbe is watching television while the embittered wife microbe shouts, 'Stimulus, response! Stimulus, response! Don't you ever *think*?'" Laughing at his own shrill impression of the lady microbe, he slid the phone to me. I chuckled to see the comic.

"I remember this one. I never really got it. I remember reading it a couple of times as a kid and being almost bothered by it."

Tapping the temple of his forehead, he said, "That's because it made you think."

He leaned forward, but as he opened his mouth, he realized that wasn't close enough for him. Instead, he slipped from his seat and into my side of the booth, forcing me to scoot over if I wanted to avoid touching him. Even that wasn't enough, of course, because he draped an arm around me to draw me close to his whispering mouth.

"Those people over there are unconscious, Cassius. They're not awake like you and I, really. And I know that sounds like a shitty thing to say," he agreed, lifting his free hand to silence me before I spoke, "but it's not an insult. It's just the way it is. People can choose to wake up at any time. There are advantages to it, and disadvantages to it, but it's always easier not to. Most don't want to, and most never will, and, frankly, some people probably shouldn't. But some people should, and will, and do."

"Wake up from what, exactly," I said, scouting out the exits from my uncomfortable position.

"It's hard to explain, because you have to use a metaphor to explain it, and the problem with metaphors is that they hypnotize you back to sleep. You start taking them literally. I read this book once, about blue feathers and movie theaters; and another one about smoke and mirrors and moonlight; and another one with a talking snake in a garden giving fruit to sexy ladies. They all pretty much say the same thing, but the more you become invested in one particular metaphor, the further you get from the actual truth, until the truth and the symbol are irreconcilable."

Barely hanging on to what he said, I asked, "What does this have to do with waking up?"

"The waking up comes when you realize the truth being implied."

"What, the hippie, 'we are one' Buddhist thing? Not that that's not a nice way to be if you get around the nihilism, but—"

"Oh, it's not nihilistic. Maybe to those entrenched in a Western mind-set, who have experienced only their egos and believe in the power of materiality to the exclusion of the power of the mind. But this isn't the Buddhist thing. Well, it is that," he confirmed, spreading his hands, "but it's not that. It's that and less than that and more that. Absolutely, we're all one, all part of the same entity, the same experience. But I'm clearly not you, physically or psychologically. Right?" He patted my arm and then touched my head and his own head, saying, "Unless you're writing about me, you don't know I'm thinking about how I want to blow this joint and go get a bratwurst at the place by the hardware store."

Laughing, I drew my wallet from my breast pocket and said, "That's fine. We should probably continue this conversation someplace more private," but he was already up and going for the door. Shaking my head, I opened my wallet and found there three thousand dollars through which I rifled, having difficulty with both the amount of bills and the bills themselves, which were one figure at first but proved different on second consideration. I'd taken the three bills in my left hand to consist of a five-dollar bill and two ones, but when I looked closely, there was a wrongness to them. I frowned until, from the doorway, my friend said, "Cassius," and I dropped the bills upon the table to follow him.

On the crowded street, Lazarus led me through downtown without a word, his eyes bright and cast on the sky, the trees, the buildings and street signs and people. He took in all things and paid the utmost attention to every detail, laughing at a sticker on the back of a Kesey-style acid bus, smiling at sunflowers laconic in the breeze. By the time we were alone in a quieter part of town, he had noticed a raven's feather lying in the black background of the gutter and snatched it up with a cry of delight.

"I have no idea how you noticed that," I said, and he grinned, handing it over to me.

"You just have to observe! That's the thing I'm trying to explain to you. See"—he led the way, and I realized he had given me the feather, so I shrugged, slipped it into my breast pocket, and followed the man down the narrow sidewalk—"there's a duty to observe the world around us. To be the most successful, knowledgeable versions of ourselves. If you're knowledgeable, and doing everything you're supposed to be doing—which is really all anybody can ever do when you think about it—then God can come into you, and observe through you."

"Isn't that fatalistic? Doesn't that leave a lot of room for people to say, 'I guess God destined me to be lazy'?"

"Sure, people will say that, but it's a middle-ground, give-and-take thing. The idea of a person erecting a temple, the idea of the body being a temple, the idea of the spiritualization of the body and the will, these are all very important. You can't host God in a cogent way without being prepared for it, the way certain molecules can only bond in certain ways with certain other molecules. That means the psychological experience which people interpret as the divine is a two-way street. God chose you because you write, because you have the proper context and set of experiences to bear the weight of this story of knowledge. Meanwhile, you're turning toward God because it's what you're meant for, like an acorn destined for the oak."

Sighing, I shook my head and said, "I really don't know about you, pal."

"Of course you don't! That's why you've been reshelving me for all these years. A—granted, excellent—singer dies, leaves behind a rock opera, and you sit on me for years just because I happen to share a name with its title, then get too caught up in your own drama to consider me for a decade."

"It seemed respectful, holding you back. The timing was poor. And as for my personal stuff—"

"Ah, fiddlesticks, excuses. You were writing about me for years before that album came out. You just wanted an excuse to work on something easier. Know what a 'zeitgeist' is? The same thing that's writing your REM Story. Ride that wave, baby." Laughing, Lazarus patted my cheek, then without so much as faltering for the overly polite, quick-to-stop Oregon drivers and autos, dashed across the street to the hardware store parking lot and the Bento-Dog stand there situated. One agitated purchase later I, at the wrought-iron table nearby, remembered what had bothered me in the cafe. "It's hard to focus with you. Jumping from thing to thing like this isn't good for my brain. This business with waking up— Hey"—I was again derailed, this time by a nakedness, an ice-white urgency which had me reaching into my pocket, then patting again and again as I sat up to realize—"my wallet is gone!"

"Just relax," said Lazarus, munching away, grimacing as onions flew from his lunch but then getting the idea to feed the birds.

"What do you mean, 'just relax'! I just had it, we just bought the damn—" I got up from the table, but Lazarus didn't so much as sit upright as he busied himself tearing off pieces of bread.

"It's not going to be there."

"And why is that?"

"It's not anywhere, where we are and the way we're being. You follow me?"

"No!" I knocked on the window of the bizarre establishment, calling, "Excuse me!"

The person who had sold us the hot dogs (unnerving resemblance to Minerva, as it happened), slid open the window. "No refunds, sorry."

"I'm not interested in a refund, but did you see a wallet up here?"

"I watched you put it back in your pocket," said the clerk, and I patted my breast pocket, empty even of feathers, while grumbling, "Thanks," before dropping back into the seat across from Lazarus.

Being angry never solved anything. That was what I told myself while I assessed this madman's face. No, it never solved a thing at all, but sometimes it felt good. Granted, it didn't make sense to be angry at Lazarus. There was no way he had grifted the wallet from me. But still, he was talking as if he knew something about it. I asked at last, "Where is it?"

"You'll get it back," he said with a wave of his hand. "Just deal with it, you'll be fine. It'll seem like another hour or so *now*, but it's the blink of an eye. You won't even know you lost it until you read the printout."

"That's a pretty big gap, between an hour and the blink of an eye."

"Time doesn't matter as much when you're in a situation like this, like I keep telling you." Dusting off his hands, he belched into his fist, excused himself, and continued. "So, what are some of the things you need in a character?"

"What the hell do you mean?"

Laughing, Lazarus asked, "When you're writing a story, what are some basic things you need from a character? What do you, as a writer, tend to write about?"

"People ready for change?" I asked, and Lazarus's eye drifted sidelong to the store across the street with its bright-pink tuxedo on display like a siren.

"Sort of, but it's more than that. You write about somebody you can empathize with, right? Somebody with whom you have an emotional tie."

"Generally—" I said, beginning to qualify, but Lazarus waved a hand.

"I'm not interested in counterexamples. I just need you to follow me for a minute, Cassius, because I'm here for something serious." He folded his hands and lowered his head. "Something which requires our focus."

Humbled, I folded my hands in a manner similar and, shifting, said, "Sorry."

"The thing is that, yeah, sure, you can write about somebody you don't empathize with, but what kind of story is that? To make a compelling character, whether hero or villain, you've got to empathize with them, and the same is true of reading. In fact, if you can empathize with both the villain and the hero, it's a lot better, since that's how life is, right?" I nodded, and Lazarus went on. "God wants to empathize with us, and God wants us to empathize with each other, because in empathizing with each other, we're empathizing with God—even, or especially, when we empathize with the worst of mankind. 'But I tell you, love your enemies, and pray for those who persecute you,' in Christian parlance."

"I hate to interrupt you, but you mean to say that God, some pan-dimensional entity so far above us we could never conceive of it, wants empathy?"

"Well, again, it's more complex than that. What God is really after is understanding, which is just a kind of pathos. Doesn't everybody want empathy? Isn't that why we read stories, why we interact with one another to begin with? To have somebody to empathize with, somebody to empathize with us? But, of course, there's no way to completely empathize with another human being, because we haven't been through every moment of their life: we don't have their brain or an understanding of exactly the type of person they are inside. We only have our own, personal consciousness. That's why I hate books that flip from viewpoint to viewpoint without an in-text explanation. That's just not how life works. Aren't there some lives you wish you could understand end to end? Isn't that why you write? So you can really understand what makes people, people?"

"I write for a lot of reasons," I said, and Lazarus spread his hands.

"That's right: lots of reasons, probably as many reasons as you have characters. And characters, themselves, are created for specific reasons, like those guys." By pure coincidence, the family from the restaurant walked down the side of the street opposite us, past that pink tuxedo. "Think about that. All their ancestors, all their friends and relatives, all the people who happened to interact with those relatives to propel them, one way or another, toward their fate. All of those countless people have had to exist just so that you and I can see this family twice today. Probably a third time later, because that's how these things work."

I shook my head, finished my sausage, and said to my friend, "You're a narcissist."

"If no one was conscious enough to observe them, Cassius, could those people really be said to exist? If they're not conscious enough to observe themselves, somebody has to do it for them."

"Is that what you mean by this business of waking up? Consciousness?"

"Absolutely." Lazarus hopped up, disposed of our trash, then uttered a delighted squeal as the hardware store's Tom Bombadil–esque busker began playing "Cindy" on his banjo. "I love that song!"

"Don't get distracted," I told him, and he laughed, catching himself.

"Multitasking is physically impossible for your brain," Lazarus told me, beginning to head down the street and adding, "Do you want to go to the beach?"

"Sure," I said, as if Ashland had a beach, not even registering that we were nowhere near the shore because I was too busy correcting him. "People are conscious, though. I mean, they're alive, they're alert and aware. You ask them a question, they answer it."

"Yes and no. They're alive, sure. But conscious? That's sort of a difficult thing to say. The more you follow the crowd, give yourself up to group psychology and society's standards of ethics, or religion, or whatever, the more hypnotized you'll be by all of this. Then, like the microbes in our Gary Larson strip, we're just sitting in our chair, watching television, acting unconsciously in response to stimuli: buying things, doing things, even creating things unconsciously, all because of the exquisite illusion pervaded around and within." He waved a hand before him, indicating everything, the fixed-gear bike shop, the trees, the prattling jays. "The illusion is that you are separate from everything else, and this is all there is, and death is the end. It's all parlor tricks. Trick of the light, if you will." He laughed at some private joke while I huffed.

"I fail to see how you can be hypnotized by reality."

"You can, though! The Hindus say, 'Maya,' or 'illusion.' I mean, sure, life is absolutely real. If I were to pinch you"—he tried to pinch my cheek, and I dodged it, barely—"you'd feel it, or if you were to trip"—this, I very nearly did, my right foot dragging as my left foot caught me—"you'd definitely feel it. All the things you do in the world, all your accomplishments, all the people you love, they're real! Absolutely. But they're also a fiction."

"That sounds like indescribably high levels of bullshit," I said, failing to recognize that we turned a corner near a yoga studio and emerged on a boardwalk populated with a murmuring sea of excited people where there was normally, I would come to find, a railroad, a field, and a series of small businesses with second-floor apartments. Certainly no beach. Never offended, Lazarus laughed, leading me past the ticket stand where I was forced to do a double take upon seeing again the family from before.

"It sure sounds like bullshit, I know! That's why there's a lot of trouble with using symbols and metaphors. Of course, that's what all words are: symbols and metaphors."

The arcade was packed but the Skee-Ball alleys were empty, so we took up the two on the end and began feeding quarters to the machines, even though I couldn't remember having change in my pocket. I supposed it was from the hot-dog clerk, but there was no placing it. As he got his first ball in the upper-left-hand corner, my friend said, "It's sort of a challenging notion to get across in words. Like I said before, with empathy, you can *know* something, or you can *experience* it. I can just tell you about me and what kind of person I am, but if you write a story about me, you'll live my life and feel what kind of person I am the way a reader who reads about me will, too."

"Right, but what about those people, those side characters, who just get ignored by God because they're a part of the crowd? Not"—I lifted my hands to do air quotes, mocking—"'awake' enough to attract God's attention. I mean, how do you even know what it is that attracts God to somebody?"

"Oh, I don't claim to! I'm not saying anything like that. God still loves the people who are off in the background, because they're all a part of God in the same way as you or I, and they're necessary to God in the same way. We wouldn't be able to have a conversation about all the people here if they didn't all exist, after all! All their friends and family, like I said before. I mean, that's tens of thousands of people, millions of them over the generations. All that, just for this conversation."

"Can you not see how crushing that is? How awful, to exist as a conversation piece! You can't mean that the whole reason these people exist is just so you and I can talk about them."

"Well, why else would they exist? God is observing them through us, and that's wonderful. God is interested enough in the fact that they exist to explore the fact that they exist based on your observations that they exist, and that's true of every stranger you observe but never speak to. God, He, or She, or whatever—'It,' say—It's not being negligent. God is just God, right?" Lazarus shrugged, made a ball in the center hole, pumped his fist, and said, "See, I think it's more crushing to consider the way you think. The whole atheistic, science-based, survival-of-the-fittest model. I mean, it's true there's no rhyme or reason, there's no grand design—"

"You just said there was," I half shouted, though it seemed normal volume over the din of the clattering machines and the chattering people.

"There's a big-picture grand design in the same way that, the more time you stare at a group of numbers or a collection of trees, the more patterns emerge. There's undeniably a sort of entity observer which operates through us, which wants to learn from us, wants to be acknowledged by us in the same way we want to be acknowledged by other people. This so-called God is mutually responsible for the living of your life and of all the things happening in it, but the trees sort of grow themselves, and the gardener comes in and maintains them, right? Think about your characters!" As the lights went off above his third high-scoring shot, my friend said, "You sort of come up with them, but it's more like they abstractly develop over time."

"It's like they come to me," I confirmed. "Like I want somebody to fulfill a certain role, and they just kind of...emerge, and take it further than I ever expected."

"Exactly right. Kind of how Michelangelo would imagine the sculpture in marble and carve away everything that wasn't the sculpture, when you need a certain character, you're sending out vibrations for that archetype into the unconscious and bringing them up to the surface, giving them consciousness and attention and energy. Assuming there is an impersonal unconscious, which essentially amounts to a kind of simultaneous ground for reality and a limitless ocean of imagination, then that impersonal unconscious shared by all entities contains all possible permutations of thought, being, personage. All people and characters and concepts already exist; what they require to be made conscious is the right context, the right amount of energy, and the right background. Not everybody's capable of fulfilling that role. If you want to write a story about a writer, say, you're not in the market for a protagonist who's a passionate laundromat worker. Unless it's symbolic."

"I suppose. But crafting a good, three-dimensional character isn't like some job interview where you just go into your unconscious and pick the best person."

"No, not at all! It's a gradual unfolding. You touch on them initially, and you'll find out who they really are later, at the end of the process, just like living life." At last, Lazarus had run out of shots, and the machine spewed pink tickets like a sick man in a bar bathroom. "It's a beautiful thing, life."

"Except for all the people on the other side of beauty." I crossed my arms because I, also, was out of shots, and had received three tickets for my efforts. "People suffering in Sudan, say, or dealing with post-traumatic stress disorder after war." At the sympathy with which Lazarus opened his mouth, I said, "Don't tell me those people are suffering just so we can talk about them."

"Well, that's not the only reason. I mean, remember, too, that people have free will. Human beings can still do what they want within the confines of the almost-limitless options given them. With that in mind, at the end, the choices they inevitably make are indelible, because a certain person can only make a certain choice: the choice they always make. Without consciousness, they're just apes, the way a computer without someone to run the software is just a hunk of metal. Let them run around, and they're liable to murder somebody, right? Every person has an individual choice to make, whether they're going to open themselves up as a channel for the universe. If they do, then anything is possible. But the more they close themselves up and hide in fear, the further away they fall. And that's not to say that God doesn't observe the evil as closely as the good, since good can't exist without evil and vice versa, but there's conscious evil and unconscious evil. There's evil that arises out of fear, like what politicians drum up during wartime, or when an abuser hits his wife because he's afraid she'll leave him, but there's also conscious evil, and that, like William Blake says, is naught but energy. And the politicians doing the drumming up, that's conscious evil only if they're aware of what they're doing, of the condition and significance of their fellow men. Most of them are just as unconscious as anybody else."

"Seems to me like it's sort of awful to be more conscious than every-body else," I said, and Lazarus, leading me to the prize counter, insisted, "It's really not. Consciousness does a valuable service to humanity. We need as many conscious, mindful people as possible. People who don't just unconsciously obey the mindless instincts and urges but who instead consciously try to gather as much knowledge as they can, like a man trying to build a fire, in hopes that the next man to come along will be able to start his own from the burning coals."

"But what is the fire moving toward?"

The ticket taker, who bore a resemblance to Chase, handed over a glow-in-the-dark yo-yo without having to be told what was wanted. With boyish delight for his prize, Lazarus refocused on me. "Like everything else, it's moving toward God."

Sighing, I shook my head and was the one who led the way, Lazarus trailing behind me as we emerged upon the boardwalk; the water had begun to absorb the atomic hue of the setting sun. "It shouldn't be nearly this late," I insisted, but my friend, unfurling the yo-yo to make it hover in stride with his step, carried on through the thinning crowd.

"You see, it's true that God wants empathy, as we discussed. But what is empathy but *understanding*? The understanding of a person and that person's motivations, specifically? The goal of the thing which we call God, the experience we call 'God,' is in part to be subjectively experi-enced and understood by the human brain, to be made manifest in the perfect metaphor. And the perfect metaphor requires a context. Gnosis. Once that gnosis, that understanding of the perfect metaphor, is had, then language and culture have both reached an apex. It means they've hit a momentum which allows for language to basically give a psychedelic experience, since God is something which can only be completely grasped by *being* experienced. A 'psychedelic' experience is just a 'mind-manifesting' experience, so when the Bible talks about manifesting the Word as Logos, it's describing an ideal where the mind literally manifests its contents externally and makes tangible what is only perceptible via language or sensation or imagination. That's why the best writers really *put* you there. You see the curtains billowing in that room with Nick and Tom and the ladies in *Gatsby*. The image evoked, the way it's evoked...words are a magician's tool, Cassius. They're God's tool."

"'In the beginning was the Word,'" I asked, "'and the Word was with God.'"

"'And the Word *was* God,'" responded Lazarus, emphatically.

At last, at the stairs which led from boardwalk to beach, Lazarus slipped off his sandals and stepped down. I followed suit, somehow unconcerned by leaving them on the busy walkway, which would have bothered me an unreasonable amount most times. "Consciousness can't arise without language, the way a program can't run on a computer without a programming language. It's why feral children, even if they do develop some language after a while, are generally just lost. Humans are animals, like I said. Monkeys. The inner light of consciousness is what we should really be identifying with, but part of the problem is that you've got a lot of Bible literalists who can only see the material. Society requires an emphasis on external, material living to progress forward. When you write a thought, you're crystallizing it to share it with another person. Freezing it. But in freezing it, we can never completely communicate what we want to communicate, because what we truly want to communicate is beyond words, which are, by and large, imprecise. When you try to crystallize the experience of God at this point, we don't have—"

"The metaphor," I said to the water which lapped across my feet. Over my shoulder, the expanse of beach had emptied, and the boardwalk, I felt, had never been there to begin with. That notion didn't bother me like it should have. Who could be bothered by anything with water like that touching your feet? When the dawning night was so cool and clear, and when I was there with my friend who squinted at the fast-vanishing sun and nodded his approval?

"That's right, we haven't found the perfect metaphor yet. We don't have the cultural context to support it. Every time we try to capture in one way or another what God is at this point in human history, it's bound to be imprecise. That's why the focus of the Word should be, not on crystallizing dogma and grasping God but on *experiencing* God. It should conjure the sensation without trying to describe. Talk around it, but not about it. It's sort of like how in Judaism there are so many names for the one entity: Elohai, Elohim, YHWH. Incidentally—" Lazarus smiled, placid as the waves upon which he stepped, then turned back to offer me his hand. As I took it, and placed a sure foot upon the water which held me like a ballroom floor made of cold crystal taffy, he continued, "the name given Moses on Sinai—you're aware how that's usually translated, aren't you, Cassius?"

"'I am,'" I said, and I faltered, then, as he smiled.

"That's the marvelous thing. 'I am' experiencing, 'I am' alive, 'I am' in love; who's doing these things? Who's experiencing these things? It's not you, Cassius."

"Not me?" I asked, barely hanging on, a tingling in my cheekbones and skull.

"No. After all, you're not really experiencing this. You're reading this, in a hospital room. But you're still experiencing it all the same, aren't you?"

"I am," I remembered with a gasp, buoying upon the waves with my hand in his, my lips parting slightly as the words left my mouth. He smiled at that, squeezed my hand, and walked toward the setting sun, which shared the sky with a low-hung moon, her white face paled by his light. I stumbled after my friend, and the words, those two words used for everything, anything, locked themselves in my head, vibrating around in my skull so hard it was as though I was going to be shaken apart by them. My stomach lurched in incredulity as I felt myself and further than myself, felt the word "I" like a column stretching up and down, an endless thread, a word I used to describe my own actions as much as the actions of my characters. If I were creating a story about a creator, and that creator created a story within that story, it would form a kind of column of perception up and down, from the top of the sky to the bottom of my feet, farther, farther still, and I took a sharp, swaying breath, and said, "My God, Lazarus."

"Do you see? That vertical motion, that's what I was talking about."

I ran my hand over my face and all but wept, and said, "But I don't understand."

"There are lots of different ways to communicate it, perceive it. Lots of different people experience it, and experience it in different ways, through different means. Sometimes you achieve it sitting under a Bodhi Tree. A guy might figure it out at a young age and be nailed to a cross for speaking too loudly. You and I," said my friend in good cheer, lifting his head toward a sky the velvet dark of natal nocturnity, "are here to help Katherine with her story, and God with God's story."

"Katherine's story," I said, and Lazarus nodded, fixed upon the face of the pale moon.

"We are all vessels for something larger than ourselves: something immeasurable which animates us, forms the ground of us, is us. We each of us have within ourselves the blueprint of our potential, as a tree has within itself its genetic code, the blueprint of the perfect tree. Specifically, the perfect version of that tree. And what tree can help but grow to its potential, Cassius, unless prevented by external circumstance?"

"What is it about Katherine's story that makes it important? What is its purpose, please?"

His gaze still upon the moon compelled me to fix mine likewise. Around it, above it, beyond it, grew stars, their light stretching out from aeons past to reach the pupils of my eyes, and when the ocean had gone from beneath our feet, we walked on space itself. Vertigo relented to delight at my fancy that we found ourselves in the pupil of some eye, greater than mine, but not the greatest, and I held up my hands, envisioning for a flickering instant some Thing, a person-beyond-persons, but not in the form of man or woman. It came upon me instead in the form of a mechanical insect, four faces and eight limbs arrayed like the spindled legs of a spider hard at work weaving, or perhaps working machinery, or maybe even typing, with six fingers on each hand and a towering miter of stars upon its head, which I knew it had fashioned for itself. The stars were numbered fourteen, twice seven, and two faces were the faces of men, and one face was the face of a woman, but the face which gazed upon me was that of a bug with clacking incisors and cheerful black eyes, its body the mahogany flame of rust or bronze. Then Lazarus was shaking me, saying, "No navel-gazing, Cassius, don't go drifting off. Don't take anything you see or feel literally."

"Sorry," I said, blinking, running my hands over my face.

"What we're doing here is important. Do you see what you are?"

I had never seen anything so beautiful as all these stars, these distant galaxies swirling in elaborate formation before giving way to the wire frame upon which reality was lain like a ground by which the dimensions were animated in hallucinatory vision of the complicity of life. "Oh, Lazarus, it's so beautiful. But why am I seeing this? Am I dead, have I died?"

With sympathy from behind a face which seemed fleetingly a skull, my friend said, "Death is only a release of energy, Cassius, a release of consciousness back upward. I suppose this is death, in a way." New tears sprang to my eyes.

"Oh, no, but Lazarus, I can't. Katherine, I don't want to leave Katherine. And I was never there for Thomas, was I? Oh, Tommy." My left hand lifted to my mouth. I was unable to face Lazarus when there floated behind my eyes the distant face of my son, my little boy. All the years I'd blown by, writing, drinking, going on book tours! And when Kitty came into our lives when the kid was thirteen, away he went with his mother in such a huff I didn't see him for four years, until at last he returned to me, tried to go to school and connect with me—but I couldn't manage it. I couldn't manage, my God, to connect with the one real life I had created. Here I was, dead, or dying, maybe, and talking to a fictional character in a conversation more profound than any I'd had with my own child, a little boy who had once struggled to see me through all the stars in his eyes. But, wrapped up in my own mythology, I never needed a child's adoration to know I was better than anything.

"You're being hard on yourself," said Lazarus, one warm, compassionate hand landing on my shoulder. "It's okay, Cassius. It's sad. I'm sorry you regret sometimes not paying more attention to Thomas, but it's the way things had to happen. The only way it could have happened."

Sweeping my finger beneath my eyes, I nodded and said, "I know," and Lazarus went on, "The only thing you can do moving forward is to really cultivate a relationship with him. Moving away is going to be the best thing for him. It'll force you both to go out of your ways to see one another. He just wants to hear from you, right, and you just want to hear from him, without either one of you judging the other. That's family. That's being with people. We all just want to be loved."

"I'm not dying?" At Lazarus's strange face, a sort of half squint and droop of his mouth, I at last clawed through the thick fog of that strange spatial Nirvana, to gasp, "The seizure!"

"There you go!" Applauding, Lazarus walked upon the planeless surface of the cosmos. "I knew you'd figure it out, sooner or later."

"You cheeky bastard. A *seizure*? Why a *seizure*?"

"Well, it was really the only way to get a guy like you believing in the one upstairs. You did a pretty fair amount of acid in college but didn't take much from it, you haven't been to Mass since you moved out of your parents' house, and you're staunchly atheist. But one for sure way to enlighten you was to take advantage of your writing, especially since ours is such a literary universe. You've got a very Western-programmed mind. Very much the American man. That's also why we have to take this route, because it would be crushing to your ego otherwise."

"Why is it important for me to achieve enlightenment, though? Why does it matter?"

"Well, for one thing, you're a writer on the verge of writing something really solid, so it's your job to disseminate for the ages the truth enclosed within the symbols of your work. If you can do that consciously, that's really the best thing for everyone. But also, I'll tell you, I'm pretty into Buddhism, and there's this saying about how no one can attain liberation from saṃsāra until the whole world has achieved enlightenment. It's true, but also symbolic, you see? On a microcosmic level, the world is a symbol for the Self, and all the people in it are components of a psychic whole. And, like I said: there's Katherine to consider."

As he said her name, her face reflected in Andromeda, morphing in the distance to produce every detail of her perfect beauty from the fullness of her lips to the almonds of her vast green eyes, which then fell free of all color on my focus. Flesh dissolved from her face and left another kind of wire frame, the substance of every woman upon whose cobalt head rose a miter greater even than that worn by the mechanical insect-god before her—one which stretched to the sky and unfurled like the branches of a tree to bow around the circumference of the sphere in which we were enclosed along with the perfect beauty of her and everything within her and myself. I wept, and leaned against my friend, who held me as I said, "My God, my God, I love her so much."

"I know," said Lazarus, hushedly, and his eyes glistened as he laughed. In the fraction of the second in which he turned away, I glimpsed a new face only half noticed before: an aged face, the face of Katherine's grandfather, I thought, and then a far younger replication, whose piercing eyes transfixed the wire-frame Feminine which gazed back down into him, us, me, for what was Lazarus but me? What was I but Lazarus, there, standing in my robe, my hands running over the fabric enclosing my chest, which I tore away so I was naked before her, humbled on my knees. I felt her in the invisible floor beneath my feet and the flesh of my body and the cap of my skull; I felt her peering up at me through the black ocean of stars; I felt her come into me, but also enclose me, as though the very rhythm of my pulse was lovemaking between consciousness and matter which opened my mouth so the warm fluid of the universe poured into me and within my mind unfurled new stars as the galaxy uncoiled from a point, then expanded like a snake, but not to strike: only to move into the shifting sunlight.

As I walked with Lazarus to a gate, he was saying, "The rest is up to you, Cassius. Help her, for consciousness lives forever, but the nature of matter, the ego, is more complex, and she will be afraid. The questions raised will be quite a lot for her; the thought of where she might go at pages' closing will keep her up at night."

"I know," I said, grimly. "I want to be there for her. I want to keep her safe, to be with her."

"You will," he said, hands upon my shoulders. "But don't keep them all waiting. They're busy people." With the kind of smile a father reserves for his son, Lazarus pushed me through the gate. "I'll see you later, Cassius, after a long, long while, but I'm sure you'll see me plenty more before then."

"Okay," I said, "okay, take care," as the stars fell away, and the night sky vanished. I was still without my wallet and shoes, but I didn't care about either. By then it didn't matter, since I was awake.

Katherine

I

I can't get ahead of myself. Or let whatever's writing this get ahead of me, anyway. It had already gotten ahead of me by convincing Cassius that Enoch was a good friend to him, even though the freak slipped him heaping tablespoons of camphor. So, fine. The seizure, which had left him like a big golden retriever puppy, for friendly as he'd become, was no doubt responsible for his poor character judgment. Likewise, I attributed his impulsive need to move to Ashland to the same incident, and humored him. A park on every block, one of the best theaters in America, and best of all, it wasn't sweltering. What wasn't to love? But what I didn't love, and couldn't humor, and what made me feel like I was becoming infected with his crazy, was when he said things like he started saying near the end of Lent, after he'd been up to his nose in six months' worth of volumes about, of all things, alchemy and magic. It had taken him that long to put together, with forensic scrutiny, the tattered sections and scattered paragraphs which, out of order, out of synch, out of reason, formed my REM Story.

"I think," he suggested gaily, lowering his glasses where he lay reading manuscript pages in bed, "that Tucson represents hell."

"In what?" I tried not to let him pull my focus from the laptop as my fingers darted across its keys, but it was too late. Still, I continued to type out of desperation to stave off the conversation I sensed to be familiar, because I had glimpsed it in that novel.

"In life! In real life. Well"—he laughed—"this life, our life."

I tapped a staccato beat upon the space key. "Reality doesn't mean anything, Cassius."

"Sure it does! Reality is symbolic of a higher order. Everything we notice, everything our consciousness observes, it has symbolism. Tucson is hell, and Ashland is a holy city."

He'd been saying this sort of thing since his seizure, and it was more upsetting every time, but that time, echoing this very page, was enough for me. I shut my laptop and unplugged it so briskly I felt the connector inside break and swore to realize that, just like the manuscript, I'd have to go to the electronic store one town over and run into that creep, Enoch. Trying to keep calm, I said, "I'm worried about you saying things like this, sweetheart."

"If I can't be forthright about my thoughts with you, Kitty, who can I be forthright with?"

"You can be forthright with me, but you can't go around saying things like that if you don't want me to worry."

"It's a beautiful thing! Liberating! How close we are to God."

Rubbing the bridge of my nose and then the corner of my eye, I felt my contact lens slip and, grimacing, was forced to shuffle my laptop out of my arm and onto the nightstand while also trying to stumble from bed. "I'm glad you had such a nice near-death experience, honey, but I wish you'd adopt objectivity with these things." Leaning toward the oval mirror, I pulled back the lid of my left eye to stare into its cornea, reddened by an elaborate motherboard of veins and growing tears. I had to get eye drops the next time I got a lighter. "People see all kinds of things when they're dying. It's all crazy."

"Oh, I know, but this wasn't really that. This happened because I'm awake. Because I have a purpose for God, see? And you do, too."

With a careful pinch, I peeled the contact from my fluttering eye, then removed its partner with a defter hand. "That's the kind of thing crazy people say. One minute you think God's given you a mission, and the next you're in a cell, insisting you're Jesus of Nazareth."

Laughing, Cassius set his book aside. "Nobody's saying I'm Jesus of

Nazareth. But you see, the crazy people who say that sort of thing are almost right. They should be saying they're Christ."

"Go to bed," I told him, grinding my palms into my eyes, then collapsing face-first into a pillow while he laughed. "For the love of God, just go to bed."

"I'm in bed!"

"Go to sleep, then."

Cackling, he leaned over and kissed the top of my head, paying no mind as I buried my face in the pillow. "It's true, though! Christ consciousness. My God, Kitty, I've lived such a long time, my whole life without realizing basic facts! Incredible. It explains everything, what I experienced."

"Does it explain why I'm going to smother you?"

"Yes. Also, for instance, why real crazy people think there are reptiles in the center of the earth, or why they believe the moon is hollow. Carl Sagan's concept of the reptile brain, Kitty. The symbolic moon in alchemy. Think about it."

When I lifted my head, his face was written with intense mock seriousness which soon melted into boyish giggling. He kissed me once again before settling back into his side of the mattress. "Thanks for tolerating me, baby."

"Oh," I wearily returned while I tucked myself in, "don't thank me yet."

"I mean it. I know it's stressful. Hey, you've got a lot going on. You're a housewife, basically," he was counting on his fingers so he missed the twitch in my eye, "and a business partner, plus all the shit you do for yourself, and this manuscript? I'm surprised you haven't smothered me already!"

"I'm just waiting for the right pillow," I said, patting his backside. "Good night."

I admit the way he was bouncing back from his predestined seizure was incredible, just like the kind of thinking and talking and working he was doing. True, he was jabbering about the symbolism of real life the way he might interpret a film, but that was fine. Better he should try to divine some meaning out of life than dwell in fear like me. Ashland was an exquisite place, but as time drew onward and I, ever closer to the apex of all this, to the scene which had so disturbed me, was getting to where I couldn't leave our periwinkle house on Starflower Lane. This felt justified the next day, as I ran around from shop to shop in tiny Ashland only to find nobody carried the kind of charger which I had indeed ruined the night prior. That meant I was going to have to go one town over, to Medford. If I bumped into that weirdo, I thought I might scream. Such a beautiful town, it only stood to reason there had to be something wrong with it. That something was obvious: Enoch.

My feelings toward Enoch were strained from the start, mostly because the manuscript had told me my feelings would be strained from the start—and because I had glimpsed more than one or two questionable things in its pages, camphor aside. This all meant that I was desperate to prove its assessment of my feelings—and of Enoch—wrong. After all, this was the ultimate form of taking a baseless dislike of someone, although I had plenty of real reason. But I couldn't stop living my life, or conform it to an arbitrary pattern because some manuscript channeled in my sleep predicted the way it would go. If I did stop living my life, that would be an acknowledgment of the manuscript's power. If it stopped me from doing anything at all, that would prove it was more powerful than I'd ever thought.

I tensed on the warehouse threshold, assessing the layout of the building and its multitude of towering aisles full of millions' worth of merchandise. It was as though around every corner lay a thousand eyes in wait for me. It was vile, that feeling of being watched. The sensation that everyone, everywhere, was in on driving me across the store, to the laptop department, past the tower of LSDs. At last, as I quickened my pace at the emergence of the wall of chargers, I was assailed by a dreamer's voice saying, "Why, Miss Beauvoir," and I fell against the assortment of display hooks, scrambling straight to maintain some dignity.

"Enoch." I nodded in grim assessment of the too-bright emerald tie upon his otherwise plain gray outfit. His face recalled, in a queer way, a young William S. Burroughs, though I was sure this man's strangeness came, not from any external drug, but an internal condition.

"I was thinking about you the other day. How are you settling in to Ashland? How is Cassius?"

"I thought he was going over to visit you all the time."

"Yes, of course, but I meant his health. A man such as Cassius seldom discusses such things with other men. We tend to discuss philosophy and religion."

So much about what he'd just said raised my blood pressure that I had to block it out and focus, my words clipped, on Cassius's health. "He's very well." Turning away to shuffle through the available chargers in hopes of discovering the one I needed, I mentioned, "Getting back to his writing and everything, although he isn't leaving the house much. He's very busy. Editing stuff for me, too."

"How pleased I am to hear of his swift recovery. I was concerned there may be long-term effects to his liver or brain or stomach lining. Would it be in poor taste to ask what he is working on?"

"It would be, if I had any idea. God only knows."

"Perhaps, but the rest of us have a good guess at it. Why, I would wager he is trying to articulate the glory of his mystical experience, either via memoir or metaphor, or a combination of the two."

"His near-death experience," I corrected, flush with irritation, still refusing to meet the beetle eyes of the intrusive stranger. "One he might not have had if he had just listened."

Laughing, Enoch teased, "A statement far more absurd to my mind than the evident notion that all this happened by the will of God."

"I wonder what Hermes would say about that," I said over my shoulder to the display of Devices, one of which was plucked up by an eager young man yammering to his mother. It was obvious to me that Hermes, the person who had exchanged initial messages with Cassius, was the man who called himself Enoch. But the question was: Why? Why all the convoluted bullshit? Why didn't he even bat an eye as I asked, "Do you think the mysterious Tetramegistus would say Cassius's seizure was the will of God?"

"My research partner? No doubt he would be the very first to say it, were I to ask him, but such things are rather beyond his concern. You two had ought to join me for dinner sometime." His tone so brightened it glared from the dusty coal of his usual demeanor like the first spark of fire. "I should love to have you both by, if you can take time from your busy writing schedules."

My first mistake might have been saying, "I've been hung up on my current project, actually," instead of telling him to let me buy a replacement charger in peace, because it was the year 2032 and we had a headband you could use to transmit your thoughts to your computer but I was still buying a charger cable every six months. Though of course, since the meeting was all preordained by a scene from this stupid book, I guess it couldn't be called a proper mistake. I don't know if anything can be called a mistake anymore, not even the way I froze, rather than exited, at the feline intensity of Enoch's stare. A smug little smile which spoke to me of a man who thought he was the wisest in the world grazed his lips, and let me tell you, I wanted to knock him out in the store, low on patience as I was.

"Why do you suppose that is, Miss Beauvoir?"

"Oh." I sighed in relief as I found and grabbed the charger I needed, hidden amid all its poorly labeled, identical siblings. "I don't know. Probably because I have a lot on my mind."

"Perhaps if you opened your heart to the Lord you would find your cup overfloweth with the waters of inspiration."

"No, thanks." I adjusted my purse on my shoulder and ducked around him. "I don't really understand it when tech geniuses become Jesus freaks. Or writers, for that matter, whether you're writing code or fiction."

"I am indeed writing, as it happens, though nonfiction. Perhaps you and I might trade work sometime. You do still have my calling card from when I left you at the hospital, don't you?"

But I didn't answer so much as hum as I rushed down the aisles, threw my credit card at the clerk, and, almost tripping over the threshold, emerged in the parking lot angry at myself because I'd fallen into a trap devised by nobody but me. All of this may have been predestined by some stupid manuscript, but it was my manuscript. It had been my brain to write it while I was asleep. They weren't God's words—nor mine, to be fair—but they were more my words than anybody else's. In the car, I wasted three minutes striking and re-striking my dead lighter, refusing to believe the black plastic was empty when I needed a joint the way plants needed water, until I remembered both having had earlier the vague urge to buy a lighter and seeing months prior brief mention in that manuscript of the whole thing. My God! What wasn't in that fucking manuscript?

At home, head aching, I stormed into our room and tossed the charger on the bed, where it bounced perilously close to Cassius's hip and made him laugh behind his laptop. "Hello to you, too."

"Where is that manuscript?" I asked. Before he could answer, I noticed it on the nightstand. My skin crawled. I turned away. "Cassius, what is it about?"

"It's really good, Katherine," he murmured.

"But what is it *about*? It seemed like it was about me having a nervous breakdown."

"Well…I mean, it is, and it isn't. Maybe, anyway."

"And you're okay with that possibility?"

"What are we supposed to do about it?" His eyebrows lifting, Cassius set aside his laptop and, beginning to remove his headband, insisted, "It'll either happen or it won't, but I'd bet it's going to happen. Which is why you ought to consider reading it." My stomach sank as he pushed it on me, going on, "Just based on my experience, that's what I recommend. It would have been a different ball game if I'd had my whole novel in advance, right? I wouldn't have been so surprised by it, or afraid, either. But"—laughing, Cassius waggled a finger at the ceiling—"ha-ha, you got me, Lord. That was a good one. Though, really, I guess I should be aiming here." Then, wagging his finger at himself, he laughed again, and I inhaled a streak of terror to see him so lacking in sense or articulation or reason that I wondered if he wasn't growing demented in the wake of his seizure. Eyes watering, breath rising to hyperventilation, I snatched up the manuscript, which got his attention.

"What are you doing?"

I didn't say anything, only clutched the pages to my breast and stormed away, but with uncanny speed despite his age, Cassius used the headboard to propel himself out of bed. Lion of a man that he's always been, he sprang on me near the door and kept a tight hold of the manuscript which I did indeed intend to destroy, as if destroying it might somehow destroy the fate hurtling in from the edges of my mind. "Be reasonable, Kitty," he said while trying to wrest the pages from my grip, digging his elbow against my ribs as I ground my knee into the back of his to try to bring him to the floor.

"I'm being reasonable, Cassius! Do you know who's being crazy? You! Enoch! Everybody else talking to me about God, okay! 'God' this, 'God' that, 'God's' plan!" Furious, I let go, and he kept pulling, visibly surprised to find himself in sole possession of the manuscript. The pages scattered into the air like so many giant, black-suited playing cards, and I glimpsed upon their raining surfaces imagery of paintings and talk of Tucson. None of it made me feel good by any stretch of the imagination, so I turned away, my hand on my forehead as I said, gasping, "Oh, Cassius, I'm sorry. I didn't hurt you, did I?"

"No, Kitty," he said with a sigh, bending to shuffle the papers together. "I understand you're scared, sweetheart, but destroying this really isn't going to help anything. If anything, it might hurt us."

"Do you really think so?"

"Of course it would. I'm editing this thing throughout the whole manuscript. See?" He laughed down at the page in his hand and explained, "This is the page where I pick up this page. What a trip!"

Yeah, it was a real trip, all right. A bad, horrible trip, one of those that came on with *la purga* and left the would-be psychonaut cradling the toilet in terror. My head swimming, I slid to the floor, feeling terrible to see him cleaning up what I had done but unable to help, unable to relate to his demeanor, which, though ruffled, remained compulsively cheerful.

"Has the story explained why any of this is happening, yet?" I drew up my knees to rest on them my chin.

"I mean, I know why my side of things happened already. You would, too, if you'd read my manuscript. I've gotten yours mostly—well, it *was* in order, thank God I numbered the pages—but maybe if you started on mine it would make you feel better."

It was the first time he'd invited me to read it since the hospital, and it was even less appealing on the floor with him as I thumbed at the edge of a page my eyes rendered illegible. "I would love to read it, honey, but I just can't. I can't even write. That bit I was writing last night was the first section I've written since we moved."

"I know," he said, leaning over to kiss my cheek. With wry caution, he assessed me. "I can suggest why this is happening to you, but you'll get mad at me."

"Why is that? Because it's going to sound crazy?" When he nodded, I laughed, wiping a miserable tear from my eye. "Well, one man's crazy is another man's normal."

"I'm not saying I know for certain, because there's really no knowing, but you just said you can't write, right? Maybe you're not writing what God wants you to write, as it were. Or maybe you need to be doing something other than writing for a while."

"Oh, Cassius." I sighed, but he waved his hand and said, "No, no! I need you to follow me here, stop picturing a bearded man in the sky. God is inside of you," he said, tapping my heart, and I rolled my eyes while he went on insisting, "the unconscious mind, or whatever you want to call it, operating beneath the will of your ego. That's what I'm talking about. That's God, as much as God is also a creator of this place: the orchestrator of these tremendous events which are happening just so we can write exactly what we do, be the kinds of people and writers we are. Be together, here."

Rubbing my eyes, my nose, then my cheekbones ready to burst from the pressure of clogged sinuses, I asked, "Why do you think God would care about us and what we write?"

"Because we're doing God a favor."

"Like what?"

"Like cosmic outsourcing! Maybe there's a story God wants to write, but can't, so we have to. Or our lives are the story. I don't know, I don't really know what it is, but take, for instance, the story about Lazarus! It's been impossible for me, but suddenly I'm a dynamo."

"Why do you think that is?"

"Well, I don't really know. I think I'm being rewarded on the one hand for diligent writing, but on the other hand I also think maybe this is why I'm here." With a fond smile for the manuscript in his lap, he said, "I'm here to help God write a book. My REM Novel, and yours, too, and maybe more. Neither of us wrote these things, Kitty."

"If it's true that God wrote these things, for whatever that's worth, and if it's true that these manuscripts mean something to God, or whatever, then fine. But that still doesn't explain why I have to experience everything that the manuscript mentioned! Isn't the fact that it was written good enough?"

"Kitty, if it's written, that means it's being experienced. And you know better than I do that when a fictional character is believable, free will becomes a two-way street. Even when you and I write and rewrite a story, when we describe events happening to a character, a fictional character is experiencing it and making choices as that fictional character could only ever hope to make. We as writers experience through the character in our imaginations. The same is true of the reader, who, reading a story, experiences the simulation in their brain the way they would experience the real-life event. That's why you get so sucked into the story: empathy, pathos, between you and the character, that's the key, the binding. So if you want to imagine as a model that God was a writer, or even just a reader whose conscious experience of a work brought it to life, then it makes sense that you have to experience everything you're going through. It might not be a causal thing, necessarily, but if a model is accurate enough, you can make predictive extrapolations using the model, right? This manuscript is a model for our reality; its writer is a model for God. We're pawns in a thought experiment."

"But to what end?" My eyes welled up with tears again, and I rose, unable to remain longer in the eerie presence of the hateful papers. "There's nothing worse than a story with no point. Just hundreds and hundreds of pages of bullshit, with nothing to it, a whole lifetime of somebody suffering for nothing at all."

"Just like real life," he said, intending to be funny, but that made me burst into tears and lean my head back against the wall. Cassius draped an arm around me. "I don't think all of this is happening to you for no reason."

"What reason could there possibly be?"

"Well, maybe by the end of the story we'll have figured it out. I've gotten it in order, but it's still kind of hazy to me. I think we're missing a part. But it's like I said before: maybe you can't write because you're not producing what God wants you to write. After you put aside thoughts of ego, immortality, success, even love of the written word, maybe the reason why anybody writes or creates anything at all is for God. And if we're all God on the inside, that's as literal an interpretation of the truth as there could be."

I was so tired of fighting about the whole thing. I could keep going until my tongue fell out; I could argue all I wanted that if everybody was God, nobody was God, but it didn't make a difference. He had lost his mind, and I was about to be dragged down with him. I would have given anything to destroy that manuscript, if nothing more than to prove that I could do such a blasphemous thing to begin with, but there would be no getting it away from Cassius. After that conversation, I used the bathroom upstairs and found that, once I flushed, it kept running. Too tired to deal with it, I threw my hands in the air, washed them like the Pontius Pilate of plumbing, and went to bed with the running water nagging the back of my skull. For no real reason, I lay awake and thought of my aunt—the dead one, not Ada—and then my mother. Should I call her? Would she pick up? What would I say? Steamed as she'd been about my moving to Tucson to begin with, and then my relationship with Cassius, and plenty of things that happened between then and now, she never adjusted, and returned my cursory Christmas cards as half-assedly as I sent them out. Wasn't a mother supposed to be more interested than her daughter in maintaining a relationship? Who was going to take care of her when she was infirm? The day was swiftly dawning.

She'd have to live somewhere. Ashland had good air. My stomach soured at the idea of Vera Vasko living a half hour's stroll away. Everything in this town was a half-hour walk. Particularly Enoch's house, the imposing castle of miniature Gothic acclaim a shade of blue darker than ours, obscured by skeletal tendrils of willow vines which revealed in insidious peep-show more of the gray slated roof than I'd seen driving by in late September, when Cassius and I had finally left town, and he'd shown me where he'd had the seizure. That house. I hated that house. That house which had turned me into a housewife. I hadn't yet been inside of that house but lay awake burning furiously with curiosity for it, and the running water and thoughts of Aunt Susan and Enoch's house and Grandpa's basement: did Enoch's house have one, a basement full of bodies, basements ugly places full of secrets one could never not know, full of terrible, awful things actually found upstairs and it was later that Grandpa killed himself. I could never un-look, face full of disturbing Polaroids, closet, a nosy girl in pursuit of what really happened, this I realized when he discovered me, trembling in the closet, sorry I found them, but, oh, how I shouldn't have been snooping in the first place and didn't want to ruin our family, and his eyes had filled with tears, echoes of shame to think that he tried to be a good person, recollections of the conversation we had made, this terrible edge. I had gotten past that, but still I was seeing them, and I would live that year a lifetime and a mistake that nauseated me as I was drowning in the awful bile of the it-didn't-matter, it-didn't-matter, and he was sorry I found them but no Christmas presents and instead could not draw anyone's attention, the ancient marriage of realization turned around on me. I was half living with my own suicidal dreams, and it turned around on me dead, but really he was dead, and this I realized as maybe my discovery had pushed him over the edge. I had gotten Polaroids, terrible, awful things I still in dreams, that dream, then twitching recollections of the conversation we had this terrible mistake as I was guilty, understood what really happened, and I would spend that year and past that, I'd thought, but still I was seeing them in the aunt I had never had, and how he tried to be a good person, and he didn't want to ruin our family or the ancient Christmas presents who instead got a face full of suicide. It wouldn't be a year and a half until we all understood having looked, and how we all, like I, could never un-look, could never not know of how his eyes had filled with tears, he was saying how he had known, and so it was as though, because I had looked, I was complicit and could do nothing, could not draw anyone's matter. It-didn't-matter because he was dead, dying, going to Cassius's voice startling me awake with a gentle, at just a month shy of the age of fifteen, Katherine. It wouldn't really matter, and anyway, and anyway, and Katherine, it didn't mean half living with my own suicidal echoes of shame, Katherine, to think that matter because it was all of six months later that Grandpa had so many problems to fit in a cigar box, Katherine, and he would never hurt me or my mother or when he discovered me, trembling, and Katherine, and Katherine, and—

"Katherine," Cassius said, hushing me, smoothing my hair, "Kitty, it's only a dream."

He'd woken me up, because I'd been crying.

2

The day after my restless night, the redwood trees jutted crooked fingers in a thousand directions, a confusion of markers all disagreeing on the proper path but all urging me away from Enoch's house. Miserable, I swayed in place, and moaned to myself, then stormed up the path of that black-gated house which I expected to contain a serial killer, or an old woman with a lot of cats, or both. Enoch, pleased and surprised to see me, urged, "Come in, Katherine. I was just having tea. Would you care for some?"

"Ha-ha, no, I think I'll be fine." I stepped into the living room where the empty fireplace seemed to echo the cheerfully anxious tones of the overture of Rossini's *La gazza ladra*, already beginning to crest as I slipped off my shoes. "You're playing Rossini, right?"

"Indeed, my dear. He is my favorite composer. *The Thieving Magpie.*" As his hand was out, I let him take my coat and found myself ushered into one of two chairs set across from the sofa. From my new vantage, I gazed out into the room, upon that oriental rug which sickened me when I identified the pale, resolutely cleaned but forever-stained shape of Cassius's stomach acid hidden among its kaleidoscope pattern. My ears rang over the music as I turned my eyes toward the back of the man who hung my coat as he said, "What occasions so rare a visit as this?"

"Oh..." I was still absorbing the paintings in the living room, one a reproduction of Albright's "*Picture of Dorian Gray,*" and the other an original, a titian-toned painting of a woman holding a cat, set above a small wall stand beside the powder room. "I was in the neighborhood."

"I would take you for the type to 'drop in' on someone as much as I would take you for the type to be interested in my company, based on previous interactions."

I drummed my fingertips against the edge of my knee while my host collected his mug and lowered into his seat. "I'm not sure why I'm here. I guess I'm worried. About Cassius."

"He seems perfectly fine to me."

"He seems disjointed," I insisted. "Like he's a different person than before his seizure."

"A near-death experience will often do that, for better or for worse, though I should say Cassius is doing quite well."

"He wanders around our house with a glaze in his eye like a Buddhist monk on acid."

At this, Enoch tilted his head, his eyebrow lightly arched. "He *is* a writer, as are you. Did you check to see if he had his headband on at the time?"

"It's not just that. It's the way he talks about these things, Enoch." The entrepreneur leaned forward, hands folded between his spread knees, as I said, "He just wants me to believe him about all this nonsense. I mean, I've listened to a lot of people talk about God, and they all sound crazy whatever they're worshiping. I thought some of Cassius's interests were kind of cute at first. He's doing all this with alchemy or whatever, writing his book and reading all these stacks of Jung you keep lending him—which, fine, that's fine, I'm glad he's got something to be interested in—but I think it might be making him crazy."

"And why do you think that, my dear woman?"

"Because, my dear man," I intoned with curling lip, "it's all he talks about. Everything relates back to it. But worse than that, it's depressing to be told reality isn't real all day." The words surprised me as they sprang out, and my breath hitching, I insisted, "The existence of those stupid stories doesn't mean anything about the structure of the universe. It doesn't mean we're fictional. That *I'm* fictional."

"Of course not. Our experience of reality is not represented perfectly in the experience of reading. The books produced by the LSD, by your mind, your lover's, these things are mere symbols of the wealth of our existence. Look around, my dear. Look up!"

I did, up at his ceiling, which, to my surprise, was frescoed. I was amazed I hadn't noticed it already, but, abused as I had been by the carpet, I had been reluctant to discover what I might find higher than the walls. Far from the black mold or suspicious (read: obvious blood) stains I'd expected from the ceiling, I was faced with an exquisite scene of two men, one on the descent as he reached toward a man of equal classical beauty, who, in the arms of an ethereal woman rife with maternal tenderness, reached toward the descending man. The solitary figure was no physically lower than his brother on the fresco's northwest corner or the putti attending the ascended hierogamy, yet he seemed ready to sink free from his plaster and set foot upon the hypnagogic rug. The work glowed in the low light of the living room, and I could not avert my attention as Enoch asked, "What author might impart, truly, a description of this fresco? Who might dare find the words to paint within the reader's mind the laconic longing of Castor, or the limpid drape of Leda's pale arms about him. Poor comfort it is to good Castor; poorer still for Pollux, who cannot see his brother but in passing, as in dreams, and fantasy. What richness of its colors, what supple melancholy shrouds its figures. But what joy exudes, still!"

He touched my hand, and I was glad of the warmth of it, strangely, in that moment. "What book, what film, indeed, what fresco, might communicate the human warmth of your hand on mine?"

With most other people, such a thing would sound like a come-on, but he seemed so priestly in that moment that it was but a pure demonstration of what it meant to exist and to feel. In fact, it was that very priestliness which snapped me out of the hypnosis of his speech, because it made me say, "That doesn't change the fact that Cassius is acting crazy. If anything, it adds to it. This whole thing with these books is making him lose his mind."

Head tilted to owlish degree, my host removed from dented nose his glasses, which he polished as he spoke. "He has spent quite a lot of time of late reading the prophetic novel you produced."

My face flushed as I recrossed my legs. "What do you know about it?"

"No more than he has told me, which in and of itself has little worth. He did, however, mention you might some merry day consider dropping by."

"If he'd stop talking about that stupid book, maybe it wouldn't be so prophetic."

"My dear woman, its mere existence indicates nothing more than a record of future events. Regardless of whether or not the record is observed, the figure which crafts it will doubtless be undaunted in forcing its conclusions upon you. But there are those times when observation of the record is necessary."

"If we were supposed to know the future," I said, my ears buzzing over the sound of the magpie singing, *Ninetta, Ninetta,* "then we would have the ability to see forward. We'd have verifiable, objective ESP, or come unstuck in time like Billy Pilgrim, or—"

"Or have a silver headband, which transcribes in intelligible form the very will of God."

"It's not," I insisted, on the edge of my seat. "Even if there is a God, surely you don't think your stupid Device is capable of transmitting His will."

"If the Lightning Stenography Device and its predictions are not the work of God, then what, precisely, are they?"

I shifted farther forward, all but falling upon the floor as I said, "It's just a story! It's a stupid piece of technology. A replacement for keyboards, that's all! It's not magic! It's not some kind of divine gift! If anything, it's a curse."

Though there were times when I worked under the assumption that Enoch was emotionless, something akin to sympathy appeared in the strain of his frown. "My dear girl," he said, at last, "what is it in that book of yours which is worse than the sight of a skull in your hands? What has the Lord showed you which seems so profane?"

With a hot sob, I lifted my knuckles to my mouth. "First of all, I'm a woman, not a girl, and I don't think that should matter, to be frank, not for this conversation or any other," and he, to his credit, politely apologized as I went on.

"It was a conversation with you. This one. I'm sure of it." I laughed and blinked at the ceiling, finding there in Pollux a solemn darkness which I did not like, which was only a result of the scarlet light cast by the Venetian lamp standing in the corner but which disfigured him to an unearthly degree. All things in the room, in fact, took on menacing aspect, and I was aware of the natures of all things, of the stones from which the fireplace had been built, rough as though they'd been just cut from a quarry, dark and beautiful like the round coffee table upon which was carved a paisley pattern seeming at that moment a mandala. Lifting my hand to my eyes, I gasped sharply, "I think it was this conversation, anyway."

He, too, was on the edge of his seat, his spectacles again upon his nose and his black eyes fixed on me. "And what was it about this conversation, Katherine?"

Blinking glistening eyes, I said, "You showed me something. I don't know, I could only skim it, and it was so disorganized I couldn't discern any kind of chronology. It might not even be this exact conversation, but there were words, names I've spent my whole adult life avoiding. I didn't like it. And I remember I say something about how I'm wondering whether or not I really had a message from God, and whether or not I'd ever written anything at all, and—" A sensation overcame me, as if, between my skull and my right hemisphere, a stick scraped my skull cavity. Lifting and trying with a silent gasp to reassure myself there was no anomaly, I said, "I'm really scared, Enoch."

Though it seemed at first as though he were endeavoring to say something comforting, he indicated at last, "If the Lord has chosen you for some divine purpose, there shall be no escaping it."

"There is no God," I insisted, my teeth clenched, and it was then that Enoch smiled in the most hateful way I have ever seen, and his face echoed the bleak expression of Pollux.

"If there is no God, surely you can tell me who it was that wrote that book which terrifies you."

Though I ran through, in my head, a hundred thousand scenarios of saying this or saying that, of doing this or doing that, there's no use arguing with a crazy religious type. They're going to believe whatever they're going to believe, and there's no getting through to them. Instead, I turned my head away, toward the gray cat which came slinking in to the living room and paused upon the threshold to clean its rear leg. "I didn't know you had a cat," I said, and Enoch smiled toward it.

"No one has a cat, my dear. Cats are sacred animals: if you are lucky, a cat will find its way into your life."

"You sound like a lunatic. Did God tell you that, too?"

Folding his hands and regarding from the corner of his eye the cat, which strolled forward to stroke its cheek against its owner's leg, Enoch said, "God has never 'told' anything, in so many words. That is not in the nature of the Lord."

"You're talking out of both sides of your mouth, saying different things all the time. Will you tell me what you mean?"

Enoch picked up the cat for all of two seconds before it sprang from his arms, bounced across our chairs, and deposited itself in my lap. I couldn't tell if my host smiled about this, or about what I'd asked him, as he went on to say, "It is impossible to explain without sounding mad. God is anything but simple. The experience of God is a most sincere and profound thing for all mankind; it is universal as language, and just as optional for the primitive man."

As the purring animal kneaded my thigh, I tried to take solace in the act of petting its ears. "That's not true anymore, though. Everybody's becoming atheist these days, worshiping science. It seems like the only religions left are the crazy, violent ones, or the Buddhists or Hindus or whatever. New Age psychos like you. All these people touting unintelligible consciousness expansion with rambling websites straight out of the nineties." I waved my free hand toward the floor and found that the cat reached forward as though to force me back into petting it as I adopted a mocking tone. "'Our Bearizzian overlords are systematically draining our energy sacks from invisible space stations in the southern hemisphere of Venus!'"

In a surprisingly real way, Enoch laughed, and I found myself oddly pleased by such a reaction from the otherwise remote philosopher. "Ah, but were you to promulgate these views, my dear," he said, ruining our tepid connection and dropping my smile to a frown, "it should find appeal to some, I am sure. As every brain is different, every individual mind is encoded to accept a particular set of symbols. Are you familiar with programming languages, Katherine?"

"Vaguely," I said, waving my hand and grimacing as the cat sank his claws into it. "When I was a kid, I went through a phase where I was kind of interested in building websites, and I still know some code for my author website so I can keep it up by myself."

"Then you will understand when I say that two coding languages may both be represented in English, but may appear completely different in terms of the symbol-set utilized. And though I may use two languages to accomplish similar tasks, some are better suited for certain tasks than others."

Just once, I nodded toward the painting of the woman and the cat with a shiver as the aggressively purring feline forced itself deeper into my lap. "Have I seen that painting before?" I asked, and Enoch took the time to say, "I'm sure you have," before he rose and disappeared into his kitchen, lifting his voice so I could still hear him. "The human brain is designed to receive stories. Symbols. It is a receptacle—a cup, if you will—with the capacity to receive and transmit narratives, and narratives are but symbol strings we experience or tell ourselves. That is all life is, is it not? The sense of ego and self which we derive over time is naught but each of us becoming more and more acutely aware— hopefully—of the true theme, the true lesson, of our personal narrative. Religion functions in a similar manner."

At the sound of rustling, I slung the cat into my arms and found it allowed itself to hang there, thorough pleasure on its face as it purred up a storm to be held. I'll say this about Enoch: he had a happy, very sociable cat. When I was small, my father told me that any person who was good to animals was a good person, but then, my mother divorced that rat for running up phone-sex bills, so what did he know. In fact, Enoch's sweet pet indicated a strange distortion: this man who, it seemed, lived like a hermit with little-to-no contact with the outside world, produced a cat which allowed me to sling it around my neck like a scarf. I had an eerie feeling of hyperclarity, reality seeming too vivid as I stood there with the cat, which, top heavy, fell into my arms so I was forced to cradle it in the manner of the brunette woman in the painting. Squinting, I drew nearer to her, and, frowning, opened my mouth to press Enoch about it when he appeared to my left from a kitchen like a Williams-Sonoma display room. In his hands was a tray of cucumber sandwiches and sugar cookies that made me laugh. "Are you an old woman?"

Chuckling, he sat again with the tray and suggested, "You'd ought to eat, my sister. I really must insist. I promise, you'll find not a crumb of camphor in the whole platter. Those tea cookies are from a box, sad to say."

"Maybe I'll have one," I allowed, setting down the cat and dusting off my hands, patting off my shirt and coming to reclaim my seat while Enoch resumed, "Religion is nothing more than a particular human computer's preferred programming language for the various functions it must accomplish in its particular life, just as his or her cultural and ego programming is, in essence, the operating system by which it functions: all of this built upon the manner in which the native language impresses upon the natal brain, like a motherboard worked upon by the hands of its creator."

Nodding, I took up a napkin and was impressed to find that the cat rested patiently aside while we ate. "I get what you're saying. But isn't religion more like a virus, or adware?"

"It can be. Being constructed of symbols, those symbols could feasibly be corrupted to become anything. But an individual language's equal versatility in banking software, websites, video games, and viruses does not mean it is an inherently 'bad' set of symbols. The programming language is not at fault for the crimes of the users, even if the crime is the passive transmission of a spiritual virus, just as your grandmother might transmit one via e-mail."

"All religions are spiritual viruses. They make people believe in fairy tales instead of focusing on the present; they cause wars and violence and all kinds of atrocities. They cause people to grow up ignorant and uneducated and impoverished; they're responsible for the oppression and abuse of women, minorities, even children!"

"Indeed, my dear friend, institutional religion has caused quite a bit of trouble over the years—but, it has also served its purpose. Were it not for the callous institutions of Western religion, the cultural, philosophical, and scientific advancements which have arisen would simply not be in their current configuration. It would be a very different sort of society. Pagan cultures are not sustainable for long stretches at a time because the archetypes of the personal gods must be constantly renewed to suit the times. The Titan Prometheus, then, is overtaken by Hermes, is overtaken by Mercurius, and so forth. An impersonal, sometimes brutal God endeavoring to make himself indistinct of character is more sustainable long-term."

All this talk of pagan gods brought to mind Persephone eating pomegranate seeds in the underworld and lingering there ever after. I regarded my cookie with vague wariness, trying to tell myself it was because of Cassius's experience in this house and not the weight of the symbol. Symbols. Maybe Enoch was right about symbols. My host left me little time to dwell as he went on, "The Abrahamic religions are in fearful revolt, for they sense their end is near. Just as dawn comes to sweep away the night, so, too, is a new aeon rising from the unconsciousness— has been rising, indeed, for many years. Evolution marches onward, for society as well as for consciousness. And you know those religious types, my dear," he said, a gay twinkle in the licorice of his eyes. "They despise evolution."

While I snorted, he continued, "The followers of the God of Abraham, Christ, and Muhammad sense this possibility of forward progress and react viciously, for progress means overthrowing them, just as a new generation of sons must supplant the old generation of fathers. After all,

Jupiter must disembowel Saturn to free the young gods from the bowels of the old. Yet a loss of the traditional, paternalistic God figure is far from tragedy; there is a better place to seek God, and it is the same place even the Abrahamic God tells us when we read His words unobfuscated by the Church, by the thick tapestry of symbols which lull the reader into trance when they so much as hear the words, 'The Bible.' This place is the location of Heaven, of Nirvana, of Jerusalem and Babylon and Mecca."

I tried not to roll my eyes. "And where's that?"

"Whence came your REM Story, my sister? From your mind? From your brain? The unconscious mind, shared by all Man? God? Is there a difference?"

"I don't know. I don't believe in God, but with all this going on, that manuscript and everything, it's just...have I ever written anything at all?"

"No," he said, so plainly I balked. "I am afraid you have not."

"I beg your pardon."

"You asked," he said, maintaining innocence which might have been comical had I not felt insulted. "There is nothing to be upset about, Katherine. I have never created anything, either, despite my dabbling."

My laugh sharpened at the painting, ready to change the subject. "It's disturbing you won't even acknowledge I've asked you twice about this painting."

"Have you?" he said, still in that light tone. "Why, that! Little more than a piece of true crime history. A case rather near to my heart. And so near to yours, in fact, that I myself am shocked you do not recognize it!"

It wasn't the first time I'd seen something I never should have seen, but the force of the revelation was undampened. What did he mean, near to my heart? True crime? A painting I'd worked so hard to avoid seeing. Stumbling up, I cried at last, "That's my uncle's painting!"

For a fraction of a terrible second, he seemed prepared to laugh in delight of himself, or the tragedy of my family, or any number of awful things about which Man should not laugh, but he caught himself. "It is, indeed. You would not believe the tedium of the channels I endured, all for a picture of a woman holding a cat."

"That's the original!" Tears in my eyes, I faced the man I saw to be a vulture. Maybe he'd done all of this to lure not Cassius here, but me. "Why do you have that? Is my family what you've projected your crazy on? Whatever it is, you've gotten Cassius whipped up in your whirlwind. Does he know you're psychotic? Condemning the violence of religions, then having a painting like that! What do you really want from me?"

"I assure you, my sister, I am not interested in you for any kind of morbid fascination for your family, though I will say your lineage is an interesting one. Genealogy is something of a hobby of mine, but literal genetics have little to do with what in you is of interest to me. That is, a potential for a higher state of consciousness. That is something which cannot be bought, nor borrowed, nor, necessarily, genetically derived; though, in some cases it may be. May I show you something? Something someone very close to me produced. It is the reason why I was so thrilled to discover Cassius would be coming to visit Ashland. And why I was so thrilled to meet you."

Already he moved toward the stairs, and I, studying the painting, then the front door, felt sure I was about to be locked in the attic dungeon where I'd be made into a woman suit. All the same, I followed, because I figured Cassius would at some point discern what had happened to me. I followed because I had to: because I had spent such a long time deliberately not reading any article that had to do with Cassius or me, avoiding any press about my family, ignoring stories in the news about the Stafford Street house in Columbus, Ohio, deafening myself to and dodging those few press questions which came, which were inevitably about how my infamous dead relatives and the so-called obvious trauma they had caused me impacted my work. I had done all of this because it was what the rest of my family, my mother and my aunt and grandmother, had done in response to the situation—what we had all done in response to the chain of deaths and revelations which had begun with my grandfather's suicide and ended with the death of an uncle neither I nor my mother nor my aunt nor my grandmother had ever known, nor ever should have known, nor certainly would have wanted to know. All those years of avoidance and fear and pain, and Enoch was right: all for a painting of a woman holding a cat. This painting had been there my whole adult life, and I had turned away time and again for fear of what it might show me. But it was just a painting, I found, and this stranger had some deeper catharsis to offer me, so it was that I followed this stranger, Enoch, up the stairs of his house. That already uncanny ascent would be the last time I felt normal until I finally had the skull in my hands.

The second story of the house proved as beautiful as its first. We moved through a hallway decorated with Ansel Adams photographs of black forests and silver beaches frozen forever in their black-and-white perdition. Even the wainscoting gleamed with refinement in the soft wall lamps, and I found myself overwhelmed by the urge to know thoroughly the contents of the house, to see its every room and furnishing, if only because I thought it might help me make sense of this man, the sanest lunatic one could never wish to meet. I couldn't understand him. Like I'd said before, it didn't make sense when rationalists became religious nuts, and the fact that he talked about other religious nuts like he wasn't one himself seemed the peak of cognitive dissonance. That, I chalked up to the poisonous nature of religion: once you're inside of it, you're always right. Disturbing that even a logical man could be infected by this insanity, this supposed experience of God, which never did any good for anyone. Even those supposedly beloved of God suffered. Martyrs, and all. I was about to bring this up when Enoch opened the door to his study, and I found such an incredible collection of well-kept books crammed from floor to ceiling that I found I could say nothing at all. The library, vast as it was, seemed to touch on every subject, one wall devoted to nothing more than psychiatric and metaphysical texts as if the two were comparable. At the opposite end of the room, a desk, though neatly arranged, overflowed with stacks of manuscripts.

"I must apologize for the state of my office. I am in the middle of trying to make sense of a series of essays in need of editing."

"I didn't know you were really a writer." He stooped to extricate from beneath a stack of papers a crocodile-skin briefcase which he set upon the desk. "I thought it was just dabbling."

"It is dabbling, in a way, but I am no writer. Not for the purposes of writing, at any rate—not for the pure purpose of the act of creation, as is desirable. I have my own scholarly pursuits, opinions on religion and so forth, and I write them and share them with those who would listen. But it is not my writing I am interested in sharing with you. Rather"—after searching his pocket for a key, he unlocked the case and revealed within another manuscript—"I have come here to show you proof of the omnipotence of God."

Frowning, I bent my head over the first page, and in the unfolding scene observed the story of a young man working at a butcher's shop when he meets an older woman. By the second page I'd paled, for it was a woman I'd met once and a man I'd never known but sometimes feared I might somehow. In the saturnine air made rancid with death, I asked, "What is this about?"

"About something which no one in this world could know. It is a glimpse into the mind of a dead man: the manner events unfolded, a confessional, a mystery hinted before us, but stopped. An aborted revelation. What this is about, Katherine, is God's unyielding love for even the most vulgar of criminals, even the most unrepentant of animals. What this is, Katherine, is a miracle, because it has no place in this world. Your aunt was a Leviathan, my sister, and what your uncle was, one cannot say."

Trembling, I rifled through the pages before me, catching glimpses of phrases and interactions and snide commentary, and I knew at once the uncle who had been hushed up under the rug and who I had fought so hard to ignore. There with all the ugliness of my aunt, too, and my grandfather, and for a few moments, I lurched randomly between pages bearing the name "Julius" and felt I spoke to him again. Death and life hung in superposition on every page I scanned. They held the venomous words of a man being propelled ever further toward an unnamed abyss: the plight of all men and women, but a plight here felt so acutely it became a source of violence.

It would have been one thing if it was just fiction, but this was a real thing that happened. Not to me, necessarily, but to my family, and to all those suffering strangers. Because of that, it had happened to me, and here it was to face me in a way I'd never expected. These were details Enoch couldn't have known, and my uncle was a person he'd surely never met. I asked him to be sure, and he told me, "No, I never did meet Monsieur Vasko in person. After all, I was but a boy around the book's first act. His inner life reveals him a wretched man I would not care to meet, a victim of his own materialist prison. Though he did have a certain charisma, your uncle," suggested Enoch, too close to my shoulder for my liking. I, too haunted, too drained by this chronicle of death, didn't lean away.

"This is a REM Novel," I confirmed.

"Every word." Again, we lapsed into silence, and I reached a point where I could no longer read because I had flipped to the end of the book and it had led me right back to the beginning. It was possible for a REM Novel to end in death. All this time I'd felt a kind of false confidence, a hope that, surely, I would make it through my story alive to narrate. But my certainty failed, and Enoch finally said, "You rather remind me of him, Katherine."

"Me?" I asked, half laughing. "I remind you of a murderer? He may be my uncle, but I didn't even know him."

"It is not so much the genetics, the shared affinity of your coloring as described, or the way you present yourselves to the outside world. Rather, it is your resolute denial of the existence of God. A laconic skepticism for the sake of skepticism, or arising from unacknowledged fear. You dare not turn your face toward God because of the implications about the similarity of you and your poisonous uncle, because acknowledging God, really acknowledging, means all the crimes against you were never crimes at all. Internalizing God means you acknowledge the fleeting nature of your own delicate life, that chain of insurmountable sufferings described by Shakespeare as 'the mortal coil.' But I warn you, Katherine"—he assessed the manuscript from so tightly within my personal space that we might as well have been conjoined—"we must all confront, at one point or another, the idea of God. If we do not confront it in life, then we will confront it as did this man: in death. For when one cannot reach out to save oneself, God will do it for you, whether one is in want of salvation or not. And I assure you, the Lord finds no higher pleasure than in the humbling of unbelievers: in eliciting a genuflection, whether out of love or terror, from those souls who turn away their faces. The question, my sister, is how long it will take for the Lord to humble you."

"You're crazy," I pleaded, as though, if I asked him kindly enough, Enoch might be the one to lose his mind instead of me. "You wrote this, surely. It's just well researched, and in poor taste."

"There are details I never could have known, Katherine, so you have two possibilities. Either what I tell you is true, and what you hold in your hands is indeed a REM Novel, unwritten by any person known to this world; or I am a man so crass that I would take a true-life tragedy and fictionalize it without bothering to obscure so much as a name. I admit, I care little for these aspersions."

Mute, I lowered my eyes toward a pile of manuscripts in the corner, and my gaze skipped over a plain cedar lockbox the size and shape of an eight-and-a-half-by-eleven manuscript. "There is a duty owed, of sorts, to God. What is it about this man, Katherine, about his pursuit and failure of the Promethean light of higher consciousness, which captured attention thus?"

He saw me notice the box, so I tried to focus on him, but my head started to pound and shadows edged into the right corner of my eye, all up toward the ceiling and across my brow. As my left ear rang with tinnitus, Enoch suggested, "If we are, indeed, characters in a story, we are symbolic. In fact, regardless of whether our world is truly a literary one, that a story has been written about us renders us symbolic, in a way, whether we want it to or not." Black eyes narrowed by his scrutiny, Enoch asked, "What, I wonder, do you symbolize?"

"I don't symbolize anything, you lunatic," I told him, by then falling away and insisting, "I'm a person. A real person, with real feelings."

"Of course you are! And so am I, my dear, and so are all the other people in the world. But we all mean something, too: to another person, to ourselves, to God. We mean something, and we mean something in the context of this"—he waved his hand around the room, and I trembled, feeling any second the contents of the office would fall apart before me—"this narrative, which your dreaming mind produced, which you yet refuse to read. Why won't you read it, Katherine? The book given you by God?"

"It wasn't. It's not that." My throat tightened as the darkness which overtook the edges of my vision rippled across my teary eyes like smoke-stained glass which poisoned the light it refracted. I waved a hand toward the crocodile-skin suitcase, and demanded, "Where the hell did you get that? You say it's a REM Novel. Did you write that?"

"My dead brother, Enoch, was the one who Received that work."

My hands lifted to my forehead as though to stop the headache as, by way of my tears, shadows warbled out of my periphery and into consciousness where they plastered across the face of my host to halo him in terrible pain-stained darkness as the migraine ground to life amid the chainsaw scream of the lights his eyes, his features, the sun-shy hue of once-olive flesh. "But that's you! It's you, isn't it?" Hyperventilating, on the verge of some terrible secret, I knew at once I'd been right about Hermes and Enoch being the same person, but I also knew such a truth was, at best, half of the reality; at worst, it was a gross, maybe dangerous, oversimplification. I knew it would be an oversimplification because it hadn't been hard to figure out. Enoch was unscrupulous in ways I could not articulate, and the idea of there being a Hermes Tetramegistus was a clear lie, yet one with a ring of truth. There was, I was sure, a separation between the entities of Enoch and Hermes, but it might have been paranoia, because I remembered then that seeing this moment in ink was the reason I had mistrusted Enoch (Hermes?) in the first place, even before he poisoned Cassius. His brother—his dead brother. Had he killed his brother? Had he killed his brother to Receive the manuscript, the way he made Cassius seize with the Device on his head? It would have been easy enough for some weird murder fanatic to write a book about my criminal uncle, but if only Enoch were that sleazy! If only he had written the book to try to cash in on a tragedy: But I knew with a glimpse that he hadn't. How had he really acquired it?

I whispered, "Is there more?"

At this, Enoch quieted, as though pondering how to answer a question he did not want to answer. When he said, "Nothing you would care to see, I think," I knew it was bad, knew without having to know, and so, clammy and paled and parched, I fell away and shook my babbling head. "I don't want to see it, anyway. That's not what I want."

"What is it you think you want, exactly, Katherine?"

Eyes darting to the door of the study, the door toward which I had, over time, leaned, I tried to straighten my mind enough to answer an impossible question. I didn't know what I wanted. What was there to want when reality was so raw and disorganized, or maybe so resolutely organized, that my psyche could only try to disorder it as though too much order might strike me blind? My hands lifting to my pulsing forehead, I cried, "I just want to know why this is happening!"

"You know why this is happening," said my host, not unkindly, but it was perhaps that very gentleness which sent me fleeing from the study with a sob and propelled me down the narrow stairs, through the living room, past the piano-seated cat which winked as I snatched up my coat and dashed out, finally, upon the street, where I gasped the humid air which portended rain, and tried to hide from God.

3

Most years, after a thing like that, I wouldn't have done anything for three days. I might have taken a few showers and cried some, but I sure wouldn't have maintained any semblance of a schedule. Embarrassment from fleeing Enoch's house aside, I was plagued by a matrix of possible scenarios, each worse than the last, each ending inevitably in Cassius's death, or mine, or both. The only way to avoid being trapped as an observer of my own mind's relentless badgering was to work. Drake Wolfram had sent a gentle inquiry about *On Orange Grove Road*, since I'd promised it to him by February, but it was well into March, and I was no further along, nor able to keep blaming the delay on Cassius's impulsive decision to move. In bed with my laptop, I drafted an explanatory letter.

"I feel like any effort is useless," I admitted to Cassius, who, beside me, edited a manuscript, half-moon glasses perched low on his nose.

"Why's that?" he asked, pen darting judgment across some unfortunate gerund.

"How can I write anything?" I rubbed the corner of my eye and fell back against my pillow, away from my laptop. "There's no point to writing anything. Do you know why I write, Cassius?"

"Yes," he said, but because I wasn't in the mood for his metaphysical bullshit, I kept rolling through like a steam engine, carrying on that, "I write to process things, okay? I have trauma! Things have happened in my life, horrible things you know about, and now an increasingly steep curve of disruptions has not only become apparent, but—"

"Represented in a physical model of the events in question."

"Exactly! So, on the one hand, it's vindication, right? But, on the other hand, if the record of the things I do is already in existence, why should I bother doing them?"

"You're doing them so the record exists," Cassius suggested, making a few brisk marks on the page and circling a word or two. "Maybe the Device's effects on consciousness are a primitive form of psychic time travel. I mean, if pure consciousness is unbounded from time and space—"

I covered my eyes and nose with my hands, hid myself from the world within the vibrating blackness of my skull. This stagnancy, this dearth of imagination—all this, I knew, would pass, but I feared what it meant when it did. I felt in me the swell of a wave, a tsunami of creativity which required the waters to draw from the shore before they came crashing back down. "I'm so scared."

Frowning, he lowered his pen to hold my hand. I stared, helpless, at my laptop. "I'm just not sure what's going to happen."

"Nobody ever is."

"But you are. You've finished it, haven't you?"

To the vanity across from us and our reflections within, he said, "Yeah, Kitty, I finished it."

"And? And do I end up okay?"

Taking a deep breath, Cassius ran his thumb along the pages of the manuscript before him, turned from me, and admitted, "I'm not...really sure."

My heart seemed as though to stop. "What do you mean, you're not sure?"

"I mean—" He removed his glasses and folded them on the stack of pages. "What I mean is that it ends with...a dramatic climax, of sorts." He set aside his work and glasses both to reach my hands, which I gave with reluctance. "There's not really a lot of clarity on what, uh..."

"I really hate it when you try to be delicate and protect me from things," I told him, my eyes narrowed. Cassius let his head fall back against the headboard.

"The long and short of it is that I've read this, and I've thought about it, and I know for a fact it doesn't matter that I'm telling you about it, so I guess I might as well just tell you that my assessment of this whole thing is that all this is happening, Kitty, because God wants you to Receive a novel."

"What kind of novel?"

"I don't know if I should go into that with you, but suffice it to say it seems to me you're being enlisted. I know you don't believe in meta-physical stuff, but that's what's happened to me, too." Laughing in a shy way, as though anxious of his laughter in the face of my terror, Cassius lifted his left hand from mine and reached to pat his manuscript. "Like I said before: cosmic outsourcing."

Quivering, I said, "Will you just tell me? I don't hurt myself or someone else, do I, Cassius? What about Enoch? Does Enoch hurt anyone?"

"Katherine." Frowning, he draped an arm around my shoulders and kissed the top of my head. "Let's sleep, all right, honey?"

"Why won't you tell me? Is it because something's wrong?"

"No, honey, I'm just tired, and you're tired, and Enoch is my friend. I'm going to see him tomorrow; I don't want to stay up listening to you rail on about him. Don't you want to sleep?"

But I laughed, because there was no going to bed. I wasn't safe in my sleep, and I knew it. After the REM Novels, my whole paradigm of who was in control of my body had changed. Everything I had been felt nonexistent. My body was beginning to act like an alien, erupting with migraines and feeling so far from me. I felt transparent, connected to myself only loosely, half transposed like an out-of-focus projection or maybe the kind of double image you get from moving during the shutter of a low-speed camera. It seemed more and more the only way to anchor myself to my body, to make sense of myself, was to write. I lay, numb, until Cassius fell asleep, then absconded with my laptop to the bay window of the living room where I wrote at least six hours that night, until my fingers throbbed and I was numb. The anxiety and dread that I felt, the horror of being so out of control, poured itself into my work in a way it never had. The whole story was still jittery, and if I was being honest, the existence of the REM Novel and the questions inspired informed what I wrote. Flashes of future memories that I'd glimpsed before I'd lost the stomach for reading still came from time to time, so I focused on inspiring a comparable sense of foreboding in *Orange Grove Road* until I recognized dawn by the tendrils she slithered through the window. Sitting back in my seat, I toyed with the empty joint pack by my side and thought again about what had happened. About what Enoch was doing.

I couldn't explain the feeling I got from our interactions. Cassius would probably call it a "vibration," but I was sure it was body language, or some tone hidden in his speech, or something about his beady black eyes. They seemed so flat and empty, even when he was laughing. And now, knowing that story in his office, I was nervous to think I even lived in the same town as him. It was one thing if the REM Novel you found in the morning was about you. But Enoch's REM Novel wasn't about him. It was as if he'd been chosen (God damn me, thinking that way, but I couldn't help it!) by some strange psychological mechanism to bring into existence a book that nobody in our reality could write, in good conscience or ethical accuracy. What was it about an individual psyche that made it possible? What was it about his dead brother's brain? What was it about Cassius's brain, about my brain, which made us capable of this nightmare feat?

The room tilted just as soon as I considered the question, and from the corners of my eyes, there grew the same darkness which had grown when considering the book in Enoch's study: that terrible book, that troublesome book. My teeth ached. How easy it was for him to lie, to say it was a REM Story when it was really a well-researched farce! After all, he was hiding all this other writing, this nonfiction. In fact, the nonfiction might be my way back into his house after leaving like a lunatic. A way back into his house for what, though? A rational explanation, I supposed.

What time was it? I ground my fingertips against my shut eyelids. When I opened them full of fireworks, they landed on the cable receiver, one of those with so much capacity it could record twenty stations while also streaming a movie, yet was, for most of its life, little more than a clock. Then, it told me it was 7:50. That meant it was broad daylight in Chicago. I swallowed my pride and, capable of such a thing only because I was sleep deprived, retreated into our spare bedroom, still stacked with moving boxes, to call my mother for comfort. Forehead against a window which revealed the luscious spread of glowing mountains, I wished with every ounce of my being that she would let it go to voice mail. She picked up on the third ring.

"Katie! Oh, Katie," she said, and I bit back a sigh, because she had decided on enthusiasm today, and I wasn't about to take the wind from her sails with reproach for my name. "I was just talking to your aunt Ada about you. How's Ashland?"

"Fine," I said, and then it was immediately, "When's the wedding?" and I ground my forehead into the glass, eyes squeezed shut against her words.

"Cassius seems to be having a gay love affair for all the time he's spending at that creep's house," I said, having described in brief detail Cassius's religious friend, but not the fact that he was a poisoner, because my mother would have let that gossip slip right out. Everybody knew the media had a mole into our family, and everybody knew that mole was Vera Eleanor Vasko. We were little more than popcorn kernels for the depraved murder hounds in the tabloid audience, but my literary identity needed managing, and even making a joke about Cassius coordinating a nonexistent *ménage* with the tech genius *du jour* was dangerous territory. As it was, my mother only laughed.

"Who, that Enoch character? You don't really think he's gay, do you?"

The year was 2032, and my mother was still scandalized by homosexuality. Probably because she was interested in it, I figured, going on to say, "I don't know, maybe. It's hard to tell with these religious types. Homosexual? Celibate? Child molester? Serial killer? Throw a dart."

"You know I don't care for those kinds of jokes," she said, so immediately cold and robotic that I felt a chill in my face, as if the phone had frosted over in my hand.

"Sorry," I said, ice giving way to the scorch of embarrassment for having forgotten myself in front of my mother. "I wasn't thinking. Anyway, he's a weird guy." Half the boxes in the room were empty; I unfolded them, phone pinned to my cheek by my shoulder. How had I let them go so long? Because I was waiting for Cassius to do it, and he was waiting for me to do it. I was plagued by the need to explain to myself and my mother. "Anyway, we've been busy here. Sorry I haven't called you."

"I know you've got a lot of work," she said in that noble, almost-martyred tone. "I understand, sweetheart. And how's Cassius getting on since the seizure? Did they ever find out what caused it?"

"Nope," I lied, "but he's doing well, doesn't show any signs of epilepsy or anything."

"You're sure he wasn't on drugs of some kind? I know they say pot isn't a gateway drug, but you *know*, Katie, it does build a tolerance. What if one day it's not enough?"

"Enough for what?" I asked, squinting into the distance, trying to make sense where there was none. At last cramming the broken-down boxes into the closet, I shook my head and sighed. "It doesn't matter. It wasn't drugs. But he's doing better, whatever it was."

"Well, good. Then, what is it about this Enoch fellow that makes you feel so creepy?"

"I'm not even sure how to begin to answer that question. I guess, 'because I feel I have to'?"

"Instinct," stated my mother, her tone one of infinite (and infinitely inappropriate) perception. "Some people are bad news."

"Yeah, but I don't want to jump to conclusions about the guy. Mostly because I'm not even sure what conclusions I'm jumping to. Like I said before, I know the joke offended you, but there's something weird about him. And since Cassius is there all the time, he's getting all religious, and—"

"Is it a cult?" asked my mother, her voice tinged with the barest hint of excitement.

"Maybe? I don't know. Whatever it is, it's not good. And they want me to be part of it."

"Maybe it *is* gay sex," she mused, and I sighed, rubbing my hand over my forehead.

"That was a joke. Please don't tell that to somebody and start the Internet gossip over again."

"Oh, honey, nobody's going to bother you all the way out there in that little valley. You're all by your lonesome! What kind of a pain would it be for somebody to bother to take a picture of you? Why would they, anyway?"

"Jesus, you're soul crushing." As she squawked in displeasure, I laughed and raised my voice so she could hear me. "Yeah, I suppose that's a good thing about living here. But it is isolating."

"Oh, I miss you," she said, and I frowned, picking at the edge of a box and then playing with the door of the guest bathroom.

"I miss you, too."

"I wish you'd never moved."

"Let's not get carried away." I laughed again, rubbing my hand over my face, and said, "I don't know, Mom. Am I wrong? Am I crazy?"

"Do you have evidence?"

"Maybe," I pondered, and she went on to say, "Well, if you have evidence, why not let it do the talking? Better to let the evidence speak for itself than try to conform reality to fit suspicion. I mean, maybe it's just stress from the move. You've gone an awful long time living alone, Katie. It's an adjustment."

Just once, I nodded, surprised by my mother's lucid advice about evidence, a word to the wise by which she herself could never abide. At least, she never had before. No matter: it set my head on straight, maybe because I was shocked to hear it from her. "Thanks, Mom. I love you."

"You're welcome," she said, before in the same breath shifting the subject to Aunt Ada and the new gossip about her son, and then my mother's friends at the art center classes she'd been attending, and then, and then, and then...and then it was 8:50, and at last I accomplished what I had meant to with that initial "I love you" by hanging up.

Of all the calls I'd made to my mother in the past few years, that had been by far the most pleasant. Maybe because everything else in my life was, by comparison, so stressful. All the stress rushed back to me when alone in the wake of the call. Her good advice was, while not forgotten, drained of meaning an hour after I had received it. It didn't seem possible that all this was the result of my stress in the face of such bizarre circumstances; it didn't seem possible that I could lose my sense of reality so completely over so short a period. Nothing seemed possible, and all things seemed menacing, when I couldn't face the source of the problem. I didn't want the problem to be me. It was not me, not some thread of fate, not some non-corporeal, multidimensional nonsense; the problem was external. The problem was Enoch. The problem, I decided as I was called by Cassius, was that Enoch had gotten it into his head that he was some sort of prophet, and that I had a mission from God. My lover, sensitive after his seizure, had been led into believing this. I couldn't bring it up to him, of course, because he took such comfort in the revelations of the story allegedly produced by his seizing brain that I couldn't bear to disrupt him with the obvious reality of the situation: Enoch, just as he had carefully researched and crafted a disturbing story about my uncle, had also crafted a convincing tale about what it was like for consciousness to experience a seizure. All of this, he had done because he believed God wanted him to, and he believed God wanted the same thing from me. He was an author in disguise, Enoch, a most convincing charlatan who had doubtless stolen the idea of the Device from the mysterious Hermes whom had never been seen, or perhaps his own dead brother. So thorough was the smoke screen that he'd gotten Cassius in on his scheme to—what? I wasn't sure. But I knew none of this could be brought up to Cassius. The best method of attack, as it were, was to approach Enoch; I had the feeling that the best way to do that was through his ego. And there's no better way to approach the ego of a self-proclaimed writer than through his writing.

The way things had gone the last time, I was surprised Enoch was willing to see me at all. But when he opened the door, the odd man was positively pleased, and smiled a smile which, though thin as all his smiles, warmed as he took me in. "Katherine! I am so pleased. I was concerned that I had offended you, and Cassius had no special report of you when he last came by."

"No, no," I said as Enoch ushered me into his home. "I'm really sorry. It was just intense for me, and I had a migraine, and—"

"You have absolutely no need to defend yourself," said Enoch, and I was just as grateful for his lack of probing as I was that he made no effort to sympathize beyond acknowledging, "The subject of your uncle must be a strange one."

"Not really. We never even talked about him. Mom and I never talk about the family, though. When she got divorced, she kept Dad's name. I thought it was out of laziness when I was little. These days, of course"— I crossed my arms between myself and the painting of a woman I recognized now as a deceased aunt by ill-fated marriage—"I see why she wasn't in a hurry to reclaim her maiden name."

"One can hardly blame her," agreed Enoch, suggesting, "Tea?" Stomach leaden, I shook my head and smiled and said, "No, thank you," as he poured himself a cup from the threshold of the kitchen. I really was very thirsty.

"I heard Cassius came to visit you yesterday." I laughed, trying to appear like an awkward girl as I shuffled off my shoes and moved around the room, leaning forward to investigate a brilliant jade vase. "I thought, 'I'd better go and apologize before they think I'm off my rocker'!"

"Nothing of the sort crossed our minds." Cheerful, Enoch put another kettle of hot water on the stove—in case I changed my mind, he said—and then turned toward me, asking, "Have you come to see it, then?"

My stomach churned at the very suggestion. It had crossed my mind that I would see the thing at some point, but had I come for it? Had I come to see this manuscript, this invasive relic of family shame which seemed alien, which had nothing to do with me, which was not written by me or for me, yet which seemed relevant to me in some intangible way I could not hope to name? Of course not. I had come to investigate Enoch. I had come to discover, one way or another, the truth about Hermes, and the dead brother, and the REM Story. Some tatter of a clue, at any rate. My eyes traced over the frescoed ceiling of the house, so out of place, and as I took it in, I said, "I was wondering if you could show me some of your nonfiction."

"Of course," said my host, gracious as any man could be, his smile perfectly placid and kind. "It is more akin to literary analysis than pure theology, so perhaps you will enjoy it. Though, of course, the deeper one plunges into a work of art, the more one sees hints of something grand at cause. And I admit a fair amount of my work regards religious texts."

As I followed him up the stairs, trying to keep my breathing regulated, I thought to ask, "How long have you been writing these?"

"Only the past two years or so. I have always admired writing, and writers, but simply haven't had time to pursue it."

"Because of the Device."

"Yes, because of the Device, and my few hobbies."

"Why do you keep insisting that this Hermes created it," I said, causing his head to turn toward me as he pushed open the door of his study, "and if he really created it, why won't he come forward? Why would he just lurk around the Internet, waiting for Receivers to contact him?"

"Anonymity is of the utmost value to Hermes," he said, annoyance flaring in me when the only thing he had to add was, "I did not create the Device."

"Why all this obfuscation?" On the threshold of the office into which he entered without a second thought, I leaned against the dark wood of the doorframe. "Why so many lies that I can't even figure out how many lies there are to begin with?"

"Can you imagine how difficult it is, Katherine, to be truly anonymous in this modern world?" Opening a file cabinet beside his desk, Enoch ran his fingers through the hanging folders and at last drew from within a dense stack of paper-clipped manuscripts. "It takes layers upon layers of deception, confusion, track covering. Often the simplest thing is to allow your identity to be subsumed by another's. Here are some of my essays." I accepted them, trying to focus on his words and their meaning while simultaneously taking in the title printed upon the first page: *The Alchemical Devil and Other Essays*. Words in audible and legible form bombarded me together so I couldn't organize thoughts of my own as Enoch went on to explain, with an even brighter turn of mood, "They lack the grace my poet-mother delivered to her works, but they are, nevertheless, my modest offering to the literary world. The collection is being published. I have only just fomented the agreement, and the ink is hardly dry, so I am loath to discuss it, but pleased to have found representation."

"That's half the battle." I flipped through the pages. "I thought you said these weren't about spirituality."

"They are not. Rather, they are inspired works, about the psyche."

"Don't you suppose the title's going to put people off?" I asked, giving the thing a wave.

At the distant whistle of the kettle which diverted his attention, Enoch chuckled. "That is just what Minerva asked."

"Minerva Reinholdt!"

"Yes, my agent." Said with a laugh. "Thank goodness for networking. I shall be back in a moment, Katherine, excuse me. Are you quite certain you would not like any tea?"

Opportunity, hot and golden, sparkled in my frontal lobe as I smiled. "Not yet, thank you."

Enoch vanished from my sight, leaving me alone with his manuscript, his office, and my pounding heart on learning of another possible lead. At once, I fell upon the lockbox, there to the side of the file cabinet, half submerged in a stack of papers; the manuscript pressed between my stomach and my knees, I crouched to examine the lock and found it so weak it was practically pointless, like one of those coin lockboxes every kid had at one point or another, with the weak hinge and little combination dial whose code was lost before their birth. I didn't feel like being discreet. There was no point to it, and, anyway, unless there were cameras in the office, Enoch would never have definitive proof it was me. I cruelly jammed a pen into the jaws of the box, close as possible to that weak lever of a lock, and forced it open with a soft gasp for the several pages which slid from their place atop it. I had enough time to read the words "Mount Ida" printed across the top of the revealed manuscript, replace those two pages, and hurriedly shut the box before Enoch reappeared.

"My apologies, Katherine—" Then, seeing me crouched like a lunatic beside his file cabinet: "Are you quite all right?"

"Fine, I'm sorry." Trying to write off my panic as fluster, I waved the manuscript. "I've been clumsy lately, I dropped an essay or two, I'm so sorry! I hope they're not out of order."

"It shall be no trouble if they are, I am sure," helping me to my feet. "You may keep those to read, if you would like. I have many loose copies, and eventually there shall be bound ones, so if you need take your time with them, please, do."

"I would love to, thank you," I said, repeating to myself *Mount Ida, Mount Ida* again and again and so struggling to maintain an air of normalcy. Attention drifting, I licked dry lips, wished I'd taken him up on the tea, and said, at last, "Uh—that book, Enoch."

"Yes," he said, solemnly.

"What do you think it is? I mean, all of this is just so strange, but then, for the manuscript to be about my uncle—"

"It has to be about someone, Katherine, doesn't it?"

"But such a cruel man! What kind of God would memorialize the crimes of this man in a work of art, as if they were worth remembering!"

"What God could abide a world where a man like this exists?" asked Enoch, shrugging, smiling in a manner not unpleasant and therefore, in context, abominable. "A God who is neither wholly good nor wholly bad, but rather who contains the sum of all things. Lives were lost, yes, but from the perspective of the divine, it may well be a matter of ends justifying means. God is omnipotent and omniscient, the fabric of reality and that which explores it, the driver and the vehicle, beyond us, also us—and yet we are so much less than God, and anything we create as human beings is little more than paltry imitation of divine glory. But what is God imitating, then? What inspires God? You, Katherine, an artist, cannot have creative output without creative input; one cannot create without consuming, cannot expel without first containing. And so, what is it, then, that we see around us but the remains of God's thoughts crystallized and walking as any character in any story of yours? Do you know *The Crying of Lot 49*? It is fleetingly mentioned in the book about your uncle, the first book he borrowed from his ill-fated wife, immortalized forever with her cat. I think often of Oedipa Maas, asking in her little notebook, 'Shall I project a world?'"

With a faint smile, Enoch gazed upon the branches of the camphor tree. "We all project a world, Katherine. Every one of us. But there are certain things which are indelible. Grounded. These things exist in consensus, as a consortium of experiences, like a work of art. What is a painting but a physical representation in space-time of an imaginary figure? What is sculpture but the same? What is a convincing novel but a projection of a world? What is food but the love of the earth for the labors of man? And what, then, is man? Woman?"

I noticed that this whole time the first REM Novel had waited on the desk for me to take notice. At last I had, and could not un-notice it, and so focused again on Mount Ida as I was drawn into the sight of these pages which seemed to bend the air around them. I hugged the essays closer to my breast as Enoch flipped through that more nefarious manuscript.

"What do you suppose it takes, Katherine, to create a world?" When I did not answer, he turned; when I shook my head, he spoke, again, to the manuscript. "It would seem it takes, to speak metaphorically, a kind of pillar. An axis mundi: the world pillar, that which appears often as, say, Mount Fuji, or the mythological tree Yggdrasil."

Head tilting to the left, and then to the right, Enoch hovered somewhere around the funeral of my uncle during the last third of the book. I reread the eulogy of my aunt with the cold sweat of recognition, the feeling of seeing a fuzzy memory captured with clarity in a video never known to exist. At last, once my eyes had scanned to the bottom of the page and the procession had begun to make their way to the cemetery, Enoch suggested, "What if the axis mundii were not physical objects of that sort, Katherine? Not some mountain or pillar, not some tower or tree, but instead a work of art?"

Darkly, I laughed. "You think this ugly book about some killer is a kind of world tree?"

"All works of art are connections to another plane: one of imagination. Say there were a very dedicated writer. Cassius, for instance, strikes me as the type of man capable of doing this. Say there were a writer who wrote a book about a writer."

"People do that all the time. I did it with *Romulus*, but the author of the book within a book in that story was already dead, and the main character's writing didn't have anything to do with it. Cassius was trying to do that with Lazarus, or thinking about it, anyway. It works in small contexts, like Shakespeare's play-within-a-story in *Hamlet*, but trying to tell this 'turtles all the way down,' hands-drawing-hands story always ends badly."

Enoch lifted a finger, letting the manuscript leaf to the beginning. "If Cassius were to write a book about a writer, that writer would be able to, in his turn, write something, would he not? Although we may not be able to perceive it, the character, by definition, perceives that he has written." As I sighed and nodded, Enoch said, "The same is true of any book, or, truly, any piece of art. Every piece of art is real unto itself, real within its own boundaries, and so if one were to write a book about a painter, that would, within the boundaries of the book's existence, make that painter's world and works real. However, the world does not stop at that boundary, at the boundary of that book, because that one book implies an infinitude of other stories. A boundless universe of stories, peoples, ways of being, all because of a single book. Why, in fact, the existence of one single work of art, Katherine, implies not just one boundless universe, but a boundless infinity of universes!"

"You're sounding crazy again," I warned him without irony, trying to keep my eyes on him and away from the book which drew me in like a black hole drawing information. "You're basically saying the entire universe, every universe, exists because of this book." I tapped the offending title page. "That's not only absurd, and disrespectful, but it's obviously wrong."

"That is not what I am saying, dear Katherine. It takes more than one pillar to hold up the Parthenon. This book"—my host's large hand overtook mine, pinned it to the stack of papers as though intending me to feel a heartbeat; I fancied I did—"is but one of many pillars for this world, rooted, themselves, in another world. Truly sublime works of art are formless, spaceless, transcendent; they exist in the realm of pure imagination in a form more perfect than Man might ever hope to emulate, yet we are given a brief cross section of this perfection, as the flatlander would observe a three-dimensional object not as a whole, but in pieces. We have the opportunity to hold on to these pieces—to make them manifest, here, with us. Not just our own works, but the works of something beyond us, which all works, of course, truly are. But you are afraid to do it, because you sense it will change you."

"That's not why I'm afraid."

"Then why are you afraid, Katherine?"

One might have heard traffic passing or a dog barking if the neighborhood weren't so quiet. Maybe I did, and wasn't aware. I knew only the warmth of his hand, a touch which felt strange but nonthreatening, as though he were an alien which either did not know how to be friendly, evocative, or sexual, or did not care. His hand was simply there, existent, real and heavy and hot, and it made me more aware, somehow, of the smell of the paper and dust inhabiting the old books of his office. I felt that he was waiting for something, waiting for me to ask a question. I didn't know what question to ask, so, at last, I tried, "What do you think God wants me to do, Enoch?"

"God wants you to erect your world pillar, Katherine, and to make one of your own Self, to connect the above and below. Pillars have an upward motion, as well as a downward one. Indeed, I would argue pillars, towers, trees, begin from the bottom up. Therefore, a work of art implies not only its own, self-contained world but also the world which produced it: namely the person, their experiences and artistic influences. These things form their own grand spiderweb of cosmic implications, and the grander the architectural majesty, Katherine, the more pillars are required to support it. It is true that, as information is lost through various iterations, so, too, can it be derived based on existing conditions, but there are still things we cannot hope to know by direct means at this stage of being. We interpret and express these things in art and music and science, and most of all, writing: for the Word, Katherine, is the vehicle of consciousness."

With a strange flash, I thought, dizzyingly, of towers, of trees, of mountains, and Mount Fuji, and then Mount Ida. Why, I'd nearly forgotten in the drowning influx of his words! Mount Ida! Mount Ida, and Minerva! The headache, which seemed ever more to be one continuous headache which only bothered the occasional break, pulsed back into my skull. Everything in me made me want to run from him, this lunatic who thought a book about a serial killer was a pillar to God, but instead I politely smiled. "I'm sorry, Enoch. I want to stay and talk more, but my head is aching."

"A symbol, perhaps, for how full it is of unwritten potential," said the man with a wink as I, somehow, resisted an eye roll. On the street I cursed him, and his manuscript, and everything but his essays. His essays, and the lockbox, and whatever it was which was titled "Mount Ida."

4

At certain points in life, a person is forced to recognize the emergence of an uncomfortable, perhaps unbelievable, pattern. The name Mount Ida was so familiar that on my walk home I double-checked on my phone's Internet what my dust-gathering college degree should have summoned offhand: that Mount Ida was where Zeus had been hidden from his father, Cronus. What this recalled was not my conversation with Enoch; rather, I was stricken by the pattern of names around me, and felt schizophrenic, but couldn't seem to help it. All these people, all ostensibly unrelated, and yet...Minerva; and Hermes; and Mount Ida; and I thought again of Castor and Pollux on the ceiling of Enoch's living room; and then, of course, of Cassius.

Cassius. That was an interesting thought: Cassius; Wagner. Cassius Wagner. I wasn't sure why, but I was compelled as soon as I got home to drop everything in the upstairs office and research the name of my lover. The strange whim that he was some carefully named imposter overcame me. Or perhaps it was only his family which had been so christened. Perhaps I stood on the cusp of a conspiracy stretching as far back as a family name. My hand on my face, I researched all the famous Wagners I knew while thinking of how he had pointed out Wagner Creek when we'd first come to Ashland, and how he had laughed, delighted by the coincidence, and said it was meant to be. This, while remembering that Faust's friend in Goethe's play is a man named Wagner: there was also the composer Richard Wagner, and the operas he wrote. Upsetting in and of itself, considering my uncle's name! (More upsetting, still, as I considered so many of my friends and family—and myself—bore the names of Shakespeare characters. This train of thought so disturbed me I dared not pursue its implications to very great a depth.) Researching "Cassius," I didn't come up with much more than the Purple of Cassius, which was sort of interesting in an offhanded way, a pigment made by a reaction of gold salts and tin chloride. It was used to color glass red, and the intensity of its appearance could allow one to determine the presence of gold. Chemistry was always sort of a mystery to me in high school; by that time, my mind had gravitated more toward English and art, but I was for some reason fascinated by this phenomenon. At last, as Cassius walked by with his laundry, I called through my cracked door, "Hey, honey," and asked as his head appeared, "why did your parents name you 'Cassius,' again?"

He laughed. "My mother liked the sound of it. She thought it was regal."

"And 'Chase'?"

"That, I don't know. I think she named him after her godfather. Anything's better than Gerda and Heinrich, right?" Then he was gone, and I was dissatisfied, fluish with paranoia. Alone, I thumbed through the essays I knew I wouldn't read, then pulled my feet into my chair.

This was getting bad. Of course his parents had named him for a simple reason. Of course the reason was dissatisfying. This was reality, not a story. I named characters with a purpose, but sometimes people barely thought about what they named their children. It was as though Enoch's voice echoed in my head, as though he stood beside me, telling me that the unconscious orchestrations of some far-off deity put ideas into parents' heads about what their children should be named. Or maybe it wasn't so simple. I didn't always have an in-universe explanation for my own character names. Often, characters grew into the name I had given them, and if there was an in-universe explanation for or about their name, it was for reasons of plot. Any attention to naming beyond that was purely symbolic, on the level of metafiction: relevant only to the story as a whole.

But, of course, it was a story I was living, or so everybody told me! I wanted to ignore it, but who couldn't help but see the patterns in all of these names? By the end of the night, I knew more variations of the mythological Hermes, and his Roman equivalent, Mercury, than I ever thought existed, even with my minor in classical humanities. I'd read about the Book of Enoch, named for a character who seemingly disappears from the Bible rather than succumbing to death as the rest of his monotonously named relatives, and told myself my research was just for fun. I caught myself somehow getting into the subject of Jewish mysticism around ten at night and chided myself, wondering what I hoped to accomplish by wandering down such a rabbit hole of nonsense. How had I gotten here? Why was I desperate for patterns in names like a clichéd lunatic pinning scraps to a corkboard?

I supposed there were plenty of people who knew lots of friends with Biblical or classical names. Names like Grace or Mary. When I thought of it, I knew more normally named people than people with symbolic names. At least, the names were explicable. Grandpa had named Ada after Augusta Ada Lovelace, the daughter of Lord Byron, because Julius's sister had also been named "Augusta"; and Vera, my mother, was named after the wife of his favorite author, whose final novel, they would be tickled to find, was called *Ada, or Ardor*. That coincidence amid this search for patterns made me uncomfortable: Nabokov was my favorite author, and Cassius's, and we had come together in part over his prose. The scheme of naming seemed troubling, seemed as if it had some influence over the course of my life. But Grandma Bernie had a normal name, and my dead aunt, Susan: her name was normal, but I wasn't sure about where it came from. Even all these years later, I wasn't sure about my aunt at all. They had talked about her very little when I was growing up, my mother and her sister, but it was always in a muttered way in front of me and, when they thought I couldn't hear, the cackling way of abuse survivors joshing about their abuser. But really, she was a sad woman. When she left me all that money, one of three properties (not the murder house), and her old pack of tarot cards, everybody figured it was because I was the only young family member she could name. Vera loudly speculated it had been a personal attack to annoy her. Nobody knew why, and I wasn't interested in explaining it to them.

I didn't meet her until Grandpa's wake at Grandma Bernie's house, which was always big and empty and sad to start with, but which had darkened and chilled to November standards despite the July heat outside. I comforted myself with a plate of hors d'oeuvres, drifting deliriously among the grown-ups at the age of fifteen, not near enough to adulthood to offer anyone consolation but too old to accept the patronizing, candy-coated gestures of kindness offered to grieving children. Placations about Grandpa being in heaven wouldn't have worked, anyway, because he had hanged himself, which was something the women in the family had refused to tell me and so something I had been forced to piece together based on half-heard whispers here and there during the funeral. I was still processing it when my grandmother and mother and aunts went up to speak, and had wept so hard I hadn't been able to see Aunt Susan's face. My perception became a stained-glass window of pain, so by the wake my eyes were dried and sticking. It was as I struggled for a place to ditch my plate to go and wash my face that I saw her for the first time. She was the most beautiful woman I had ever seen, and familiar, too, her dark-red hair, so unlike the rest of our family, piled on her head like a crown. She scanned the crowd as though for someone particular, but then saw me and smiled, eyes and mouth and cheeks all crinkling.

"You're Katherine, aren't you. Vera's girl. Your mother was the one who called to tell me Julius had died. I don't think anyone else would have. She's a good woman, your mother."

Finding no help in a room where everybody wanted help of their own, I realized I was trapped in a conversation and nodded. "Mom's cool. I want to be a writer like her someday, I think."

"As noble a career as any. I know a lot of writers, and actors, and photographers, and—painters," this, said with a distant glaze in her green eye. But it was not her addendum of painters which caught my attention. It was photographers. The idea of photography had curdled my blood for the past six months. Every owner of a camera or a cigar box or a family photo album was a suspected pervert. Horror was everywhere, and I was transported back upstairs, my stomach cold, to the back of Julius's closet. I knew then why she had felt so familiar despite the crystalline colors of tears, despite the bleak and blackening haze of grief suffusing the grand marble room, its dusty piano clinking beneath murmured conversation as its keys were brushed off with intent to play a song. Shocked at my estranged aunt, I gasped, "It was you in his pictures, wasn't it?"

She faltered, my aunt Susan. I'd gotten the feeling in the two minutes I'd known her that she was a woman who never faltered: the kind of unflappable woman who posed for marble busts of Hera back in Ancient Greece. What I asked so quieted her that I feared for a second I had done something wrong. Finding my mother occupied by a cousin, and Grandma Bernie busy along with Aunt Ada accepting condolences from a few psychiatrists, Susan observed softly, "He kept them. You saw them."

Feeling drained just to acknowledge it aloud, and yet somehow empowered by the acknowledgment, I nodded once. Her brow collapsing into furrows of sympathy which I have been told was not a common sight, Susan took up my free hand to squeeze. "Oh, Katherine, I am so very sorry. He didn't—did he?"

"No," I said, softly, flushed, shaking my head, forced by my trembling free hand to put my plate down on the telephone stand where there hadn't been a telephone since 2011. "No, he didn't. But, I..."

My eyes darted around this room of family and friends and strangers who didn't know or understand what I had seen but for one person proving all three of those things at once: who understood what I had seen better than I did. Tutting at tears I only then realized I was crying, Susan drew me from the living room, down the hall, and into a clay-tiled foyer empty except for the occasional guest coming or going through the side entrance.

"I shouldn't cry," I sobbed at the foot of the steps. "He didn't do anything to me, my God, but I still saw. Was that him, with you?"

"Yes," she said bleakly. Her hand squeezed mine. "You have every right to cry, my darling. You saw something no little girl should ever see. Something no person should ever have to see. I am so sorry." The muscles of her neck strained to show her age, and, with a shallow breath which resembled in so many ways a hiss, she said, "I threatened him so he would destroy those awful things. He promised he did, that son of a bitch. I don't know why I believed him, I..."

Lapsing into silence, Susan's lips rested, parted, until she asked, "Were they here? Was it here, in this house, that you found them?" At my nod, she rose, taking me with her. "Show me, please."

Stomach twisting, I frowned at the soft bustle of the wake, then up the darkness of the stairs. I couldn't bear to mount them until, at last, with a sharper squeeze of my hand, my aunt said in a patronizing tone, "Didn't you love Grandpa Julius?"

"That's why it's so horrible," I said, choking on my tears, wracked by a rattling gasp that echoed wet in my lungs like pneumonia. "I loved him so much, he was like a dad to me. My dad never wanted to see me, Susan, but Grandpa always did, and he was always so nice to me. He never hurt me, but now I feel like I need to hate him. He was so sorry, but I feel like I have to hate him, for your sake."

Both her expression and her grip softening, Susan stroked my face with her free hand, frowned in a slight, strange way, and said, "You don't need to hate him, darling, not for my sake or anyone else's. Not even for your own, if you don't want to. I don't hate him."

"You don't?" I asked, my throat so tight I could barely breathe, and my aunt shook her head.

"No. I used to, of course. I thought about killing him every night, sometimes even while—ha-ha." She caught herself and waved her hand. "Here I am, going on like you're my therapist, and not a fifteen-year-old. Oh, to see such a thing so young. Katherine, I'm sorry."

There was a strange kind of catharsis in that, in that shared sorrow from someone who had been victimized in a manner so much worse than I. I couldn't understand that sympathy. I couldn't believe she had any for me, had any for anyone but herself, after what she had been through. But it emboldened me, enough so that when she suggested, "Since I know you love your grandpa, you wouldn't want his reputation besmirched," I felt only the barest twinge of reluctance about leading her up to a chic, "modern" bedroom whose low-set, black-and-white furnishings now belonged to Bernadette alone, much like the contents of an overflowing closet not yet cleaned out. Toward the back of the walk-in storage was a series of platforms which one had to climb like a treacherous-if-broad set of steps to reach the attic crawl space. These were cluttered with all manner of things: old board games, dusty boxes of files, abandoned CDs, stacks of framed paintings, tatters of hats, neglected religious icons. Beneath an ostensibly, offhandedly tossed shirt pinned under the dust-covered case of Grandpa's abandoned violin lurked, not the once-hoped for Christmas presents pursued by a nosey girl, but the foul cigar box which I did not open, rather dutifully tucked under my arm as I navigated my careful way out of the closet and back to the aunt who waited with her lips in a tight expression I could not place. Maybe an uncanny combination of grief and disgust and victory, or maybe that was just what I projected on her. Either way, she dropped the odious contraband into her purse and said, "Thank you, Katherine. Never have I been more thrilled for a hotel suite with a fireplace. It shall be a happy bonfire tonight."

"You won't tell anyone about them, right? That I saw them, or brought you here." I felt once more the greasy sense of complicity I'd suffered for making the discovery to begin with. Susan smoothed my brow.

"That would be as awful an experience for me as for you, if not more. Better they're gotten rid of quietly." With a terse sniff toward her purse, she verbalized what I had thought for six months: "Bernadette certainly can turn a blind eye, can't she. It's criminal. The worst thing a person can do, Katherine, is to ignore the shadow following them around, even if it's only their husband's. Why, after all, the Bible teaches the Christians that they are to become one flesh on marriage: therefore, the shadow of one's husband is one's own shadow. Never marry, Katherine," said my aunt with a gay laugh, turning toward the door and shaking her head. "If you do marry and expect independence, be ready for a temporary arrangement or a nasty shock. But never blind yourself to what's really happening. If you must marry, marry the man you know you can trust; and if one day you find you can't trust him, don't feel obligated. If you ever get the sense you haven't the whole story, never settle for feeling that. That's the problem with the Vasko women, why I've let our relations lag. They would rather their heads in the sand than admit air is made of oxygen."

"Mom's name is 'Beauvoir,'" I said, absently. "She said she didn't want to change it back to Vasko, she didn't like the sound of an alliterative name."

"And you, Katherine? 'Beauvoir.'" She smiled at that, then said, "'A fine view,' is what that means. I think not of the philosophtrix but of Baudelaire. A *beau fille* deserves a *beau voir...*" She must have made the decision then, as she smiled at me and turned away. "*Et les dames d'atour, pour qui tout prince est beau, ne savent plus trouver d'impudique toilette, pour tirer un souris de ce jeune squelette.*"

That was what she recited as she left the room, then the house, and then, about a year and a half later, the earth, so that I, just-turned seventeen, would meet Cassius at her funeral. The rest, they say, is tabloid history. The unhurried blossoming of our love would take years, but there was no stopping it. He had always been a man I could trust, could love. But with the REM Novel in the house, I forgot that completely. And there had arisen the feeling that I didn't know close to the whole story.

I suppose that what occurred next only occurred because I was so paranoid. Of course, I can't blame the book for fating my paranoia, because I hadn't read the thing. But knowledge of its existence, regardless of whether I had read it, was a plague to the soul. Acutely aware I was tied to a track, I could only keep surging forward in careful study of Enoch. It was as though unraveling the mystery of Hermes with which he shrouded himself would somehow save me from that which otherwise allowed no salvation. As the walls closed in, I hoped for some explanation, some clarity that might assure me this was not all some strange, targeted assault which meant in the end that I was a dream and my life was worth nothing. But wasn't that true whether I was living to begin with? Far out in the future, I would be less than fictional in the eyes of the living. My headstone would be worn to a nub, my books would all be lost with no Nag Hammadi vessels to conceal them, my name would be unpronounceable under the dull light of the blackening sun which would have, eventually, no face to shine upon. I would exist only unconsciously, book or no book, world or no world, and that notion, coupled with the notion that my demise might be forthcoming, made me jumpy. Was the book an accurate model of reality, or was my reality a result of someone using me to write the book? With the causal relation of existence muddled, I found myself obsessing over every small action: Is this in the book? What, if anything, does this mean? What does this symbolize? I began, also, to obsess over Cassius's movements. When he went for his next visit to Enoch, I got it into my head to follow him.

Have you ever tried to tail somebody in a community full of friendly neighbors eager to greet one another? You feel like an asshole. Everybody already thought I was an asshole, anyway, I'm pretty sure, but as I traced Cassius's path to Enoch's house, sunglasses on, I lowered my head, avoided all smiling eye contact, and felt as if I were violating some privilege imparted by being in the last of America's comforting towns. Scrub jays in the distance laughed at me as I, like an idiot, made my way down B Street and then realized that it was going to be a tough number, eavesdropping in any successful way. What did I hope to prove, exactly? What kind of conspiracy did I think there really was? The license plate of the car across the street ended in 944, and I felt strange on seeing it, thought about any other fours I'd been seeing lately, about cars, Volkswagens, Ted Bundy's Volkswagen Beetle, Ted Bundy, killer of women, who imparted the advice that the best way to get away with doing something you're not supposed to be doing is to look like you're supposed to be doing it. That was what I decided to do. Chin up, even though someone was coming from the end of the block and somebody else across the street had just exited their house, I strode through Enoch's gate, made an immediate right past the garage to avoid the living room window, then took a wide berth around the house as though I intended to enter through the back. I even shut the gate, quietly, behind me, and thought to myself how funny it was that so private a man didn't bother to lock his back fence; but then, that was the community for you. Low among the rosebushes, I crept past the glass patio doors which opened to the empty kitchen. I was out in the thyme by the gazebo when fleshly shadows moved in the dim house. As Enoch threw open the window over the cramped sink, I ducked, trapped behind the gazebo in the corner of the garden where at the very least I could be seen by no neighbors. Neither could Cassius and Enoch see me, unless they were particularly attentive. Unless this was a scene in the book, which, I realized with an ugly feeling, it probably was. Did that mean they knew I was there?

"For R. D. Laing," Enoch was saying, his voice carrying through the backyard, "the crucial test of whether a patient was psychotic was a lack of congruity between his reality, or the reality of person A, ostensibly sane by society's standards; and the reality of person B, who is not sane by what he called 'common consent.'"

"Do we have to open the windows?"

"Far too beautiful a day not to take in the wind, good man," said Enoch, and my lover sighed.

"I know, but—"

"Yes, my neighbors can be quite nosy." There was a pause as though for emphasis. I didn't like it and was on the verge of going when at last one chair scraped the floor, then another. The men sat at the cramped kitchen table as the host assured his guest, "They will mind their own business."

"Right." His face audibly in his hands, Cassius said, "That definition you gave doesn't make me feel less insane."

"You are not insane. You are a mystic. Your reality does not disagree with common consensus in any meaningful way. You are simply seeing things from a new perspective. The subjective experience of what the Western mind has been trained to think of as 'God' with a capital *G* has also been deeply tabooed by those who would claim to be closest to Him." As if apropos of nothing, he said, "Has Katherine been reading my essays, do you suppose?"

"You gave her essays to read?"

If ever the sound of a man sucking his tooth could be put out, this was, and I, head low, took the opportunity to dart along the side of the house, where, poised beneath the window, I would be invisible in the shadow of the rosebushes. Enoch grumbled, "I suppose she shall begin them when she is ready for them. At any rate, they require a certain familiarity with Jung, and the symbols of alchemy."

Laughing, snapping his fingers, Cassius said, "Whenever I try to talk about that, I sound like a lunatic. He was a cool cat, but only he could articulate what he did in the way that he did."

"Nonsense, dear man. Someone need only pick up his work where he left off. The same is true of any artist. That art thou—decide the thing, become the thing. Life is a process of perpetual change, and that is a fact which holds true regardless of topic: sometimes, that change can be severe, very serious, and when it is resisted it comes on like a rhinoceros charging, its black scythe of a horn cutting through the air. We must change with it; we must accept our inherent nature. We must know ourselves. The better man knows himself, the higher he climbs upon his tree of knowledge toward a perfect understanding of that which we might call 'God.'"

"The Holy Spirit, Trystero," said Cassius with a chuckle. There was a genuine smile in the tone of Enoch's response.

"No author did better than Pynchon in dancing around a depiction of that which cannot be depicted. There is a certain aspect of the unconscious which, by definition, cannot be brought fully into consciousness, and it is this from which the Word buffers us. It can, however, be experienced in one form or another, for better or for worse, and communicated with a series of symbols *in context*. That is what life is: a narrative we build to defend our egos based on a collection of more or less arbitrary vignettes selected to provide us with the context for our own being. When we feel ourselves becoming something we cannot or do not wish to justify, we are stricken by cognitive dissonance and find ourselves forced to face that which we never expected, never considered: that the existence of our shadow is dependent entirely upon our own existence.

If we did not exist, nor would our shadow; if our shadow did not exist, we would not, either."

"I suppose I don't understand what Katherine's shadow is. What's chasing her?"

"Isn't it obvious, good man?" I stilled at that, because it was not obvious to me, either. When Cassius had no response, the host of the conversation said, "She is terrified of mortality. Hers, yours, the concept in general. But hers more than anything."

"We're all afraid of our own mortality," Cassius said, but I, heart in my mouth, lowered my unseen head against my chest and considered the garden gate. I shouldn't have come, but there was no taking it back, no leaving the conversation early, because they would most certainly hear or see me leave, assuming they didn't know I was listening. It was entirely possible, even likely, that they were having this conversation for my benefit since they'd read the novel. For all I knew, they could be in there with printed copies, reading lines from the manuscripts like actors preparing for a play. It made my scalp itch as Enoch insisted, "Katherine's role is one of profound significance in all of this, going by what I have read in the novel."

That sealed it. Cassius had allowed Enoch to read the thing. They really were in on this together. I barely had time to be vindicated as he carried on. "I am very curious about Receivers, because I am not one, myself. I do not think that one is more important than another, but what I do think to be important is that Receivers experience the Device in various conditions."

"Like a seizure."

"Or enlightenment, perhaps," suggested the younger man, and this fell between them, and me, like a soft and blasé confession.

"I just don't want her to be scared the way I was when I woke up from my seizure."

"But it was worth it, Cassius, wasn't it," said Enoch, as I, white with fury, trembled and wondered if I could stir up enough shit at the police department to get the old camphor poisoning reopened without seeming vengeful. "Think of what we Received from suffering you did not consciously experience!"

"That's why I made sure they left it alone. But what I'm saying is that you can't do something like that to Kitty."

"I have no need to, Cassius. She is doing it to herself. We need only be there at the right moment, and see what unfolds. I am very curious. That book upstairs—"

"That book upstairs shouldn't be read," said Cassius above the drum of his fingers. "That book upstairs, I mean, at best it reflects badly on me. I brushed shoulders with that guy."

"And you do not yet understand why you had that encounter."

"Do you?"

There came again protesting floorboards as Enoch rose. He carefully said after some time, "I do not presume to know anything anymore, myself. I do not presume to know even why I do the things that I do, even when I believe I know why I am consciously doing them. In general, this attitude works quite well for me. But so far as the case of Monsieur Richard Vasko is concerned"—the creaking drew near the window, and I pressed tighter to the house, my eyes closed against the agitated wasps visiting white roses near my ear—"he most certainly did not achieve enlightenment in life. His is an important lesson, but there is more to it than that, insofar, at least, as its relevance to this situation is concerned. He is, after all, a direct relation of Katherine's, as was your late friend."

"Yes, yeah, and my great-grandfather on my mother's side was a farmer. What relevance does his farming have to me?"

"Precisely as much as you allot it. The amount of significance Katherine places upon having an incestuous serial killer in her family may be, suffice to say, unhealthy, and may be part of the reason why she makes such a fine Receiver for whatever it is that the Lord wishes to impart. I cannot be certain. You said she is experiencing writer's block? Perhaps she feels overwhelmed by internal pressure. Or perhaps she senses that another, better project is soon on the horizon. One which will require her energy, her receptivity to new knowledge."

"I don't think she wants any knowledge. I think she just wants to feel successful on her own merits. Like she's really in control of her life."

"Of course. But to achieve that goal in a substantial way, one must have the unnameable, objective-in-subjective experience. It is one thing to know the thing, another entirely to experience it. Imagine being raised in a house where words were never spoken and music went unplayed, yet you were taught to read both language and music. The model without the reference. Likewise, we have the Bible, the Koran, the Tibetan Book of the Dead, and none of them have true meaning to us until we have had that semisecret, wholly optional human experience of divine ecstasy. This is the rationalist flaw. Evidence of 'it' is not so much a problem of concrete physical evidence of the sort they demand; rather, because 'it' is an upward movement of consciousness, the experience is strictly subjective and tangible only in results, not in evidence. Those results can often be attributed by the rationalist mind to something more materially explicable. William Blake wrote that man is enclosed by the five senses which experience the world; we are like Helen Keller, blind and deaf and dumb to all which is above and around us while our seemingly omnipotent teacher, desperate to break through our darkness, sends us every sign, any sign, pressing words into our mouths and hands until at last comes that day we hold our fingers beneath the tap and connect the sensation to the term 'water.' From thence comes our true light, the true light which brightens the world. From the Word."

"Yes," breathed Cassius over the clink of glasses.

"You and I have had our experiences, for which there are no words. But that is the goal of the Word, you see: to find and disseminate, at last, that perfect metaphor for that which cannot be named. That which must either be boiled down to a symbologem as obscure as a stone, a fish, or a crucified man, or which must be experienced long-form as a progressive series of symbols in a piece of interactive art, a psychedelic experience, or a participatory religious mystery. I am not so sure," he added in a wry way, "that, done right, there is any difference between the three, but that is another discussion. At any rate, I think there is something you had ought to read, my good man, and something I had ought to discuss with you upstairs, away from the neighbors. Would you follow me?"

I knew exactly what he was doing. He thought his manuscript and whatever secret it held was in jeopardy, and the only way to maintain control was to preemptively share it. God only knew what was in "Mount Ida," but I had a feeling it was an explanation, at least in part if not in full, to the mystery of his connection with Hermes. At the very least, it would be some carefully crafted story that would justify whatever happened, whatever the symbol of Mount Ida represented to Enoch. And Cassius, compassionate and malleable as he was, especially after the seizure, would accept it. Skin crawling, I waited for them to make their way up the creaking stairs, then made little effort at discretion as I burst through the gate, catapulted across the front lawn, and went running down the street.

I never doubted there was some knowable explanation for all of this. That, maybe, was why I had no issue with pinning the thing on the lover who'd been with me almost thirteen years, whose life and marriage I had disrupted. I had loved him but refused to give all of myself to him, all so what? So I could someday say, "Aha, I've caught you, sharing a mystical manuscript with this strange man I don't trust, who I think has done something terribly wrong, only I can't be sure what"? I didn't know what I was doing. I felt terrifically alone because I was making myself alone but didn't know how to stop. Why had he shared it? At home, I locked myself up in the office again and buried myself in the essays, hardly able to read hot as I was with betrayal to think that poisoner, that viper, knew what I would do.

And not just a viper but a lunatic. The essays began with a four-part apologia on the Christian devil which devolved from academic tone to rambling about God. Then came several essays about the operatic works of Wagner, Handel, and Rossini; a handful of film analysis; and a set of essays on literature from Shakespeare to Pynchon, which I studied for a while, attempting to derive some personal meaning until Cassius jolted me with a knock on the door.

"I hate to interrupt you, honey," he called from the other side, having returned without my notice, "but did you want to go out to dinner tonight?"

"I can't," I said without getting up, without unlocking the door between us. "I'm sorry, Cassius, I have a lot of work tonight."

"Katherine," he started, but then thought better of it, or maybe thought about the manuscript, and just said, instead, "I love you."

"I love you, honey."

"Kitty," he said after another few seconds in which he had not moved. When I answered him, he asked with petulance, "Can I at least have a kiss?"

It was cruel of me to feel put-upon, and I tried not to. All the same, I threw down the essays and tromped up to unlock the door through which I presented myself, thrusting my face toward his as though it were less a kiss and more some assault. Hurt bloomed in his eyes, but I didn't care. I was tired of people keeping secrets for me to discover, and that this one should involve my life so personally was inexcusable. That he should have shared the details of my future with Enoch hurt. So, I hurt him. Even stung as he was, Cassius bent to kiss the corner of my mouth, then my lips. "I love you, Kitty, oh, Christ, I love you, hey."

"I love you," I said, starting to shut the door again. "There's your kiss, have a good dinner."

"Are you working on your novel?" he asked me before I could close it all the way. Restraining a sigh, I left it cracked enough to say, "I'm editing something."

"Oh. Well." In an annoying, fretting way, he refrained from finishing his thought, hesitated in the doorway, and at last settled on, "Well, good luck."

"Is something the matter?" Maybe it was more of a bark than a question, but I couldn't be made to care. "You seem nervous, and it's making me nervous. What's wrong?"

"Nothing. Nothing's wrong. I just wanted to have dinner with you."

"And I have to work."

"Katherine, I just don't know why you're so angry today. I'm on your side, baby. I know you're scared, but I'm just trying to help you. Would you talk to me?"

My office door shut. I couldn't stand to hurt him; sooner or later I'd feel empathy, and then I'd really be trapped. Then I'd be going to dinner, functioning and having normal conversations instead of sealing myself in my office with King Crazyland's literary vomit. It could hardly be called nonfiction, or fiction, or useful; it was a bunch of literary analysis elevated to the level of gospel, as though analyzing art or film or poetry was some religious act. As if art could be objectively defined against some universal standard. It was an offensive idea. As bad as saying there was no free will, as bad as the thought that there was something out there which knew how I would behave in a certain circumstance, before that circumstance arose. The only one who should have known such a thing was me, and I, of course, had no internal, organic way to predict the future and no way to know how I would act in it. But somewhere, something did. Something deep inside of me, some strange, antennae part of my right brain. Was it making sense of cosmic background radiation? Probability? It had to be. It had to be making sense of something. Surely, there wasn't an intelligence actively writing.

The more I considered, the more it seemed writing was the solution to my thinking about this. After all, I didn't know 100 percent of the time what a character was going to do or think before they did it. That was the way it was with a good character. They surprised you. The fact that the printout I had received allegedly matched reality meant I was getting what was essentially a final draft of reality—or close to it, at any rate. But that final draft's existence implied the possibility of prior revisions, and I wondered if there had been a time when the so-called author of this didn't know what I was going to be doing. Maybe they had once been like me: just along for the ride. That would mean I had some small agency (maybe vaguely imaginary), which meant I could change things. There was nothing indelible in the book so far as I was concerned because I hadn't even read the thing end to end. But I still remembered the paragraph that had chilled me. That left me first avoiding, then scrambling for explanation:

The skull, alarmingly round amid its oblong cousins, conjured Cassius's seizure, and Castor and Pollux, and the names Enoch and Hermes in parallel. I was less sure than I had ever been of Cassius's friend—whether he was Enoch to begin with, or Hermes to begin with, or both, or if there was a difference, and what it meant. Had he killed this man? Why else would there be a skull there? Why else would I feel so cold and afraid and alone? Why else would I be sent here to find this skull, after all—sent by the novel, by God, by my dead aunt and uncle—if not to uncover some crime? But, a crime by whom? What was this skull? What meaning, if any, could be derived?

I read that and pretty much stopped doing anything. I stopped writing, stopped editing, stopped being able to think anything but those lines. They had disturbed me even before I'd met anybody named Enoch. What about finding a human skull isn't disturbing? What about reading of your lover's seizure? Maybe it was true I'd gotten bitchy over the past six months, but could I be blamed? As if it weren't enough that we'd uprooted entirely in hopes of living out a dream in some fairy-tale town, I had been plagued by worry that the skull belonged to Cassius. My name shouldn't have been Katherine, I lamented in my office, and his shouldn't have been Cassius; mine should have been Cassandra, and his, Agamemnon. But was Enoch really a killer, or just odd? It was hard to say. He was an unreal man, out of touch with the worries of others. At least, with the worries I carried. He had described some divine mission, but how could I produce anything important with a human skull floating in my future?

I couldn't sit and wait to find the skull's owner through tragic inaction because nobody listened. The more I read the essays and the illuminated treatises to which they referred, the more I felt I wasn't the crazy one. I had to hang on to that. I only felt insane because I was isolated in a new town with new people: because my lover had been psychologically destabilized by a near-death experience and we were both shaken by the uncanny implications. Someone crazy was taking advantage of that destabilization, and I couldn't stand by and let it happen.

A few hours after my encounter with Cassius, I took up my keys and my purse and asked myself what I expected to do. What could I do? I had evidence: for what, I wasn't sure. More and more I thought of a short story which had chilled me as a girl, about a lady who buys a jigsaw puzzle from a thrift store and puts it together with an increasing sense of déjà vu until, at last, she realizes the puzzle depicts her, sitting in her room, putting together the puzzle whose final piece depicts an awful face, staring at her through the window. When I read that as a girl, it terrified me, and now I understood why: I was surrounded by these pieces, feeling more and more that putting them together would only end in a disaster.

Yet there weren't even enough pieces to form a picture. Nobody knew anything about Enoch. Most of the articles about him and the Device had him living in California, not in Ashland; everybody knew "Azarias" wasn't his real name; and everybody, it seemed, knew that he was really the Hermes he had begun to reluctantly admit was his research assistant. All were content to nod their heads agreeably when he claimed that Hermes Tetramegistus lived elsewhere, in solitude. Eccentric geniuses had their reasons.

I wasn't sure what I was going to do—grill Enoch for information, maybe, or go for a walk which would inevitably lead by his house and result, more than likely, in another round of creepily trying to listen in on his activities—but as I slipped from my office and down the hall, the sound of Cassius on a video call downstairs caught my attention, and I held my breath to hear Minerva.

"I have to hand it to you, Cassius. It's an interesting concept. It's not a whole book, though."

"I know it's not. That's part of the reason— I shouldn't be telling you this. You might not even like the idea, anyway, but Katherine has something similar she's...working on." I tried not to be overwhelmed by frustration at the thought of him sharing information about my REM Novel with her, of all people. "I'm thinking that maybe this book should be a collaborative effort."

"What does her book have to do with it?"

"It's the same sort of thing, uh...a metafictional thing."

"With the Device."

"Right."

"Maybe we could spin it as an anthology on the future of writing." Minerva hummed as I worked my way down the stairs, back to the wall, and crouched to stay out of the lens of the camera lest Cassius notice me even from the distance of his open office, where I could only see the white-blond back of his head. His agent continued musing, "Sort of a Hunter S. Thompson thing, this blurring of reality. Gonzo fiction, psychedelic fiction. A couple of writers writing about themselves but about something that's clearly fictional."

"I'm not sure I'd label it an anthology. It's all one smooth story, Minerva. If you put it together in the right order, it's like the reader is reading about me reading the other stories in the book. And I don't know if I'd call it 'fiction,' necessarily."

"An exquisite corpse is a kind of fiction."

"Kind of, but let me see if I can get Kitty to share it with you."

That was what he was saying as I, breath hitching, noticed the dreaded manuscript resting upon the living room coffee table, its paper softened and beginning to curl from the intensity of Cassius's scrutiny—and Enoch's. I, mouth dry, slipped past the doorway and into the open room, compelled to touch the pages. It was the first time I could stand to since Cassius and I had struggled over the ordered document. Before that, it had been perhaps the full six months since the seizure. My God, half a year, half a year. I held in my hands the result of that seizure, the result which predated the cause, which at once foretold the seizure but never could have existed if my lover hadn't had a seizure in the future to begin with. Cradling it to my breast as I might a child, I studied the foreign house around me, the dark stone of the fireplace and the soft rose of the walls and the plate depicting Demeter which Cassius had brought from his home in Tucson. All of this seemed existent because of the thing in my hands; all of this seemed to have been projected outward, yet would continue to exist if I cast the thing in my hands into the fire. There would just be no proof of the phenomenon which had illustrated it. Which seemed as though to cause it or, if nothing else, predict it. I had always had a hard time grasping the idea of quantum entanglement. Maybe this was what it meant, or, at least, how it felt. I had become entangled, or had always been entangled, my condition inexorably tied to the condition of something which had nothing to do with me, because it wasn't a person, or a part of me. It was just a book. Distantly, I was aware of Cassius and Minerva going on in the other room, with Cassius pitching the book in my hands as, "Sort of a novella about a nervous breakdown, which'll be a lead-in to something else. What, I'm not sure yet, but that's also what Katherine's working on."

"And what is the point of this story, exactly?"

"Expanding the reader's consciousness, I guess," laughed my lover as I and the manuscript slid around the couch to avoid the office en route to the garage. "Enoch told me you're giving him a shot, and he's on board with this project, too, actually. He's got this short story, "Mount Ida," that would round out the book, although it's...." Cassius's voice dropped, and, though I was in the kitchen, I froze to hear. "I don't know, Minerva, I'm also kind of wondering if these stories should be published at all."

"You can't offer these to me and then back off, Cassius. What's wrong with them?"

"It's not that there's something wrong with them. It's just that...the line between truth and fiction is hazy, right?"

"Honey, I don't really care if it's fiction or not. Who would believe that you put the LSD on your head and wrote a story in your sleep? I sure as shit don't. I think that Enoch is a crazy cultist who's getting you embroiled in his bullshit, to be perfectly honest, but I think his essays will sell to other crazies, and in the meantime, if he's finally getting you to get your shit together, I say, more so the better. Just remember, if he gives you Kool-Aid to drink—"

"Oh, we're way past that." Cassius laughed. I found nothing funny about it, and was in the middle of asking myself what I meant by my plans for a night drive when what I needed was to have a come-to-Jesus talk with my lover when, at last, he asked Minerva, "So how's Tommy, and Tucson?" and I realized with a chill what I was meant to do. "I warned him you'd visit if he wasn't careful."

"Fine and fine, though you'd know that if you ever called him since your move, just like you'd know he wants his parents to visit occasionally."

"Oh, Minnie, for Christ's sake. You didn't visit him for three years after he moved back to Tucson because you couldn't risk running into me by surprise, and you're going to blame me for—"

By then I was out in the garage, the argument silenced by the door. Trembling, I jotted a note on the back of the manuscript's temporary title page, so that one side read "Katherine" while the other sneered in trembling hand "*I suppose you know where I'll end up going.*"

Then, my body carried me. In the strangest way, my conscious mind turned off, and it was like the flow of highway hypnosis, or ghostwriting something boring. Here the flow arose from fear rather than muscle memory. By magic, I was in the driver's seat of my manual Saturn, and the garage door was opening. The house was well insulated, so it didn't surprise me much that Cassius didn't hear me. What does surprise me was that he didn't know, or didn't care, or couldn't help that this argument was the one where I left the house. I expected him to come barreling out. But maybe, I thought with a start, he'd told Enoch. Enoch, into whom I nearly backed as I emerged in the alley. The sight made me choke on my tongue, but when he smiled—maybe it was the way he smiled—I felt certain he was only a ghost, a figment of my mind, a trick of the light, and yes, of course, it was only the trash can of the people across the way and some garbage as revealed when the headlights properly fell on him in my backing up. But I could have sworn I had seen him stooped there, the devil, and was questioning my sanity when the just-closed garage door opened again, and my foot slammed the accelerator so I careened down the curving alley, around the corner, and off through the neighborhood.

On the breathless road, I wondered what I was doing. Easter was three days out, which meant travel would be a nightmare, and the pass out of the Rogue Valley might still be in questionable condition. I hadn't checked the weather, or packed clothes; I also hadn't taken the Mercury, because Cassius was the last to have the keys, and because it, as an auto-navigating death trap, had all kinds of override features and potential security problems which came into play when one owner was effectively trying to steal it from the other. Car-napping, maybe. It just seemed sensible to take the Saturn, but crawling through town, I found myself wondering if the sensible thing wasn't just to stay behind. The thought of Cassius on my tail, for some reason, sent a chill through me, and the thought of Enoch was so much worse. My head swam and my jaw ached with the want to call my lover, but I could barely drive, let alone think about a conversation with a man who had offered up my story without my asking. The story in the seat next to me, the one happening to me: the bargaining chip that would get me proof, one way or another, that Enoch was not who he said he was.

5

The first ignored call from Cassius came forty-four miles after the California border. It was a holiday weekend, but there was an advantage to my leaving at such an odd hour; save for truckers and early drunkards, I was the only one on the dark roads. Though it was true my stomach was tighter every turn, and a few curves' urgent lines manifested too suddenly for my liking, the Golden State soon relieved me when the winding mountain turns ironed out to nice, boring fields, their velvet hillsides mere pictures on the drive's distant walls rather than obstacles to be surmounted. The landscape was quiet: all the livestock slept out of sight (out of my sight, anyway), and up high in the sky the romantic heavens spread themselves full of dazzling stars which I dared not admire too long, forced to keep my eyes pinned to the road, to the passing trucks, to the ever-present threat of sleep or disaster: mine, or someone else's doomed to become mine.

I was so afraid. I laughed at myself, alone in the car, for being so afraid, yet going and doing some terrifying thing all the same. Was that brave, or stupid? Was that right, or wrong? Was following the novel I had only partially read, could only stand to half perceive, going to lead me to or away from the skull? The truth? I couldn't imagine. I could only finally get a hotel room in Bakersfield, nine hours from Ashland, where I slept for the first few hours of Good Friday and awoke wondering what was so good about the day a messiah was crucified. I didn't understand it, that or any religion, any more than I could understand the price of a toothbrush and toothpaste from the hotel, or the way my hands trembled as I neared Tucson as though it hadn't been my home for over a decade. The trembling might have had to do with Minerva, who I had seen twice since she started the divorce proceedings, and who had a documented disdain for me anytime we weren't working together. That disdain was visibly apparent when she, of all people, was the one who opened the door to her son's Tucson co-op apartment on Bellatrix. As if, in coming to stay for a few days, she had already become owner of the place.

"Cassius told me you would probably be coming. I just wasn't sure when. I didn't realize you'd be so...bedraggled."

"Thanks," I said, reminding myself that I fucked, almost every night, the man who was once this awful woman's husband. Feeling better, my attention focused to the man on the couch who, like a more compact, far younger Cassius, turned bright eyes toward me and returned my brief greeting with a cheerful, "Hey, Aunt Kat, come on in. Want a beer?"

"No, thanks, I drove. Listen, Minerva, I really don't want to take up your time."

Despite her son's invitation, she was still half in the door, and I was forced to stand in the concrete breezeway, windbreaker whipping as I waited for her to move. Instead, she said, "I normally don't let clients talk to me without appointments, let alone their girlfriends."

"Oh, Mom, let her in."

"Last time I let her into a house, it was a disaster," said Minerva. At last, I grew agitated enough to wave the manuscript under her nose, which made her wince away.

"Do you recognize this smell?"

"No?"

"That's because you've never smelled this much money in your life." I jerked it back from her. "I heard Cassius talking to you about the manuscript. This is it."

With a sly double take around the breezeway, Minerva at last stepped aside to let me into the small two-bedroom apartment. It seemed to house the contents of a hoarder's storage unit. Evidently, not having a sufficiently-sized patio, Thomas had opted to keep his worst purchase decision to date, his used Mustang motorcycle, in the corner of the room. I hadn't known him to use it more than a couple of times, and not once since he moved into this place, which was the last time Cassius and I gave him any money. While I hovered on the edge of a nightmare of milk crates, dirty socks, and dusty books, Minerva unhappily stepped over an abandoned pile of mail to drop into the couch whence her son scrambled.

"Sure I can't get you something?" he asked, and when I told him no again, I think he detected the haggard shade in my eye, or the exhaustion crackling my voice. Between the two of us, he said at last, "Why don't I go ahead and leave you ladies alone."

"That's fine, sweetheart," said Minerva, picking up her bottle of sangria and filling a glass which had surely been filled at least twice before. "I'll come and get you when you're wanted."

That got a snort out of both Thomas and I, but the boy said nothing as he left. When he disappeared down the hallway, sent to his own room in his own apartment, I sank into the armchair across the cluttered coffee table and threw down the manuscript, happy to have it out of my hands. "You can have that to read, and if you think it belongs as part of a novel with Cassius's section, then fine, be my guest and throw it in. But I want you to do a favor for me."

Though her eyes had been bright on the manuscript and her hand had been stretching toward it, my declaration made her stop and laugh. "Oh! You want me to do a favor for you, do you?"

"Yeah, I do. Or else this is going to be a simultaneous submission for Drake Wolfram, and I can tell you he's going to snatch it up. And Cassius's part, too, and Enoch's." Her lips tightened but she said nothing, only waiting as I demanded she "Tell me everything you know about Enoch. He's your client. You must know something about him, more than Cassius and I."

"Why, exactly, do you need to know anything about Enoch?"

"I can't explain it without sounding insane," I told her, calmly, or in a way which I thought was calm. "I can't explain it, but I need you to trust me, and I think, when you read that book, it will all make sense. But for me to let you read the book, and for it to make sense to you, you have to tell me something about Enoch."

"So you want me to reveal information about an intensely private man, who came to me, expecting my confidence, all to satisfy some hunch that's so crazy you won't even tell me about it because you admit it sounds insane. And you say that if I just lean on you and have faith that I'm betraying this person's confidence for a reason, I'll discover the reason when I take time out of my busy schedule to read your little book, which may well not be worth a second of my time?"

"It's not my book!" I half shouted the words, catching myself at the end, and repeating again at a normal volume, "It's not my book. I didn't write it. It's written in my voice, it's about me, but it's about things that still mostly haven't happened yet. It probably even documents this conversation!" Agitated, I snatched the manuscript and flipped through it, trying to thumb its pages without really reading it, and found that Cassius had not just organized it into linear fashion but cut it into chapters. I kept an eye out for that *M* name which had filled me with such dread over the years, and when I found enough repetitions of it somewhere about two-thirds of the way through, I slowed until, at last, with a grim sense of victory which did not resemble victory, I found this page and showed it to Minerva. She lifted her glasses atop her head, scanned the paragraphs and then, leaning forward, scanned again, her once-narrowed eyes like headlights. She reached for the stack of pages on my lap, but I slapped a hand on them and leaned back in my seat. "Tell me everything about Enoch."

"I don't know why you expect me to know anything of substance. He's a recluse. I know he's from Colorado," she suggested at last, and that brightened me significantly because it was new information. Drumming her fingers against her jaw, she said, "Well, he's obviously full of shit, just talking to him about Cassius, so he might be lying about this, but when he was pitching himself to me, he told me that his mother was some poet I'd never heard of, uh...hold on."

Because everything I asked of her was a chore, Minerva sighed as she rummaged through the purse on the back of the couch (selected as the cleanest place in the room, no doubt) until she produced a phone on which she tapped. "You sure do have some balls to demand anything of me."

"That was why I came in person. There was no way you would do anything for me over the phone. If you couldn't see how desperate I am."

"My doing this for you has a lot less to do with you than you'd think. Here she is: Leda Anatida."

The name set off an alarm bell in my head, and I remembered, then, seeing the book on display in the shelves of Enoch's living room, faced out next to Baudelaire, Ovid, and other poets who were, to a dutiful son's mind, no doubt of lesser significance than his mother. It made sense. I had thought he was just being pretentious, favoring an author of whom nobody had ever heard for the sake of seeming unique or trendsetting. Of course, Enoch was all of those things, but I realized he was, with that small gesture, paying homage to his mother, the same way he did with the name of the software running the Device's tutorial. As Minerva shrugged and put away her phone, she said, "I don't know anything else, Katherine. Sorry to disappoint."

"No, no. That's fine, it's perfectly fine." While she drained her glass, I placed the manuscript between us. "You said he pitched himself to you, though. I thought Cassius recommended him to you—or am I wrong?"

"Oh, Christ." With annoyance at the glass in her hand, really meant for herself, Minerva sank back into the cushions of the navy couch which had never been vacuumed once in its life. "As soon as Cassius told me you were on the way here, I started drinking. That's never a good idea...it was Enoch who set the whole thing up in the first place. Insisting Cassius get on his next book."

My stomach tightened as Minerva went on. "Enoch contacted me about his Device and explained he'd come into funding. He wanted to set some aside to bankroll the marketing campaign for Cassius's next novel if I could get him to write it using the Lightning Stenography Device. Legitimize it. He told me if I could get him to finish a draft by the end of last year, he'd pay me a finder's fee."

"Did he?"

"Did he ever! He didn't say anything about psychologically torturing you, but it's not surprising. You can see he's got 'I'm a little shit' stamped on his forehead if you talk to him more than twenty minutes. That's probably why he's so reclusive. He can't maintain a mask of sanity."

"Do you think he could ever kill someone?" I asked softly, so that Thomas, who I was certain listened in, couldn't hear me. Minerva didn't care in the least and only barked a laugh.

"That mincing little man?"

"He's near as tall as Chase," I insisted, adding with a sigh of exasperation, "Plenty of killers have been smaller than average. Wiry, at least."

"I suppose you Vasko stock would know all about serial killers," she sneered at last, and time slowed to accommodate registration of both the ringing in my ears and the chill in my face, so cold it burned like coming out of a sauna and sticking your hands into snow on a freezing Illinois day.

I licked my lips, and kept it to: "You've got a lot of nerve."

"I never liked your aunt," she kept on, maybe realizing this was an opportunity she'd never have again. "You want to be perfectly honest, I always figured she would be the one to seduce Cassius away from me. Struck me as kind of a slut. I think it was that Chase met her husband, Lewis"—waving her mostly empty glass, dregs swirling in its base—"at one of those...oh, Dale Carnegie courses, I think, or some shareholders meeting, or something like that. Who knows. So Chase and Cassius, of course, being easily taken in, stayed friends with Lewis's widow when he died. Know how he died?" she asked, chortling like a lush. I scowled.

"Stringing up Christmas lights."

"'Oh, no, honey, I'm so sorry I bumped the ladder,'" she said, in so close an imitation of my dead aunt's chocolate croon that I found myself back with her, at that one meeting with her, that one moment in time which somehow tipped the scales of my life toward an unfathomable combination of favor and misfortune.

I, hot in the face, snapped, "She didn't kill anyone. People like to speculate that she killed her father because he was beating her, but it's a lot of talk. Nobody knows. Nobody knows about her, or anybody else in my family, for that matter."

"Everybody knows, Kitty Cat. The verdict is in; it's been in for almost twenty years. It's a fact. Sorry if you're sensitive about it, but I knew Susan personally and I can tell you she was not the sort of person you should ever spend time around. Ugliness and bitterness, all this foulness was in the air around her. I hated when Cassius spent time with her, even if I was there. But then the girl to whom she left her wealth turned out to be a skank like she was, so I'm thinking maybe it's just Lewis's money that's cursed. Or, like I said, it's just you Vaskos."

Full of trembling rage, full of wishes for violence I could never enact and wondering what it was that drove my notorious relative to kill, I breathed, "I think you're still just bitter about before. Cassius and I."

"You are unreal. Of course I'm bitter!" Minerva flipped her auburn hair, almost the same color as when we met. "It's amazing to me. I brought you into my house, agreed to let you stay with us at no cost to you because you were a family friend who needed help while finding a place, and what happens? Barely four weeks!"

"Your marriage was ready to end before I showed up," I said to her at last, and Minerva narrowed her eyes.

"Displaying orchids with copies of *The Flowers of Evil* and *Lolita*. Very cute."

"Now who's crazy. You forgot about Ovid's *The Art of Love*." I tried to say it in a sneering way, but it fell flat, because I had done exactly that, I remembered: those exact books, and exactly for that reason. Was that what Susan would have done? Susan was clearly of whom we both thought when Minerva huffed, "You Vaskos. The apple doesn't fall far from the tree."

"Maybe you're an agent and not a writer," I said, standing up so quickly it was as if my body were snatched by some invisible hand, "because you can't help but resort to clichés."

"Oh, yeah, everything has to be Ovid with you or it's not good enough, right?"

"If you bothered reading him sometime, maybe you'd see why." I laughed, shook, snatched up my keys, and said, "I've been noticing a lot of strange names lately, Minerva. In Ovid's version of Arachne, Minerva throws a tantrum because Arachne is a better weaver."

But my jagged laughter was returned to me like a snake mistaking its own tail for a twitching mouse. As Minerva leaned forward, she reminded me that, "And what does Arachne get for her talents? Slashed across the face by Minerva's shuttle, so that she hangs herself, and gets turned into a spider, anyway. You may have won Cassius—woven a more alluring, enduring life, or had a better relationship, or whatever you want. But you've deformed yourself in the process, like all the rest of your awful family members."

My heart pounded in my throat as though I were about to vomit it up as she said with a sneer, "I sort of hope Cassius is right, going on and on with his little theory about the foundation of consciousness being in language, in literature."

"And why is that, exactly?"

"Because, then, that means it's true, all that shit that the Buddhists and hippies say. That we're all God. That means I'm God. I'm every good thing and every bad thing. And if you're some main character in your own narcissistic little story, I'm especially every bad thing that happens to you. Every flat tire. Every misstep, every tragedy. Sure, that means I'm the good things, too, I suppose, but you really have to make those yourself in life, I find." Minerva crossed her legs, smoothing her crisp black button-up like a man at the end of a business meeting, and I realized I had lost all the feeling in my hands. There was a kind of visible static in the air, something about the way my eyes were focusing, maybe, I don't know, but I grew afraid, terribly afraid, as Minerva said, "If I were God—if I were really God, if I were some writer writing your story—I'd think you were a shit who deserved to be punished. But"—

she reclaimed the sangria bottle—"seems like you're doing that well enough on your own, don't you think?"

I didn't think that. If I ever had, ever truly had, I couldn't anymore. None of this was coming from inside of me, and the sight of Minerva filled me with new terror. What fate had I invoked with my allusion? At the time of our indiscretion I had felt, yes, like I had been come upon by some incredible Jovian figure, Cassius; but, of course, he was only a man and I was only a woman, and the things I had felt, the things we had projected on each other, were just symbols, ways we wanted to interact, ways we expressed our desire and bonded, through literature and poetry and finally, then, physically, but it was truly just projection. That was the basis of any relationship. I had pined a lifetime for some grand romance, some mythical literary romance that would wash me up and away, and I got one. We were two true writing peers, two true partners who, despite their ages, overcame the odds—but we had never bonded completely because I hadn't allowed it. I had moved out once the divorce was over to have my own space and continued the relationship with Cassius because I wanted the best of both worlds, to be with him without being smothered by him. To be with him without compromising with him. But would any of that have happened without the funeral, and without the eventuality of this skull's pursuit? This difficulty, this pain, all of this: Was this me? Was this coming from inside of me? From outside of me? Or was it a meeting point?

In front of the apartment, in the lukewarm Tucson night beneath stars drastically faded from the standard Ashland display, I questioned my decision to take the Saturn and stared down at the keys in my hand. I didn't want to acknowledge the possibility of living in a literary universe: I focused on the weight of the keys, the texture of the plastic in my palm and the cold metal sliding between my fingers, and my hands trembled as I thought of putting those keys, of which I was so hyperaware, into the ignition. How could I drive all the way to Colorado, and for what, and how? Why? I couldn't do it. My palms and forehead slickened with sweat as I considered what Minerva had said. Yes, yes, you had to make the nice things in life, the good things, the true things.

But I didn't know how. I could find no means of escape—maybe because I could envision no place to escape to.

Feeling fluish, I thought to call an auto to take me to the airport, and then said no, no, what if that was cause of my future discovery? Although I hadn't read anything in the novel about me being in a car accident, I shook, and my teeth were chattering, and I couldn't make myself believe that I wouldn't get into an accident if I got into a car by myself. The manuscript, I'd left with Minerva, so I couldn't check how it all worked out. I felt in the grips of a dream and squinted at the smogged stars, trying to see them, hugging myself and feeling small and bleak and alone. That was the reason why, I suppose, I finally called Chase, whose surprise was audible from the word "Hello?"

"I know this sounds weird." As I tried through rapidly blinking eyes to recognize how the astronomers of antiquity discovered shapes in the stars (I saw no cluster of bears, no hunter or bull, no scorpions, no brothers), I rambled, "Would you come pick me up? I'm in town. I need help."

There was a long pause before he asked, "What are you doing in Tucson, Kat?"

"I...heard Minerva was in town and wanted to pitch her something Drake wouldn't want," I said over my shoulder at the apartment, its living room lights the only illumination as I leaned against the dusty car, where I scraped my boot against the tire's edge and felt like I was ten. "But I just can't be in a hotel tonight, and I can't—"

"Well, sure, you can always drop by. Why don't you just call an auto, though?"

I gritted my teeth, dropped the keys on the hood, and marched into the Tucson dark, struck by inspiration enough to suggest, "The bank wasn't expecting me to be in Tucson, either." There was, in there, an attempt at an awkward laugh over my shoulder at the abandoned Saturn. "They froze my card, and it's late, and I really don't want to deal with it."

"I keep telling you and Cassius to switch banks. Weston Grand has no fee, and they're not as sensitive to potential fraud. Which is not always a good thing, of course, but—" And then I was stuck, nodding and gritting my teeth while Chase had the opportunity to both lecture me and try to sell me on what I was sure was one of his investments, which were two things he rarely had a chance to do in tandem. It was rare enough for us to speak just the two of us to begin with. I was going to have to do some ass-kissing to get him to come out of his way to pick me up, and the farther I got from the Saturn, the better, so I let him talk to me about banks for a solid two to three minutes before, at the corner of Calle Bellatrix and San Regulo, disoriented in the dark and lost from not having visited Thomas much in the past two years, I took a right for no real reason and said to Chase, "So can you come and pick me up, please?"

"Sure," he said, and I breathed a sigh of relief which I'm sure was audible as on Calle Betelgeux I took a right while trying to get back to the main street, either Wilmot or Twenty-Second. "Where are you, then? At Thomas's house?"

I opened my mouth, but it was then that I, with a drop of horror, found my body had led me to a street I had known to be there but had forgotten all about: East Calle Castor. It startled me so that I lost my conversational place until Chase said with that agitation to which I'd long since grown used, "Hello, Kat? You there?"

"Uh, I— yes," I said. "Yes, I'm here. I'm at, uh...on Wilmot, near the corner of Twenty-Second."

"Jesus! You couldn't be farther away. Let me order you an auto."

"No!" The word burst out of me like spit-up from the mouth of an infant, and tears emerged along with it as I, trembling at the corner of Betelgeux and Castor, felt obliged, somehow, to follow this synchronistic street even though I knew that it was the wrong way, even though I remembered vaguely from my time in the area that I would be let out on a different main street from the one that I wanted. But I felt forced, as if in following Castor I would discover in the names of the streets some revelation. I, tearful, half whispered into the line, "Please, I don't want to be alone, Chase. I can't. I need another person, please. Someone I know. I know it's so far away, but would you come."

With a put-upon sigh, Chase said at last, "Let me call Naomi. She lives closer. She or Alex can bring you up to me."

"Oh, no, Chase, I don't want the pregnant woman coming to pick me up. She's going to have the baby any minute."

"Too late," he barked, and I grimaced, squinting in the darkness-huddled houses as though their stucco faces would offer me some missing divination, some symbolism which I could find nowhere else at all. As to the left there opened the mouth of a street which I did not recognize, I lifted my phone to reflect its light off the sign: "Calle Leona." I chose to still follow Castor, taking Chase's bullshit as he carried on, martyred, "I really do like to get to bed around eight or so. I have an early schedule."

"Cassius and I usually get up around four in the morning and get to sleep at seven, so I know what you mean. I'm sorry to keep you up," I said, for once able to one-up him on something as I carried on past the dull houses, brick front, and blessed the odd streetlight placed at San Regulo. My pace hurried as if someone followed me; light brought into relief nothing but my own shadow, and was not reassuring in the vast dark. "But thank you, Chase."

"Of course, anytime I'm awake. Where are you, again?"

"I might walk down toward Golf Links."

"Are you drunk? Why don't you know where you are?"

"No, I haven't been— Will you please just have Naomi call me, or Alex, whomever you get?"

"Fine. See you soon," he said, and as he dropped off the line I frowned down at the phone, then up to find myself adjacent to a park where a big gazebo invited me to wait in shelter. I thought about it, but Castor had turned into South Avenida Del Sol, and I was somehow bolstered by the thought of following the sun, so I kept along the path I was on. I started making jokes to myself in the dark, as, almost past the park, I passed Cappela, and still on Del Sol said, "I certainly am a cappella, aren't I," like I wasn't alone, like there was someone to hear me, because it made me feel safe to speak aloud and laugh at my own stupid, unfunny puns. Soon I passed Dened, and then Herculo, but it was when passing Luna that I felt an eerie throb in my head. Trembling, mouth dry as cotton, I studied the green street sign: "East Calle Luna." I got out my phone, then, and thought back to the ones I had passed. I thought of Leona, Regulo, Cappela, and none of these seemed, somehow, as important as Dened, which stuck out at me, and which my phone stubbornly corrected to "Deneb" to reveal that this, like all those others I had passed, was a star. I laughed, my eyes filling with tears, to find it was the brightest star in the constellation Cygnus: the swan. Cygnus; Anatida; thoughts of Leda and her sons. What kind of map was this, Tucson?

Standing there on the corner of Luna and Sol, laughing and crying, my phone rang, and I was almost expecting it to happen at that very second so wasn't startled at all. As I picked it up and said, "Hey, Naomi," like I was normal, like everything was fine, her voice filled the line like the pink light of dawn.

"Kitty! I'm so happy you're here, what a nice surprise it was when Daddy called me! The car and I are comin' to getcha. Where are you?"

"I'm in a gazebo," I told her, wiping my cheeks with the back of my free hand, smiling for reasons I couldn't comprehend, "in a park, off Del Sol. You know how you go down Wilmot, and there's Castor? Castor turns into Del Sol," I emphasized, as if it were a revelation to anyone but me.

"Oh, yeah, I sort of know. Okay, I'll find it on the map and be there in a minute!"

She was always so happy, Naomi, even nine months in, disturbed and disrupted, and I tried to absorb that on the phone, feeling stirred and no longer alone even as the dead line left me there, laughing, wondering if all of this was real. But I still hadn't hit a main vein of Tucson, was still wandering, a stranger in the dark through neighborhoods I didn't know, lured by street signs on and on. On, to the last turnoff before Golf Links. It was then that I stilled, my hands running cold before that final street along the path laid by Castor: East Calle Mercurio. Mercurio, Mercurius, Mercury. Hermes. I trembled, and the light from my phone reflected off the sign so it seemed to wave to me as at that very moment, Naomi arrived in her golden chariot, pulling off Golf Links, blinding me with light before slowing, sticking her head out the window and laughing. "Hey, pretty lady! I thought you said you were in the park!"

"I was going to be. I didn't realize you lived so close."

"Oh, no." With a blushing giggle of guilt, Naomi snatched her grocery bag from the passenger's seat. Inside lurked a chocolate ganache cake, a wheel of brie cheese, and a bottle of ginger ale. "I was just dying for some snacks, and Alex is still working, so I was actually at the grocery store on Wilmot when Daddy called. Funny, huh!" With a big grin up at me, she unlocked the doors, patted her protruding stomach with her free hand, and said, "It's like the baby knew his auntie was here to visit."

It wasn't the baby that knew, I thought while studying Mercurio. Or maybe it was. A conspiracy of unborn babies and long since arranged street signs, a surreal fractal organized long before my birth on some other plain of being, some dimension I might never comprehend. Or maybe I could. Maybe they were right. Maybe, I thought, climbing into Naomi's gold Taurus, there was something to this idea of living symbolism, of my being edged ever onward by something inside me as much as outside me. Maybe it was only inside of me because I had once seen it outside of me and had made some choice which let it inside of me. Or maybe I didn't do anything at all, and it had come into me because I was convenient, and molded me to its silent purpose. But as Naomi pulled into Mercurio and reversed out of it again to turn her car north toward her father's house, the peaking wave of anxiety broke with an uncanny sense of calm. My body, my intuition, had not rebelled on me. Maybe I very well would have crashed the Saturn had I driven it, or maybe I wouldn't have. That was irrelevant, because what had once seemed to me a kind of rebellion, I realized, was a sort of guidance. I was being guided. My fear and failure, my paranoia and possible psychosis, all of this was guiding me upward, forward, and into something I was beginning to have no choice but to accept. By following the path of Castor, I would be led to Hermes. Of that, I was more assured than ever. And what did that mean? Why was it important? *Why me?* I asked, not of God, but of myself. *Why me?*

But no matter who I asked, me or God or Naomi and her unborn baby, there would be no answer forthcoming. So, whether to me or to God, I supposed it wouldn't matter in the end.

6

For an overdue pregnant woman forced to eat a wheel of brie in her auto on the way to her crabby father's house at eight at night, Naomi seemed in a stupendous mood—but that could have been because she was excited to see me. "I didn't know you and Cassie were coming," she said at last, having spent most of the thirty-minute cruise talking about Alex's job at the casino off the freeway, potential names for the baby (lots of *L* names—Lucia, Lucretia, Lucius, Linus...), and her struggle to get strangers in restaurants, grocers, and theaters to stop patting her belly without permission. Her conversation so lulled me I had almost forgotten what had sent me to Tucson, and found I had to grasp for an explanation that would keep everybody off my case until the truth emerged.

"Cassius is probably still in Ashland," I admitted as the car rolled to a halt. Agitation of the curtains marked movement in Chase's living room. "Maybe, I don't know."

"Uh-oh." As the car dozed off and relinquished its key, Naomi lowered her three-quarters-eaten wheel of cheese and asked softly, "You're not having a fight, are you?"

"Well, no," I began, the "but" unformed as the front door of the house opened to reveal Chase's six-foot-five frame rendered a shadow by backlighting, time unwilling or unable to shrink him the way it shrank most lesser men.

"What the hell is going on," he called, and because we couldn't hear him from inside the car and he had to repeat himself once we were outside, it was with aggravation. "Haven't had this many calls in one night since I got rid of my landline. I just got off the phone with Cassius. Did you flee Ashland without telling him?"

"I didn't 'flee.'" All the same, shifting her groceries from hand to hand, Naomi gasped, and I was forced to turn a plaintive look upon her. "I had to come here. I had to ask Minerva something, and I couldn't let Cassius be involved."

He wasn't going to let me keep it at basics. "You couldn't have Skyped her? You came all the way down from Ashland. How did you even get here?"

"I drove," I said, and, his massive hands raising above his head, Chase asked, "Well, why didn't you just drive yourself here, then, if it was so damn important you come!"

Tears forming in my eyes because I knew it didn't make sense and there was no way to make it make sense, I took a breath and said, "Please. I've come because I'm very worried about Cassius."

"I am, too, after hearing him on the phone. He's on his way to the airport." My mouth drying as I crossed the threshold of Chase's house, I struggled to hear him over the ticking of his clock, too loud or too fast as my irritated host went on. "I can't believe you made me call my nine-months-pregnant daughter—"

"Dad, it's fine."

"It's not fine! You're only ever thinking of yourself, Katherine," barked Chase, and I, throat tight and eyes tearful, practically screamed, "I'm doing this for your brother! He might be in danger. Consorting with a lunatic, and I don't mean me. I mean a real, dangerous individual. You're a genealogist, right?"

"Right," said Chase with caution as Naomi shut the door behind us and lowered herself with a hefty sigh into the nearest armchair, big and bright and ridiculous, like everything about her father.

"I need you to do me a favor: Would you research the Anatida family for me, in Colorado?"

"Just what is this about? What does this have to do with Cassius? Why isn't this something you could have e-mailed me about?"

I touched Chase's bicep. "I need your help with this, and then I need to go right away. You're a very rational man, and none of what's happening makes sense without any context. Even rational things sound irrational out of context. I need information, all the information you have about the Anatida family in Colorado, please."

Contemplating the boxed ganache still in the bag before turning attention to the phone on which she typed, Naomi asked, "What's special about Colorado?"

"I'm not sure. I just know I need to go there."

"Are you sure you're feeling okay, Auntie?"

"Naomi, please, please be on my side. I need somebody to be on my side on this. Chase, please. Just humor me. Find the family for me."

"Okay, and? Do I have a city? Do I have birth dates, death dates, first names, anything?"

"Leda Anatida," I answered before I froze as epiphany crushed me under the weight of my own stupidity. "There's a Mount Ida in Colorado, isn't there."

"Of course there is," scoffed Chase, as though every human being had ought to know the exact name of every geographic impression across the United States, but I didn't care about his attitude anymore and with fiery enthusiasm asked, "And what county is it in! That's where you'll want to search."

"We'll see," said Chase, lumbering through the living room and into the small office filled with wooden animal carvings produced by his late wife. Naomi shuffled in behind us, pulling her dandelion cardigan tighter around her and crossing her arms at the frigid temperature of the room, both of us crowded behind him. After trawling a database for all of five minutes, he said, "Here."

In a line upon the 1960 census, two-year-old Leda's name was reflected one line beneath the name of her father, Basil Anatida. "You're damn lucky it's been digitized already; the 1960 census was just released this year. They have machines reading all the text now, humans just do the editing."

Hijacking his mouse, I scrolled across the row of information to the address: "19660 W. Brook Freeway." I stamped it into my frontal lobe the same way I had once stamped Mount Ida there, everything on the verge of coming together like the threads of a tapestry tightening, at last, to form its image. Vindicated, I took a shallow breath and lightly patted Chase's back. "Thank you, thank you so much."

"You're welcome," he said, gruffly but not unkindly, as I slipped my phone from my pocket and checked the time to see it was just after nine. I had been thinking about going to the airport to swallow my fear of flying, but with Cassius jetting in, maybe the best option was to take an auto to Phoenix and depart from there. Was he landing in Tucson, or Phoenix?

"I'm really sorry I wasted your time and bothered you, Naomi," I said. As she insisted again, "No, no, it's no trouble, I was out already," Chase copped to my intentions, shuffling as I was toward the door, and spun in his chair like an executive in his twenties. "Where do you think you're going! You need to give me some sort of explanation."

"Not really, I don't."

"For all I know, you've gone off your rocker and you're on your way to murder someone." Over surprised Naomi's sharp reprimand, Chase went on, "Or you're just going to end up hurting yourself somehow. Well, I won't be responsible for it. You need to tell me what's going on."

Maybe I needed to make a break for it. Run as far and as fast as I could and explain it all later. Better yet, they could call Minerva and ask for the manuscript, which could explain it better than I ever might, even if it sounded like me doing the explaining. Instead, I made the mistake of saying, "That woman, Leda Anatida. She's supposedly the mother of Enoch."

"Enoch Azarias?" Chase lifted his eyebrows at his daughter as the air conditioner kicked in to blow more cold air down my neck. "What does Enoch have to do with any of this? You mean the guy who created the LSD, right?"

"Yes, the Device. As far as what he has to do with anything, I'm trying to get to the bottom of that."

As his daughter was again distracted by her buzzing phone, Chase leaned back in his chair to assess me from behind crossed arms. "Trying to make a break in the case there, Sherlock?"

"Don't patronize me, Chase. Enoch is a dangerous man. I'm almost sure of it. I don't even think his name is Enoch. I think he's really the Hermes who he's told the press is his silent partner."

"And what makes you so sure?"

My mouth dried at that. Feeling foolish, I explained about the REM Novel: what it was, what it was about, and what it was about it that had made me stop reading. Amid my explanation, Naomi lifted her phone to her lips, her sympathetic expression not near so implacable as that of her father. Not that I could blame Chase. The longer I talked, the crazier I sounded, and the crazier I sounded, the crazier I felt. At the end of it all, Chase asked, "So where's this novel?"

"Minerva has it."

Naomi pressed her phone to her heart, expression bright with astonishment. "I believe you, Kitty."

"I have to go to Colorado. I have to see what I can find there about Hermes."

"That's absurd," said Chase, and as Naomi sighed at him, he went on, waving a huge hand. "Well, it is! It's paranoid! She's gotten drawn into her own fiction. No book can predict the future. These things aren't predestined to happen."

"That's what I used to think," I said, running my hand over my face and feeling myself back for a moment on Mercurio. "I'm really starting to question some of that. But logically, even if we do have free will, if we can only react a certain way to a certain thing, and that's the way we're going to react, right...oh, God." I was giving in to it, giving in to the crazy, sounding like Cassius and Enoch, and it made me sigh as Chase rose again, face narrowed with annoyance.

"I don't care for discussing philosophy with you, Katherine, when you're insulting my friend—"

"What?" Shocked, I dropped my hand from my face. "Enoch?"

"Yes, Enoch. Who do you think invested in the damn thing, even if it truly is going to be ridiculous for writing! It's what people want, so it's an excellent investment. Somebody's going to market a successful Device like that eventually, anyway, so it had might as well be the guy I met at the genealogical society conference a few years ago. I think I know the man, Katherine. I'm a superb judge of character, and Enoch Azarias is trustworthy, even if his silent partner might be dubious. But who cares about that? He's not bothering anyone."

I wanted to scream. There was madness at work here, whether mine, or someone else's. I was in a crucible, and all this felt more intentional by the second. Directed right at me. Trembling, I breathed to Chase, "I didn't realize you invested in his company. I don't understand. At dinner that day with Cassius, you completely trashed the Device."

"Because I knew that would be the only way to make sure Cassius tried the thing. He's an old man, of course he's going to be stuck in his ways. But if I was against it," said the older brother with a positively devilish grin which made my hand jump to my cheek so quickly I almost slapped myself, "I knew he'd climb right on board. And what could be better for my investment than having it used and publicly lauded by Cassius Wagner."

I recognized the significance of what Minerva had said about Enoch having come into funding before he approached her. Lips trembling, I exhaled, inhaled, exhaled, tried to focus on my breathing, and ended up only able to say, "I can't believe you're part of it, too."

"You're being irrational, Katherine. This isn't some conspiracy." His tone wasn't unkind as he reached toward my hand and then sighed in disappointment as I pulled away from him. "Enoch's not going to do anything to Cassius! These things aren't predestined, and you can't let some stupid book you woke up to one morning push you around!"

"I'm trying to avoid it. I'm trying, but I feel like—" I laughed, and my eyes filled with tears, and I turned away. "I'm sorry, I'm sorry, I really have to go."

"Not until Cassius gets here, I keep telling you."

"You can't control where somebody else goes, Daddy," chided Naomi, but he went on. "My pregnant daughter brought you here, went out of her way, even though you could have called an auto, and that's only after you've scared the living hell out of Cassius, acting crazy all the while. You're not going anywhere until Cassius gets here, and you're definitely not going anywhere until I know you're not a threat to yourself or anyone else."

"Daddy, she's not your daughter. Auntie doesn't owe anyone any more explanation than she's already given. Kitty." Sympathy furrowing her brow, she said, "It would put your mind to rest a lot if you could go to Colorado, huh."

"Yes. Thank you, Naomi." I sighed, backing toward the door. Chase barreled after me, insisting, "I won't have it, you wait right here!"

"What are you going to do to detain me?" I challenged, and ferocity rose in his eye. What happened next occurred so fast it was impossible to make sense at the time of its occurrence. Chase was closing the distance in seconds and making a grab for my arm; I was yelling a protest about kidnapping and ducking away, trying to be heard over shouting Naomi, who likewise protested that her father had ought to let me do what I wanted until her voice pitched up to a cry of surprise accompanied by that universal splash signaling the coming of new life, and Chase released me to our mutual gasp as Naomi cried, "Oh! The baby!"

"See what you've done," began Chase, but Naomi, fire in her eyes, fell back against the edge of the desk, then stumbled forward to grasp her father's shirt with the ragged demand: "Get me to the hospital."

"Of course! Come on—damn it." He remembered me again, narrowing his eyes and saying, "Damn it, Katherine. I'd tell you to stay here, but I'd be that much angrier when you were gone once Cassius arrived. You're coming with us."

As he made another snatch for me, I ducked away. "I'm not, and that's final! I don't understand how you and Cassius can be from the same family. He's such a nice and gentle man."

"You're a fine one to talk."

Hackles raising, I started to open my mouth, but Naomi, not at all herself amid her urgency, roared, "Shut up, Kitty!"

I did. She, still clutching her father's shirt so tight he choked, turned her raging eyes up toward him. "Daddy, the hospital, please!"

"I know, baby. We just have to convince your—"

"Leave Auntie here! The hospital."

"But—"

"She's an adult," screamed Naomi, and at last, Chase hopped to it, but not before casting me a narrow-eyed sneer.

"Mount Ida, huh. Colorado. I'll be sure to tell Cassius to change his flight. Assuming, of course, your little 'REM Story' hasn't told him already."

If he weren't carrying a woman in labor, I would have considered punching him in the back of the head. It seemed I might have, anyway, in that instant. But I'm sure I never could have done it, never could have done anything but cried. Is that good, or bad? Having these urges, these furies rise, and leaving them unexpressed. Wasn't it better to not have them at all? To not feel all the ugly things? Didn't feeling ugly things make me an ugly person? I felt vile, and it was as though Chase had some power over me, some ability to make me see myself reflected as vulgar: a befouler of all things good, a madwoman who had forced his daughter into labor through insanity and high-strung emotions. One flesh, my husband's shadow—I rotted with guilt to see him whisk her down the hall. "I'm really sorry, Naomi," I called, trailing after them.

"It's okay, Kitty," she said, gasping, then laughing as her father opened the garage door and supported her down that singular concrete stair as if she or it or both were made of glass. "You made my baby come! We're finally getting him out of me, the little monkey."

"You're so sure he's a 'he'?" I asked, the doors of Chase's car sliding open on proximity of his key. Naomi grinned as he lowered her into the passenger's seat with all the care one might use to transport a wedding cake.

"I peeked," she confessed, the playful tongue poking between her teeth the last vision I had of her until after Easter, a whole lifetime later, once I had divested myself of my fear. As the door shut, Chase studied me from the corner of his eye, then crossed to the controller's side of the car and said with an accusatory jut of his finger, "When you irresponsibly leave, the house security code is 6-4-5-7-2. Don't forget it and don't send me a text asking for it because I won't answer. I would appreciate it if you would set it up," he added gruffly, perhaps recalling one of a thousand arguments had about the difference between a request and a demand.

"I will," I said, crossing my arms. "Thank you."

Then he, too, vanished into the car, and the garage door snarled open while the Plymouth cruised backward down the drive, its three passengers headed for the hospital. Maybe Cassius would be diverted by the baby's birth and give me time to get ahead. To get to Mount Ida. The garage door closed, and, my head swirling with numbers, I scrambled inside to jot the security code on grocery list stationary left near the kitchen's entrance, that set of numbers being freshest, and less important to keep in my memory than 19600 S— Or was it E, shit, shit— Breezeway Highway—

"Son of a bitch," I said, racing back to the computer. Of course, it had locked itself, registered, like all Chase's property, to have high-security features. Hissing, I wasted precious time repeating the process he'd undergone on my phone, which was not as easy because I didn't have some members-only site. This left me with a national directory which didn't have a search function as nice as the site Chase had used. Between clunky controls and the tiny phone screen, by the time I had regained the information (19660 West Brook Freeway, yes, how could I ever have forgotten an address so unique when inundated with other input) I was broken from my search by the sound of tires outside.

Nausea scaled my throat. It was Chase, I was certain, back from the hospital already, having dropped off his daughter, come to retrieve me or hold me for Cassius. Worse, it was Cassius and Enoch, having arrived by some supreme time dilation, or because they left earlier than they'd claimed. Why, what would have stopped them, after all, if this business was in the book? Maybe it was even the cops, called by Chase, who, so desperate to detain me, had decided to call them to place a false claim about a home invader, or— The knock on the front door startled me into a yelp. I peered around the edge of the living room drape, squinting to see through the interior lights' reflection on the dark window. Outside sat a car so familiar I faltered in recognizing it, amazed to find my purple Saturn in subtle relief against the black backdrop of the Tucson night. Agog, I threw open the front door of Chase's house and found Thomas, who, with a canine smile that reminded me much of his father, said, "I think you forgot something at my house."

"Thomas! Oh, Tommy, oh my God, you're a saint!" One subject I had wasted precious moments in ignoring was the problem of reaching the car, and what I was going to do once I reclaimed it. But here it was, solved for me without my even trying, and I, on the verge of happy tears, threw arms around my nephew's neck and kissed his cheeks and said, "Yes, thank you, oh my God. How did you know to come here?"

"Naomi was texting me. At first she just wanted to know if you were all right, but by the time I noticed you'd left your car outside, she was saying how I should probably come pick you up because Uncle Chase was getting crazy. His arthritis gives him anxiety," said the young man apologetically, handing me my keys. I kissed his cheek again with that grimace-inspiring, bruising force my aunt and grandmother used to apply to me.

"You're incredible, Thomas. Thank you so much. Hey, would you tell me, have you heard from your dad yet tonight?"

"Actually, yeah." Rubbing the back of his neck, Thomas's eyes flickered between me and the mimosa tree. "Is there something going on with you, Aunt Kathy?"

"I don't know." I felt stupid, laughing and crossing my arms, feeling more exposed in front of more people than I'd ever felt in my life up until that very moment. "This sounds insane, I know, and your mom came out for Easter and all, but..." I laughed again and batted my wet eyes, and gasped. "Do you have some time to help me get to Larimer County, Colorado?"

He laughed at first, but then marked my adamance. "How far is that?"

"Fourteen hours, about. If we take turns, we can do it straight through. I can pay for everything—gas, food, new clothes if you need them for the trip—but we have to go this instant. Please. I need your help, Thomas. I can't do it alone."

"We've got to get you an auto." Contemplating first the Saturn and then, regretfully, the keys already in my clutch, Thomas ran a hand over his cheek. "Are you sure you're okay, Kath?"

"I am so close to solving this thing. You heard me talking to your mom. Did she show you the manuscript?" I was amazed when he shook his head, mostly that Minerva had the decorum. "But you do know, right? I mean, you heard."

"Yeah, all that, even the whispered part. Sound carries in my house. The walls are paper thin, even if they are just painted bricks. Anyway, Kathy, I don't know."

"Please." I took up his hand and squeezed it. "I have such a long way to go, and I'm scared. I'm scared for your father," I emphasized, not adding that I was most scared for myself.

"Because of that Enoch guy," observed the boy.

"I know you have no reason to help me. You have no reason to do anything at all for me. All I did was ruin your childhood," I whispered, eyes watering. "Oh, Tommy—I'm sorry."

"You didn't ruin anything! My dad ruined it, that shit. But we've mended fences and everything, it's fine. It was never your fault, really. You didn't see their marriage before. Things are better this way."

With sharp breaths still hitching my shoulders, I fell into a humiliation spiral to think I couldn't collect myself in front of this person I'd known since he was a kid. I felt like a kid, myself, standing there pathetic and crying. Not interested in waiting for his uncle's neighbors to crawl out of the woodwork, Thomas ushered me back into Chase's house and shut the door behind us. There, he hugged me and said, "It's all right, Aunt Katherine, I love you. Hey, it's all right."

"You're a good boy, Tommy," I told him, pulling away and reeling for the box of tissues on the adobe coffee table, crooked beside the hand-carved wooden wolf. "I'm sorry. I feel like I distracted your father from you. Like I took him away."

Studying the thin mesquite bookshelves of Chase's living room, which featured presidential biographies, books about the World Wars, and a collection of travel atlases, Thomas said, "He made his choice. You didn't force him to do anything. But he was always like that, Kat. Even before you showed up, he was always in his office." Thomas laughed and shrugged, his hand running over his jaw. "It doesn't matter, but I remember the first conscious time I ever puked. I had some flu and I'd had, like, hot dogs or something repulsive for breakfast because it was all they could get me to eat, and while Mom was at work, Dad was busy working. I started to feel sick. I go to him and I say, 'Dad,' you know, 'I think I'm sick, can I have some water?'"

It was a story I vaguely recalled hearing before. The boy went on in bass imitation of his blasé father. "'In a minute, you're fine, you're fine,' he says. And I say, 'No, Dad, can I have some water, my stomach really hurts, I think I'm going to puke.' Then it's 'You're not going to puke,' all of three seconds before I project hot dogs and God knows what else all over the carpet, all over the edge of Dad's desk. Then he realized I was sick."

"Oh, Thomas," I said, frowning, arms crossed. He laughed it off, though a certain slate hue faded his Cassius-blue irises.

"It's not a big deal. I just mean to say, work's always been more important to him. His capital-*W* Work. Not his family. You just gave him an excuse, pretty much. And you gave Mom an excuse, too. I don't think she was happy, either. She used to want to be a writer, too."

Blanching to remember the insult I had hurled in a heated moment, I said, "I had no idea. Your father never said."

"I think he felt guilty. Like he chased her out of it. He wouldn't take the time to read anything she wrote, she says. She's still bitter. She'd read everything, every little thing he gave her, and he read nothing, didn't care, and so finally she focused on her career as an agent, which was more important to her then, anyway, but"—Thomas crossed his arms in a mirror of the way I'd long since crossed mine—"more and more I get the feeling that anytime somebody says somebody else made them do something or kept them from doing something, it's just trying to shuffle off responsibility for personal desires. Whether they know it, they wanted an excuse to succeed, or to fail. You know what I want to be, I think, Auntie," said Thomas at last, and I perked in surprise. "I want to be an architect. I want to build for myself, and then, I want to build things that will endure: homes for families, buildings for generations to live and work, testaments to withstand the test of time. I know it's not painting or writing or something, but will you help me?"

Relief! Sweet relief! At last, yes, there was something I could do for someone. My eyes filled with tears again, and I felt myself saying, "Of course! I said I would. Pick anything to study, and I'll support you. I just don't want to see you waste your mind. You're so talented, Tommy. And architecture is an art, my God." I laughed at him, and then at myself, emotional as I was over the opportunity to help him. I felt for a second like the Wagner I'd denied myself the privilege of being, because I somehow wasn't worthy, because I had hurt people by needlessly inserting myself into a relationship which had been perfectly fine before I showed up. But the thought of Cassius isolating himself day in and day out in his office—I believed it. One of the reasons we had spent so long living separate lives was to facilitate both our work. My work, anyway. And here we had been drawn more tightly together than ever by neither my work, nor his, but the work of something else. The human balance of Love and Work once seemed impossible to me. Somehow, by some tremendous act of conjunction, the two had to be combined; perhaps we seemed on the cusp of managing it because it was a Work about our Love, but there was still one more problem to be worked out before the states could be superimposed. A problem waiting in Colorado. Catching up once more my future son-in-law's hand, I reiterated to Thomas, "I'll help you," so that, in a wan way, he smiled.

"Then I'll help you."

7

That was how Thomas and I ended up on the road to Colorado at ten at night on Good Friday. As we hit the freeway and I once more left behind that sprawling network of lights in the bottom of an arid mountain basin, I remembered the town's beauty for the first time since seeing it at twenty-two out the window of a train, there against the night, vaster than it was when I first knew it all those years ago. More than two people ago, if you considered that the body replaced all its cells every seven years.

What had happened to those two Katherines? Better, what were their names? When I'd come out to Tucson, I'd been Katie. I had changed myself to Katherine the year prior, or began insisting on my full name more often, at any rate, but I hadn't become Katherine yet. I was still Katie inside, and then Katie, say, gave way to Kat, and after Kat, who? Kitty? Kathy? Was I Katherine? Who was I, inside of myself, and who was I beyond that? I couldn't keep fooling myself anymore, after all. I couldn't ignore the intricacy of what had been arrayed, like the eeriness of obscure roads in some nameless Tucson neighborhood interwoven with the particularity of a star-shine constellation. I couldn't ignore it any more than I could ignore the care I put into my own stories, any more than I could ignore the way the REM Novel had interrupted my life. Was it the REM Novel that was to blame, though, truly? After all, it had been that image of me, myself, there, with that skull. I could imagine it as if it had already happened and trembled in the passenger's seat, covering my eyes with my hand.

"Are you okay, Kath?"

"Do you believe in God, Thomas?"

Thomas laughed, gazing out across the road before us, a dark highway outlined by reflectors which implied the road, rather than demarking it in any meaningful way; he craned his head up before he responded, and the breath caught in his throat. "See the moon," he intoned, and I did, lips parted to see the pale orb, expectant in the sky, and was instantly back in the streets, reading "Luna." The Easter body of Sol's sister glowed in pure radiance, and I pressed my cheek to the cool glass of the car as though in some effort to feel her light filter through my flesh. My teeth chattered to think of what she meant as we passed beneath her dreaming face. Disturbed as I was by the skull, I was troubled ever more deeply by Enoch's book, which I had not read but which I knew nevertheless would confront me with the troubles of my long-dead, disappointing relatives, and myself—for I was like my uncle in ways I could sense, though I kept my bitterness in my heart and meted it out in my writing. Yet, Enoch's book chronicled, also, the suffering of my aunt. I thought of her beneath the radiant moon. She was not a good woman, but that did not mean she should have had to die. But then, I didn't think my uncle should have had to die, either, or my grandfather, or anyone. Was that terrible of me? Was it selfish of me to wish that tragedy could be erased, that everyone I had once believed to be good and pure might someday remove their masks of pain and perversion and reveal themselves as the shining lights I always knew they were? Was it pathetic to wish that everything beautiful remained beautiful, was perceived as beautiful—and not in that heart-rending way, that *mono no aware*-ness that makes your lips tremble in the dark of night and forces you to hide your face from your friend?

"Sorry," Thomas said, as if the poetry of nature merited apology. He considered the question I had asked, humming. "I do, I guess, believe in God, but not the Christian God or anything. I took acid once," he admitted in a meek way, expecting reprimand, not realizing I had consumed quite a few psychedelics in my time, "and had this beautiful, visionary experience of understanding. About the words 'I am,' and how we're all God, really, sort of, in a way. The feeling faded because it does if you don't integrate it, but the lesson stuck with me. What else could we be? What else can there be?" He shrugged, gesturing toward the desert landscape with its the miniature forest of cacti. "If God is omnipotent, omniscient and everything, then God is everything. The material basis for everything, and the actual everything. That means you, and me. But there's knowing it, and there's feeling it. You can know it in an intellectual way without really feeling it. But I think that just means you're not intellectually understanding it all the way. Someday I'll feel God," said Thomas, nodding, assured of this notion, confident and more comfortable in it than I could have ever imagined myself being. "Without having to die, or take acid, or have a near-death experience or a seizure like Dad, I'll be able to have the experience of God in the world and hang on to the experience of God in the world. What is it called in the East? Being in the Dao? That's probably what I mean; someday, I'll consciously be part of the Dao, the flow of things. I think that's probably all God wants. God wants to be conscious of God, right? God just wants enlightenment, too. Just wants to know."

Amid the spread of utmost serenity, I nodded. The presence of the skull in the REM Novel had weighed so heavily on me that I had missed the big picture: that if my life was really a book, then there was some pathos involved. Some catharsis sought. And my catharsis? My relief? Would it come with the relief of the mystery of Hermes, some understanding of what it was that Enoch hid from me? Or would relief have to come from elsewhere: someplace within me, the place from which catharsis always emerged in the end? I knew the answer and I didn't want to admit it, because I was desperate for someone to realize it all for me. To feel it all, and do it all for me. Maybe that was what God really wanted. God wanted us to experience the ugly things in life so He wouldn't have to. Wanted someone to realize what He wouldn't, or couldn't, or only could once we had, the way pathos with a fictional character comes with the empathy of shared revelation.

At last, long after I had thought of it and accepted it, Thomas suggested, "If Dad's read the novel, and it has the scene of you going to Colorado, he might have just flown straight there."

"I know."

"What if he's waiting?"

"I hope he won't get in my way."

We did very little talking across the vein-thin highways through New Mexico and into Colorado. As we journeyed ever north, the sun at last rose, blooming like blood from a wound across the flat scape of the desert, dunes and scrub soon succumbing to the treacherous beauty of mountains, beautiful like Oregon, that place for which I keened. And— Cassius. But what I did, I did for him. I sensed he waited in Colorado, and in my breast and throat there lodged simultaneous dread and hope, fear and wonder, and love. Most of all, love. Soon it was the middle of Holy Saturday, and we found ourselves wandering, dwarfed by the might of the mountains, and I swear, of all of them, I knew the distinct peak of Mount Ida without having to be told. As my tongue and cheeks numbed with fear, my heart high in my chest, Thomas confirmed, "That's Mount Ida. Uncle Chase brought us to Estes Park, once, to go hiking in Rocky Mountain National Park and everything. We saw the most beautiful bighorn sheep."

Somehow, we ended up in that town when we got turned around, about the time I started to wonder if I really was crazy, or being led on a (for lack of a less infuriating term) wild-goose chase. Did all this hinge, somehow, on my belief that any of it was possible? What if I stopped believing? What if I made the choice to say, "Thomas, let's just turn around, or maybe get a cabin here, and wait for Cassius." What would happen? Would I still find the skull? Was it even possible for me to suggest we turn around? Would turning around be what led me to the skull? My head ached and my mouth was cracker dry, but at last in the grocery store we found a nice old man who explained that the road to the ranch we wanted—it was in fact a ranch we wanted, wasn't it—well, the ranch we wanted, if he was thinking of the same thing, was a place up the highway, off one of the switchbacks and down a ways, though nobody'd lived there in quite a while and so far as he knew the place was abandoned five or so years ago. Funny fellow who owned it after the writer died usually sent his brother to town for him, or maybe it was his boyfriend—you never did know these days, he supposed.

"You never really do," I agreed, managing along with Thomas to cobble together a feasible route from the tatters of the clerk's rustic descriptions until, at last, at the lowering of the shade of night, we came upon the flimsy chain which served as a poor gate for a fence unused for cattle, or even privacy, for several years. Turning up the heater and checking the top button of the flannel jacket I'd bought him in the park, Thomas asked, "Is this really the place you want?"

I didn't know, so I didn't speak. I left the car and, between it and the swaying chains, surveyed the property as twilight stretched starry fingers from distant Mount Ida. An old property, I was sure: there was no way something like this would be allowed anymore. As I stepped over the chain with utmost caution, the view swamped me properly. How incredible it was to be so close to the park, and to be so remote with nature. Well could I envision the pastures tended, full of lambs and cows and goats—but all was silence, and the whistle of the frigid wind. What had once been the ranch house stood empty before the remains of two barns. One, though decayed, was more intact, slumping inward beneath the pressure of its rot rather than immolated as its sibling. Heart racing to see some foreshadowing, some meaning which no one else might have seen but me (and, perhaps, you, if you can be called different from me on reading this), I penetrated the belly of the house.

Inside, my phone's glow illuminated the remains of someone's hand-me-down life: the furniture had been cobbled together from the tastes of at least two, maybe three, people, with pueblo-style chairs and tables in the living room, rustic hunting lodge adornments in the den and one of the bedrooms, and a particularly modern bedroom with a low, flat bed and no adornment on the walls save for row upon row of empty bookshelves, their contents having long been whisked off to some new home—a home I knew, with a ceiling painted in fresco, Castor and Pollux, and Castor in the arms of Leda, and Leda, wearing the soft and tired face of the woman who gazed from a photograph above the dining room doorway, out across the flat oak table and the window behind, beyond the ranch which had been inherited from the father who had once filled out the 1960 census and who happened to leave it to his daughter, who happened, at time of the census, to be barely two, barely alive, barely conscious. And all so I could stand in the dust of the house: nothing confirmed, no documents left behind, no pictures but the one of Leda on the wall. Nothing telling. No proof, no personage.

In the cold of the night, I turned my attention to the barns. First, I checked the one which still hung on, which still pushed itself from the ground as though to evade a fate so imminent not even the groaning wood could deny it as I pushed open the door and found cobwebs, dust, a cough, a trick of the shadow in the light of my cell phone which made me jump, but which ultimately meant nothing. But in the burned barn (which had once been, but existed only as suggestion of itself, the way an optical illusion, a set of shapes, does not form the cube it implies) I felt a pulse of intuition. The dirt floor did not appear as the floor of a barn, tromped by anonymous ungulates. It wasn't the same as the floor of the barn next door. I frowned at the patches of grass and weeds which had cluttered together, certain I had found the key to everything. This dirt was no more a floor than was any grave.

Was there a body buried here? Was this where someone had died? Did I stand upon a corpse? Trembling, I retreated to the house only long enough to collect a shovel found in the downstairs broom closet. By the time I emerged again, Thomas had come from the car to lean against the fence and call, "Did you find anything, Katherine?"

"I want you to get some money out of my wallet, find a place to stay, and come and get me in the morning, all right?"

The frown in his voice carried through the night as he called, "Katherine."

When, five minutes later rose the distant retreat of the car over the choking of my spade, I knew he had given up waiting. I had meant what I'd said and was relieved to be alone with my thoughts, but felt even in my early hour Easter Sunday solitude that I was not by myself. I trembled, the taste of copper in my mouth from where I'd bitten my tongue in my digging, and when I hit the first bone it was like a revelation—so much so that I fell upon my knees and scooped away the dirt by hand, cursing myself for having relieved Thomas, yet feeling on some mad and fruitless vision quest. Some effort which I knew I could only undertake alone. With bare hands, I examined the bone and thought it might be a femur, and soon found another like, and other, shorter ones; I, knowing nothing of bones, thought perhaps they were the bones of men until I found the first horse skull. The discovery brought tremors all the same, for how right had been my intuition to excavate the floor of a barn burned so its ashes might further cover evidence of some odious shame! Yet, it was not my intuition which had guided me to the barn, was it? It was the REM Novel. It was the course of my whole life up to the discovery, and after, and all which would continue to happen, probably, beyond its end.

What would happen after the end of the time the novel chronicled? Would I notice any difference? Some sense of jamais vu, or some feeling of having lost a burden? Would I receive any of the catharsis afforded to my readers if this was the dream of some author far above me, typed out in a book or played out on a screen? What would I be when it was all over? What would I be then, and what would I be after death, and what would I be after that, and after that, and, and, and— "Too much knowledge makes one old," as Baba Yaga said to Vasilisa the Beautiful. And I felt, to be certain, the weight of years when at last the bones of horses gave way to the unmistakable bones of a man.

The skull, alarmingly round amid its oblong cousins, conjured Cassius's seizure, and Castor and Pollux, and the names Enoch and Hermes in parallel. I was less sure than I had ever been of Cassius's friend: whether he was Enoch to begin with, or Hermes to begin with, or both, or if there was a difference, and what it meant. Had he killed this man? Why else would there be a skull there? Why else would I feel so cold and afraid and alone? Why else would I be sent here to find this skull, after all—sent by the novel, by God, by my dead aunt and uncle—

if not to uncover some crime? But, a crime by whom? What was this skull? What meaning, if any, could be derived?

"I found it," I whispered, taking it up in my hands, cradling it and turning my tearful face toward the stars, to the distant peak of the mountain which, impassive, offered no response while I breathed, "I did it. I found the skull. Now? Now what? What do you want from me? What can I do?"

Maybe it was because reading the scene of the skull's discovery had provoked me into dropping the whole REM Novel to begin with, but I found myself paralyzed as to how to proceed. I had seen this one moment, this vision of myself and this skull, and this one moment had collapsed me, somehow, acting as both guide and goal, terror and treasure. But what catharsis, this! What answer, what help? So it was not a skull I had made. So it was not Cassius's skull. So? How would I explain it to the police? How could I explain the discovery? How could I receive a catharsis from a thing so paltry as a human arrest? How could I share any of this, which had happened, which was so true and real and vivid to me, and yet which was relegated to fiction on a page, ever, at best, a half-truth as any memory?

"Katherine," said a voice, so familiar that I responded with a cry as the skull sprang into the pit with its relatives. I looked back to find Cassius standing above me. He had arrived in silence. "Kitty," he said again, beginning to crouch, and I, helpless, choked like a girl waking from a nightmare.

"*Cassius*," I said, at once afraid but also desperate for him, to touch him, to be in contact with he who knew better than anyone what plight I'd surmounted. As I lunged to grip his shoulders, then the lapels of his sport coat, I lowered my head and sobbed, the tears coming in relief as much as confusion, as much as fury. "What does it *mean*? I don't understand what it means. Oh, Cassius, I don't know what to do. I'm so confused. Where did you come from?"

He smoothed back my hair, trying to fix its flyaway strands, then smiling at the futility as the wind picked up. "I've been in the house.

Spooky, huh! Not long, just a while. Good reading time. Enoch dropped me off to wait for you."

My mouth opened and shut, and I sobbed as much as laughed. "I don't know what I expected, I guess."

"Me, neither." His tone was agreeable as his chuckle. "Will you come inside with me? Kitty?"

Limply, I nodded, and Cassius, holding my right arm, drew me to my feet. Arm in arm like a bride and groom navigating the aisle after their wedding, we proceeded toward the house, dark and quiet in the night. "I'm so glad it wasn't you," I told him, barely breathing. "I was so afraid it would be, I wasn't—" I laughed and shook my head. "Maybe I should have read the book, after all."

"Horror is always easier when it has a face," he said, nodding. "When you can see it."

"But what do we *do*," I pressed, and he grimaced.

"I know it seems bad, but nobody was murdered." At the arch of my brow, he sighed. "I promise. If there were a real murder, I'd be the first to go to the police. Granted, what happened still wasn't good, but...let's just say it's a situation which warrants some cleaning, and Enoch is going to clean it so we can publish the book without a legal problem."

My head swam at my longtime lover's relaxed reaction to the skull. "Is he really Enoch?"

"Does it matter?"

"I want to *know*," I insisted, and Cassius laughed, pushing the protesting back door with his free hand.

"That's what's fantastic about you, Kitty. Hey, when was the last time you wrote something?"

"I've been too stressed to be inspired," I admitted, deliriously taken aback by a question from nowhere, claustrophobic in the dark house. I squinted as my eyes adjusted to the lack of starlight. "So busy in pursuit of this."

"But this *is* inspiration, you see, Kitty? It's all a big game, sort of. And all of it for you."

"For *me*." I almost laughed the words but was so disturbed I could find no humor. "For *me*, from whom?"

"That's...complicated. And it has a lot of answers. But you know, Kitty"—he took me down the stairs of the cellar and toward a softly glowing light, and I realized he'd been hiding down there all the time I'd been searching—"that's why it's good we're writers. We're the best people to answer the question. Will you do something for me?"

At the bottom of the stairs, he stopped, and I stopped with him. Past the banister, in the dusty office he had arranged for himself, a battery-powered laptop glowed softly in the light. The LSD sat attached, inanimate yet so imbued by then with a meaning beyond itself that my stomach hollowed to see it.

"One more time, Katherine," he asked, lifting his eyebrows, "while we talk. For me?"

Mouth dry, I regarded the Device, and, after making my way across the cold stone floor, I lowered myself into the seat. Cassius drew my hair away from my eyes before crowning my head with the thing, which I realized was mine. "What do you want me to write?"

"You don't have to write anything, honey. I just want to talk to you because I know you're scared. I know it seems like there's something strange going on, and I suppose there is. I mean, none of this is normal, right? But here's the rub: this is the way, secretly, things have always been. We just didn't have the context or the knowledge to appreciate it. It's like interpreting a dense book, *Ulysses* or whatever: you come back to it throughout your life, and every time you revisit it, it reveals more of itself. That's what wisdom is. And the REM Story you channeled, along with mine, these things are things that come from someplace beyond human imagining. Transmitted, somehow, from someplace beyond comprehension. But that's true of all stories, of all life. Everything that is and was and will be is all eternally present, like reality was a book in the hands of something beyond perception. But we, within the proverbial book, or reading an actual book, can only live this moment, the next moment, the moment after that, in linear order. We can only read one page—one word, truly—at a time. It's the only way to make sense of it."

I might have wrung his neck, might have given up the whole game then and there, but instead I just tightened my jaw and let him go on: "What are the dimensions, Kitty?"

"What is this, seventh grade?" When he just watched, I sighed. "There's—call it, 'a point.' A dot. And then the second and third dimensions are spatial, and the fourth is time."

"Linear time," emphasized Cassius. "But you need to be in a dimension above the dimension you're observing to observe it. What do we use to measure time, Katherine? Our sense of it. Our perception of it. The fifth dimension." He lifted his hand, showed me four fingers and his thumb. "We can't observe eternity because that's above our material standpoint, but we *can* observe our own perception, if we're conscious enough. We can decide where we want to be, what versions of ourselves we want to be. But better, still, is to learn the patterns at work, see, Katherine? Not the forward and backward motion of a human being growing up and considering in retrospect, but the upward and downward motion of awareness. And we can use the low portion of the pattern to anticipate the higher part. Like a writer, writing a character trying to find God. Like consciousness, pretending to be a human in search of a skull."

He touched my hand, held it, squeezed it. "I love you so much, Katherine. And you know what? All of this, everything—the way you've suffered, your refusal to move in with me all these years, my seizure—has brought us right here. You see? It's a game. A model. And you're the most important part of the model, in a way. You're not the part that understands in principle; you're the part that understands experientially."

And he was right. I both experienced and understood, there, in that moment, where time stretched limitless and the laptop begin to stutter with overwhelming input. I opened my mouth and contained in my open mouth the world the way the open mouth of a cup, empty of contents, contains all things for its emptiness. Why, I cannot possibly know, but that image of myself as vessel, for whatever reason, was at last the one which struck me like a match white hot down my spine, and in the instant that I lifted my hand to my mouth and cried, "Cassius, oh, Cassius!" the cursor blinked with the unfolding of a world.

Felicity

I

In the beginning was the Word, but before the beginning was the Space, infinite potential so pregnant with possibility it was nothing as much as it was everything. So delicate was this fabric that mere acknowledgment was sufficient to shatter its sanctity, to divide it into two, then four: light and dark, then also observer and observed. The first observation was observation itself, and for an observation to have been made, someone must have observed it. It was the distinction between observed and observer which resolved itself into Consciousness and Matter, the Conscious realization of Matter's Space. Consciousness, bright and gleaming, was without company, seeing planets and stars all too distant to contact. Who, then, might observe him? Naturally he could observe himself, and of course he would have to, if his light was all that was. This was a problem to be solved. He could not make two of himself, could not contact the twinkling crystals distant in the void. But, by reflection, he came to the answer, and Consciousness cast the light of his golden eye upon the empty slate of the moon.

"Are you awake?" he asked, and all at once I was, awake in this body of a woman, the space around me still half-formless. Had I been the observer? But it seemed he, standing over me, had created me, for I had not existed before he saw me within the bowl of the moon.

"I am," I marveled. I roused from the pool in the center of the temple which birthed around me like the unfolding of a lotus blossom, its nine columns and marble ceiling coming into existence alongside me. His voice came, distant: "How are you feeling?"

"Why are we here?" I asked into his golden face, taking the hand he extended to help me from the silver waters pooling at my feet.

"I thought that maybe you'd like to make a world with me," he said, and I, reaching out, touched the bitter-cool air of the naked moon and found it felt like glass shards.

"Will it be warmer than here?"

He laughed. "Yes," he said, turning his bright gaze out to the planet swirling blue and green beneath us, "it'll have to be. For the animals."

"I love animals," I said, and he smiled, reaching over to take my hand, his own massive and warm, hot as the face of the sun. "I love you," I told him, and a twinkle became his eye, and a sad twitch tugged his lip, and he kissed me.

From our kiss was first birthed life, which trickled out of me and across the surface of the earth below. We stepped through the gateway of my temple and emerged upon the surface of the planet, observing the mass existence of flora and fauna teeming in the primordial chaos of indistinct life where biological forms thrived like pulsing stone awaiting the chisel of a master carver. Our chisel took the form of words, and with our words, he and I carved shapes into the land and divided earth from sky, male from female, plant from animal. We divided the animals from one another—bird from fish from mammal from that alien fourth, insect—raven from dove, shark from squid, lion from leopard. The ravens were my favorite, and as he and I set across the world to see it was to our liking, six followed in entourage. There were seven beautiful continents which graced our land, and across them all we were astonished to see what vast mountains, what torrential waterfalls, what sumptuous forests all rolled across the mossy landscape.

"What do you think we should call it?" he asked, but I shook my head.

"I don't think we should call it anything."

"Nothing at all? But how will we talk about it!"

"We don't have to talk about it. We can just experience it. We've been talking about it, without calling it anything but 'it.'"

"Don't you think it deserves a name, though? Everything else has a name. Your birds have names." As he reached toward the raven upon my left shoulder, its inky breast puffed at the indignity of touch.

"My birds have names because if we don't separate them, how will we be able to distinguish them from other animals? They'll be lost in the miasma if I don't have a way to think of them as separate."

"And you don't think this planet deserves a name to separate it from the rest of the soup?"

As the irritated raven alighted from my shoulder and carried up into the sky with its fellows, I lifted my hands to my hips. "Isn't that how the trouble always starts? Trying to distinguish one world from another? Besides, there's nobody to use the name except the two of us. What does it matter if it's named or unnamed?"

"Well, there's nobody to use the name, but there might be somebody later."

"What do you mean?"

"People! Don't you want some humans here, sweetheart? Think of all we could do if we made our own people! They'd see how great we are. It's like somebody to give us feedback, right?"

White horror sank my heart to hear him say such a terrible thing, as though I were once again breathing the needle void around the empty moon. "I thought this was a world for us."

"It is, honey, but, I mean, you can hardly have a world where nothing happens."

"Why not! Don't you love it here?" Sumptuous sun roses burst at our feet, crimson and tangerine buttons glowing on the rich emerald earth which faded into the wide plains of grass and arching oaks about which played our creatures. "It's perfect! There's no war or famine or pain. All the animals are so happy! Do you think they'd be that much happier with human beings to encroach on their territories and pollute their environments?"

"Well, are you going to have a story about a talking squirrel?"

"Don't be ridiculous. This is life, let's just live." Above us, the ravens' song rose to a clamor. "Do we need a story?"

"What's the point if we don't have a story?" I spread my hands in amazement for his question as he continued, "What could we possibly learn? Did we come into existence just to stare at each other for eternity?"

"I have no idea! You tell me: you're God, aren't you!"

Mouth paralyzed in brief shock, he soon barked out a laugh. "Me, God! Hell, sweetheart, I thought you were God."

"I obviously can't be God," I told him, waving a hand toward my white eye hanging in the sky. Was its majesty diminishing, or was it my foul fancy? "I was created second, wasn't I?"

"Were you?" My hackles raised as he lifted a hand to stroke his jaw, a mockery of consideration. "It's hard to say. Anyway, I can't be God. I have a body, don't I?"

"If we're talking bodies, that counts me out, too, doesn't it?"

"You're Matter itself, aren't you?" With a dubious cock of his brow, he pointed out, "I'm Consciousness, sure, but would I exist if I didn't have anybody to observe?"

"I could hardly know I existed if nobody was here to observe me."

"So something else must be God," he posited, and my face above blackened amid the rising cries of my angry ravens.

"This conversation isn't about who's God and who isn't! This is just like you, always turning arguments into other things. This is about making people! You want to make people! Why do you want to ruin this place? Look: maybe we can make them but keep language away from them."

"Honey," he started, his brows knit, but I was desperate because he was on the verge of ruining our perfect time in the solitude of our private world. I snatched up his hands and begged, "Why is it so important that there be people? Why can't we all just live in peace and quiet, watch the life flow in and out like waves?"

He stroked my cheek. "Sweetheart," he said, laughing, "life can't exist without change. Conflict. Right? Think about the monkeys running around in the jungle. As long as time keeps going forward, they're going to evolve, aren't they?"

"No! If I'm Matter, I get to decide the rules. If I feel like keeping down the human brain so it can't develop language, then that's what I'll do. Time won't even exist until they become conscious. So, see!" I half laughed, desperate. "If they never become conscious, nothing ever has to change."

His sympathy was eroding to irritation, and we both knew it, but I could hardly stop myself. In the sky, my eye was narrowed by pain as he carried on. "I know you just want to have a nice time with me, and we can still have a nice time!"

"No!"

"Honey, what do you think is going to happen?"

"I think all of the wonderful things will go away! I think you—you'll go away." My eyes watered as I clutched the ruby silk of his robes and hung, sobbing, from his neck. "Please, we can't let them evolve. They'll distract you so I might never see you again."

At last he sighed. "Let's do what you said. Let them evolve, but no language. Does that sound all right?"

I nodded away my reservations, hanging in his arms. "I don't want you to be mad at me in a place so nice," I told him, feeling like a child. He laughed as he patted my back.

"I'm not mad at you, honey."

"I guess I must be, then," I told him, and he laughed at that, too.

"I just told you I'm not."

"No, I meant *me*."

"Why didn't you say that, then! 'Me' and 'I,' two very different things."

My face tensed in annoyance. "I don't want to play word games with you."

"Is there any other kind of game, really?" he asked, a twinkle in his eye as I, disgruntled, turned away to take up the clay of my earth and make statues, men and women. Into these I poured my breath, which they took into their hearts in a deep pulse that echoed the vibrations which trembled through the world. These animals, fleshy and hairy and ignorantly naked, came to life in a series of gasps. Their eyes darted with the ferality of apes, alive but unconscious.

"Beautiful," cried my lover, but I was not entirely convinced of it, for although they bore our image, they were less than us, could not speak as us or walk or think as us, and I would see to it that they never could.

It began in a slow way, though it happened as I expected it would. Just as I spent hours of time with the birds, so, too, did he spend much time with his own favorite animals. Once, those beloved animals had been the lions of the savannah and the wolves of the forest. Now my lover spent an increasing amount of time in the company of the ape-men. They delighted in his arrival whenever he appeared, and mine, too, undeterred by my open displeasure to have to lure him back into my company. But then, one day, my laughing lover showed me something.

"What's that?" I asked, paling as I recognized on my asking the dagger of bone in his palm.

"They're hunting! They caught dinner."

I had felt the death of the bison, but had thought nothing of it, for although I loved my animals dearly, they grew weary with their many adventures, and had to be renewed, or die to feed other animals— but it was an understanding they did not mind, and many, like the squirrels, took it as a game. I had not supposed this death would mark the true end of peace. I might avoid giving man language, but they, being apes, had capacity enough to develop tools. Still, it shocked me that such a development had been beyond my awareness! That I had not felt the earth of them succumb to the urge to produce a tool, as I felt the earth of all things succumb to all urges of instinct, was a disturbing development.

It was not long after that I returned, and on my arrival my lover excitedly clasped my hand, dragging me to the cavern where the ape-men made their homes. "Come and see," he said, and to my horror, they had made art of their murder. The hunt of the bison was depicted in detail, clustered figures chasing a beast ridden by someone whose head was clasped by a halo. The scene, it seemed, carried on to one of sacrifice, depicting the murdered animal displayed before a feminine figure as tall upon the wall as an ape-man might have risen had one stood before us.

"I think they made it for you," he said, and I, pallid, gripped the fabric of his robe.

"We aren't letting them evolve."

"I know, sweetheart! I'm not responsible for this, I promise. One of them must have been inspired. I'm sure they think you're a thousand times more beautiful than any of their women."

Just what I wanted. Grinding the tips of my fingers into my shut eyes, I stormed from the cave and hissed at the nearest group of ape-men, who scattered away like a group of startled birds. As my lover let out a noise of displeasure, I reached an arm toward the sky for my ravens. "If they get any further along, I'm going to destroy them."

"You wouldn't."

"Try me! I'll destroy this whole stupid world. Even my ravens." I caught the raven which had intended to land upon my arm and devoured it in flame. The ape-men howled in terror at the sight, and as the remaining ravens cawed above us, I narrowed my eyes at him. "I mean it. Anything in this world with Consciousness is going to bring conflict."

"You're the only one bringing conflict." His tone was sharp as a blade. I winced, but he went on. "All I wanted was to have fun with you, to make a really profound and beautiful world with you. To do that, we need people. We can't have profundity if we don't have people. Talking dolphins. A sentient weed! Anything! Don't you want to see the kinds of stories these people will live out?"

"A story has conflict. What if I don't want conflict?"

"If you don't want conflict, then why are you being contradictory!"

"I'm not being contradictory. I'm not doing this just to get in your way."

"Then why *are* you doing this?"

The heat filling my face rendered me so blind I could not see my eye in the sky, could not see it was pitch black. "I am doing this," I said with careful enunciation, "because I love you. Because I want to spend time with you."

"And you are, sweetheart. I'm right here." He touched my shoulder then, and I felt him more solidly than ever, and I ached to kiss him but forced myself back.

"But where will you be when all men are Conscious, not only you and I?"

Again, that sympathetic affect became his eyes, and he took my face in his broad hands. "I won't be going anywhere. I promise, I won't."

"But I won't be able to see you," I said, trembling, and he squeezed me to his breast, insisting, "You will!"

But I could not imagine he was right, could not fathom finding him anywhere but in his own body. Fearing he would become lost in the sea of people, I insisted, "Please, no. I don't want them to take you from me."

Sighing, he kissed my forehead and said, "Okay, sweetheart," but they were hollow words, and we both knew it.

The fateful day of his first life's ending came when, one evening, I could find no sign of either my lover or the apes he cherished. With a twinge of terror, I set out in search, and could not uncover them for twelve hours' work, until, at last, from the mouth of a cave in the center of the desert there emitted a curl of smoke. As my unkindness let up a scream of betrayal, I uncovered him within, with his apes, instructing them in the art of cooking over an open fire he had taught them to make.

"Honey," he began, but I could only feel rising rage sweeping over my eyes, the fangs of a wolf in my mouth and my heart as I shouted for his silence. The hooting apes retreated into the darkness of the cave, whisking away women and children so I and my ravens could meet my lover alone in the light, where I gripped his robe and demanded, "Why are you doing this!"

"Well, they need *fire*, obviously, sweetheart."

"They don't need fire, they're perfectly fine! They *didn't* need fire before they learned how to craft tools, when they were eating berries and fruits."

Sheepishness became his expression, and shame bloomed in me to realize the truth of what had happened. With a gasp, I accused, "You showed them how to make tools, didn't you."

He lifted his hands to touch me, and I swept back from them, eyes narrowed against his obvious hurt. "It's not a big deal. It's just something to help them."

"Something to help them, sure. But what about us?" My eyes boiled over with tears, alone as I was. Neither raven nor sublingual ape could validate the absurdity of this conversation. "This is our world. I thought we created this so we could be together. I thought you wanted to make this world so we could spend time together, or play a game together, or something! Not so you could ruin it with people."

"I'm sick of this fear. People don't ruin the world, they make it. You wanted to talk about God the other day: God isn't possible without them." He waved into the darkness, indicating a family of huddled cave dwellers clutching each other for fear of my fury. "You and I can't exist here without people."

"Why not?"

"What would be the point!"

"I never asked to be alive, and when I realized I was, I just wanted to be with you." More pathetic than ever, humiliated for ever having wanted something like being with him in the first place, I wiped the back of my brisk hand beneath my eyes. "Isn't it enough to just be together?"

Exasperated, though with a softened expression, he ran a hand over his sandy cheek. "It is. I love you. I love you so much that being with you is all that matters, and that's why we need people: so you and I can be together. And I mean, really together. Really one flesh."

"I don't see how they'll do anything but get in the way of that. Right now we're perfectly equal, and happy, and you want that to change. Maybe you only want to have people so you can be worshiped! You want them to feed your ego."

"No! I want them for you." This time he made the mistake of reaching out for me, and my fifth raven descended upon the extended hand while his two brothers swept upon my lover's eyes, and his two sisters caught the stones which the howling apes threw at the sight of their god having the Matter torn from his sockets; red-and-white ocular ooze smeared over black beaks to add the sultry sound of viscous fluid to the symphony of shrieks and squawks. All this happened before me as though I dreamed, and I felt nothing as the ravens, beaks sharper than the knives of men, pecked apart the limbs of my beloved, swallowed his tongue, and flew off into the heights of the cavern above our heads. Indeed, I felt nothing as, from the darkness, the savages emerged to investigate the ruins of their god, probing bloodied limbs and fleshy torso. One noted the scarlet hidden beneath flesh and grunted to the others, who had been taught by my lover it was a crime to waste meat. Solemn, they took his remains to the fire. It was then that I came to my senses, and I, with a piteous sob, realized what I had done, and what was happening—but it was much too late, and they cooked him, my beloved, and devoured him with all the thoughtlessness they would have shown devouring that bison from their hunt. From the hunt he took them on. Their mouths were filled by his flesh, and new light chased the darkness from their eyes. As sight of me fell away, one noticed the dancing flame. He gasped, with each gasp looking around himself in a new direction like a man coming awake, then gripped the arm of his comrade and murmured something in his ear. I retreated, leaving behind even my ravens, for I knew that the whispering ape had just named fire, and that the first Man had been born.

As I stepped from the cave to the whistling desert morn, thoughts of my beloved came to me. I, full of tears, relived in cycles what had happened. What horrors I had wrought! He had done naught but love me, love what we created, but I had refused to consider or compromise. Even if I had been right, what did it matter? He was not there to see the pain people would beset upon the land. He was not there to see the sadness which wracked me as, barefooted, I trudged across the sand, turning my eyes away from the harsh golden light of the sun, which, without its soul, seemed to wish only to burn, rather than illuminate. All Matter, devoid of Consciousness—oh, my heart! From the tremors of my feet fled lizards and snakes, desperate to make their escapes from me. Not even cacti bloomed in my sight, withered, rather, at my pain. Would I truly never see him again? It seemed impossible that he who had come before me could ever be gone, that I should be alone, made to wander in the empty wastes in a world I had once loved to life with him. Matter, without Consciousness!

It was true enough to say that it was still his world, and mine, that he had contributed as much to its making as any father to the making of his child, and so was present in its every facet. Even hidden in the light of the stars. But I had become attached to his way of being, his active existence in the light before me, in me, fleshly with Matter in the form that I knew. To go without was heartbreaking, for I could always remake his form, my lover, but wherefrom came that spark which lit his eyes? Where gone? Scattered. That lost spark was him, more than his body could ever have been, and I could find no trace—not in the desert, alone as I was. For ageless times, I wept and wandered, lying in sand wastes and wishing for a death that seemed never to come, for I felt neither thirst, nor hunger. Even so, I ate the thorns of prickled bushes lining my dunes, and hardly slept for the agony of my heart. And when at last I collapsed beneath a palm, I yet had no rest, for I was awoken by a distant, pained scream which reminded me so of my own that I burst again into sobs for want of that spark of my lover. My tears, falling upon the ground, became mirrors of lachrymose reflection, and each which fell seemed another trap to hold me: a trap I had lain myself, to dim the world once brightened by my lover's light.

But perhaps I could find it among those creatures I resented. Perhaps that spark still burned. Perhaps, in man, my beloved might appear again, for the ancestors of all men devoured his flame to light their own. With a spark big enough, I might see him emerge once more. I might do penance for my crimes against him: for so destroying him in my bitterness so that all which was left was mere stain upon stone. But would he want anything to do with me, assuming I was successful? I had to believe he would, that there was forgiveness in his heart. If I lost that hope, I was as good as dead.

2

The first thing for me was to return to the world of men, and I emerged from the desert to discover they had built themselves seven civilizations—a world more complex than I could ever have hoped to create by myself. They had taken the substance of me and used it as the material to produce all they could ever need, and used it to divine the laws of existence in the land. They had forgotten how to see me, these men and women, so I walked invisible among them, but they kept my lover's voice alive in their mouths, just as his spark burned in their hearts. With that spark, they had surged through many ways of being, civilizations rising and falling in aeons of increasing ability and intellect. These aeons seemed to me an eyeblink, yet endless, with no order but what nature demonstrated. Ageless, unseen, I waded the miasma of men and women, of sensation and being, until at last there rose before me the seventh Kingdom in the Western Lands, whence emanated the echo of a sound like a bird's coo. I came to find its source within a glade, in the Forest of the Kingdom, a land I did not know.

The gift of all those who walked my lands—speech, for which he had given his life—was the same which allowed me to come into a human's spirit as I might move within my own, and for a time forget myself in mortal guise, see the spectrum of their thoughts and theirs alone; but when I tried to penetrate the heart of this sound, I could find no way in. By squinting and focusing, feeling with ghostly fingertips, slowing the pace of the energy with which I had hastened through space and time, I focused on a most exquisite savage: a woman, clothed in the skin of a deer. She slept beneath a towering oak, curls of supple black night sky tumbling over pale shoulders as she sighed in speechless slumber. I was stricken by the peculiar notion that she had been born of this tree, for she was far too perfect to be born of any human pair. How might such a thing be in this world that I had made?

Hand upon my heart, I backed from her lest my phantom's touch awaken her in panic, but she stirred of her own accord, rolling upon her back to stretch her limber legs. She lifted her lids, unveiling eyes beautiful and dark, the color of her hair or the bark of Forest trees. Curled in the roots of the oak with her arms crossed over her breast, holding her bow like a lover's frame, she gazed through me, seeing no apparition but the morning star through the branches of her tree. This, she regarded for a time, her lips curled in the sort of half smile one sees upon an impish kitten, and my heart ached so that I wished a moment I'd had a daughter. But, of course, she was my daughter, and she was my mother, because through her, perhaps, I could experience this world and what it meant: what my lover had left for me. But, lo, as she gazed upon the glittering star of morning, and as I touched the center of her forehead, I found to my amazement that she had no tongue but the one in her mouth.

"What manner of woman is this?" This, I asked myself as I dared to touch her cheek, but she had no answer. Shivering at the caress of a ghost, she smiled, laughed, hugged her elk-gut bow, and sprang to her feet. She darted through me, and I was the one who was chilled, falling to pieces and coming together to see she ran with the abandon of a child, perhaps to play in the stream near the redwood, which, with a moss-covered finger, steered our way. She reached up her hands and waved to dawn's birds, even pursed her lips at them as though to kiss, as if she knew these things from some place beyond words; but she did not speak, nor think in words, and I felt from her mind only the rippling of needs, indistinct flashes of instinct pooling in a vast space which contained within it everything and nothing at all. I could not inhabit her if she did not have language. Even if she did not speak the languages I knew, that did not matter, for I heard all languages of men the same; but she had no language of men and instead knew only the languages of her body, and the animals, and the trees. I, fascinated, decided to watch her.

At the edge of the stream, she stopped and smiled and, with a sigh, caressed the water. It chilled her so that she laughed; then, falling upon her rear, she slid her bow from her shoulder, and quiver, too, to frown at the four arrows. Her chest was beset by the same urge which my lover once taught men to feel: the urge to make tools, to plan, to produce in advance. I knew well that urge to create but had not felt it since the creation of the world and all its life, and wanted in that instant to remind myself; so, from the muddy loam of the opposite bank, I created a stag which peeled itself from the clay and shook its head with a snort like the north wind.

The girl's body stiffened at the wondrous sight, a black deer shaking free from the earth, but it was only for an instant that she was stunned; she whisked up her bow, and the stag across from her stretched its limbs, bowed to where I stood invisible, then sprang off into the thick of trees to tumble through curling locks of vines. Herself a creature of the Woods, rather than a daughter of man, the girl darted across the stream with grace such that the tips of her toes barely grazed the water as she leapt from stone to stone. Her heart pounding in her ears as much as mine, she burst through the terrain easy as a villager might move through his cottage, rounding after the deer and at once drawing an arrow from her quiver. Undaunted by tangled root or patch of thorn, she pursued like a hunting dog the thunder of the deer which, too terrified or perhaps too thrilled with its new life to ease its tread, left a trail of clear sound to guide her to her quarry. At last, in the microseconds in which she was presented with a clear shot, she took it; despite myself, I emitted a cry of delight as the projectile penetrated the throat of the hart, which stumbled over the moss-consumed body of a fallen cedar and rolled to a violent halt. Was this what my lover had felt, seeing Man take its prey! Sweeping after it, the girl stood with one foot propped upon a nearby root, the other on the soft dirt upon which the wounded stag dragged itself. With her mouth solemnly set but her eyes narrowed by determination, she took from her belt a jagged piece of horn. She gripped, grimacing, one of the antlers which the beast thrashed, its snorting head turning so its rolling black eyes might find hers and show her the hatred of a dying deer was a more powerful thing than the weapons of man. Indeed, it seemed as if she was taken aback by the intensity of the rage with which the animal regarded her, and from her arose a soft, "Ah," but she released the feeling quick as it came and slit her prey's throat with a hand like a viper's head.

Relentless! A beauty, be certain, but no gentle woman by any means. It took tenacity, after all, to survive in the Forest!

What might this girl do, though, were all creatures not so hapless as a new-made stag? I felt through them, touching the spirit of each until I came to one furred animal, full of fang and claw: my bear. I was not sure the girl could kill such a beast without being killed, herself. What would she do? Would she try?

Stroking the cheek of her kill so entranced the girl that, at the outset, she did not hear the hunger-driven beast hurtling through the trees in pursuit of blood. When she did hear it, the tenderness with which she mourned the deer vanished, and what was left in its place was the cold, hard face of a Huntress. It thrilled me so that I forgot myself, as though I were in the way of the scene unfolding. As the thunder of the beast grew, the Huntress tore from the throat of the deer the arrow which had killed it; the shaft snapped in her hand, unmendable. The muscles of her body tensed. She gazed into the Forest and was soon rewarded by sight of the shadow raging within, lunatic with bloodlust. Terror sallowed her face, and, crying out for the wasted deer at her feet, the Huntress galloped into the trees.

This was a beast she knew from the experience of her senses. This beast, like all things, nameless to her, was to the world at large "bear" but to her naught but terror. This bear was not like the bears which the Huntress sometimes encountered; this bear was savage, and seemed not to want the fruits of her labor, but rather her, undeterred as it was by the stones and roots and groping branches which turned against the Huntress to falter her escape. The girl's bow caught upon the branch of a tree and was pulled from her grasp. She cried out, tarrying to grab it back and, for that delay, was forced to duck around the trunk of a gnarled ash tree the size of a small house. On its opposite side was a crack wide enough for a creature her size, but not for a creature the size of the one chasing her. By holding her breath, she wiggled within and even made it halfway before the piercing claw raked her flesh. The shock of pain elicited a scream, for her shoulder exploded in hot agony; but there was little the bear could do. Though it scraped her, it had done so with claw, rather than mouth, and by some miracle the Huntress forced herself farther into the hollow, farther into safety, so the beast could only moan in fury and, despondent, work no more than a single paw into the trunk. Gasping, clutching her bloodied arm, the Huntress fell back and gave an echoing shriek when falling back meant also falling down. In the roaring darkness, she squinted, waited, panting, tilted upside down. As her eyes adjusted, she found the tree the mere entrance to something greater: a cave, which sloped into the earth. The still-snarling bear which tried fruitlessly to force its pursuit rendered the darkness more welcoming.

Into its depths she marched, stooping low to avoid hitting her head—though, the deeper she went, the taller the cave became. Soon, she managed to walk again, walk and turn her head and breathe without fear of oppression, but a chill had begun to fill the tunnel, for its depths were cold. With no exit in sight, sweat broke across her forehead, even in the face of that frigid air around her, but the darkness finally gave way to a glow which brought with it relief.

It was strange at first. Difficult to notice, for her eyes had grown used to the nothingness around her, and the somethingness came on so slowly that it was like the soft arrival of the sun to warm the Forest trees. But this was not light like the sunlight of the day, nor light like the moonlight of the night—it was its own peculiar brand, the slate of seawater, though the Huntress had not seen seawater that she then remembered. Seeking its source, she hurried her pace, and the winding tunnels of the cavern gave way to cries most curious. Never had the Huntress heard an animal make noises like these, funny babbling she could not discern, but, had a human from the City been listening, they might have realized it was a man's voice, crying, "Hello? Is somebody there? I hear footsteps!"

Of course, the Huntress did not understand that. She did, though, understand the tone of the thing which spoke, and it made her want to hurry along to its source as though it needed her, though she was the one in need of many things—a seat, a drink of water, an exit, a few friendly plants to help her with her wounds. She had no sense of those urges, though, when confronted by the sound dominating her conscious-ness, and could only scramble after the source of light which had begun to soften the darkness. The tunnel soon widened, and the Huntress gasped against both the sight and stench, hovering at the edge of a new room as her eyes sought for focus.

A cavern: one the breadth of the glade which was her home, and high as the trees which made it. The Huntress, it seemed, had come quite a long way, and stood a tiny, pale atom upon the edge of an alien space bathed in cyan light. Upward, her eyes sought the figures of bats, though of course she did not see "bats," but black spots of motion flickering between stalagmites, some unfurling wings to swoop, squeak-ing, in search of food. Beneath her feet, the light illuminated the soft source of the foul smell: the excrement of those cave dwellers which hovered and chirruped above as Forest birds. Such limitless filth made the Huntress gag, stumble a step, and turn to leave, but the voice called again, "Wait! Felicity, it's me!" and though she knew not the words, she knew their feeling. With a jolt of urgency, she adjusted her attention between the ceiling and its wretched floor, and discovered in the distance a stone upon which lay a metal thing the Huntress did not recognize.

Her frown giving way to grimace, the Huntress waded into the guano to the tops of her ankles, each step warm until it was cold. More than once she felt something wiggling against her heel that made her want to leap. But on she marched to the source of that light; at last, before it, she stood in awe.

"Am I glad to see you," uttered the noise from beyond the Huntress, inspiring a curious frown. The sounds emerged without evident cause, but so loud it was as if this shining thing beneath her produced them. Like a great sliver of stone. It hardly seemed the sort of thing to make a sound.

"Well," said the inanimate thing, its tone beginning to rise in a combination of agitation and excitement, "aren't you going to help me? You do recognize my voice, don't you? Felicity?"

But the Huntress could not have answered had she understood the words, for the gleaming thing enchanted, as all alien artifacts. So glittering was this thing, indeed, that it reminded her of a flower. Tentative fingers stroked the valley where blood would run from the time she picked it up until the demise of a woman whose existence was yet unknown to the wild girl.

"Easy! I'm not sure what's what anymore, God only knows what you're touching. I— Hey! Ow!"

The sharpness of the thing's noise caused the Huntress to yank her fingers from that which they'd touched upon the Flower, the crimson gem which, many faceted, was more beautiful than the morning sun and glimmered magenta in the wan azure light. At the gem, she frowned, and at the Stone Flower, she tilted her head.

"Well, I can tell you for certain: that was my eye. You can say anything anytime," it carried on, oblivious to her linguistic condition. "To be frank, you're beginning to worry me."

With a sigh at the noise beginning to disturb the chattering bats, the frustrated Huntress scanned once more for the source: for some animal which uttered so strange a set of sounds as these. She found nothing living. Nothing at all, indeed, but for this object before her. Her lips pursed, she studied this thing to try to place it. It was not like the things of the Forest. It was not what a person with words might have called a tree, or rock, or grass, or even, truly, flower. No flower, this thing, though it had a stem like one. But what was its use? Part of its stem gleamed in the blue light like the face of the moon; this was the part she had touched before, which had foretold the coming of more noise.

She thought on that a moment, that connection, and then, carefully, touched the tip again.

"I told you, be careful!"

"Ah!" The Huntress felt as if she had awoken from that force which claimed her every night, which tucked her down against the ground and filled her closed eyes full of visions. The noise had come from this thing! This Stone Flower. With a curious tilt of her head, she touched it again, her finger running down its edge. Excitement filled her to have discovered this special object which, in the manner of a stream, made sound with no mouth. Her excitement led to her drifting attention, and, rapt in wonder, she discovered that the edge of this Flower was deviously sharp. Another, softer cry peeled from her lips, and she jolted away on the supple light's bruising to vulgar red.

"There, see! You'd ought not to be touching that if you don't want to be cut."

But hot upset had surged over the Huntress, and she plunged her wounded fingers in her mouth, shocked that this Flower, of all things, had bitten her. The Stone Flower was no good; it stirred fire in her head and mouth and she gave a shout, a noise with no distinct meaning but the feeling of the cut.

"Well, I'm sorry that you've gone and hurt yourself, but you've only yourself to blame, going around pawing swords. Come on, Felicity. Stop being a child and let's get out of here."

But she was already leaving, turning away from the foolish Flower with its invisible teeth. She would find a way out of the cavern which, perhaps, would not lead her back to the bear. Behind her, the Flower was crying, "Wait, wait, won't you come back! Oh, you can't leave me here. Not after all this."

Of course, there was no convincing her with words. Teary-eyed to consider her options—to stay ankle deep in bat guano and be plagued by the shouting of a mordacious Stone Flower, or go back where she started and face the claws of the bear—the Huntress hugged herself and squinted through the reddened light in hopes of seeing some way out.

The only way out was the way in. Furious, she kicked the floor of filth, hiccupping, and frowned down at her bloody fingers.

"Oh, dear. You look how I feel. Or how I wish I could feel, at any rate. It's a curious thing, but since she put me here it's rather like I can't feel as vividly as I used to. Emotionally, anyway. All quite dulled. I suppose that's good, considering. But I've never seen you like this, Felicity." For a time, the Flower was quiet, and the Huntress cried over her fingers, and the bats filtered back into their places. At last, it said, "I suppose I'm deluding myself, expecting you to be you. Poor Felicity! She only took my body. But she left your body and took everything else."

It was a strange thing, that Stone Flower. The more she thought of it, the more she wondered about it. How strange, that a Flower should babble like a brook! And what strange manner of babbling, and biting! Why, the Flower seemed to her as the arrows she fashioned from the black stones found sometimes near the stream or the roots of trees. But it seemed made neither of those materials, nor bone, nor stone, truly, but rather quicksilver made slow. This Silver Flower's sharpness made her wonder if perhaps it was not something akin to her arrows, something that might be used to kill hart and bear alike, and much else, besides. It was anchored by some wretched metal vine, but, if its bite were powerful enough, perhaps it might gnaw itself free. Blood welling upon the tips of her fingers, the Huntress returned to the side of the thing and reconsidered it. The part of the Flower's stem which was not silver—the part whose base housed that lighted gem—seemed made to be held, if only because the grip of her bow bore a similar feature. With a tentative hand, she reached toward it, touching again the softly lit ruby set within the pommel, and a gasp of shock overcame her as so, too, did a vision. The face emerged first in her mind's eye and then seemed to take her from the cave. This face, one she recognized as similar to her own, yet altogether different, wove implications to crown her psyche like a diadem of need; its image, exquisite, projected upon the walls of the cave, left her breathless amid the recognition that, much as there were she-bears and he-bears, and female birds and male birds, so too did her being a woman mean that there must, somewhere, be a man.

Oh! Man! She had never seen a man before! She clutched her heart and gazed up at him, squinting to see just where the Man was, for it seemed he was everywhere and nowhere at once—a fragrant dream blinding her eyes, yet a nothing pinpoint glinting in the back of her brain. He was not real, this ghostly image that startled away the bats and glowed in the depths, but, oh! Beautiful! With the face of a noble oak and eyes which glinted fire, though the color of water—indeed, filled with water. He suffered, and much as the Silver Flower beneath her, he was bound. She knew then that whatsoever had bound the Silver Flower bound, too, this tortured man, garbed in a garnet robe and bedecked with a circlet of four thorny roses which scraped his forehead bloody. As though in refusal to submit, he gritted his teeth and glared somewhere beyond the Huntress's point of observation, his defiance so intense she remembered the dark-eyed, outraged stare of the dying hart.

"Ah," sighed the Huntress, her hand on her heart, her eyes filling with tears and turning urgently toward the Silver Flower. "Ah!"

"You remember him, do you?"

With her throat going tight as it did in times of danger, she reached toward the image which broke up, then, with an explosion of bats, and reformed as they swooped across the opposite side of the cave. "Ah," said the Huntress, with an attempted grasp of the ghostly image which, miles above her and a dream even then, was impossible to touch from the belly of that cave.

"You don't remember." The Flower sighed as the Huntress bit her lip. "I was hoping he would jar your memory. To forget even the King! You're not yourself at all." It hummed and chuckled, and the Huntress turned to the babble, which seemed to require attention. "Perhaps this isn't so bad. You might not even remember any of this once we get it all sorted out. Why, you're like a toddler, aren't you! A girl, a little girl in a woman's body, with no memory or language or—oh, Felicity." This delighted the Silver Flower, which chortled away, and this noise made the Huntress excited, because she understood that it was laughing, and so laughed along with it, since it was something she did when animals were very funny. She thought, perhaps, that she had done something very funny, and if she was funny enough, the Silver Flower might take her to Man. This laughter, the Flower found even funnier, but as its gasps rose to a crescendo of, "Oh, no, darling, please, I can't take it, this is already too much," the cave rumbled, and the image of the King disappeared, and the Huntress whipped her head in the direction of its absence.

"There's no time for that. Pick me up, girl," said the Silver Flower, its voice rising in urgency. "Come now, hurry!"

She sought the new sound, the sinister rumble-whispering which came from the very blackness of the cave itself, all that which lurked at the edges of the light. From her shoulder, she drew her bow, checked its string to confirm it unharmed by her escape from the bear, then notched one of her arrows.

"If that's what I think it is, those aren't going to do any good. You'd ought to try picking me up."

How she wished that thing would hush! It was only going to draw attention, and whatever Beast lurked in the darkness seemed massive. The rumbling carried on, until, with horror, she realized the filth of the cavern floor was the monster's home, and so stumbled back upon the stone with the Silver Flower. At the edge of its light, the dark creature burst massive from the muck with a deafening roar which rattled the cave's very ceiling. As screaming bats scattered like an explosion, the Huntress uttered a cry.

"That should be a familiar face! Not that you can understand me, but it belongs to the Witch. Remember her?" The Flower's voice couldn't compete with the noise of the monster which was, at best, only one-fourth illuminated by the light to reveal glistening umber pustules arranged in rows along the body of a leech, visible along with only one terrible claw which transmitted to the Huntress the certainty there were yet many more. A leathery wing, too: and as a head thrashed somewhere above, it lowered enough that she glimpsed part of a horn, it was toward this that she shot, because if that was a horn, perhaps nearby was the head, and she might learn its proximity by the Beast's reaction. Though the arrow pierced the darkness, the creature acknowledged no pain.

"Girl," begged the Flower, "won't you pick me up! It spits venom, you know."

That, of course, she did not know. What she did know was that she had no interest in charging into the darkness and going anywhere near that vile thing which made her heart hammer and the pores of her forehead pour sweat down her brow. She felt a rabbit on the verge of ensnarement and could not stand the thought of greeting this Beast which was so much more awful in its shuddering than the bear which had chased her to begin with. Though it would be nothing to cut the Silver Flower loose with its own bite, it wasn't something she could throw, nor something she could shoot. To use the bite, the Huntress would have to draw close to the thing in the darkness, and the thought of that rotted her stomach with nausea. But she was not certain of the choice she had, because a liquid thick as tree sap and the olive drab of dying grass dripped from above. It sizzled through the guano only feet from her, burning down into the excrement, its sulfurous stench so vile the Huntress could only gag.

What fate, this! She had eaten so many creatures of the Forest! What would it be like to be eaten, herself? It would hurt, she was certain. She did animals the dignity of killing them before eating them, but animals were never so kind to each other. She was going to suffer and felt it all in a flash as if it happened to her then and there; but the horror of that suffering forced her to move, to snatch up the Silver Flower. At the moment she did, so, too, did the venom of the Beast trail toward the chain; in the end, she needed not cut the Flower free, for it was the Beast which did it for her. The chain sizzled, loosed with a snap, and she bounded toward the darkness, toward that sliver of monster; though it roared, she plunged the Flower into its flesh, for it was that or death, and perhaps still death. But if she had even the smallest of chances to avoid the fate of the hart, then it was the right thing to do, the only thing to do. She had never held a thing such as this, but her body knew what to do when it was in her grip. In fact, it seemed as if the thing possessed her limbs and swept her toward the Beast of the darkness, the tip of the Flower poised to meet the wall of scales.

As the Flower penetrated the Beast, it erupted in a cry sharper than the screams of thirty tortured mountain lions. The Huntress gasped, as did the Silver Flower, and she jerked her grip upward toward the innards of the creature, then slipped loose the blade from its guts once they were well perforated. With a more wretched cry, the Beast shrank away, but, to the Huntress' wonder, a new sap poured from the wound before it withdrew to the darkness. This cerulean ichor dripped upon the guano floor, and from these pools of blood and shit sprang the purest and most beautiful crimson roses the Huntress had ever seen.

"My God," marveled the Silver Flower, "is that all?"

The Huntress winced to face the darkness, wondering the same thing without words, but it seemed the Beast had withdrawn into the squalid blackness of its home. With a cautious eye kept forward and the flat of the Flower balanced on her knee, she crouched to pick three roses, each more beautiful than the last. The third contained, of all things, a spider, which crawled from the petal's cradle to leap, harmless, upon the muck, into which it disappeared.

"Well, girl, you can't sit around cooing at roses all day. Come along."

The Flower hardly needed tell her that, and not least of all because it didn't do any good speaking to her—certainly not now, because the Huntress realized with a start of fear that the voice of the Silver Flower was inside her own ear, where once resided mere nature's impulse! It terrified her, and yet she felt as if she could not put the object down. If she did for even an instant, the Beast would return and she would be dead. She gave a soft coo, an attempt to shush it, and turned the way she'd come, the tunnel which had let her into the strange black cave and opened back to freedom—and the bear. Though, it might have grown bored. And even if it had not grown bored, she knew the Flower could banish not just Beasts of darkness, but Beasts of the Forest, too. What was this Beast of the darkness, after all, but a Beast of the Forest above? With her bow again over her shoulder and the Flower in her hand, the Huntress trudged back, the tunnel's darkness lit by the pallid glow of the Flower which chattered in her ear without least intent to stop.

"As fun as it is for me to see you less than your best for once, Miss Perfect, I'm afraid we have to do something. Get your memory back, that's what we need. Why, it's like a nursery tale! An adventure. We shall steal back your memory, and see if we can't get you talking again, too. To make you mute! That heinous woman. I appreciate what you did for me, or what you were trying to do for me, at any rate, but you really ought to have pushed that old banshee off the horse and saved yourself. Father would have been a lot happier. Not to mention the City!"

Oh, what was it going on about! It was like a bird awakening too early, alert in its nest and singing her awake before she was ready, but somehow so much worse. At least birds stopped for breath! And a brook, at least, was a pleasant, murmuring sort. So what could be said of this thing which bit and babbled and seemed to do nothing nice but cut down her enemies or sometimes show visions of Man?

Ah! Ah, Man! The thought of Man crowned by roses of the type she carried stopped her stride, and while the Flower sighed, "Oh, dear God, what is it now," she felt her throat close, beset again by the image, almost as she had been when the Flower had shown her, though somehow less clear. The feeling of him came more as when she, say, hunted a boar, and in that instant felt the accumulation of all the boars she had already killed, and thus had the knowledge and impressions required to kill the present prey. Any memories she could be said to have came to her without consciousness, unsorted perceptions swelling to form the basis of instinct without personal meaning. No images she had encountered in her life stood out, yet one single day had given her two moments which crowded her mind: the embittered hart and the crucified Man.

"Ah," sighed the Huntress, gripping tight the handle of the Flower, "ah!"

"What are you going on about?"

"Ah," came another, sadder sigh, and her free hand lifted to her heart, patting there.

"You're...sad. Hurt? Lonely."

The babbling wasn't helpful, wasn't showing her the image of Man again. Irritated, she considered the walls of the tunnel. Her free hand lifted to pat the nearest, and upon her toes she stretched to touch the stunted ceiling. "Ah!"

"Dear God, I'm in hell. You like rocks? Rocks? Are you talking about the tunnel we're in? Yes, this is a tunnel."

"Hm." Falling back upon her heels, the Huntress patted her head because that was also where she had seen Man, and where she heard the babbling of the Flower. Could she be clearer? She arched one eyebrow at the silly thing in expectation of its understanding, only to decipher a sharp sigh before another inundation of babbling.

"Ridiculous! Am I to read your mind? Realistically speaking, I'm sure I could, if you had any capacity for language. But you don't, darling. And while you are, of course, more delightful than ever before, I'm afraid this is not going to be helpful to our communication. Oh, sure, I can get vague impressions, but whatever you're going on about isn't getting through."

The thing just wasn't understanding. Biting her lip, the Huntress sorted through the rocks at her feet. The oblivious Flower carried on, "I'm sure we could work out a system of pictographs or some elaborate symbolic language. We can get basic expressions across. Danger, for instance!"

The image of snarling wolves came over the Huntress, a vision so urgent that she gave a cry and gripped tight the Flower. As she did, the panic of snarls relented to the soothing rush of a waterfall, and she sighed as she clutched a piece of black rock, narrowing her eyes in a critical way for her companion. It could frighten her, but not show her Man when she pleased!

"See," continued the Flower, unaware of her displeasure, "we have no problem communicating basic things. But what about higher-level concepts? For instance, oh…economics. Politics. The shape of the stable boy's rear. The important things, my girl! I've not had a civilized chat in ages."

With her tongue between her teeth, the Huntress clutched her rock of choice and thrust it against the wall of the cave, her lines sharpened by urgency as much as displeasure. As the Flower babbled, she drew, and then, stepping back, swept the chatty thing up high that its gem might see the message she had to impart. "Ah," she emphasized to interrupt it. As its useless words halted, comprehension was marked by a gasp.

"Oh! The King!" She lifted the Flower higher to allow it to see the sketchy depiction of the crucified figure, a black halo emanating from its skull as she had seen the roses crowning Man's. "Yes, yes, my girl, the King!"

It was no use. The Flower was no more capable of understanding her than perhaps the birds, or the deer. But, as her hand lifted to touch the image which she had produced, the King came upon her with the same vivid intensity as before: no memory, this, but an image given unto her by the Flower which she clutched when confronted by the image of Man straining to release himself from the inky manacles which bound him.

"Ah," cried the Huntress, patting the stone wall as though it were his face, then giving another, far sadder cry when she remembered he was not there.

"I know. I miss the old man, too. That's how desperate I am! It was so good to see him again after all we went through, then we get home and what happens?" Had he still a head, he might have shaken it. "Consider yourself lucky you were out of commission for the horror show. It was like nothing I've seen, or want to see again."

The Flower could babble on all day, so long as it kept showing her images of Man. The heave of his chest inspired in her ears the phantom beating of his heart, along with the fear those phantom beats might end. Her hand still on the face of the image, cold upon the wall of the cave, she cried at the Flower and shook it, tried to draw its eye closer to the dream.

"Girl," it shrieked, "let's be calm, Felicity, if you please! The King, yes. Do you know where the King is, darling? Here." Its empty words rang between her ears, their reverberations clearing away the King, whose image faded into a black spire which rose amid ruins dancing in chartreuse flame. She gasped at the vision, the sight of this Tower in a desolate landscape, and squeezed shut her eyes against the yawning terror it instilled in the pit of her belly. It seemed to her for all the world she stood beneath that Tower, yet also above it, and beside it, infinitely small and large at once. Just as she started to panic under the force of the consuming sight and all the terrors it somehow represented, it vanished, and she stood with the Silver Flower clutched in her white-knuckled hands, alone in the tunnel beneath the tree, staring at the crucified shadow of Man.

"You understand, now, darling," asked the hopeful Flower, "where he is?"

The Huntress exhaled a mixture of relief to be back and disappointment at the Flower, then patted its brass hilt, the color and texture of the setting sun on a clouded day. In the condescending fashion of true ignorance, she shook her head in pity and marched on, and the Flower was left to sigh, itself.

"I had serious doubts about you until you and the Witch rescued me, and even that wasn't the wisest move, O Wisest Woman in the Kingdom. But I don't suppose it does much good telling you that. There's no point in showing you, either, not without context. Supposing I just showed you all the details of your former life. The state you're in, without any background or sense of yourself, why, it would not only seem like it all happened to somebody else, but it would terrify you, I'm sure! You're practically a walking baby. My God, what are we going to do! What if you never reach the Tower?" The Flower's gasp was so melodramatic that, had it hands, it might have slapped them upon its own mouth. "What if you simply spend eternity wandering around the Forest, picking berries and rolling about in your little deerskins! Oh, Felicity, no-no, we mustn't let that happen. There has to be some way to get you understanding. Do you see, girl, that the King is in the Tower? You like the King, don't you? I— Oh, ugh, what is that smell?"

The Huntress had been aware of the odor for ten feet or so, rising like the scent of thunder across her olfactories, and it had narrowed her eyes as much as stifled her breathing. This was the smell of no bear, she marked. This was a far more terrible, more rancid stench: an acrid filth that clung to her sinuses, burned her eyes, and reminded her of the cave whence the Silver Flower had emerged, though it was as if that scent had been compacted a thousand times over. It was with horror that she marked the rumble as, at her feet, stones trembled.

"Girl," gasped the Flower, in similar revelation, "I think we'd ought to go."

But there was no need to tell her, because she was off, sprinting with her head as low as she could keep it, skipping over stones and grateful more than ever for the new light which revealed every crack and nook and rock over which she had once tripped. Now all was clear to her, clear as the glimpses of the Beast closing in behind her, its body slithering through the tunnels, clawed hands sinking into rock to propel it after her, desperate to have her, screaming like a woman awakening from a nightmare yet groaning like a man dying from liver failure. The Huntress released a cry of her own, pumping her arms and rounding one last corner to see a white sliver of light within the shrinking corridor. As the Flower cried, "Oh, God, thank you, God!" the Beast behind them swiped out a filth-coated claw to rip a lewd tatter from the leather of the Huntress' breastplate, by some luck or dexterity only taking part of her armor and neither her flesh, nor her bow, which she feared might break, anyway, as she thrust first the Flower, then her own body, through the impossibly tight crevice of the tree which had sheltered both the Flower and the Beast. Face-first, the Huntress burst from the bark with a gasp and fell with the Flower, stumbling forward, using its silver stem to clamber over a gnarled root in escape around the edge of the tree just as the foul-smelling shadow penetrated open air. Scrambling back against the bark, she hyperventilated, clutched the Flower, then caught the sound of another furious animal raging through the underbrush.

"What is it now," whined the Flower, but the Huntress was rapt as the bear charged from the trees, finding instead of the Huntress the semi-living Beast which tried, inch by black inch, to extricate itself from the depths of the earth. Driven by bloodlust, perhaps, or by the still-nearby scent of the Huntress (however faint beneath the guano of the Beast), the bear descended upon the monster, sinking first claw, then tooth into the terrible flesh and receiving in repayment the burning venom which dripped from its mouth. Huge-eyed, the Huntress watched with the silenced Flower: the bear tore apart the monster, the monster dissolved the bear, and when what was left of the Beast receded, mindless, back into the depths of the tree with all the skittering of a half-dead cockroach, the bear let out one last moan while sizzling in its own innards. Rising to trembling feet mere yards from the puddles of gore and half-dissolved flowers blooming in the dirt from the creature's sapphire bile, the Huntress held the Flower to her breast as though it were an old and traumatized friend.

"I hate this place," it insisted, its voice at a high pitch. "I hate this Forest, I hate that cave, I hate these animals. I hate everything here. Oh, Felicity! I was a Prince, once!" The Flower moaned in outrage as the Huntress backed away from the vile scene, her stomach burning as she shook it from sight by dint of the thick trees into which she faded. "I'm not certain I'm going to make it. It's not exactly as if I can die of thirst or hunger or exhaustion anymore, but maybe if I try hard enough I can die of pessimism. I know you ladies went through quite a lot of work to get me back and all, and I do so appreciate it, but what kind of life is this? What, exactly, am I to do!"

What was anyone at all to do, to begin with! Only what they needed at the given moment. What the Huntress needed at that moment was what she had needed from the outset of the day: the bath she had been after when she first awoke. Oh, the touch of the stream! Let her be rinsed clean, free of the filth of the night and the hunt and the cave! Let her feel like an animal again, and not like the Beast!

That Beast. She trembled to think of it, realizing that it came upon her with the same feeling as the image of the Tower rising high to pierce the sooty clouds. Were they related? She felt toward the Beast the way she might toward a baby bear, assessing the Tower. It seemed to her as if the black spire were a thing of evil: the inevitable development of the Beast, or perhaps some concentration of it. The very idea sickened the

Huntress, but the violence of her stomach gave way to another, similar rawness, and she remembered her abandoned hart, uneaten and lost. Sacrilege. But, wasteful or not, she still needed to feed herself, and it seemed priority over even a dip in the stream. With narrowed eyes and attention focused away from the babbling Flower, the Huntress followed the messages of the trees and stones and moss, all familiar friends pointing the way to one of countless food sources. Indeed, it was not long by her reckoning before they emerged in a familiar grove, smaller than the one which was her home but where she found with joy that the fruit trees had, of late, been unmolested by the birds.

"What fortune"—the Flower's voice bounced as the Huntress leaned up to caress fruit hanging from a low bough—"apricots. My Father, but aren't they delicious."

With a gentle hand, the Huntress set the Flower tip-down on the earth, its pommel against the tree. As she grasped the fruit which she had tested, the Flower lamented, "I used to love apricots. They were my favorite when I had a mouth. Remember the ones in Father's garden? Naturally, you don't. But I certainly do, so soft and sweet, and small, but more flavorful than any peach...oh, you don't care."

First one, then two, fruits rested in the hands of the Huntress, who fell upon her rear before the Flower. She took a bite, first the right one, then the left, and delight lit her face like the glow of aurora as the Flower, near outraged, moaned, "Apricots, apricots! Eternity in this form for one more bloody apricot! Oh," it sighed, not noticing how the Huntress had lowered the fruit from her lips and come to stare at him, chewing, her eyes keen with the intense focus she devoted only to birds, or images of the King, or bucks, or wolves, or bears encountered in the underbrush, "I wish you could speak. I wish you could tell me if they're decent, if nothing else. I miss my apricot tree," it said, and, at last, to get its attention, the Huntress shoved the Flower so off-kilter that it fell to the ground with a startled cry.

"What is it?" it demanded, and the Huntress, poised upon her knees, presented to its jeweled pommel the palm-size fruit.

"Apricot," she said in the most careful of ways, in a near-giddy way, the word bubbling up like the babble of a brook. She laughed, and fell upon her backside, while, thunderstruck, the Flower gasped.

"What? Yes! Yes! Apricot, yes, that's right, girl! Apricot!"

"Apricot," she said again, and the Flower laughed in delight.

"Oh, tree! Tree, I could shake your branch. My girl, yes, that fruit you are eating is an apricot. 'I eat apricots.' Can you say that for me? 'I eat apricots.'"

"Apricots," she babbled, enchanted by the fruit as if they were all which existed. As she cradled one to her heart, she nibbled the other and regarded the Flower with pacified doe's eyes.

"I am terribly pleased by the breakthrough, but with us on the other side, let's see progress. Oh," it exhaled as she did, each for individually motivated exasperation. "Girl, I know I had ought to be easy on you, but I remember your voice from before all of this. It was nice enough, all considered. I'd like to hear it again. Say 'girl' for me. Do you know who 'girl' is? Girl, girl."

"Girl," parroted the Huntress, and the Flower gave another sigh, but this, for relief.

"Yes, girl! 'Girl eats apricots,' you see? You're the girl. Girl."

Slowly, the Huntress lifted the fruit which she had cradled to her breast, then jumped at the sharpness of the Flower's tone as it chided, "No! No: 'girl', not 'apricot.' 'Girl,' do you know 'girl'?"

"Girl," hummed the wincing Huntress over her shoulder, at the trees, the vines, the weeds and grasses and bugs, and then, at last, down at her own body, at which she laughed. "Ah! Ah, girl! Girl?" She patted her heart with the fruit and the Flower might have clapped, had it hands.

"Yes! Girl! Would that I could kiss without drawing your blood. 'Girl eats apricot,' you see? 'Girl eats apricot.'"

"Girl-eats-apricot," she tried, the noise coming guttural, untrained, but soft and beautiful for all its time of salvaging. She covered her mouth with a surprised laugh, dropping the mostly eaten left apricot to the forest floor. "Ah! 'Eats'!" With delight, she ravaged the remaining apricot, overjoyed by her small understanding of the Flower's noises. Perhaps that would soften the ones it was always making.

"Yes! That's just so, ha-ha, you little barbarian. Ah, dear girl, I'm so pleased. Yes, my girl, yes, you enjoy eating your apricot."

"Apricot," murmured the Huntress again, smiling, not at all for her companion, but just for herself, and for the succulent fruit, ripe, half-devoured, in the palm of her pale hand.

What funny sounds the Flower made, and how funny they were to repeat to it—funnier even than chirping after the birds as she so often did in the morning. Babbling seemed to please the Flower, and had quieted the thing enough that she was able to eat in peace. But all this noise had her thinking of noises, and what they meant. There were many funny noises in the Forest, after all. The Huntress had heard birds singing and elk groaning and bears snarling, and yet it seemed she had never heard her own noise. What noise, exactly, was hers? Each creature had his own. Perhaps Man could teach her their noise. She smiled at the thought, at the dream-image of him where she lay for a time after eating, but soon shook herself from it, for the tree above was rich in fruits. It seemed sensible to collect more for the journey, but birds were always helping themselves to things from high in the trees, so perhaps they knew something she didn't. Staring down at herself and over her shoulder, the Huntress frowned at the Flower.

"Yes? What is it, you delightful girl?"

"Girl," repeated the Huntress, reaching over with her free hand to wiggle a thick brown vine curled around a tree near the apricots. Finding it sturdy, but flexible for her purposes, the Huntress fell back a step, lifted the Flower, and, amid metallic protests, hacked at the vine.

"Ah! Blast it, Felicity! Do you think it's a picnic, being a sword? Not at all! I do feel every impact, I—oh, that's fine"—it dropped to the ground so the Huntress could free the vine—"no, don't worry about me, Felicity, just leave me here. I'll be perfectly fine."

Humming in mimicry of the birds, the Huntress studied the Flower and set to work with the vine, wrapping it around the hilt, then removing it so she could sling it experimentally around her shoulder. "I suppose I'd ought to get used to it, being an inanimate object and all. Oh, sure, it was refreshing to see a human face, but now that I'm out and about we'll see what it amounts to. Being dropped on the ground will be the least of my problems if something happens to you and some stranger gets their paws on me. You hear me, girl? Nothing can happen to you."

Tongue in the pocket of her cheek, the Huntress tied one loop to be slung around her chest, then added a second for the Flower, modeled after the thong which held the quiver upon her back. This thing had always been there for her to carry her quiver, so it seemed a fine example, and, in the end, she fashioned a second thing in the image of the first: lesser, but still perfect because she had made it. Pleased, she turned and showed it to the Flower with a sparkling, "Ah!" of pleasure.

"And just what is that supposed to be?" asked the snotty weapon, but it had its question answered as, cheerful, the Huntress whisked up the Flower, slipped it into the smaller loop, and strapped it to her back.

"Girl-eats-apricots," she sang, "apricots, apricots."

"Ah," uttered the Flower, faltering as the Huntress assessed the apricot tree, "I see. Very well, thank you, darling. You have always done a fine job considering me."

Oblivious to the backhanded praise of her companion, the Huntress reached up and, hand on branch and foot on root, mounted the tree. "Be careful," nagged the Flower, but the Huntress could not be distracted, since this was a task requiring utmost concentration. One could never be too careful climbing a tree! The art of tree climbing was a worthwhile venture, however, for the Huntress found the farther up they were, the more succulent the fruit, thick apricots bursting around tiny pits until all the way at the top of the tree the Huntress discovered apricots with flesh as sumptuous as its seeds microscopic. It was these which she took with cries of triumphant joy, forced to poke her head out from the thickly leafed branches to have some sense of direction while she picked. As balanced as she was, she was just as focused, and so might not otherwise have noticed the black thing which cut the distant sky—but it was such a vicious and ugly and terrible sight she could not help but see it, and found, indeed, that the distant Tower rising above the other side of the Forest dominated her attention as soon as she, gasping, recognized its shape beneath the bleakly colored clouds.

"Aha, there it is! You see, Felicity? That's where she has the King."

"Girl," said the Huntress uncertainly, cradling one apricot to her breast while another tumbled to the ground below her.

"I know, she certainly is a wretched— Oh, why do I bother? It's rather like talking to one's dog. Felicity, oh, my dear, I never knew I could miss you. You *are* in there, you fluttery, fair-hearted thing. You have to be in there somewhere."

"Eats," whispered the Huntress, thinking of the putrid Beast from before, then, again, of the Tower. The Huntress had not even known her Forest to have an end, let alone that its end should give way to something so wicked!

"Eats? No, girl, good God. She's not going to eat him. Not literally, anyway. Although"—here, the Flower paused, sucking on teeth it no longer had but still felt in the phantasmic manner of amputated extremities—"she *is* a Witch. That doesn't necessarily imply cannibalism, does it? Oh, dear."

Anxious, the Flower turned its gaze, and that of the Huntress, toward the King: even though he was still bound to the wall, he was also in the arms of an exquisite woman most terrible, whose dove-white flesh further deadened her stare, whose hair was the night bereft of stars, and whose gown was the abominable depths of a sea home to creatures too terrible for the sun's eye.

"Ah," said the Huntress, heartbroken to see Man in the arms of Other while she was helpless, unable to free him from this place which he seemed to so detest. His bearded face tensed as his pale eyes turned toward the cold amusement of his captor, to whom he said something which the Huntress could not hear and would not have managed to understand. It hardly mattered. What mattered was the slick blackness of the wall to which Man was bound. Why, she knew that awful stuff! The Beast was of that stuff! The Tower was of that stuff! Man was held, surely, in the depths of that rotting black fang which dwarfed the Mountains far beyond impenetrable trees. Awe sowed the seeds of terror in her heart as the vast world grew all the vaster. She, shaking her head, pressed against the thick branch which supported her, and flattened further when it seemed the bone-white woman turned briquette eyes toward the Huntress as though she knew she was being watched.

"You can hardly be afraid of a bit of effort, girl. You live in a Forest!"

"Girl," repeated the sullen Huntress, thinking of the woman who caressed Man's face.

"Oh, you're not just a girl, Felicity. A very clever young woman: a lost Queen who is going to get us across this Forest, free our King, and retrieve your memory and my body, and who is so kind and sweet that she will turn a blind eye to all of the things I've been saying to her, assuming she remembers them at all."

"Apricots," she said, which, had she been feeling herself, might have been an assurance of her memory. Humming, she gazed beyond the trees, beyond even the distant spire, which inspired again the face of Man and a throb of love for how terrified he must have been. It seemed to the Huntress she needed to save Man. She had been the one to wound the Beast, after all, before the bear sent it scuttling back into the dark of the cave for what she hoped was for good. If this Silver Flower of hers could conquer a monster, perhaps it could conquer the woman who surely animated it, whose blackness of night and whiteness of bone pumped cold terror into the Huntress's veins. Newly dedicated, she descended the tree, taking two additional fruits and half listening to the musical babble of the Flower as she planned their route across the Forest.

"She's no joke, my girl, regardless of how little power she may have actually had when she was just sitting in her shack in the swamp. I've never seen anything like it. You don't ever expect magic to be real, do you? I thought all that Witch business was a myth. But apparently there's really something to it, seeing as I'm a sword, and all. Really turns your world upside down."

Lowering upon the ground, the Huntress shifted hair from her face and scrutinized the sumptuous canopy. With no conception of time and hardly any of abstract distance, the Huntress only knew that the black spire rose from a place she had never been, never seen, and so she was not certain how, exactly, she might arrive. But the only way for her to get anywhere was to begin, so into the trees she marched, her keen ears tuned to the sounds of the Forest, and her eyes set to pierce the foliar shade with the pale light of the Flower.

3

There was no way to know how far they marched that day, nor to recount all the words tumbling from the Silver Flower which, alone for so long, seemed to have noise stored up inside. Or perhaps that was just the way of Flowers which made noise? The Huntress had never seen such a thing before, after all. What was she to know of the language of Flowers when she herself was a silent creature? If only she had noises of her own. Perhaps she might sing back to it, instead of whistling and twittering in the background like a bird as she moved between dense trees, hoisted herself over collapsing logs, and drew ever deeper into parts of the Forest unknown, darker than the parts she loved and full of strange new insects, black-eyed beetles observing her with mechanical wing twitches from the golden spiral of a fern.

"Such a mess." The Flower's sounds emanated from her back, where its eye gazed the far way they had come. "All these plants, this mud and the dirt...and the bugs! Ugh." A fly landed upon the Huntress's forehead and was swatted away without a second thought. "Absolutely wretched. Speaking of: When was the last time you took a bath, Felicity? Remember those?"

While it was true she did not know what a "bath" was, a bath was yet what she imagined as, in the humid hothouse of the deeper Forest, smaller weeds were replaced by bunches of white and orange mushrooms which sprang amid the flowers and shrubs. As the Huntress bent to examine a few to determine their suitability for eating, across her mind flashed a pleasant doe who ate a different one and died soon thereafter. It seemed to her there was no knowing which mushrooms would bring death and which wouldn't; so, stomach growling like a wild dog, the Huntress reached into her quiver in hopes of an apricot and instead pricked herself upon the thorn of a forgotten rose. A hiss of upset twisted past her teeth, and, withdrawing her hand, she gazed accusingly at yet another wound, and at the ground which played host to the lost drops of blood. But even her blood, it seemed, was different that day, for she gasped as it gathered itself together, each drop combining with its brethren. As she stumbled back, it pulsed to life, growing into the body of a red-and-green Serpent, perfectly formed, upon the ground before her.

"Girl," said the Serpent, and, "apricots," so that the Huntress would find it well-disposed. Though her hand had been upon the hilt of the Flower, it relaxed at the animal's voice, and she laughed slightly, still leery of nearing. The Serpent regarded her with equal caution, retreating just so to a plume of peonies. Amid all this strangeness clamored on the Flower, whose noise rose like alarm bells through the mind of the Huntress.

"My God! A snake, emerging from your blood, as though it were normal."

"It is normal," insisted the Serpent, and the Huntress gasped, "Ah!" because she realized by the similarity of their noises that what was on her back was not a Silver Flower at all but rather something quite like the Serpent at her feet. This, she fretted over, for she knew that snakes were slow killers, and in consequence wondered down at the hand which the Silver Flower had nipped when first they met. In her fancy, she felt a pulse of distant, infectious pain and pictured with immediate panic that the wound would be far worse than it was.

"Dear God," said the Silver one, its ruby eye filled with the instinctual imagining of the wound and tricked by it, taking the image for reality even though her real, cleanly cut, and only slightly dirty hand was visible to the naked eye, "it's infected? How is it possible? I'll have you know I may have been trapped in that cave, madam, but I am quite clean despite the bats. There is no way at all that an infection so vile and so fast-acting is any of *my* doing."

"Ah," she cried, holding her hand to her breast and unable to examine it for fear of what she might find, "girl, girl!"

"And what is the matter with girl?" asked the amused Serpent.

"At the very least *you* can speak. But can't you see? This must be your doing. You came from her blood only after she pricked her wounded hand on that rose, and that rose came from the Witch's Beast, so I think it is more than evident that this is your doing, vile snake."

"I am still not entirely certain what injury you're on about. Her little cut, you mean?"

"Girl," cried the Huntress, fearing her time at its end, feeling as one of her arrows might just before impact. Oh, she was filthy! How cracking and crumbling she felt! If only she'd had time for just one bath before she met the hart's fate, before she fell to pieces amid the plants of the Forest.

"See? You've broken her heart, wretched snake!"

"I can hardly be held accountable, my dear Sword, for I was only just born into this form; though, I have seen all things. Can be all things. Perhaps it is better to say I have just come into the world."

"Just like a snake to play games like that, girl. Get away!"

"Apricots, girl," said the Serpent, tone charming as possible. "I remember you've some sweet apricots in your quiver. Maybe you've one for me? I'm very hungry."

"Nothing for snakes," insisted the Silver thing, and in that moment, with another soft, "Ah," the Huntress made another linguistic connection.

"Snakes!" Between the one upon her back and the one on the ground, she gasped and nodded and insisted again, "Snake," but then paused, wondering about the Silver one. Was that so? Was this thing truly a snake? It was more rigid than one, and its invisible teeth were all over. Though she learned about new things by comparing them to known things, there were perhaps some labels which were simply not suited. But, still: the word "snake" felt closer than the image "flower," which in turn felt closer than the void which had existed before gazing upon this object. Now her mind was filled by the sound "snake" when she thought of it, and so it was that the Flower had become to the Huntress a Snake, and the sound floated through her mind in the color of silver.

"Wonderful," grumbled the Silver Snake to its ground-bound cousin, "now she thinks I'm a snake."

"You could hardly be a snake, my good man. You are far too lacking in finesse, and far too clever for your own good. Or hers."

"Here I thought snakes had the market cornered on cleverness."

"Not at all. Why, the wisdom of a snake arises almost exclusively from the fact that it slithers on the ground. Hardly a clever mode of transport. Of wisdom and cleverness, the latter is more comfortable, to be certain. Better to be a Sword strapped to the back of a comely lass, in need of a bath though she is."

"In need of a bath and an antidote," insisted the Silver Snake again, fearing the poison and reigniting ancestral fears in the fluttering heart of the Huntress. "Whatever you did when you came out of her must have caused her putrefaction. Horrible—like an opened grave!"

"Perhaps consider looking at it," suggested the helpful mistletoe-colored Serpent. "Or, she could."

Livid, the Silver Snake turned its attention to the Huntress, who groaned as arose another vision of her surely rotting hand. Fear filled her so that her stomach writhed in nausea of what must have been the venom of the Serpent, or perhaps even the overdue stuff of the Silver Snake. So faint that she stumbled against the nearest oak, she glimpsed, from the corner of her eye, her muck-ridden hand—and it gave her pause. Frowning, she lifted her hand, turned it this way, that way; then, after scraping with her nail some of the muck from near her cut, she scowled over her shoulder at the ridiculous Silver Snake.

"Snake," she chided, brandishing her hand to prove her companion had allowed their imaginations to run away with them. "Girl! Snake eats, no."

"Well you've learned 'no' fast enough," muttered the Silver Snake before it emitted a cry as both it and its sling were dropped to the ground. "I beg your pardon, Felicity! You may be a little savage, but I think you can at least find it in you to have some courtesy."

"One can hardly be expected to show courtesy to so rude a Sword as you, good man," said the Serpent in laconic fashion. It slithered down the flat of the blade to wrap about the hilt, where its chin lay against the pommel while the Huntress retrieved from her quiver an apricot. "Or perhaps I had ought to say 'boy,' as you insist on diminishing the woman who rescued you."

Had the Silver Snake a face, it might have burned, but the ruby upon which the Serpent laid its head seemed to serve that purpose. "I beg your pardon? You certainly seem to know it all, so you had ought to know who I am."

"The very same might be said to you," suggested the Serpent before rearing its head toward the Huntress. "Remember my voice, Huntress, Felicity, Queen? This face and form are foreign, but something in me speaks to you familiarly, does it not?"

So far as she was concerned, she had never seen the Serpent in all waking memory, and thus could not have answered in the affirmative had she understood anything but the word "Felicity," which was becoming a popular noise for snakes to make, and more curious still because she could not tie it to any one thing. A curious noise, considering she was far more used to such creatures hissing! As though reading her perceptions, the Serpent's eyes glittered with delight while the Silver Snake insisted, "Of course she doesn't remember you. She's never met you. I certainly haven't."

The girl, meanwhile, asked, "Felicity?"

The nodding Serpent met her eyes. "Yes, my dear: Felicity. A fine name for a woman in your state," he added, eyes twinkling in lieu of the smile whose permanence rendered it bereft of meaning. "Girl eats apricots, Felicity?"

"Girl," affirmed with a nod, beginning to nibble on the fruit in her hand.

"Well, she shall eat far more than that when we reach the City."

"You know the way?"

"I do, though our Huntress fair does, too. Have you no faith, though she found you hidden in the squalid depths of the earth?"

"Forgive me for lacking faith in somebody who articulates with the capacity of a rattled toddler."

"Her tongue will find its way back to her in time." Unwinding from the Silver Snake, now, the Serpent glided across the Forest floor to experimentally slither near the Huntress, who stiffened; a Serpent was still a Serpent, and no apricot, however soft and delicious, could distract her from the potential danger of its presence. "Just as she, in time, shall find her way to the City. Frankly, it would be far easier for her and me to find the City without you, but she shall have some difficulty in its navigation once there without your help. You'd ought to keep a clear head."

"How could you possibly know anything about what's going on? You just sprang out of her blood!"

"As I said: I am of the world. I have knowledge of many things which happen on its surface, and of all occurring in its depths. And because all things occur, in truth, in the depths, I do, indeed know all."

"Then why not share some of it?" asked the irritated Silver Snake, while, in experiment, the Huntress broke off part of her apricot to set it before the Serpent, which made no move to strike.

"There are certain forms of knowledge which may only be received by firsthand experience—thank you, darling—and all forms of wisdom are this, in truth. For it is one thing to know something, but an entirely different thing to experience it." Jaw unhinged, the Serpent consumed in one swallow the chunk of apricot. This inspired a giddy laugh from the Huntress, who had never seen a thing so silly as a snake eating fruit.

"Snake eats apricot." The Huntress giggled, and the Silver Snake snorted.

"Whoever heard of a snake eating apricots. What sort of snake are you supposed to be?"

Crooked jaw dangling upon its head, the Serpent slurred, "No snake, my good man," with a grunt as its jaw popped back into place and a few seconds' pause as it worked it back and forth. "No more than I am truly the blood of our Huntress dear. Recall, won't you, whence I came?"

"Yes, yes, a load of nonsense. A snake, springing from blood." The Silver Snake gave a sigh of irritation as the Huntress wiped her hands upon her knees, then bounced to her feet and bent to claim her weapon. "Since you seem to be so unhelpful regarding the matter your substance, could you at least tell me why you're here?"

"If you consider it logically, I was never not here to begin with," suggested the Serpent, slithering after the Huntress as she set again upon her quest. "But as to why I have emerged, that is a perfectly simple matter: our Huntress pricked herself upon the rose of the Beast."

The sigh which overcame the Silver Snake was a belabored one, indeed. "Oh, yes, flawless logic, old chap. How I didn't see it before is beyond me."

"And me, as well. It is basic arithmetic."

That said, the Serpent fell into the pattern of its slithering and found pace just ahead of the Huntress, where it led the silent way for quite some time. Into the depths of the Forest, the Huntress marched, armed with her bow and Silver Snake, her eyes and ears alert to all things; but she found to her awe and anxiety that the Forest seemed silent, that all which lived that day was the trees, and the ferns, and the mushrooms. Darkness fell, and glowing beetles faded in and out like stars stuck near the earth. She rediscovered the light of the Silver Snake as, beneath the sagging boughs of a poisonous yew, it illuminated her through the night. A good thing; there was no sleep for her, no way for the moon to do its work on her while she hid from the darkness in dreams. By the time the eye of fire returned for the day, her own eyes were just as dry and aching as her body. But in the night, in her exhaustion, she'd dreamt awake of Man while the snakes slept quiet at her feet. Inspired by her dreams of him, she had removed the roses from her quiver to construct a crown the likes of which rested on his head. With artful grace, her fingers danced between the thorns, and with the edge of her nail, she split the stems of each so all three might be woven together. Then, cautiously, she crowned herself, smiling in the eerie glow, pleased, and thinking of Man.

"What a lovely crown," commended the Serpent on waking next morning, as the Huntress shared her second apricot.

"An awful thing," complained the Silver Snake, its eye blinking awake. "Don't you see those thorns? You'll prick yourself!"

But, of course, the Huntress paid no mind to either and ate away as the Serpent reset his jaw. "Surely a few thorn pricks are worth the beauty of a crown such as hers."

"I would expect you to say that; you're probably hoping to get siblings out of the matter."

"Even if a thousand snakes sprung from her blood, we would be but one, my friend. But suffice to say my motives are for the good of our dear Huntress."

"They had better be, seeing as she created you."

"Is that so?"

"You sprang from her blood. Not a normal occurrence, obviously caused by the Witch. Therefore, I can only suppose that our Huntress has created you by some...unconscious, magical means, or some such; either Felicity using the tools of the Witch without realizing it, or the Witch working on Felicity, in which case, you are an evil spy. After all, there's nothing snakelike of Felicity; that a snake, of all creatures, should spring from her blood, is patently absurd."

"Yes, I have developed along with the Huntress, but my presence in her blood is mere consequence of the manner of her most recent birth by way of our mother tree. In truth, I knew her long before and was once independent of her, though her friend. Side by side, we've blossomed under the boughs of our righteous oak, and while she has acted, I have watched. Now, however, it would seem help is called for, so when the rose of the Beast pricked her, I thought it time to emerge."

"Then you admit you're a monster implanted in our perfect Felicity by the Witch-Usurper."

With a laugh so merry the Huntress picked up on it and laughed along with him, the Serpent shook his head. "My good man, for casting so bright a light as you do, your understanding of these things is woefully simple. By that logic, you, too, were created by the Usurper. Or were you born with one ruby eye to start, O Prince?"

"The condescension is quite tiresome," insisted the Silver Snake while the Huntress licked clean her fingers.

"Far better my condescension should be occasional, my dear Prince Sword, or else I should be rather more like you and miss small details while blinded by the light of my own cleverness."

"Oh, yes? What details are these?"

"For instance, you seem keen to point out that no snake has sprung from the blood of a woman in this Forest, but whence came the Forest to begin with?"

Oblivious to the argument, the Huntress peered through the fingers of trees and over her shoulder, toward the side of the Forest which was yet untouched by sunlight. She remembered how she had seen the fang-like spire which held Man rising amid the Mountains, and how the Mountains had been on the side of the Forest opposite the sun, who, at the time, had traveled in the direction of his home for sleep. Now that he was waking up, it meant she was to walk toward him to find the spire, and so she did, sleepy snails retreating and nocturnal bugs retiring amid the unceasing babble of the serpents. Here and there she grasped a few scattered words.

"I suppose I'm not sure what you're asking," the Silver Snake admitted at last, and the Serpent, who slithered by the Huntress's side, chuckled.

"At least you can admit one small parcel of mind where your light cannot shine! But that is the way of the Usurper: she has muddied your memory with her filth, so you think the Forest was always here. But even I, who live bound to flesh as consequence of our Huntress's rebirth, recall plainly that this Forest did not surround your Father's fair capital. Once, my good man, what lay in this spot was a City, which was surrounded by the fields of farms—and beyond that, a patch of Woods. But it has overgrown, and you mistake it. The City is not where you think it is."

"Why, the City is still there!" Triumphant, the light of the Silver Serpent turned the prideful gold of the sun. "Oh, poor Serpent! You've no faith. You think the Witch really has such power? Please. Father's City is so well built that my only concern is how we'll reach her Tower if we make it past the walls. I'm not worried that she's turned it into a bunch of trees."

A most convenient thing that the Serpent's mouth was in a permanent smile, though it still turned its head to hide the expression lest the Silver Snake take offense. "Some things must be experienced, I suppose."

"Well, I mean, really. This whole thing is absurd enough: she built a giant spire, turned me into a sword, put a snake in a woman's blood, and, oh, yes, resurrected that woman from the dead. And I don't mean the 'daring journey into Elysium' resurrection like I got, more the 'soul-stuff wrenched violently from the death-beyond-death' sort of resurrection. Or did you forget that part of the story, know-it-all? If you were to say that the Witch created an old-growth Forest and made me believe it was always there, that would practically make her God."

Though the Serpent seemed eager to make a response, the word "Now" was stuck in its open mouth as its attention was snagged to a nearby tree. The Serpent emitted a hiss which so startled the Huntress she leapt away as it said, "See there! All creatures of this Forest arise from the Usurper!"

As the Huntress and the Silver Snake turned their attention to the shadowy tree, a towering raptor concealed in its branches descended in a flurry of screams and necrotic feathers. Amid the cries of the trio, it snatched the Serpent for its prey.

"Ah," cried the Huntress, sprinting after it, but the Silver Snake moaned.

"What are you doing? Helping the snake!"

"Snake," she cried. "No eat Snake!"

"Let him go! Good riddance to awful rubbish!"

Tears of panic filled the Huntress's eyes. It was not often, after all, that one met so pleasant a snake as that; nor was it often that a snake sprang from one's blood, a most curious phenomenon which endowed in her a responsibility toward it: though she knew she had not created it, it was nonetheless her friend. She cried out, chasing after the dark interloper, keenly aware that she had only two arrows in her quiver, and that to waste them when she had so little time to make more would be her undoing. Her shot had to be clear, and it seemed as if the Forest only grew darker for as quickly as the eagle flew. Pounding heart propelling blood to burning legs, she followed the shouts of the Serpent while blocking out as best she could the staccato drumbeat of her steps and the chiding of the Silver Snake, who seemed for some reason to disagree with her pursuit. Was she wrong to do it? Was the Serpent unsafe, going to hurt her in the end?

But only one of the snakes had bitten her, and it was not the Serpent. More dedicated to helping the kindly reptile, the Huntress slipped free her bow and hastened her pursuit, stumbling through patches of blackberries and brambles until, at last, the stygian eagle alighted atop a cherry tree, dead and apart from its living fellows, the ground beneath its roots bereft of little more than dirt and glistening wax mold. Serpent thrashing in its talon, the terrible bird of prey bent to gut the creature in its clutches, and the Huntress let fly her second-to-last arrow, and the Silver Snake said, "Oh, splendid, whatever would we have done without him," for her shot, motivated by plight of her friend, would never miss. Indeed, it struck the eagle through its eye with the wretched thunder crack of shattered skull, and bird and Serpent together tumbled from the tree. Casting aside her weapon, she circled the trunk to find at her feet the dead eagle and no Serpent; it was above her that she discovered her friend, hanging from a forked branch which had caught his long body on the way down and supported now his dizzy frame.

"Marvelous shot, my girl," he applauded muggily, slithering down from the branch and into her waiting arms, where she cradled him to her breast and cooed like a worried dove beneath her rosy crown.

"Ah, snake," she hushed through tears, assessing scales for injury as he slithered upright in her arms, pleased to be crushed against her bosom. "Ah, snake! Snake, sh."

"Ah, girl." The Serpent laughed, draping his body around her shoulder as a human might an arm. "I am quite fine, you see, my darling?"

"'My darling,'" mocked the Silver Snake, its light having reduced once more to passive teal. "I can hardly believe you're buying this, Felicity. He's clearly a spy from the Usurper. Maybe even the Usurper herself, in masculine, serpentine guise!"

"You sound downright paranoid, friend," said the Serpent, gently, as the Huntress reclaimed her bow. He was close to saying more when, in the distance, arose crashing as if of animals, and cries which sounded to the Huntress's ear to be the language of snakes. She perked, attention toward the thunder of boot falls and trio of deep, tree-bark voices which disrupted at last the lush placidity of the whispering Forest:

"It was over here!"

"Are you sure?"

"Maybe it just dropped dead."

"It didn't just drop dead. An arrow took out one of that bitch's eagles like it was a carrier pigeon hit with a rock."

"I doubt we should call her a 'bitch,' since this whole Forest is made of her ears," said one of the voices as the Huntress drew against the dead tree with her hand, for safety's sake, upon the hardened tail of the Silver Snake.

"Maybe we should keep our voices down," answered the third voice, which the Huntress recognized by the sound "Maybe," which became its name.

"Will you give it a rest," began the first voice, which stopped as its source emerged from the trees to see the Huntress, and she, with wide-eyed surprise, saw it. The source of all the noise had not been giant snakes as announced by their language, but, of all things, men. These men, all three different, were nothing like Man, of course, but the sight so astonished her that she froze.

"My God," gasped Maybe, who was short, and blond, and the grubbiest of the three, "is that who I think it is? I mean, I've never really seen her, but—"

"Nonsense," scoffed the second voice. "I sincerely doubt she's come crawling all the way up from the underworld." As this middling, black-haired man spoke, the Serpent whispered the word "Doubt," so the Huntress would know this to be the man's name. Doubt, meanwhile, went on belligerently insisting, "She's clearly some woman they've sent from the City to trick us. Some doppelgänger."

The man with the first voice—tallest, with wild brown hair and a beard thick as the eyebrows shielding his blue eyes—all but roared, "Will you listen to yourself! Will you look around! Will you look at that eagle!" The word had erupted from him so many times by then that it was clear the man's name was "Will," and Will was pointing with vigorous insistence at the body of the eagle. "You really think that bitch is going to let anybody shoot down one of her eagles just to get one over on us?"

Turning his wild eyes upon the Huntress, Will threw down the tool in his hand, a sharp, flat rock attached to a stick. The edge stuck into the ground in a way that made the Huntress jump with surprise, but though she tensed for conflict, her muscles tensed further with unresolved expectation as the man collapsed at her feet and exclaimed, "Your Majesty! Oh, no dream, nor spell, could ever concoct a face so radiant. My very Queen!"

"Thank God." The Silver Snake sighed, and the Huntress knew for certain that only she and the Serpent heard its words, for the men did not turn toward it as one turns toward abrupt sounds, as the Huntress turned over her shoulder toward it even as Will, weeping tremendous tears, kissed her dirty boots.

"You're going to seem very foolish when she speaks up and we discover it's just some peasant girl from the City outskirts," insisted Doubt, stepping over the body of the eagle and nudging it with the toe of his shoe. "But I suppose there's something to be said for her shot."

Maybe, who had been observing beneath the boughs of the nearest living tree, drew closer. "I've never seen the Queen in person," he said again, hushed, "but she's so beautiful, like her paintings, and the statues. Surely it's her."

"How could it be her! She was killed, remember? Left to die in the underworld when she went to get the Prince, if you believe the official narrative, or did that memory toddle off, too?" Doubt was reddening about the face by then, arms folded over his chest as he, in the most literal sense, talked down to his young companion. "I certainly remember! I remember the whole bloody thing. The Queen's death is what got everybody into this mess."

"Maybe the Witch brought her back," suggested the hopeful boy, while Will finally righted himself enough to be called "genuflecting" rather than "prostrate."

"Your Majesty." Hands clasped, he admired the face of the Huntress, who gazed back, uncomprehending. "What say you, my lady? Surely you can offer us some word to set at ease the minds of my companions."

"Snake?" asked the Huntress, trying to determine how the men had learned language, and whether they had learned it from the snakes or the snakes had learned it from them.

Doubt waved a hand. "She hardly speaks."

"The Witch has done wilder things than make a woman forget how to speak," answered Maybe, his voice soft with awe. "I've never seen such hate in my own mother's eyes. How could she do that, the Witch? In one second, all those women..."

Will insisted, "I tell you, it's not worth considering. The Queen's not like other women." Rising to dust off his hands, he took those of the Huntress and gazed down into her eyes. "My lady, I know you've been away quite some time. And coming from Elysium must change a woman. You'll return to yourself soon, I'm sure, but I know the face of my Queen. And I won't let anything happen to you, my lady—that much, I promise."

"You're not the only thing that's changed," said Maybe, frowning as he came to Will's side. "The whole City is practically destroyed: half the buildings, razed to the ground, and the Witch's Tower has taken up the market square. You know, marm, where the fountain is? Where your coronation was, and all."

"Oh, King's bollocks." Doubt fell in line with his companions. "I don't even care if you aren't the Queen. Do you know how long we've wandered 'round these bloody Woods? You've got to know them better than we do. Someone must. How long's it been?"

"I've no reckoning," said Will, shaking his head. "We escaped the City with the other lucky men and banded together, the three of us. I don't know that the rest were as well equipped to survive—seems like most of the men stayed behind to fight, and were either imprisoned or lost."

The Silver Snake impressed itself upon the mind of the Huntress, who knew not his words but was visited with images of the three men running fearfully away from a wild throng of creatures like her—not men, but women, some in fine dresses the colors of paradisaical birds in the far-southern Forest, some in dusty gowns the color and texture of earth, some barely clothed, some swamped in the dowdy garb of priestesses—all of them with eyes lit emerald in fury: "A trio of cowards, these three!"

"Shush," urged the Serpent under his breath. Doubt was alert for every sound.

"What was that?"

"What?" asked Will.

"Our lady sighed," said Maybe.

"Is that a trophy?" Doubt gasped as he noticed the Serpent hanging around her neck, apparently dead. "My God! Some royal jewels."

"More proof that our Queen is none other," shouted Will, beating his breast with his clenched right fist. "To have slaughtered the bitch's eagle, and her serpent, both!"

"Are you certain it's dead?" asked Doubt of the Huntress, who could not understand his question, and only smiled away at he whose companions were so friendly.

"Dead," parroted the Huntress conversationally, the word being one thrown around quite a lot, but which, like "Felicity," she could not connect to any one object or action.

With another, victorious bellow, Will jostled the Huntress and beat his chest again, and she got so caught up in the thrill of his approval that she did it along with him, victory surging through her in nameless pulse of adrenaline. Doubtless they applauded her graceful rescue of the Serpent!

"You see," insisted Will, draping an arm proudly around her while the Silver Snake sputtered in disbelief, "our beloved Queen is more herself than ever. Perhaps a bit scattered after returning to life, but, why, who wouldn't be!"

"Perhaps she could tell us why she made such a fool's bargain, if she really is the Queen," sneered Doubt.

"All in due time," said Will to the sky left bare by the dead tree above them. "We'd better get back on track. Daylight's only just shown up, and we're already losing it. Your Majesty," Will moved along with her toward the tree line, gently insisting, "you'd ought to come with us. Though I still think we're better off in the Forest, we're making all the progress in the world, and I'm sure we'll be at the City within a few days."

"He's been saying that for more than a few days," said Doubt, but Maybe hurried his pace to run alongside Will and the Huntress.

"Maybe with you here, Your Majesty, we'll find our way faster! Four heads are better than three, aren't they?"

"Six heads," muttered the Silver Snake, pettish, all but rolling its eye, "but who's counting?"

Though it was true the men could not hear the Silver Snake, nothing would stop them—particularly Doubt—from admiring it, and the lithe man happened to be admiring it just as it spoke. "What an incredible Sword that is," he marveled, and Will nodded.

"Fine craftsmanship. Where did you receive your Sword, Your Majesty?"

Making no connection at first, the Huntress studied the man, who seemed to speak to her, then, the Silver Snake, which drew his attention. "Snake?" asked the Huntress of Will, who laughed.

"Why, madam, do you mean to say that snake there gave you a Sword!" Energetic man that he was, Will pointed to the things he named—first "snake," then "sword"—and then he slapped his knee in a bark of jovial laughter. As he did, the Huntress made another connection with a gasp of surprise for the Sword, seeing it clearly for the first time under light of distinction.

"Oh! Oh, *Sword*! No Snake!" With a sprite's laughter, the Huntress slapped her own forehead, then chided the Sword. "No Snake? Girl!"

The Sword sighed, annoyed, the gem of its pommel glowing red. "My girl, my dear, my sweetest Felicity, I must pick my battles, mustn't I? I figured you'd get the details in time. I'm really just focused on getting us to that City and getting Father freed so I can have a pair of blasted hands again!"

"*Snake*. Apricots?" She gasped as she realized perhaps she had misunderstood about them, too. "Apricots!"

"What's she going on about?" asked Doubt, to whom Maybe could only shrug. The Huntress herself was about to try to ask of Will whether the thing in her quiver was indeed called an "apricot" when a creeping kind of infected-boil, Southern Jungle-rubber stench overwhelmed again her sinuses. Nauseated, the Huntress gave a cry of terror as Will asked, "What in the bloody hell is that awful stink!"

"Beast," cried the Huntress, which was what the Sword repeated at high pitch in her mind as she slipped away from Will and drew her weapon.

"What sort of beast?" asked Maybe while Doubt gagged. The Huntress had no way or time to answer, sweeping back the way she'd come while chasing the black eagle to discover the path she'd once intended to take now marked with the filth of the Beast, the guano of its trail tarring all luckless flora to have been in the way.

"My God," breathed Will, emerging behind the Huntress, gripping the weapon which she still had not heard named but which she knew was not a Sword. "I saw something fly out of the City, but I thought I dreamed it in the chaos. This stink, though; I know this stink."

In the distance, the Forest rumbled with the force of the Beast, and the Huntress, her Sword gripped, marched in the direction of the sound until Will gripped her arm.

"Your Majesty! Where are you going?"

"Beast," she said, trying to pull herself away. "Sword!"

"It's not safe," insisted Will, dragging her in the opposite direction along the path of filth. "We've got to go the way it's come from and regroup before it decides to go back. We can't follow it."

"Maybe it's going to the City," suggested the boy as he arrived behind them, and the Sword, annoyed, shouted in the Huntress's head, "Yes, of course it bloody is! That thing kidnapped me and stuck me down in its hole for ages. I think I can tell what it wants."

"Let her go," insisted Doubt, the sound of his voice drowning the soft, condescending chuckle of the Serpent for the Sword. "If the loony woman wants to fight it, let her fight it! Less skin off our nose."

"She might really kill it," suggested Maybe. "If that's the thing that's been rumbling about for the last day, don't you think it's worth a try?"

"No! We have to protect her." Will kept steering the Huntress away, and she, irritated, tried to escape only to find herself clutched tighter in the man's burly arms. "You have to trust us, marm. We know what's best."

"Beast," insisted the Huntress, sharply, waving her Sword. Will only shook his head.

"That's no good, marm. Give that here. We'll hold on to it until we've got some time to get you into your right mind." Meaning well, Will reached forward to try to take the Sword, and it was in the moment of her cry of protest that the Serpent sank its fangs into the offending hand.

"Bloody witchcraft," cried Will, falling away from the bite and assessing his immediately swollen hand. "Lord, no! Your Majesty, you said it was dead!"

"You see!" Triumphant, Doubt drew his dagger, falling back three steps and saying, "I told you, I told you both she can't be the Queen! It's by witchcraft that she wears her face. She's the Witch herself, for all we know!"

"She can't be." Tears in his eyes, Maybe insisted, "She must be the Queen. I've seen her face in marble. My ma and pa said she used to be a farm girl who lived down the road when I was only small. I know it's her."

"That bloody snake!" Panicking, Will tore from his sleeve a bandage of fabric and wrapped it as a tourniquet around his wrist. The Huntress, Sword high, darted from the men and after the Beast, oblivious to Will's calls after her: "Your Majesty, come back! The Serpent isn't dead! It'll kill you! It's been sent by the Witch to end your life!"

Doubt, pale, seemed poised to run away if he was going to do anything at all, and looked toward Will in expectation even while the man dressed his wounds. "Well, we can't just let her get away. She'll get back to the City, and we'll be dead for certain, if we're not already. I certainly wouldn't bet on us."

"*She'll* be dead, more like. The City's dangerous, madam! Don't you see? We're better off staying in the Woods."

"These are the Witch's Woods, you fools. And not Woods anymore, but Forest." The chiding of the Serpent was more for the sake of the Sword than the men, who were by then out of earshot of the snake's soft voice. He shook his spade-shaped head as the Huntress pursued the Beast, saying, "Men of that sort are no good. They'll never reach the City for the same reason you would never reach the City, Sword, were it not for the placid wisdom of our fair Huntress."

"And why is that, then?"

"For they only see themselves as right, and give no mind to the words of their brothers, nor the wisdom of serpents; they see themselves only as masters of nature, and not as her humble servants. Their presumptions are good as carved within their minds. They cannot see that City and Forest are two parts of the same thing; just as they cannot see that the Forest has no end; just as they cannot see that they are as much animals, a part of the Forest, as they are men of the City."

"Do you ever say anything that isn't impenetrable nonsense," moaned the Sword, its lilac light distressed. "I still don't know why she had to save you from that poor eagle. It was doing us a service."

"For how else would our Huntress see all men but Our Lord, the King, as imperfect?" asked the Serpent of the Sword, and it had fair point, for thoughts of the King resurged in her mind as she trailed after the filth of the Beast. She felt certain this foul creature would lead her to him. She was increasingly convinced of her need of him, and his need of her, for those men were not like the Man she had seen upon picking up the Sword; they bore none of his silent grace, none of his beauty or his noble suffering. None of the light which shone from his being, even crowded as he was in darkness, had showed from the hearts of these men.

"Just what is that venom of yours going to do?" asked the Sword, voice low.

"They shall be reminded of the closeness of man and animal. Perhaps both Doubt and his young friend shall be slain by maddened Will. Or, perhaps not."

"A pity, that uncertainty." The Huntress, sure she had lost her pursuers, slowed in the exhaustion of her pace, hand upon her ribs, mouth burning with thirst as the Sword went on. "When it turns out that the City you're talking about isn't the City I mean but is instead some ridiculous metaphor for death, I am going to be extraordinarily cross."

Chuckling, the Serpent shook his head. "Your thinking is perhaps closer with that joke, friend, but I assure you the only one who shall be dead upon commencement of this operation is the Usurper, our vile Witch. Even then, that depends on one's perspective on these things."

"Oh, girl." The Sword reached into the mind of the exhausted Huntress to show her images of herself strangling the Serpent. "Won't you shut him up?" The Serpent's muzzle tied shut with a bow; the entire creature stuffed in a sack and buried at the bottom of her quiver. Despite herself, the Huntress laughed and prodded the gem in the hilt of the muttering Sword. "Incredible, how you've forgotten all decorum along with name and memory."

"Incredible, how you have yet failed to see the truth I have tried to impart so very many ways."

Oh! All the Huntress had ever wanted was a bath! Up to her ankles in the muck in which she trailed the Beast to find the King, she sighed at the thought of taking a bath with him: of together being cleansed of their woes, sinking into one another in the same pond, instead of being there, where, hand upon her face, she wept for her thirst, and for her loneliness. Both Sword and Serpent had attention diverted.

"Dear madam," cooed the Serpent, breathing the salt of her tears with its tongue, "you are never alone. No matter how alone you think you are, we are with you."

The Sword was less adept at consolation and, more used to criticism, struggled to come up with something supportive. "Don't do that. We'll find the King soon, don't you think? And the City, too, if this ridiculous Serpent will tell us where it is, rather than making up a load of nonsense."

"My dear Sword," cried the Serpent with a glare for the pommel stone, "if I have told you once, I have told you a thousand times and am not certain how much clearer I can make it. Perhaps if you would only close your wretched eye, you would see what I mean. It is so bright it blocks the light of the sun, so not one of us can see the truth of the matter."

"And what truth is that," sneered the Sword. "How am I to see the truth if my eyes are closed? I'll be blind!"

"See you not images in the mind's eye of our Huntress fair?"

"I can't very well trust the way she takes things. Up until a few moments ago, she was under the impression I was a blasted snake!"

"What matters most: the words and symbols with which her mind processes her surroundings, or the actual significance of those symbols?"

"Meaning what?"

"Meaning, close your eye, and see the change in the Forest trees."

Dark with the rage of an advance decision that nothing would happen, the Sword shouted, "Fine! Fine! I'll close my blasted eye; I'll turn out my light. Then you'll see how much you need me. Felicity will be like a little animal without me in her brain. You should have seen her when she found me. Positively feral! And to leave a feral woman like that alone in the dark, you're asking for trouble! Things are going to come from all sides! Bats! You want another eagle to come and swoop you up? This time Felicity won't have light to shoot with! You don't realize how dark it is in this part of the Forest without my light!"

"Clear your mind, my good man, and close your eye," commanded the Serpent, patient, gentle, "and see the truth."

At last, the Sword's light dimmed, then vanished. The Huntress, left in the darkness of the deep part of the Forest, gasped to see how the trees shrank and changed, how their thick leaves thinned and burned and vanished to reveal a sky of permanent night which made the womb of a cherry moon. The Sword gasped, "My King," and the Huntress, "Snake," while the Serpent lifted its head toward the City unfurling far around them, barren and dust covered.

"Your light has served its purpose, my good man." The Tower drew itself from relief, brick by brick, against the black and starless sky, distinguished from its backdrop by the oil-slick substance of its facade. "But there are times when it is better dulled, lest we all forget it is but a lamp. After all, lamplight serves rather more to distort the darkness than illuminate it. Wouldn't you agree?"

4

What a strange day this was for the Huntress—stranger, even, than the day before! Never had so many curious things happened. She found herself in a part of the Forest which seemed most unnatural, where trees were bent and twisted and sometimes collapsed, and others were woven together and combined with rocks to form strange sorts of caves. Some of the caves had large holes in them which shimmered with a kind of solid water. The Huntress touched one of these panels and frowned when her hand came away dirtier than before, blackened by the same stuff which covered all the surfaces in this part of the Forest. Because none of the trees or caves had any leaves, she got the idea that there had once been a fire here—fire, of the sort set by lightning. The fire had consumed all the leaves, the moss. Everything.

"How queer it is to see through her mind," said the Sword, which gagged as the Huntress shifted his hilt to her newly dirtied hand. "Oh, for—no, Felicity! That's filthy!"

"It's only ash," said the Serpent as the Huntress made her way down a path laid in blackened stone. "You shall live, good man."

"Are you sure about that?"

"Only if you are," said the gay Serpent, lifting his head and losing his humor when the Huntress stopped short, attention raised by the distant but familiar sound of a string's tension. As she scanned the rocky caves, the Sword whispered, "What is it? What's happening? I can't see a thing!"

But the Huntress saw it all with ease: upon the distant mound of collapsed stones rose the nimble body of an archer not unlike herself. Unwilling to find herself a doe, the Huntress leapt aside, between the squat bodies of two less-ruined structures, as the stranger let fly her arrow.

"Was that an archer! My God, I preferred it when it was all vicious animals and rumbling Beasts and intrusive, cowardly woodsmen!"

"Who goes there?" The feminine demand rose high in the air. The Serpent opened his mouth to speak when he recalled the smallness of his lungs, and the difficulty of being heard over such distance. He gazed into the keen face of the Huntress, then studied the black eye of the Sword.

"You're really going to detest this, good man. Just remember I am part of her at the end of the day, in a manner of speaking."

"What are you talking about?" asked the Sword, but it was as this question rattled around and as the Huntress opened her mouth to shush them that the Serpent coiled to spring between her lips. With wild eyes, the Huntress tried to yank him from her jaws, but the reptile rammed himself far into her throat. In so doing, he became a new tongue, growing indistinguishable in all ways from her old one; in becoming her tongue and her language, the Serpent also became her. He cleared her throat, then, as the Sword screamed, panicking in her mind, "I knew it! I knew it, I bloody well knew it, you bastard!"

"Do be quiet," the Serpent bade with fresh lips as, for the fourth time, female voices shouted that if she did not emerge, the Huntress would be hunted and killed. With a deep breath, and a keen awareness of all that the girl had observed—still observed, indeed, in awe of herself for her speech and in awe of the Serpent for his overtaking it—the Serpent called, "I am a messenger of the Usurper, the Black Lady, the Witch: the one who dwells in the Tower who you have never seen, yet whose eyes lay upon all who dwell on the earth. If you kill me, there will be a terrible price to pay. But, if you spare me, you and your sisters shall be left living, and rewarded."

"You're an idiot," hissed the Sword. "I knew it, you bastard."

Ignoring the Sword, the Serpent considered the entrance of the alley in which they had taken shelter. While enjoying the Huntress's enthrallment to experience so clearly the City, he lifted her hand to strip away her gear. At the resistance of her body, he caressed her mind with surges of affection and images of the King, and, as the distant women murmured among themselves the plausibility of the account, the Serpent called, "If I surrender unto you my weapons, will you consider leaving me alive?"

More whispering bubbled. Full well ignoring the protestations of the Sword, the Serpent removed it from her back and took, too, her quiver, and bow, as the leader of the women called, "Give us everything, and we will leave you unharmed, and you will have every opportunity to prove your words are true."

Nodding, the Serpent tossed first the quiver, then the bow, and then, with particular relish, the Sword, which skidded across the cobblestones and flipped facedown with an altogether ignoble series of profanities. "I detest you," came its admonishment, while the Serpent followed, the Huntress's hands above her head and her eyes possessed by a new intensity as they scanned her charred surroundings. Seven women emerged from the ruins around them; their leader, who had first shot the arrow, was en route, and made no move to discourage her women from taking aim on the newcomer. At last, the General stopped, a foot taller than the Huntress, muscles like that of a tiger wound beneath her tawny flesh. With narrowed eyes, she surveyed the interloper's stoic face, and then, at last, spat upon the Sword.

"You claim yourself a messenger of the Black Lady." She leaned close as a snarling animal. "But I know your face. I know it because we destroyed it a hundred times all over this City, 'Your Majesty.'" A title delivered with a sneer.

"It was only in a past life that this face I wear belonged in busts of marble," lied the Serpent, gazing with meek air into the face of the General. "Now, I am a humble Huntress, and all by my rebirth at the hands of the Black Lady."

"Is that so."

"It is! And I have come to spread word of her wonders, to reward those who have proven loyal and punish those fools disobedient. That Sword is her gift to me, and with it I shall rend her enemies. But know this—" The Serpent tilted forward the head of the Huntress, whose voice dropped to a charcoal murmur which forced the General nearer. "Any enemy of the Black Lady is an enemy of mine; all those who stand against me are enemies, likewise, of Our Queen. And all those who are enemies of Our Queen shall perish in the wrath I have brought with me from Elysium, that I might repay She Who Dwells in the Tower for her kindness in wrenching me from death's cold grip."

The whispers of the surrounding women rose as they speculated whether it was true that the Queen had died at all in her efforts to retrieve the Prince. If it was true, perhaps what stood before them was a demon, or a test from the Woman in the Tower. Their anxiety filled the air with the density of smog, and the Serpent parted the lips of the Huntress so he might taste it, her eyes falling closed as he bade her appreciate a sensation of which she would otherwise have no perception.

"How do I know you're not lying?" asked the General. "You've no proof you've been sent by Her. In fact, you've come from the way opposite Her Tower. You're just down here, one of us. Worse, you've the cheek to claim you're anything like us! A 'Huntress.'" With a sneer, the tremendous woman stepped back to assess the small frame of the disarmed girl before her, filthy, clad in the skin of a deer and crowned with a crooked trio of roses fused to the matted tangle of her hair. The General laughed at the sight and shook her head. "You're no more a huntress than I am a princess."

"If you would like to be a princess," offered the Serpent, arranging the Huntress's lips in a placid smile akin to the permanent manner of its own, "you need only act as one, and others shall treat you as one. Once, I may have been a Queen, but no longer. Indeed, I've no memories of that former life. Do you see that arrow," said, with a nod to the one remaining.

"Yes," said the skeptical General, following along.

"That arrow is crafted of the bone of a stag I killed only a fortnight ago," estimated the Serpent, rifling through the series of vague impressions littering the Huntress's disorganized mind, suffused in unconsciousness as it was before the Sword. "You are a perfectly adequate archer, yourself." He studied the General's arrow, still jammed between two cobblestones. "Had I not reacted on instinct, I would be dead with the glory of your shot. What a pity that would be! But if you would have it, I would arrange a contest: we shall both shoot toward Our Lady's highest window, and whosoever hits the closest is clearly in her favor."

All around, the women continued to whisper, and one distinct voice agreed to her sister that, "It feels like it's been ages since Our Lady came into us."

"And I shall show you how to call her into your hearts again," said the Serpent, a small, not unkind smile upon the Huntress's lips. "Once I have proven through grace and cunning that she has sent me."

Snorting, the General tore from the ground her misspent arrow and drew once more her bow. "If you are to leave Our Lady's favor to each woman's personal skill, then she has no favor for the poor, or the weak, or the stupid. Thus, she has no favor for you."

"We shall see," said the Serpent, smiling plainly, stooping to retrieve the bow of the Huntress and her final stag-bone arrow. The craftsmanship of the arrowhead was so fine, its tip so well keened, that it seemed a pity to spend, but it would be no waste, no matter how it seemed. One of the women retrieved the Sword, which had fallen silent: a mercy for the Serpent, but a source of dread for the Huntress, forced to watch as the party approached the towering spire. The air around it seemed to warp, and the blackened stones with which it had been built breathed and glistened like the scales of the Beast. Though she was overwhelmed by fear, she could make no escape, for the Serpent drove her, and placed her at the foot of the quivering Tower with the General at her side.

"Allow me to shoot first," requested the Serpent, and the General stepped away with a small, malicious smile. The Serpent, eyes narrowed, assessed the impossible height of the Tower, and the force of the wind, and the mediocre physical strength of the Huntress's arms, and made a concerted attempt, even with all that in mind, to botch the shot, forcing the Huntress's normally steady aim to falter and send the arrow but a quarter the height of the Tower, where it stuck, sad, in the wall. The General and her women laughed, and, with a massive arm, she shoved the Huntress aside.

"Hers may be a tall Tower, but that was the saddest shot I've ever seen. Surely you can hit at least the sill of her window!"

"In wind like this," suggested the Serpent, innocently lowering the Huntress's bow, "I am not certain anyone could. Even you, dear woman."

"We'll see about that." The General laughed. After little more than a few seconds' aim, she spent her shot toward the eye socket of the Tower's highest window. All present were breathless in silence as the arrow ascended high, higher, ashen tail feathers wavering in the wind until, at last, it struck the window through.

"Hah!" Delighted, the General spiked her bow and turned to the Serpent, angry face written in triumph. "You see! I told you, you're nothing but a liar," were the last words she ever spoke as, from the top of the Tower, there grew a quaking roar. From the violated window burst a red lion which, wingèd, swooped down upon the screaming woman but targeted only the General, who had begun to run when the creature first rent her flesh. The scattered women stumbled from the scene, could not escape the plaza fast enough, but the Serpent tarried to retrieve the arrows of the General from her abandoned quiver before backing away, appreciative of the lion's might.

"I feel in admiration of that noble creature," remarked the Serpent. Exiting the plaza, it came again upon the terrified women, who, chattering in a cluster near the remains of a market stall, fell into deep silence at the Huntress's appearance. The Serpent surveyed the horror of their faces with her narrowed eyes, giving special assessment to the sixth, who, through nothing more than poor luck, clutched in her hands the Sword.

"I'll have my weapon," said the Serpent at last, and this terrified mouse dared extend it with trembling hand before falling away to her comrades as the Huntress gripped its hilt. "Let this Sword be the symbol of my power," suggested the Serpent to the women, who nodded in chorus.

"We shall never doubt you again, never touch it or take it from you," promised the one who had given it up, who, with a tearful shudder toward the sloppy sounds of the gory meal in the plaza, begged, "Please, madam, O Prophet of She in the Tower, won't you let us thank you for sparing us? For coming upon us so graciously?"

Though the Huntress screamed in her heart with images of Man in the faces of all these delays, and how he suffered, and how keenly she wished to free him from his misery and hold him in her arms, the Serpent was given pause by these offerings of recompense. "It has been quite some time since any of us have had a decent meal," he said to himself, and to the Sword, which spoke up.

"Absolutely not. That's been your game all along, no doubt: get us into the City and get us trapped here forever without bothering to see the King."

"Paranoia is unhealthy, my good man," murmured the Serpent under his breath, before, with a smile, he patted the hand of the nearest girl. "I would be honored by your hospitality, my daughter."

A smile overcame that woman, who shared her relief with her sisters. Soon the entire sorority had gathered around the body of the Huntress, all talking excitedly and asking in a symphony of six voices all details they could think to ask of the Usurper, who they had not seen in ages, and who, indeed, they could not remember. The Serpent turned it around on them.

"Do you remember when Our Lady last spoke to you?" asked the Serpent as they were guided by the women to the remains of the barracks.

"It must have been ages ago," suggested the fairest of the women, who had been the one to bear the Sword, and was most favored by the Serpent. "Perhaps even before the Forest grew around our City."

"Have you ever explored the Forest?" asked the Serpent, but the women only laughed at that, as he had expected they would.

"Not us," said the cleverest. "There's no finding a way out of this City, but even if there were, the Forest is full of untold dangers. Worse than that, men."

"What is so bad of men that you should cast them into the wilderness, apart from you?"

This gave the women pause outside their barracks. The wisest studied the Huntress. "You speak as though you were not a woman yourself. Not a messenger sent by Her Majesty."

"I have been away an ageless time, and Our Lady has awoken me only recently to teach you her ways and bring her into your hearts. I have heard secondhand what occurred in my absence, and at last see the effects. So I ask you, all six present, how is it that things came to be this way? How is it that the men and women came to separate themselves, and why?"

The youngest spoke up at last: "At the urging of Our Lady, we cast the men from the City, for they proved traitors and oppressors."

"I see. And what was it the men did to oppress you?"

"They ruled us," said the strongest, her mouth in a tight moue of displeasure. "They bade us raise their children and keep their homes that they might live as men, and forced us to live as mere women. They condemned us to a life of passive, bestial servitude in their presence, so it was only right we should throw off their yoke and cast them into the Forest. They are no better than animals."

"But there is one man in this City," suggested the Serpent, at last, as the women came into the barracks and set about in preparation of their meal. "Indeed, that very Man who once ruled men and women alike with equal fairness. Our Lady has taken him captive." The eyebrows of the Huntress lifted at the Serpent's bemused behest. "Surely you ladies, and indeed the rest of the women hidden about this City, would prefer men of your own to the monotony of feminine company day in and day out."

It was the bravest, then, who spoke up, removing her gear and suggesting, "It is Our Lady's privilege to keep a man, is it not? Regardless, no man may enter this City, as no woman may enter the Forest."

"What stops them?"

"They cannot find the way," the wisest explained, opening the doors to the courtyard to reveal the fire over which roasted a heifer. "There is no way for women into the Forest and no way for men into the City, no more than there is a way for a rook to swim alongside salmon."

"All that is consequence of frame of mind. Should the rook develop a taste for salmon, I assure you, my girl, he would have himself gills in a fortnight."

A few of the women laughed together, and even the wisest was amused, though she turned her face toward her table-setting sisters to hide her pleasure at the humor. "You are a quite amusing messenger from Our Lady, O Huntress. Has she sent you to reward us, only, or to lighten our moods in times of war?"

"There is no reason the answer cannot be both," said the Serpent, feeling all the time more jovial. "Our Lady's heart may be black as night above, but that only means her shadow must be all the colors of the rainbow."

With a titter, the fairest, who until then tended the hearth, bounded to the side of the Huntress. "And she deserves to be adorned as such. Aren't there all those old garment shops in the ruins of the north district, Melody?" As the girl asked this of the wisest, the Serpent briefly stopped listening. At the influx of thoughts of silken gowns and precious anointments and rich feasts, the Serpent somehow forgot himself, and that he had not, in fact, been sent by the Black Lady to luxuriate among the City's women. It seemed to him, after all, that he had been sent among these fine creatures for a reason. It made all the sense in the world that the Black Lady would desire his presence, for were they not in her City, so near her Tower that the Huntress might toss a stone to it? Yet they suffered no ill. Had not the Black Lady's lion attacked the General and left alive the Huntress, he asked himself, forgetting his own wisdom for cleverness. Smiling, he patted the hand of the fairest as he announced, "Let us have our feast of fellowship, my girl. We shall worry over petty details like dress once we've something in our stomachs."

"And then?" asked the girl with starry eyes. The Serpent leaned down with a smile.

"And then, I shall teach you how to feel the Black Lady in your heart, how to awaken her inside of you again, the way she awoke the first day."

It was as the girl squealed that the Huntress removed the Sword from her back, and the blade fancied it was mopping its own brow. "Serpent, dear man, I'm receiving all sorts of keen insight into your intentions with you properly in our Felicity's head. I must say this seems a bad idea. I much preferred it when you were disturbingly calm and in control of the situation outside by the Tower."

Though the Huntress's eyes narrowed, the Serpent kept most of her face under control, beginning to lay down her weapons without conscious thought. The Sword, though, went on, "Think of it this way. We've got to get all the way to the top of that wretched thing, haven't we?"

Beneath the distant murmuration, the Serpent hummed, "Not necessarily."

"Excuse me! 'Not necessarily'! I know I've been harsh with you this whole time, but you'd ought to know I was just *joking* with that business about your being sent by the Witch. I didn't think you'd start a bloody cult!"

"Nor did I," replied the cheerful Serpent, "but life takes us many strange places."

"And what, exactly, do you think will happen? You're going to stay down here forever? Felicity does have a mortal, corporeal form. Regardless of how many times the woman's been pulled out of the underworld, she does have something akin to an expiration date."

With a patient chuckle of condescension, the Serpent shook his head. "While it's true my dear Huntress is but human, I have the utmost faith that, should we fulfill her will to the letter of her mind, the Black Lady shall reward our dear Felicity. Forgive her. Maybe even render her immortal."

"Would you listen to yourself!" The Sword screamed in the Huntress's head, and the volume came on with a shock of pain which stirred the girl, who had been lulled into a kind of hypnosis by the distant actions of her own body. She who had become an observer in herself emerged and frowned at the Sword in her hands; then she thought of Man, and felt her throat itch with sadness.

"Girl," she said into the quiver in her arms and the final apricot there, waiting for the King. "Girl eats apricot. Man eats apricot."

It was as though the Sword felt itself choking up. "Poor girl. You just want to climb the Tower, don't you. Just want to see the King."

But it was then that the Huntress was swallowed up again by the Serpent, who reappeared in her face, in the hardness and determination. Wrapping the palm of the Huntress's hand around the gem, the Serpent called to the women, "Might one of you come help with my weapons? Perhaps find someplace out of sight, that our feast can go uninterrupted by the unseemly presence of tools of violence. A closet, say. Someplace where we needn't worry for them."

5

So it was that the Sword found himself in a closet in the back of the barracks at the behest of the Serpent, stuck once more in darkness while distant laughter rang as if mocking his inability to reach the Huntress from isolation.

Over the sound of something, somewhere, dripping, the Sword tried to think the problem through. "Oh, what in the hell am I going to do? I'm pathetic. No arms or legs. Not even a face! Maybe if I had a mouth I might shout a bit. But, oh, no, that blasted Witch. Blasted Serpent! Oh, that bloody Serpent. You know, Rat," it addressed the creature which had poked its black-eyed face from a hole in the back of the cell to which they had been condemned, "I told Felicity from the start, nothing good would come of that snake. What has he done for us? Oh, only forced us to run into a trio of incompetents and then gotten us to this bloody City, where I...just a minute, now."

As the Rat sat at abrupt attention to wash his whiskers, the Sword realized, "That bloody snake didn't get us to the City. *I* got us to the City!" Excitement bubbling in his metaphorical heart, he shouted, "By God, Rat, I was the one who got us here! That means I can be the one to save us! Hah! Ah, Felicity, you can thank me later! Let's see...see, see... ah! Yes, if I open my eye—"

As its eye opened and cast excitable plum light in the closet, it realized that it had been in no closet at all: rather, abandoned to lean against a tree; and that the Rat was no rat at all: rather Doubt, who leapt a foot to see the blade appear before him while buttoning his fly.

"Bloody hell," shouted the former thief, and the Sword cried out, "Yes! I've done it! I've truly done it, my Father's bollocks, I'm bloody brilliant!"

"Eric! Eric, get over here and see this!"

The young man called "Eric"—whose real name was, of course, "Maybe"—emerged from the nearby thicket of blackberries with blushing face turned skyward. "This isn't going to be another rude joke, is it, Douglas."

"No, this time it's something real. See? It's that imposter's Sword!"

With a gasp, Maybe turned his mossy eyes upon the blade. "It is! Maybe she's around."

"Hello," called the Sword, "can you hear me, either one of you?"

The answer was evidently no, for Doubt went on to say that, "If she is, I'm not sticking around. Frankly"—his voice dropped—"I've half a mind to bolt, anyway. Brutus has been acting a right lunatic since that snake bit him."

"Maybe it did so in service of the Queen," suggested the boy, worrying his hands while the older man, snorting, bent his dark head to investigate the Sword's bright eye, which appeared to him as nothing but a beautiful gem the way a bird has no appreciation for an object's nature beyond color and size.

"Which Queen is that? Good Queen Felicity, or the Black Queen of the Tower? Or, do you suppose both?"

"What do you mean?" asked the boy, gasping as his comrade snatched up the Sword, which shouted, "There! Can you hear me now? Damn. Obviously not, since you're not screaming."

Anxious, Maybe suggested, "Perhaps you'd ought not to touch Her Majesty's Sword," while the thief went on undeterred, hardly of mind to listen to a boy, let alone a blade.

"If you'll recall, lad, this all officially happened because of a magical kerfuffle with the ladies. Isn't that right."

"Well, yes," allowed Maybe, "but there was more to it than that.

My family and I came into town to watch the execution. Don't you remember what a big deal it was?"

"Right, but all the women in town were in on it, weren't they? The uprising."

"No! It was a Witch they were executing, remember? It's a funny thing, I can't quite seem to remember it all, but—"

"Ah, scamp, you're a cute lad, believing in witchcraft and the like."

"You realize," observed the Sword, unheard by the man who indulged in graceless fencing practice, "that I am, in fact, your Prince."

But Maybe went on. "You said when Brutus was bitten—I mean, you believed it then."

"In the heat of the moment, sure. But having had time to think on it, I've recognized the simplest solution has been staring me in the face all this time."

The thief, oblivious, continued, while the young man by his side gazed petulantly into the trees: "You're too old to be believing in business like that. I know you and your mum and sisters all lived together, but you're among men, and it's high time you learned men's truths: that wasn't witchcraft." He planted the tip of the muttering blade into the ground and posed, triumphant. "That was a coup."

"Like for chickens?" asked the young man.

"No! Not a 'coop,' a 'coup'! A coup! You know, an uprising?"

"Oh! I think it's a silent *p*," suggested the boy, and the thief scowled.

"No need to be correcting me, lad, it's a word I've only seen in books. Not exactly a lot a high-talkin' philosophical types in the thief's guild."

With his arms crossed and his lips pursed in a frown, Maybe concentrated on the tip of the Sword embedded in the earth, then tensed all the further when it was withdrawn and tossed into the air as though it were the blade of a circus performer rather than a deposed Queen. "Would you stop! I'm trying to tell you: my mother and sisters, their eyes filled with green fire! They've blue eyes!"

"A trick of the light," insisted Doubt, lazily waving the Sword. "I was there, too. I saw the smoke, the fire, saw it light the eyes of everybody there, saw the whole bloody thing. There's powders to turn fire green," he said, and by then the boy's eyes were tearing.

"My family wouldn't do that! We're farmers, innkeepers! We'd hardly been to the City before! How was my mother supposed to be a part of any stupid coup!"

With a low sigh, the thief, having once had a mother, himself, gave in to his kernel of sympathy and was about to comfort the boy with a hand on his shoulder when the Sword said, "Since this fellow is such a skeptic and can't hear my voice, I suppose I'll just have to show him."

The Sword closed his eye, and shrieked to find that, outside the hand of the Huntress, it was rendered truly blind when its gem was blackened shut; the thief likewise cried out, trapped in a tiny closet of weapons, where he would otherwise be delighted to abruptly find himself were it not for the chestnut horse with which he took company. The colt, which seemed just as startled, whinnied in terror as the thief screamed and the Sword opened its eye; Doubt stood back where he had been in the Forest.

"Bloody hell!" Eyes whipping all around, the thief confirmed he was back and placed a hand on his heart, half panting as the boy beside him cried, "Are you all right, what is it!" while, in the underbrush, the thunder of footsteps stormed in their direction. As the Sword fretted that it had seen nothing at all, not even the impressions of the thief, Will burst from the trees, eyes wild, his still-bandaged hand held to his breast while, with his left, he brandished wildly his axe.

"That bastard Beast. Get out of my Woods, you shit-fucker!"

Sighing, Doubt waved the Sword. "Would you calm down, you dolt. No, it's not the Beast, I—" Frowning, he insisted, "I had some dream, or..."

But the volume of the woodsman's gasp shocked the thief into losing all memory of the vision, as Will asked, "Is that Our Lady's Sword, Douglas!"

"The deceiver's Sword," corrected Doubt, trying to add, "and it's mine," though Will wrested the Sword from him with such ease that Doubt might as well have meant to hand it over.

"To hold Our Lady's very Sword..." Tears filled the burly man's eyes, and, as Maybe patted his shoulder, he wiped the dirty tourniquet across his cheeks and beneath his beet-colored nose. "I should be so lucky, to hold such a thing before I lose my hand."

Maybe spoke up, leaning around the man's tree-trunk arm to get his attention. "I can't help but think that if the snake's venom were going to rot off your hand, Brutus, it already would have. At least, you'd be awfully tired."

It was not, however, Will who was tiring, but rather the Sword, tired of being passed from hand to hand, ogled and groped, and still rather irritated by the thief's ignorance. Who could find themselves in a closet of weapons with a living horse and take it for fancy! But the woodsman, sweaty and huge and edged with serpent venom though he was, did so love the Queen. Surely if anyone would recognize the City, it would be him! Surely if anyone could realize what was wrong with Felicity, this woodsman would be he!

"All right," said the Sword, shutting its eye, "maybe if I can't see, at least you can!"

The Sword was right: the woodsman did adore his Queen, and if there was ever a man well acquainted with the City, it was Will, for its odor had disagreed with him since he was small and proved a cause of his intimacy with the Woods. All manner of strange things had happened since their growth into the Forest, not the least of which being a man finding himself in tight quarters with a rat and a horse and the distant sound of women laughing as if at some dinner party.

"Lightning's eye," cursed Will, wild, as the rat squeaked in surprise to observe itself and its company and the colt rolled its eyes in equine whiplash. "Our Lady's Sword has brought me to the City!"

"Yes!" The Sword grew so excited that it opened its eye in hopes of seeing the man with some sense in him. "Yes! That's exactly right. Can you hear me?"

"Cor," shouted the man, seeing again the arrival of his friends, and the Forest, and not hearing one word of the Sword, "brothers! You'll never believe what I've seen! Our Lady's Sword has shown me a vision of the City!"

Panic struck the Sword as he realized the implications of this statement, and he all at once found himself shouting, "No, no, that's not quite right. I *took* you to the City. Or awoke you to it? We're already in the City, yes, that's right! I...I can't explain it like the Serpent can. Not that he can explain it either, really—"

"This is a sign, lads," shouted Will, jostling Maybe with one arm, brandishing the blade with the other. "We'll come upon the City any day!"

"And the Queen?" asked Maybe, inspecting closely the Sword.

"Surely Our Lady is already in the City! Why would her Sword show us its vision?"

Sighing, the Sword told itself, "Well, he's close," while Doubt had grown exasperated enough to say, "Listen here, brother. I saw that City same as you did. But one of us here isn't deluded enough to think it meant anything, right?"

Face reddening, Will snapped, "Care to elaborate?"

"What's to elaborate? You're seeing things. It was a dream. Like the pictures you see in your sleep? Remember those? Or maybe a hallucination. It was a trick of the light I saw, but I think it's the snake's venom getting to you."

"You listen, Douglas," said the woodsman darkly, stooping forward so as to be nose to nose with the slim thief. "From the start, you've done nothing but whine and hold the lad and I back."

"I don't feel held back," helped Maybe, but Will went on, his words rising to a snarl. "We've been wandering what feels damn well like bloody years now trying to find this City; we catch sight of it, and you can't even believe it!"

"Excuse me for skepticism of the man who's been leading us around in circles! Some bloody woodsman you are!"

"Some bloody thief! What kind of man's an *ex*-thief, anyway? Who the bloody hell gets thrown out of a thief's guild!"

"People with authority issues! Which, incidentally, is why I don't have much issue with you, outside of your getting us lost and keeping us lost, since you aren't much of an authority, are you?"

It was this which pushed Will over the edge, and which turned his ruddy face purple; but, of course, Doubt can only be held so responsible for the type of inner turmoil which drives a man to the solitude of the Woods in the first place, and so can only be held so responsible for the fact that this was the moment when Will forgot himself, threw down both Sword and axe, and lifted both fists, even the damaged one.

"That's it, you wee-nosed weasel. Put up your fists and we'll see who's the authority around here."

"The authority at what?" asked the thief, paler than usual, craning his chin up as if hoping a ladder might drop from the sky to lift him to safety.

"The authority at kicking in your teeth," shouted Will, throwing a punch which Doubt, through years of practice earning and dodging strikes, ducked by slim margin.

Maybe, however, was not interested in a fight which, serpent venom or no serpent venom, had been a lot of wandering in the making. He was more interested in the Sword, over whom he was free to crouch, and of whom, beneath the din of the brawl, he could ask, "Are you all right?"

And the Sword, who until that very moment had been lamenting his fate in silence, cursed to spend eternity in the hands of three buffoons or the weapons closet in the City, gasped. "Lad! Oh, you can hear me!"

The boy frowned as Will tackled Doubt, using full strength to pin the man by the solar plexus. "I must be silly," suggested Maybe into his shoulder on the off chance one of the fighting men might have state of mind enough to notice the boy's moving lips, "but I can hear you. I heard you all the way back when we first met Her Majesty. Are you real? Or is this like how Grandma Rita kept insisting skylarks were sending her messages through the teakettle?"

The Sword might have wept for joy. "No, my boy, you're no madder than I am! I know that doesn't seem very reassuring, but trust me. Who's ever heard of a mad Sword, after all!"

Behind skepticism, the boy whispered, "I wasn't sure at first. I thought I was making it up in my head. Giving you a voice. When I was littler, we used to pretend the animals had voices, my sisters and I; we'd talk for them as if they were people for a laugh. I thought I was doing that with you, but it's really you talking, isn't it?"

"Yes! Yes, it is, it's me, and, lad, I have had faith in you from the moment I first clapped eye on you!" This blatant lie seemed to fool the pleased boy, and the Sword gasped. "My God, you've such sense for someone your age! You can help us! Would you like to help your nation, your City? Your King and Queen, lad?"

Patriotism sparking courage in his bright eyes, the boy clenched his fist. "I'll do anything. What's happened to Our Majesty, Sword?"

"Pick me up, have the faith in me that I have in you, and everything will all be fine, Maybe."

With a glance at the fighting men, then down at the Sword, Maybe took a deep breath to steady himself and lifted the blade in the final moments of twilight's glow. As the men paused in Doubt's sound beating, the Sword opened its eye, and the farm boy found himself in a closet with the Sword, a rat, and a wild-eyed wolf.

"Open the door," screamed the Sword. Panicking as the wolf bared its teeth in a snarl, the boy hurtled from the closet like a comet through the atmosphere and rushed down the hall in which he found himself. The pounding of his feet upon the stone floor caught the attention of distant voices, one demanding above her companions, "What is that din!"

"That's him," shouted the Sword.

"Our Lady is a 'him'?" asked the baffled boy, yelping as the wolf snapped his heels so he leapt around the corner, rather than skidded.

"No, no. The thing that's taken her tongue is a 'he,' I think. The Serpent who bit your friend."

The lad was about to answer with astonishment when the wolf knocked him through double doors to the ivied courtyard where once dined an army but now ate seven women, six of whom cried out to see not just a wolf, but a boy, and, close behind them both, a rat scuttling after the same food which distracted the rabid lupus.

The seventh woman, however, with dark hair and calm eyes and the radiant face of the pale, dead Queen, did not scream, though she did leap atop her chair, expectant hand outstretched. "I'll have my Sword, lad, and your interruption will be forgiven."

As the wolf launched itself from the shoulders of pinned Maybe to rush upon the fresh-roasted meat in the center of the banquet, the rat took interest in the legs of the fairest, who shrieked and kicked and fell away from the table with cries that her sisters help. She who was bravest became distracted by helping the fairest pull the rat from her skirts, and she who was strongest hurried she who was youngest away so only the wisest and cleverest were left to deal with the wolf devouring their meal.

"We'll make a trap," said the cleverest, but the wisest stamped her foot.

"That will take too long. Fetch our weapons! We ought never to have locked them up."

Clearing the throat of the Huntress, the Serpent suggested, "There is indeed a weapon in the room, knives and forks of our dinner table aside."

"Serpent, you bastard," called the Sword, as Maybe stumbled to his feet and brandished rather inadequately the mystical blade, "lock me in a closet, will you! Well, joke's on you: all your flimflam about the City being the Forest and the Forest being the City and men being animals and up being down works both ways!"

"Those are my friends," realized the boy with a gasp, a crimson tourniquet tight around the right paw of the wolf. "Brutus! Can you hear me?"

"He is rendered less than animal," snapped the Serpent, and it was as all this happened that the Huntress frowned behind her own face, shocked by her tone and the way she felt when the Serpent used her to speak. "I suppose you were the horse I heard earlier, lad? A stroke of blind luck that you've found my Sword at all. Give it here."

"The Sword told me you're not really Our Lady," said the boy, stepping around the table to put the arguing women and ravenous wolf aside so nothing might come between him, the Sword, and the Serpent Queen. "But surely you are Our Lady, too. Will you let her go?"

The smiling Serpent patted the Huntress's shoulder with her own hand. "Our dear Felicity knows this is the surest way to a wonderful life for the both of us. The surest way to help our people."

"But the King," insisted the Sword, and that word, which so often accompanied images of Man, stirred the heart of the Huntress, who reached up and felt the crown of roses upon her head, and felt her eyes well up with tears.

"No." The Serpent extended her other hand. "Give us the Sword, boy."

"Don't give me over," begged the Sword. Dismayed, the boy faced the wolf who was once his friend, who had helped him in times of need, who had been quicker to anger than ever before since the Serpent's bite. How he'd suffered! All the woodsman had wanted was to reach the City to see if his grandmother was alive; having arrived, the boy was not certain his friend was there at all, was able to see it, overtaken as he was by a wolf. So, tearfully, as the Serpent demanded with the mouth of the Huntress, "My Sword," it was with a flaming heart that the boy avenged Will by slipping the blade's tip into the mouth of the Huntress to cut out her false tongue, which dropped to the floor and became again a Serpent.

"Girl," cried the Huntress in shock, falling back. "Man!"

"Oh, Felicity," sang the Sword, as the Serpent, thrashing upon the floor, lamented, "My head."

"My Lady," gasped the wisest, drawing the snake to the attention of her sorority. "Sisters! We have been betrayed!"

"Man," insisted the Huntress to the Sword, who said hurriedly, "Yes, yes, the King! We shall bring you to the King. Boy, you may release me," began the Sword, but the young man could not get the weapon from his hands fast enough, and, terrified, threw the blade, then turned to run as the women shouted among themselves, "She's no messenger of the Black Lady! Why, she can't even speak for herself! A snake did her speaking all this time!"

"My nature as a snake makes nothing I've said less true. It was all true, in a way," mourned the Serpent, attempting to shake its head free of pain. With a chuckle after the retreating farm boy, it gazed up at the Huntress, who brandished the Sword at the wolf but glowered down at the Serpent.

"Beast eats snake," she said, pointing at the wolf, which smacked its lips and lifted its head.

The Serpent assumed as plaintive an expression as possible. "Dear Huntress, I never meant to do you harm, my Queen. I was carried away when I took the place of your tongue! Why, our dear Sword should be able to appreciate better than anyone the kind of pleasure I found in arms and feet, eyelids and smell." Drooping, it gazed at the Huntress, then rolled upon its back to show its belly. "I shall never again, Your Majesty, take such liberty with your form. I only meant to elevate you and give you glory among your fellows. But I know how wrong I was, and how my own lascivious ways—"

"Just bloody pick him up," said the Sword with a sigh of disgust. For one reason or another, the Huntress got the message, and snatched the Serpent just before the wolf tried the same. With the Serpent in one hand and the Sword in the other, the Huntress vaulted the table, dashed through the courtyard, and burst back into the barracks. At the end of the hallway waved the boy from before, calling, "Follow me, Your Majesty," before, with widening eyes, he urged, "Hurry!"

"No need to tell us twice," insisted the Sword, feeling nauseous for all the swinging he did as the Huntress tore after the young man. She spared one look over her shoulder: six angry women; a scampering rat; and a bounding, starving wolf. As she rounded the corner, the Huntress found the young man stopped there and cried out, pointing with her Sword and meaning that he should come along.

"The closet, Lady," he insisted, pushing her toward it to stand between her and the crowd. "Your bow and quiver are there, please hurry!"

The Serpent said, "Tell us your name, lad, that we might, if nothing else, remember it," as, urged by the Sword's fearsome images of devouring, the Huntress rushed toward the open closet and its sundry tools.

The boy, eyes alight with bravery, lifted his chin. "My name is Eric Hope."

The Sword seemed to roll its eye, as, with relief, the Huntress swept bow and renewed quiver from their fellows, "'Hope' would have been a much better name than 'Maybe,' Serpent. You might have asked him sooner."

"I prefer to allow Felicity to make her own decisions," said the Serpent. Over his mistress's shoulder, the wolf descended upon Hope, who held back their pursuers as a dam did water. The Sword, bound to the eyes of the Huntress, could only ask what sight so filled the reptile's eyes with bleakness. He could only be denied an answer, for the Serpent thought the sight too grim to share and turned his head away, saying, "Onward, to the Tower."

"So you can betray us?" asked the Sword as the Huntress burst from the barracks. With a gasp of the dusty City air, she faced the blackened spire which chilled her to the bone but drew her forth as a bat toward the moon. The Sword clutched to her breast, the Huntress studied the Serpent resting across her shoulders.

"Snake," she said, softly. "Sword and snake and girl."

"Yes," said the Serpent.

"And Man," said the Huntress.

"Yes," said the Sword.

"King," suggested the Huntress, touching the crown upon her head and thinking of the crown upon his. Of all the suffering of his eyes. Feeling her own fill with tears, she rushed toward the terrible black Tower, forgetting the lion still at its base, fluttering carmine wings of such a span one flap could make the Northern Wind. She remembered as she skidded to a halt in the plaza, as the Sword had begun, "We'd ought to stop and think of a plan to deal with this— Stop!"

But, of course, it was too late. The Huntress found herself in the plaza with the lion above the skeleton of the General, laconic at the outset and then, upon seeing the potential of a second meal, stretching to its feet with a roar which shook the earth it trod.

"Father's eye," profaned the Sword, as the Huntress took a breath and planted wide her feet. "Do you see its size! Nearly big as the Beast which hid me underground!"

The Serpent, unimpressed, slithered down the Huntress, her body his ladder to the dirt. "Not half so big as that, good man."

"Where are you off to? Running away before you lose a scale?"

"Not at all. As I was trying, earnestly, to tell you before, I have realized just what it was I allowed to happen. And I am sorry." With a solemn lift of his head, the Serpent gazed at the Huntress. "Allow me to make it up to you both."

"How do you propose to do that—" began the Sword, but it was as he did that the Serpent started its long slither toward the lion. This drew the creature's attention sufficiently, and if the predator could have laughed, it might have to see such a tiny thing approach, this sad little lizard striped red and green which could only crawl on its belly on the ground. The lion roared again, and the Huntress cried out, "Snake," but could not step forward, for the Sword showed her if she did, she would be devoured.

Calling back, the Serpent said, "You must promise to trust me, though I know it is hard after what happened in the barracks. Suffice to say, my dear, I will never let such a thing happen again. And I promise you: there will be an 'again.'"

"What are you blathering about?" demanded the Sword, who, in the business of demanding, missed the second in which the Serpent was snatched up in the teeth of the lion. The Huntress, however, did not. A sharp cry of grief—his name—wrenched open her throat, for her friend, for all the tribulations caused and companionship given her, was no more. Her beloved friend had taken death upon himself, as though to be devoured by the lion so she would not succumb to its claws.

"Oh, dear God! Felicity, run! Would you please run." The begging Sword showed her that lingering would be the source of her end, but, overcome with grief, she could barely move, and instead stood trembling, her eyes filled with tears and her stomach at her feet.

"Snake," she said amid her tears. "Oh, oh, snake."

"Now's not really the time," urged the Sword as the lion prowled ever closer, slowing as it neared to savor the fruits of her prolonged terror. It was as though the Huntress were frozen to the spot. In the face of her pain, she forgot how far she had come, all that she had done and was going to do. She only felt the pain of losing the Serpent and guilt for not having better served him as a friend, for not having protected him from the lion, as though she ever could have. The Sword protested, and the lion encroached, but still, the Huntress wept, and even fell upon the earth to bury her face in her hands. She did not see when the lion ended its approach: when it stopped before her, fangs bared to devour, and instead stumbled to the right, then again to the left, and then fell, dying, flat upon the ground.

6

The thud of the lion's collapsing bulk coaxed the Huntress from her grief; she lifted her head, then gasped to see it panting out its final breaths before her. Frantic, she gripped the Sword as though to better show him, and he, too, professed, "If I keep swearing like this, the gods themselves will slay me, but what am I to do? This past day and night has been the strangest I've ever lived, and that includes my so-called rescue from Elysium."

All the stranger, too, as the crimson fur of the dead lion began as though to mold. It seemed a kind of algae, or rot; the putrefaction of dead flesh beneath its rust perhaps lent an odious texture to its carcass. But then, all the quicker, it bloomed the living color of moss on Forest trees; the supple prairie outside Hope farmstead, once north of the City, near where Felicity had been a peasant; the vibrant emerald of the luxuriant sea, awash with the thriving beauty of nameless multitudes; and the lion began again to take breath—or, more appropriately, the Serpent took first breath as the Lion, for he groaned, still facedown upon the plaza cobblestones, "If only I could describe the taste of my own mouth. Like pus and bird excreta."

"Snake," gasped the Huntress, clutching her heart and gazing wide-eyed at the Lion. "Snake!"

"'Lion,'" he corrected, using forepaws to push himself up with a groan and a stretch and a flap of new wings. "Try 'Lion.'"

"Lion," she formed, gasping then, and throwing down the Sword to wrap her arms around the creature's mane. "Oh, Lion! Snake, Lion!"

"Don't mind me," said the Sword, rolling nonexistent eyes. "Perfectly comfortable, thank you. Good to see you back, chap. Thanks for... I'm not entirely sure what it is you've done," it admitted with audible consternation, "but then, I've given up trying to understand anything."

"You've yet to give it up, and you never will," said the playful Lion as it draped an arm around the Huntress and lay on her cheek a doglike kiss. "The day you cease your efforts to explain just what it is that is happening is the day we shall have to call the doctor."

"Can you blame me? A fellow could feel like he's going mad, all this business going on!"

"He's only going mad if he believes he is. The more happily he goes along with things, the surer of his sanity he shall be."

"That's all well and good, but let's not forget that we've still a very real issue before us, consisting of that—why, yes, that Tower!" The Sword laughed, tickled by his epiphany. "Dear Lion, you can just fly us up there, can't you!"

With skepticism aimed at the Sword, the Lion said, "I am not certain that is wise."

"It makes perfect sense! Why else have you a pair of wings if not to fly us up the Tower!"

"Why was the Tower built with stairs of such a spiraling height if not to find them used?"

"Point taken, but, even so! I mean to say, it seems a rather convenient development. It would be silly of us were we not to take advantage of it. What's the harm? If anything, we reach the Witch faster and have more energy to deal with her, not having climbed hundreds of steps and fought off who knows what sorts of monsters."

"It may be better to enter it from the bottom, that we might see exactly what sorts of monsters lay in wait, and take care of them as we come to them."

"What? No, no! We can deal with them from higher ground! All we've done and been through, all we're capable of! You're a Lion, chap!

My God, we can do anything at all, the three of us together. Don't you think, girl?"

"Apricot." The Huntress frowned into her quiver, wondering if they would reach Man before his fruit spoiled.

"I'll take that as a solidarity statement, pet," decided the Sword, then saying to the Lion, "Well? Are you going to keep us waiting down here until Felicity's apricot spoils? Or are you going to fly us to that Tower window and help us take down the Witch once and for all!"

Trapped between the waiting Sword and the earnest Huntress overcome with imagery of herself flown to the highest window to find and free Man, the Lion sighed into the sky, lowered himself, and begged, "Please remember: I told you no good would come of this. I can only do so much."

"Of course, of course. Onward and upward," called the Sword as the Huntress gingerly mounted the Lion, her fingers plunging into its fur, her head lifting toward the top of the Tower. "Let's see what this Witch is made of!"

Body winding tight with the coiled muscles of his new nature, the Lion bolted off, its wings flapping, its tremendous body rising as the Huntress gave a cry of half delight, half terror and gripped all the tighter its thick mane. The beast laughed. "Careful, my dear."

But she, of course, could not help herself, never having dreamed of being so high. She gasped to find around her the circumference of the City, so wide and once beautiful despite its blackness that it stirred something in her as she might feel stirred standing in her favorite trees, a sentinel of the Forest. There was familiarity across it all, as if she had seen it before, and she gasped, whispering, "Lion?"

"Yes, fair girl?"

"Forest, Lion?"

"Yes, my girl." The Lion craned its head to the stars, then down upon the City over which they circled higher with each pass around the Tower. "Forest."

Too quick, the Sword insisted, "You ass, you can't just tell her any old thing. Felicity, darling, that's not Forest, that's the—"

But, faltered by deep curiosity, the Sword blinked his eye open that he might be the only one to see; he found himself in the hand of a dreaming Queen, herself in the hand of an angel flying surely, beautifully, over the trees of the Forest, with the City and its Tower far off in the distance. When the Sword once more blinded itself, and through the eyes of the Huntress they were naught but a girl and her wingèd lion, the blade fell into marshlike silence.

"Sword," asked Lion, as if he did not know what the blade had seen, "is something the matter?"

"It's all Forest, darling," agreed the humbled Sword. As the Lion chuckled, the Huntress nodded, because she had figured that out quite some time ago.

"Forest," she said, kissing his closed eye.

"Oh, girl. I'm rather going to miss this journey of ours when it's over. You can be charming. But do be careful. I remember she's very powerful. Oh, I wish you could understand me!"

Fleeting images of possible deaths crowded the Huntress's mind, put there by the Sword's frustration. In fighting the Black Lady from the vision of Man, she might be stabbed through, immolated, aged in an instant, dismembered, defiled. She clutched the Sword, and said, insistently, "Man," and was rewarded with thoughts of him. She imagined what it would be like to feel the touch of his hand upon her arm, her cheek, to feel his kiss and be held by him. Emboldened, she gripped her blade, and the Lion chuckled and said, "Yes, my fair girl, Man," as they exploded at last into the Usurper's bedchambers, viridian wings flapping wildly as it realized there was no proper place to land; all the room breathed and pulsed with the beating of a heart and horrid flesh like that of the Beast. Cringing, the Lion set down a tentative paw and felt it nearly submerged in twitching muscle. Tearing it free, he suggested, "Perhaps a fire is called for," only to see the Huntress's attention had been captured. Crucified upon the blackened wall, just as promised by the visions of the Sword, was the King. Man.

"Man," she breathed, "Man, oh! Oh!"

"Felicity." His voice was a thousand years old from suffering but no less beautiful than imagined for its pains. More beautiful, perhaps, sweeping straight into her heart to make her laugh, which made him laugh and cough and say, "You shouldn't be here, but I'm so happy to see you. Oh, it's been a lifetime."

Undaunted by the beating floor, the Huntress slid from the back of the Lion and, gasping, sprinted for the King. Tossing down her Sword, she threw her arms around his feet and kissed them, wonderingly touched his legs beneath the tatters of his robe.

"Did you just throw my son to the floor?" asked the King, laughing, and the Sword said, "Never mind, Father. It's been happening quite a lot. You don't feel much when you're a blade. It's perfectly all right."

"Well, I'm glad of that, at least. And glad to see you."

"If I could cry, Father, I would positively weep."

"Let's not get carried away." The King chuckled, ever dry, as the Huntress slipped her quiver from her shoulder and dug into its acquired arrows to produce the still-good apricot. She held it to her breast and retrieved again the Sword with which she cut down first one hand of the King, then the next. The black walls of the Tower bled from its wounds as the Huntress tore away the ventricles binding his legs and then plunged her Sword into the floor, ignoring the hisses and pops of the structure while she pulled him into her arms.

"Apricot?" she asked, and the King laughed at that, weakly, sagging in her clutch.

"At a time like this? I've never much cared for apricots."

The Lion deigned to land upon the floor at hearing that, but the blade was the one who spoke first. "Wh—never cared for...Felicity"— if Swords could pale, this one might have—"girl, put him down. That's not—"

Just as the realization of danger is often the most dangerous moment of all, so too was this revelation too late. The charcoal Tower hummed, universal, even when the Sword opened its eye to illuminate the room; but the body in the arms of the Huntress, when illuminated, belonged not to the King but rather the Witch, who turned such a wicked gaze upon the Sword that it was stricken blind and screamed, "My eye!"

"Sword," cried the Huntress, her attention then diverted down in terror as the King in her arms first began laughing, then was no King at all, blackening and whitening, becoming soft in flesh yet gaunt in bone, more beautiful and cruel. Having dropped the body and scrambled toward her companions, the Huntress cried to realize that which she'd held was the source of her strife.

The Lion, undaunted, held high its head as it placed itself between Huntress and Usurper. "What have you done with the King?"

The blackened woman rose to her feet, smoothing back her hair as the Huntress reached for the Sword; the Usurper smiled when the floor snatched it first, a dark arm emerging from its pulsing surface to toss the blade down spiral stairs in the center of the room. While the Sword made its screaming descent, the Tower's creatrix neared the Lion.

"The King and I are one in the same, so long as he and I are together in this Tower. I expect you will protest and deny my privilege, but my King is a part of my own heart. See?" She waved a hand, and from the west wall emerged, truly, the King, his rosy crown askew, his agonized eyes locked on the Huntress.

"Man," gasped the girl, but the Lion stayed her movements with a flickering tail and warning growl.

"You call him 'Man' as if he is only that. Can't you see his sovereignty? But of course you can't." Delighted, the tittering Usurper clasped her hands. "You remember nothing at all. All signs have pointed directly to it; people have spoken to you of it again and again, but you haven't even felt it! That is a forgetting beyond forgetfulness. Why is that?"

"For your interference," accused the Lion, and the Usurper smiled thinly.

"That's right. For my interference. For I have taken her true tongue, and in so doing, her ability to be all that she was. I have taken the light from her eyes and from her spirit, have drowned her in the wilderness of my Forest as I have tangled the City in the grip of the trees and hidden from its women the light of the sun."

"And the Men cast into the Forest?"

"Let them have the privilege of living in the light; in the darkness, they are naught but animals."

Shaking his head, the Lion said, "Would I could give you my eyes. Would I could save you, myself! But that is for the grace of one far greater still than I."

Baring her teeth in thin smile, the Usurper demanded, "Who is that, then? 'God'? The King?"

"Only that very same who gave you the power to weave all this tragedy," suggested the Lion, not without compassion, for he knew full well the pain which filled the heart of the Usurper in the face of rejection. "The very same spirit which you pulled from Elysium to taunt the King who wronged you."

The revealed King, who had until then listened from his place against the wall, panting for breath in semi-silence, lifted his head. "I truly am sorry."

The Usurper watched as he was swallowed to the neck by the Tower wall. "You're only sorry because I have you and you've no other recourse."

"Perhaps you could see His Majesty's contrition had you not sought to punish him from the first," said the Lion as a chair rose to become a black Beast with bull's horns upon its head. It charged the wingèd cat, knocking it aside to leave the Huntress exposed for the Usurper, who was upon her in an eyeblink.

"I have watched you from the first, girl. As has he: your King. I begat you, in fact, that we might together watch, but I did not think you would reach here. You wouldn't have, were it not for the bumbling guidance of your friends. What are you worth on your own? What merit have you, what value above that of any child? Only by luck and kindness have you come this far, and only that I might have the pleasure of murdering you with my own two hands."

"Pneuma," pleaded the King, taking a ragged breath despite the compression of the wall, "please."

"Watch," insisted the many-voiced Usurper, that single word spoken by invisible chorus. With an easy grip, she dragged the Huntress to the top of the spiral staircase and forced her to confront the abyss, the drop of impossible height filling the girl with terror which engendered new struggle. Clutching the smoke woven into the Usurper's gown, the Huntress cried out to discover she could not grip that which gripped her; her hand went through the body of the Black Lady. Cackling, the Usurper snatched her by the throat and dangled her over the drop, the fountain of the City plaza at the Tower's foundation a distant pinpoint in the center of a bleak mandala.

"I saw into your heart, dead girl," the Usurper taunted as the Lion was thrown from the upper window and the Huntress cried out, craning her head to see whether he got his bearings, "and all of this began because you wanted a bath. So, have one."

The Usurper released her grip. Within the wall, the King screamed; from outside the window, the Lion roared; from the base of the Tower, the Sword shouted. All of them, the same word: "Felicity!"

The Huntress, eyes wide, fell to her death.

It seemed a dream. Her body slammed into the pool of the fountain where it lay as if it had always been there, a twisted wreck facedown like the wretched buildings of the ruined City, eyes half-open, unblinking, uncomprehending, into the infinite base of the fountain. No sound arose but the ring of tinnitus; the Tower, its captives and invaders and slaves and rulers, fell into uniform silence. The Huntress felt no pain, nor fear, though she felt very much as the hart, and wondered, not in so many words, if the hart really had been defiant, or hateful. Perhaps its eyes had held surprise. Perhaps that was what her eyes held. As they struggled to focus, she recognized something must have broken her fall despite the limitless length of the Tower beneath her, for it appeared she hovered in space. What was it that had saved her? A body: a body she could not feel, poised beneath her own.

Whose body was this? This cool body, this woman's body. This bleeding woman's body. Twitching, with pain like a knife in her nerves, she turned her neck to see the Sword lying in the water, there, atop another Sword. Her lips trembled. She faced the impossible fall beneath her, then realized what had happened. She was on the floor. This woman beneath her was her, she, herself. She understood why the fall had seemed so limitless: the bottom of the pool was a mirror of perfect glass, revealing to the Huntress her own form for the first time in a comprehensible way. For the first time, the world unveiled the meaning of the word she had often heard, but not yet placed to anything at all. At last, she understood the word she mouthed in silence. The word everyone had used over, and over, and over again: "Felicity."

The Huntress was just a wild girl. The Sword was right. But in the mirror, beneath her, was Felicity. And her, then? What did that make of her, she who watched? After all this time, why, she had been neither Huntress, nor girl! But who was she, then? Who was she who watched Felicity? Felicity looked harder, her eyes narrowed against a pain so great she had ceased to feel it, narrowed against the rattling of bones in her shifting body as she lifted her head and met the gaze of her whose eyes trained far above, to the height from which the girl had fallen. As her eyes welled with thoughts of her King, those very thoughts—the faith which she had felt in the knowledge of his rescue—changed the texture of her tears. Not water; they grew white like sea-foam, the likes of which the world would never see again. At last, Felicity recovered language, and as her dense tears struck those of her reflection to bounce from the water as perfect pearls, she asked that reflection, "Who watches me?"

Felicity asked this not of herself, but of me. She had seen me because she had seen herself, Felicity, staring into that mirror to face her observer. And because she had seen me, I awoke, and realized I was Felicity, watching myself from the mirror's other side. Breathless, I told her, "I do," and she laughed, and smiled. Amid the sounds of scattering pearls, forms more perfect than any diamond, my awakening in her heart suffused us both with light, and together, we finally remembered:

7

Once upon a time, I was a peasant girl on a farm with my father and three sisters. This was in the days when there were Country people and City people, long before there were Forest men and City women. I had been born last in my line, and my delivery killed my mother. I survived to be crucified by my family for a murder I could hardly have been said to commit, and became their slave, toiling day and night, from the time I was small, to care for them, clean for them, and cook for them. Though my father still handled the farmwork, I was made to do as much as I could, and more than that besides. Through endless days, I labored and prayed this might not be my true lot. Why wouldn't it be, though, I often asked myself, alone at night in my dingy attic room. One window framed the Northern Lands, the distant Mountains and the sea beyond which I did not know then to be my fate; but the window by which I made my bed, and the window out of which I gazed to dream and hope and sigh, was the window to the south, which revealed the City glittering gold and pearl. My sisters dreamed of living in such a place, themselves. My sisters also dreamed of adventures, of excitement. What made me special? I was a mousy girl, or so I'd been told, and not worth much more than the tasks I fulfilled. It was my special duty to tend the fire, but anything that needed doing in the end was done by me, and it happened one winter that I probed the coals as my eldest sister found me.

"Felicity," she began, hands on her hips as if she had discovered me lying about, "there's been a wolf in our fields, picking off our sheep. You'd ought to do something about it, hadn't you?"

"I suppose," I told her, frightened I'd be met with the beast's claws and unsure just what I was supposed to do to catch it. Soft girl of fifteen in pearlescent fangs: it seemed unlikely I would do it in without being eaten, myself. But that, I realized while pacing the kitchen, was my ticket to catching the thing! Aflutter with excitement, I collected as much wool as I could and, feeling silly, kitchen knife tucked against my heart, I dressed as a sheep and hid among the flock at nightfall. I waited, absurd, in the darkness, trying not to giggle at myself, a little lamb. Just as I started thinking my sister had been having me on, something moved. My squint resolved the pointed ears and stiff tail of a diligent wolf which, quiet as the night which hid him, crept between the slats of our fence and into the field. My muscles tensed. Above the pounding of my heart beat the creature's footfalls as it moved amid the sleeping sheep to find the one which suited its appetite. When it found one near to me and opened wide its jaws, I threw off my disguise and sprang on its back, satisfied by the animal's yelp.

"A devil," it cried, bucking, "a demon!"

"The only demon I see is the one trying to pick off our sheep."

"*Your* sheep! These sheep don't belong to anyone, any more than I belong to anyone."

"You belong to your Woods," I chided, knife glinting in the moon-light. "You never should have come to our farm."

"I never should have listened to that stupid rat, is what I never should have done. If you let me go, I'll never come back to this field long as I live—but the same can't be said of that blasted rat, and I can only tell you what he's up to if I'm alive."

"What rat is this?" I asked amid his babbling, lowering the blade but tightening my grip on the wolf's fur. "If this is a trick, you'll be dead in an instant."

"No trick, girl. Go see, see your pantry! You thought I was bad, eating sheep? The rat is worse than I am! A downright pig. If you don't do something about him soon, he'll have all his relatives moving into your house. Then you and your family will really starve."

Lips tight, I considered the house, shivered without my sheepskin, and pointed the blade at the neck of the wolf. "If I ever find another sheep missing," I told him, "I'll make it my business to kill every wolf in this area."

Giving himself a shake as I dismounted him, the wolf said, "Sheesh! Take a little food and everybody gets sensitive. It's not worth the effort."

"Go on," I told him, kicking some snow across his face. He snorted, sniffed, then wheeled around to rush off, leap over the fence, and be gone.

Irritated to have a new problem to grapple, I faced the farmhouse, a smoke-emitting smudge against the dark night sky to which I and my knife retreated. Inside the matchbox kitchen, I dusted off my boots, lit a small lamp, and, creeping to keep from disturbing my family, I began checking foodstuffs in our pantry only to recognize the wolf was right. A bag of oats had been torn into, a hole in the back causing its contents to spill out, and the same could be said of our rice, and salted meats, and even our flour, my God, as though it were worth eating on its own! That wolf hadn't lied: the rat was a pig. Such a pig, in fact, that I found him buried headfirst in a bag of flax, loudly snoring from where he had fallen asleep midfeast.

"I'm rabid," cried the rat as he awoke in a panic, caught by his tail between my two fingers. "Let me go or I'll bite you so many times you'll never be able to stand the sound of rain!"

"If you were rabid," I told him, whipping him by the tail as if he were a rattle, "you wouldn't have half a mind to warn me of it, would you?"

With his pink hands curled into little fists of consternation, the rat twitched his whiskers. "No more than I've half a mind to warn you of the spider living in this house."

Exasperated by the unfolding chain of events and wondering if I would ever get sleep, I stuck my free hand on my hip and said, "Let's hear about this spider, then, and I'll let you go. But get it straight, buster;

if I see you around this house again, I'll make sure the pantry floor is covered in mousetraps."

"Girls today have no sense of gentleness," cried the indignant rat as I carried him outside and set him upon the back porch, where he scurried into father's rocking chair to clean his tail of the stink of human. "A fellow's got to eat, hasn't he!"

"The spider," I insisted, tapping my foot, and the rat rolled his eyes.

"He's living in the outhouse," he said, jerking his thumb toward the small, repulsive little shack. "You'd ought to thank me for telling you. It was only a matter of time before he bit somebody on the backside and caused a family tragedy."

I snatched the broom leaning against the doorframe, muttering to myself that, "I wish it had gotten you," before the guilt set in, and I corrected, "I'm really sorry; it's just that we can't have wolves eating our sheep, or rats eating our stocks."

With an indignant squeak, the rat exclaimed, "That shyster! A fine way to show your gratitude," and tore off into the darkness to find the animal who'd sold him out.

Attention dominated by the outhouse, I gripped the broom and pulled open the warping door. In the dark of night, its interior was like the soot of our fireplace, but the light of my lamp burned bright enough that in the back corner of the floor glinted a spider's web. Muscles tense, I readied myself to destroy it until a soft voice above me asked, "You don't see me going about setting fire to your home, do you, my girl?"

Frowning, I found, indeed, a fat caramel spider on the ceiling, its front legs working before its twitching incisors as though finishing its most recent meal. With the broom clutched to my breast, I drew back a step, trying to be courageous as I said, "No, you don't, but I'm also not the sort of creature to go about biting others."

"Not true at all. Why, my girl, think of cows! Or me, of course. Your broom is worse than your bite, I think." As I grew aware of my makeshift weapon, he asked, "Don't I deserve a home as much as you?"

"Of course, and wolves and rats need to eat, too, but you all can't do it here! You'd ought to go make homes of your own, elsewhere. This is my home, for my family."

"When humans build a home, keep cattle and grain and comfortable, dark spaces, they invite implicitly all things which also crave those comforts."

"I'm not trying to be mean, but just because you invite yourselves doesn't mean we want you."

"No," suggested the spider, lowering himself by a silken thread to spin precariously near my face, "but we can be useful."

"And how's that?"

"Well, the wolf told you about the rat, and the rat told you about me. You would have never known of me had you not spared the wolf, indeed, had you not hunted it to begin with. Why, do you know how long I've been in your father's outhouse? Since before you were born! It was only a matter of time before I was found to mutual unpleasant surprise, or had a curious spell of appetite."

"I suppose that's true. It would have been terrible if you'd bitten one of my sisters."

"Are you so sure about that?" asked the chuckling spider. "I've heard the way they talk to you, seen in your eyes the way it makes you feel."

Frowning, I leaned half from the outhouse. "How did you know about the wolf, and the rat?"

"I know many things." Dropping to the floor, the spider crawled toward his web. "All the secrets in the world. I can tell you an awfully important one, if you'd like."

"If I let you go?" I asked, but I could already see that the spider was beginning to devour his web in the manner of a salesman, pitch rejected, packing his wares to leave for the next customer.

"Well, my dear, I can certainly tell you no secrets if you kill me. But I can see in your heart that you won't." Pausing in its work and turning to me with his front legs folded beneath him, the arachnid assessed me with glittering ebony eyes, the likes of which I would not see again until I met the Serpent. "A warmhearted girl, sweet and kind. One must learn to be unkind and even cruel, living among cruelty, mustn't they?" This was asked so softly, so gently, that it saddened me for myself. I nodded as the spider returned to his work. "The time will come when you throw off isolation like the cloak it is."

Anxious that someone might overhear us even though my family slept and not many people heard the speech of animals, I whispered, "What was your secret," and then had to crouch and bend my head at the wave of a tiny arm.

"To make a diamond," said the recluse, winding the final thread of his web around his spindled hind leg, "one need only take a piece of coal, and force it to endure tremendous pressure and unspeakably intense heat."

"Why," I cried, delighted, "is that really all?"

"Yes, my hearth keeper, an operation so simple even I could perform it." It nodded sagely on its way between my feet and through the outhouse door. I followed him with my eyes, mystified by his knowledge as I was surprised by his courtesy. Biting my lip at the sight of his departure, a burst of courage sparked aloud the question:

"Could you help me make one?"

The spider's trek paused in place. "A true diamond is made within the earth," he suggested, "but if you bring me a coal, perhaps I can help. Would you still see me sent away into the snow, even if I did this favor for you?"

With fretful moue on the edge of the outhouse, I hummed. What were the odds of such a polite spider biting someone? Still uncomfortably high. At last, I said, "You can live in the attic with me, if you'll only promise you won't kill me."

"Should my fangs ever meet your skin, my girl," said the too-cheerful spider, crawling upon my shoe for a ride back into the house, "I promise, you shall find yourself with little more than an itch and a few days' rash."

Not the least bit reassured about it or my decision-making, I carried it inside and wondered if this creature told the truth. The previous two had, despite the odds. As it dismounted my foot to follow me into the living room, it said, "You've a lovely home for a girl treated so poorly in it."

"I just want us to have a nice place to live," I told him, using a poker and pan to knock from the fire a coal, which, while burning, became the center of attention for my new friend, who wrapped about it a web as though weaving it into a heatproof sack. "They're my father, and sisters, and they may not be very nice to me, but they're family. I have to be good to them, don't you think?"

"It is one of the King's rules, that the people of his Kingdom should honor their parents," he agreed while crafting with his thread a rope with which to drag the sack, "but there is more to a parent than birthright. One can honor the idea of someone without honoring the someone in question."

He skittered off, the coal insulated in its chamber of webbing, dragging behind him as he plunged into the snow. Though I worried for him, I could not make myself follow, for the night was dark and cold and I could not yet believe any spider, however courteous, could be trusted. When he didn't return for hours, I started to think my misgivings well placed, but just before dawn, another trail approached in the snow, and I leapt from my vigil at the kitchen table to let him in. The shivering spider clambered upon the porch, hauling a diamond like the tip of my thumb.

"Why," I cried, "that's incredible!"

"I am so pleased you like it," he said, eight eyes on me as I unwrapped the gem to turn it this way and that in the glow of my lamp. "I thought it to be rather sloppy; I have not brought anyone a diamond in some time, since people rarely talk to spiders living in outhouses. But perhaps soon enough I shall make you another, if you are patient."

"How wonderful," I cooed, burning with curiosity to know why we had to wait but reluctant to ask lest he take my curiosity as lust for gems, rather than thirst for knowledge. Smiling, I lowered my hand to take the spider into my palm, then lifted him to my lips to lay a kiss upon his back, which seemed, I'd say, to please him, for his tiny forearms stroked my chin.

"I shall bring you a diamond every time I can if you persist in giving me kisses like those, my girl," it jested as I, with my treasure, retreated to my room in hopes of some sleep before the day began.

I was no fool: no good could come of sharing my diamond with my sisters, or my father, so I kept it hidden, always, in the toe of my shoe, regardless of whether or not I wore it. It was hardly as if it was some tremendous treasure, after all; the spider was right. The diamond was certainly beautiful, more beautiful than any I had seen, but it was still far from a perfect diamond. If I tried to bring it to the City, it was hard to say whether it would be worth anything at all. That was how people came to live in the City, if they were not born to it, or brought in by a relative; they found or made a treasure worthy to sell in the plaza markets in exchange for a house. This diamond might be worth a shack on the outskirts, assuming it was worth anything; worse, I would become reputed for subpar diamonds, and the worst thing was to be in the City, but only on its edges, for then one missed so much one hardly knew what one was missing. And still all that was only if my friend was not offended by my exchange of his gift! He might be disappointed that I had made my way into the City by means not my own, and if I sold or revealed my secret to anyone, my friend might bring no more gifts. So, although my sisters and father berated and used me as they always had, and although even that flawed diamond might allow me to move, I remained where I was, in the attic, with my diamond and my friend. A year passed, and on the anniversary of the day he had brought me that first diamond, my friend bade me take a coal from our fire; this, he took away again, and he returned the next morning with a second diamond, bigger and far more beautiful than the first.

"How did you make this?" I asked him that night, for we had been friends for a year, and he knew I was not greedy for anything but knowledge.

"I did not make this, dear girl," said my friend, settling into his web in the glass of my window. "You've no horses here on the farm, or else you might come watch me. Have you been to Hope farm, or their inn? A most lovely family, with one horse for each family member, and room enough in the stables for thirteen more, as many horses as they have rooms for travelers; the biggest horse is a stallion with furred hooves the size of boulders. He weighs so much one need only encourage him to crush a red-hot coal to make a diamond, though it is an endeavor of such strength and burns his hooves so seriously he can only manage it once a year."

"How wonderful," I said, admiring this diamond, the size of a peanut shell. "Why does he help you, this horse?"

With a positively wicked laugh, my friend, who was, of course, still a spider, asked, "Have you seen what a burning coal will do to a pile of hay, my girl? If he did not help me in making the diamond, Hope farm would be ash in an hour."

Well, I thought to myself, it's a good thing he is my friend, and not my enemy! Most would have been horrified by the spider, I am sure, and most would not have liked to keep him so comfortable in their room. I admit that more than once I awoke to find I'd been bitten in my sleep and had some itching lump on my elbow or wrist, but any harm my friend did was temporary at best. Since it seemed the cost of our friendship, I made no complaint but to once ask about his appetite, which I had thought to be for flies.

"Flies, of course, sweet Felicity. But what creature can resist indulging its sweet tooth!"

We laughed, and I was touched in a strange way, and all the time the spider and I grew closer—but the closer I grew to the spider, the more my family resented me. It seemed to them that I idled time alone like a madwoman, and in too good a humor for all they had known of me. It was around this time my eldest sister was married off so just the three of us were left, but Chastity had done so little around the home, beloved as she was by Father, I hardly noticed her absence. I admit I had also taken the advice of the spider, which had become necessary as time went on; my family seemed crueler by the day no matter what I did to please them, and I often thought that, if they had known about the diamonds, I would have been ridiculed for having such crooked gems, or for thinking them worth keeping. For thinking I could amount to anything but a farmer's daughter, plowing in the muck, chasing off wolves and rats, confiding in the spider which bit her at night. Day by day I neared wit's end, and my family became all the crueler. Now more than ever, my sisters broke pottery or stole silver to sell someday in the City, and I would be held to account. I often faced my father's wrath and wept through bruised eyes to the spider, which would hum from his weaving on my windowsill.

"Were I you," he said one day, "I might set this place aflame and find another family."

A sob burst from me; I wished at that moment I might slap my friend, whose callous advice seemed at such times especially ill-advised. "They're my family," I insisted, "and they might not be good to me, and they might not care, and I might not know how to connect with them, but I—I remember when I was a little girl, don't you? You've been here all this time. When I was very small, weren't there times? Times when they were kind?" I struggled through my tears to recall and, hiccupping, lay my head upon my pillow while the spider tsked at my inconsolability.

"Why, sweet Felicity! Of course this life of yours has given you as many good things as bad." Strolling across the wall to lower upon the corner of my bed, he rested at the edge of my pillow, one of his eight legs extending to catch a teardrop as it fell. This, he crammed into his mouth. "I suppose perhaps I was being rather harsh when I suggested you kill them. The logic of spiders cannot always apply to human girls."

"It would be criminal. Even if it was something I could bring myself to do, I would never survive."

The spider turned, pensive, to the window, his eight eyes dreamily unfocused. "The laws of men, most curious things. It would seem to me an open-and-shut case in the face of your plight. Does law not work both ways, my dear?"

"What would I do if my family was punished for the way they treated me? What does it matter? They, imprisoned, leave me the farm—and then? A whole life doing what?"

"You might bond with the Hopes. Young Eric shall be quite a handsome lad in a few years' time."

"I don't want to live on a farm! What can I learn here? What can I be here?" Heat filled my face with my wretched sob. "If I'd never been born, there never would have been any trouble. My mother would still be alive, and my sisters might all be working in harmony together, and—"

"And there would have been no one to find me in the outhouse until it was much too late," said the spider, so ominously my tears quelled. Legs working in eerie synchronicity, the creature scuttled up my arm to sit below my ear, where it whispered, "I was growing bored when you found me. If you did not exist, sweet Felicity, I might that very winter have found myself with uncontrollable appetite, and taken one of your sisters for a glutton's feast. Then the next, and then the next, and then your parents, too."

I clutched the hem of my dress. "Why haven't you done something like that to me?"

"Why, between the sweetness of your tears and the odd taste of your blood here or there, a spider might live forever! Not to mention what pleasure it is to have your conversation, to see your delight in things so simple as those little diamonds. No, dear Felicity, you are better alive for a lifetime of nibbling than dead as a one-time meal of grief. Had I my way, you'd live a hundred years!"

It was then that an idea possessed me, although I could not say whether it was worth anything, or whether it was treachery on the part of my imagination. But it seemed to me this spider was far more than a spider, though I could not explain why, or how. It was not the talking which was the tip-off, for all animals in the Kingdom spoke if only one knew how to listen, though passersby might think one mad. No, there was something about the spider which made me think he was not just a spider, and in retrospect, I suppose it was the diamonds he brought. It took a very particular kind of animal to know the secrets of nature, after all. Many animals might know the secrets of other animals, but for this one to know a secret of the very earth itself, and to be able to replicate it on the planet's surface, why, that seemed neither the work, nor the knowledge of a commonplace spider. Perhaps that meant that he knew other secrets: human secrets, and the secrets of whatever creature he really was, and more than that, perhaps, besides.

Whatever he was, I realized I was valuable to him. Brave, or foolish, I sat up primly, heedless of the creature on my shoulder. "You shan't see me live another month if you cannot help me carve a life more tolerable than this farm."

"Felicity," gasped the spider, "my girl, let us not be absurd! How crass, to make a joke on your life." He intended to bite me in punishment, but before his fangs could penetrate, I swept him away so he bounced across the pillow with a cry of shock.

"I'm making no joke," I told him, rising. "I can see nothing to hold me to this world! Perhaps it's me! Perhaps I'm sad and broken, wrong and vile!"

"Felicity—"

"To be born on a farm! Born on a farm for naught but abuse, and why? To kill my mother and keep my family in half comfort! Who can be comfortable in a house like this, on a farm like this, in a place like this, knowing this is all that they are, all they'll know!"

"Why—"

"There's so much more to see! To do! I can't stay here! I can't be here! If I must, if this must be my life, with a spider my only friend using me for food as much as friendship, why, then—I'll open my veins in the kitchen next month, and see myself down to Elysium!"

"But my girl, you haven't a horse, and you know what happens to suicides! They have no guides. The Ogre shall eat you."

I laughed sourly. "Better to be eaten all at once and have the misery over with than face a lifetime of little bites, poison building in my blood! What kind of friend are you? To tell me to hurt those I love! To bite me at night and drink my tears! No earthly friend, no friend by man's reckoning!"

"I have brought you diamonds," suggested my wearied companion, as humbled as a spider could be while I snatched off my shoe to let both gems fall in my hand.

"What, these? Diamonds! Rocks! Coal tromped by horse's hooves! What do such things do for me but glitter in light? What good are they if they can't bring liberty, knowledge, happiness?"

"They can bring all those things, and more. So can I."

"Then do it!" I fell to my knees and clasped my hands upon the bedside. "Please. Do me this kindness, and I promise I'll always do as you say. I'll live a long, good life and dedicate my blood to you, for whatever it's worth! You can have all the blood and tears you'd like."

Thoughtfully, the spider tilted his head. "If I do you this kindness, my girl, you may well never see me in this form again."

My heart twisted, for the idea of losing even this friend was a painful one; after all, he was my only friend, no matter why or how or what he was. "Why?" My eyes brimmed. "Can't you find a way to help me and still remain my friend? Did I so offend you?"

"Oh! Dear girl, I shall always be your friend. No offense at all; I love to see the spark of fury in your heart. But, I shall have to come to you as something other than a spider, for if your life is truly to change, a change in circumstance shall require an alteration of wisdom."

"You'll really do it," I said, gasping.

Sighing, the spider made his way up the wall. "Yes, of course. I'm left with no choice. It would hardly do to see you devoured by some Ogre. What else is there for me? Wait another century in another outhouse for another girl clever or lucky or quick enough to find me?" As he had that first time, he bundled up his web. "No, that simply won't do. I do, indeed, know just the way to help you, and I suppose you are quite right: no one wants to spend one's life living in a farm, if they are keenly aware of all else there is. But know this: I cannot change your life for you. After all, I am but a spider. All I shall do is provide you with the opportunity, the circumstances, to allow you to change your life. You must recognize them and grasp them yourself, knowing what I have taught you."

"How will you be when you return?" I asked as I opened the window to the cold.

"Who could say? Not even I. But you shall know me, feel me, when I return to you, when your life is better, different. Then, we shall begin our friendship anew—in a better, different way."

Tearfully, I leaned out the window to lay upon his fuzzy abdomen a kiss: a twinkle lurked in eight black eyes. Too soon, he left, and I was alone in my cold attic room, and the winter wind cut to my bones, so I, weeping, shut my window.

8

Would the spider do as he'd said? I could never be sure. He had been a good friend in many ways, but an arachnid could never be entirely trusted. Not one so honest about his worst intentions, anyway. Even so, I had to believe that he would help me; if he didn't, I was lost. I would stand by my word. I would rather feed myself to the Ogre at the gate of Elysium than stand another helpless season of suffocation in the dark. All I could do, day in and out, was work and pray and wish over my two little diamonds, my two gifts from my friend, whose third gift came twenty-nine days after he departed, when we received a visit from the King.

When it happened, I was outside, bundled against the cold while shoveling snow to a main road flattened by many weary horses. It seemed the snow would cover my work in a few hours' time and I would be at it again, and I might have cried for frustration if the cold hadn't stung my eyes with my own tears. I was exhausted by my efforts and blinking snowflakes from my eyelashes, focus failing, when there appeared in the static of the snowstorm first one shadow upon its horse, then another, and another, until twelve such figures rode in procession—though on only eleven horses. All were bundled under such an immensity of furs and weapons that I could not see their faces, and I stood still, fearful as they approached. As the man who drove the black stallion at the head of the line rode his horse before me, the beast pawed

at the snow and snorted in the cold in a way which inspired an affinity
for its plight.

"Is this the Hope farmstead?" called the man from beneath thick
cloaks of scarlet fox fur. I shook my head, pulling down my scarf so he
could better hear me as he explained, "We're after their inn!"

"No, sir! We're shepherds here, and farmers. We've hardly any rooms
to speak of."

With a glance over his shoulder at the eleven men and ten horses
idling in the road, then toward our house, the man asked, "Are you
sure you've no room to take us, lass? There's no seeing in this storm,
and my men are exhausted. Their horses, too. See that one, with two
men upon it!"

"Aye." I squinted through the storm, at the two figures upon the
final horse.

"My guardsman's mare fell dead of spider's poison three days ago,"
he shouted. I felt myself pale against the apple of the cold, but the man
didn't notice my fleeting, tearful pain as he went on, "The spider was
stomped dead by my horse, but that means we've a rider with no horse,
and a horse tired for his second rider. I see those old stables in the field."
He waved a hand—to my surprise, for how well he saw through the
snow. "Perhaps my men and I might put our horses up for the night,
and crowd a time by your fire?"

"I would love you to," I told the obscured man, who had no trace
of malice in his voice, indeed radiated warmth from his scarlet furs amid
the white noise-storm, "but it's not my home to offer up to strangers.
It's my father's."

"The man who cares for a place is the man who owns the place,"
said the stranger, in thought. "Who is shoveling the path to the house?"

"I am, sir."

"And"—his blue eyes squinted to better see the cottage—"there's a
good deal of firewood beneath that sheet. Who was it who chopped
that?"

"I did, sir," I said, the snowstorm beginning, but slowly, to
diminish.

"And the cooking, the cleaning, and the washing! I see three lights on upstairs, three rooms. Do three people help with all of that, or does the girl who stands before me do all of that, as well?"

Unsure whether to be affronted for the sake of my family or startled by the man's perception, I said nothing, and only clutched my shovel tighter. A smile brightened his voice. "I'll say so again, my lady: the man who cares for a place is the man who owns the place. And the man who owns this place seems to me to be a lady."

At last, I laughed, for it seemed all I could do. He was right to put it like that, and I felt very silly to have let my family make me think I was anything but the owner of the house to begin with. After all, I lived in its very topmost room, like a queen in her tower! Delight filled the stranger's eyes on my laughter, and he extended his hand; I realized belatedly he awaited the shovel, which I passed.

"Let my men and I relieve the burden of your work in exchange for a night by your fire," he said, gently, as both our grips lay upon the handle. For some strange reason, though I did not know this man at all, I felt as if I did; and felt as if I knew not just that I could trust him, but also that I would have no trouble with my father for letting him and his companions stay, however many there may have been.

"I would love to have you stay with us," I said, and so it was that the cloaked man whistled to his fellows, who dismounted horses which waited obediently, unhitched, for their masters to tromp through the snow and meet their leader.

"This is not the Hope family's inn," called the man, "but this is a home that welcomes us. Let's help the lady, and earn our keep."

With the wave of a magician or a maestro, the stranger swept his men to work. As they took out their weapons, swords, axes, and glaives for use to shovel snow, he dismounted his horse, took me, laughing, by the waist, and set me upon his saddle. "There's a lovely sight! Stay warm, my lady, and we'll be through in hardly any time. But before I start"—he paused, one hand still on my hip as I settled on his stallion's back, his lapis eyes bright upon mine—"will you tell me your name?"

Flushed, I told him, "Felicity," and this he smiled at and repeated to himself as he turned away with my shovel in his hands to do for me my work.

I cannot say how long I sat upon his horse, but it surely could not have been more than ten minutes. Miraculously, in those ten few minutes came the true death of the storm, which revealed charcoal sky full with embers of the setting sun. As the men worked, they chanted songs, and one drove me to tears as the jet stallion whipped his mane. It was a song composed by the red-clothed man upon his horse's killing of the spider.

O brother, prophet, my regrets
For what I did today;
With your eight legs, like God's own arms,
I had to do away.

Eight seers' eyes shall see no more
No silken webs shall weave;
But neither more your wicked core
Nor fangs to make men heave.

As I turned away to hide my sadness, the tail of the horse flicked my knee as if to pat it in sympathy. I dared not confirm its intent; it was a roundly known fact among those who spoke to animals that horses only spoke with other horses, preferring otherwise to listen.

They were nearly finished when my family noticed the noises outside and the first face appeared in the window. Knowing Shame and how she loved an excuse to chastise me, she checked with glee to ensure dinner would be late. Instead, our eyes met from my place upon his gilded saddle, surrounded by the men who had the path almost cleared, and her expression bloomed with shock before disappearing, along with the rest of her, from her window. It proved mere minutes later that my father burst out, shouting, "Felicity! Get off that stranger's horse this instant!"

The crimson man paused with a spadeful of snow. "She's warmer on the back of my horse than she would be standing out in the snow, waiting for us to finish our work."

"It's Felicity's work," corrected my father as the eleven men lowered their impromptu shovels to lean while observing the scene's unfolding. Their leader, patient and cheerful as ever, approached my father and sisters crowding the doorway. His horse followed him with me upon it, unbidden by any means I had been able to perceive.

"Perhaps it was Felicity's work, but we've made a trade, you see. Your daughter has offered us a night by the fire and the use of your stables in exchange for her work."

A gasp rang between my sisters, and my father, red in the face, shouted, "Felicity! You know better than to offer our home to strangers!"

Tears of panic already forming in my eyes, I opened my mouth to explain, but the man laid his hand upon my leg, and I, shocked by the touch as much as comforted, hushed. "Your daughter only meant to give twelve weary travelers a place to stay," he said. My father scoffed in condescension.

"Twelve travelers, or twelve robbers, more like! Robbers or worse. Felicity, get down from that horse and get inside. I'll deal with you after I've figured out something for these men."

"You would turn twelve men and their horses out in the cold for your own mistrust?"

"It's not mistrust driving me, but lack of foolishness. I'm not stupid enough to invite strangers into my house. Not that we've room for you to start with!"

"We're very compact," said the wry man, having my father on, which was never a good idea and only made him stomp his foot like the ridiculous troll he was.

"I won't abide strangers in my house," he insisted, and it was at last that the man lost his humor and said, tersely, "Aye, but what stranger stands before you, brother? You have not even seen my face. For all the world, you might know me, and be embarrassed by yourself before your daughters and your pride."

"I know no man but the King," snapped my father. "No friends have I, no man is good enough to have my company, and my daughters only barely. Felicity, certainly not—and certainly no fellow she thinks to invite without my say-so! No, sir, I'll not be having a stranger in my house."

"But your King?" asked the man, and my father snorted, saying, "When he shows up, I'll give him my very bed to sleep in, my own food to eat, and one of my daughters to marry. Until then, I'll be keeping no company."

It was then the man unwrapped his scarf, which fell from his face to reveal a beautiful white mouth upon more perfect a dark-bearded jaw than any sculpture could demonstrate. With deft hand, he stripped off his fox fur and the hood over his head, tore away all the clothes of winter to stand in the snow, the King, bared in flaming mantle, crown glittering like the gold fire of the sun which burned yet on the horizon, sinking ever lower in deference to the glory which made me and my sisters and my father all gasp, made my sisters clutch their skirts and retreat into the house and my father fall weeping to his knees while I stared in wide-eyed, widemouthed awe of this man, this King, to whom I had been hospitable because it was simply the thing that was done.

"Your Majesty," began my tearful father, reaching to kiss his robes, "I didn't know, please, I'd no idea you would come in disguise!"

"A King finds no clearer window to the hearts of his people than in the guise of a traveler in need of a rest; I have seen into your heart to find it a disappointment from the first of my arrival. See your daughter, shaking from the cold?"

"Not the cold"—I laughed, almost afraid to correct him, meaning nothing by it but playfulness—"but for your glory, O Lord, you who have come to visit us! Oh"—tears welled in my eyes to realize what it was my friend had done for me—"oh, you've come to *visit* us."

"By happy accident," said the King with a fond pat of my knee, not realizing or, perhaps, not acknowledging the causality set into motion by my dear friend. Returning his attention to my father, his expression hardening, the King said, "Even if your daughter had not already given her word we would have a place to sleep, I believe you but a moment ago offered me your bed, did you not?"

"I did, my Lord, I did indeed!" Hurrying to his feet, my father rushed inside. "And a stew. Go, girl, Felicity! Come down from there and make things ready for our guests." He turned to me a forceful smile, and I dared touch the King's mantle.

"May I, Your Majesty?"

"Of course. You and your sisters run along; I should like time to speak to your father by myself." My heart fluttered with trepidation at that, for I knew Kings to be as wrathful as kind, but I also had faith in him to do what was wisest for my father: for this King, the Red King of the West, was a man who ruled with his people in his heart. He kissed my hand and helped me from his horse. I rushed inside to meet my sisters, who gossiped in the kitchen, then stopped to stare as I emerged before resuming as if I were not there at all.

"Madness," said my second-oldest sister, Phobia, who should have been next to marry off. "The King's obviously taken pity on a pathetic, sooty waif."

"Witchcraft," accused my third-oldest sister, Shame, staring into the stew. "Perhaps she's been enchanting us all this time."

"I'm not surprised, really, but I'm appalled she would let the King think our father is some brute. Why, Felicity"—Phobia studied me, her chin haughtily lifted—"you've never complained before about doing work around the house. Why let the King cast judgment on father without saying anything?"

"A travesty. If Chastity were here, she would be very disappointed."

For some reason, their words, which normally might drive me to tears, did not so much as touch me. I kissed Shame's cheek, then stuck my hands on my hips and laughed aloud. "Why, we've hardly more than five bowls to start with. What are we to do for sixteen! Four and four." That made me laugh all the harder, then, for I thought of my late, eight-legged friend, and laughed and twirled in the kitchen, and not thirty minutes later the living room was crowded with the King and his men, my father and his daughters, and me, who found herself with a mug of stew sitting at the feet of the King, in my father's armchair by the fire which danced in the rubies of his crown. He, of course, had been one of the lucky ones to have a bowl, and I was likewise lucky to have gotten a mug, for there were those with the misfortune to receive flower vases and well-washed pails. I and all the men but my father laughed together, while my family, less than pleased, sulked in the silent reverberations of whatever conversation had been shared between the King and my father.

"I see a father, and three lovely daughters," observed the King during our meal, "but where is our lovely mother?"

"Under the willow boughs, near the Woods," said my father, truly saddened by the thought before he turned a bleak eye upon me. "Felicity saw to that."

"And what would Felicity know of her mother's death?" asked the King. I, dark-faced, trembled.

"Her life was the cost of my coming to the world," I lamented, and the King's curiosity melted to sympathy.

"Why, Felicity! And Phobia, and Shame, poor girls. It's been no easy time without her, I would wager. I lost my own wife on the birth of my son."

"I recall," said my father, eyes dim. "I am still so very sorry, Your Majesty. The Kingdom will never recover."

I, turning my face upward, asked, "What was she like?"

My father and sisters hissed softly their disdain for my question, but the King took no offense, in fact shook his head, lifted a gloved hand, and said, "Every voice in the Kingdom would leave Sophia forgotten in her grave, as if I wished I had never had a wife to begin with, rather than had and lost one—but ah, I miss her! I wish, always, to speak of her."

His gentle gaze fixed on me, he said, "She was beautiful as you, though in many ways, most different. Her hair, like gold, and her eyes, like seawater. Not like you, Felicity—black, your hair. Black as the feathers of ravens, and eyes like the bark of an oak. But she, like you, was clever and wise, both—so wise that she was not too clever, and clever enough that she knew the truth of wisdom. And her heart! Warm and honest, and full of stars." Pain filled the King's face, and he lowered his bowl with a damp sigh. "I blame myself for her death, for it was the birth of my son, and the hand of my concubine, and the curse of my parent, which caused it."

"You shall not find her like again," said my father, sympathetically, and the King shook his head.

"No, not again. I shall find another, different Queen, with the noble qualities to make the right ruler, but beauty and being enough she should not be mere shadow to her predecessor: instead, partner in my adoration, a partnership separated by time and heartbeat." With a small smile, the King returned to himself. "As it happens, Father, I recall mention of not just a bed and a stew, but a daughter, too."

The old man perked. "Why, you would really have a wife from one of my daughters!"

"From any man's daughter, truth be told. Her parentage matters not," said the King, carefully watching as I listened, focused on the fire. "Not half so much as the sharpness of her mind, and whether she can do unto me a service of my choosing."

At last, blushing, Shame spoke up, lowering her glass candy dish. "And what sort of service would you have, Lord?"

"A challenge, good lady, a wager." Setting aside his bowl, the King sat forward, hands folded. "I may not seem it, but I am a man who loves to gamble. And I take the matter of my bride with utmost seriousness. Any woman who hopes to win my heart should realize likewise the seriousness of the matter, and the cost of failure."

As my sisters edged forward on their couch cushions, the King said, mostly to my father and to me, "I will have you do me a task which can be done by only the cleverest, and the wisest—a work which must be completed by the dawning of the sun this morning. Those girls who take up my challenge will commit themselves to it and find no turning back. They will complete the task I have given them by the dawning of the sun, and I will have their hand in marriage, or, they will fail, and I will have their head."

"Why," gasped Phobia, "what sort of King are you, beheading the ladies you court!"

Laughing, the King lifted his eyebrows. "How else am I to impart the seriousness! No one is forcing you to try for my hand. You can just as soon say no and sleep tonight as if nothing had been offered, rather than staying awake to try the task."

"I will," said Phobia, flouncing to her feet. "I would rather live a thousand years with father and the sheep than risk my life for something silly as a crown."

"It isn't silly," I burst out at last, surprised by myself and drawing like shock from my sisters. Still, I went on, insisting, "It's not just a crown, just a thing. Do you know what it means to be a Queen? To be the bride of the King? What knowledge! What beauty! Oh!" I turned, setting aside my mug and forgetting it completely as I clutched the robes of the King's lap. "Please, sire, what would you have me do? What task might I take on to commit myself to your heart?"

With a smile, the King smoothed a strand of hair from my cheek. In a most soothing voice, as if he knew perfectly well what it was I knew and didn't know, the King said, "I would have for my wife whatever woman in the Kingdom could make on this night the most perfect diamond ever seen."

A gasp rose from both my sisters and my father, and Phobia cried, "That's impossible!" while I, trembling, tried to stay calm, and said nothing. What did this mean? What would happen at the end of this night? I vibrated with such excitement I felt I might jump from my seat and go running, screaming, through the house, but I could not so much as smile, or even breathe, for Shame studied me close as one might a painting. I rose to collect every empty vessel in sight, bowl or mug or vase, juggling them in my arms while Shame said at last, "Well, a diamond's got to be made some way, hasn't it?"

"Indeed, it has. It is not so impossible, though only a task for one who is brave, to be certain. Especially considering the cost of the failure."

After contemplation, my sister said, "I've always been embarrassed, living here," and while Phobia gasped in indignation, Shame insisted, "It's not exactly a palace. But, why, I'd live in a palace if I did this, wouldn't I? I'll find a way," she said before coiffing her curls to smile, winsomely as she could, at the King. "I would love to make you a diamond. Death would be better than staying here."

"Mind that your words don't wound your father mere hours before your passage to Elysium. Hubris is a poison worse than that of the spider which killed my man's horse. What of you, Felicity?" The King watched as I, one foot over the threshold of the kitchen, seconds from leaving the room, was forced to freeze with the cluster of containers in my arms. "Would you take up my challenge, my lady, and make me a diamond?"

"I would," I said, mind spinning. "I'll try this for you, Your Majesty, though I cannot promise I will succeed. I have never made a diamond before," I admitted, and he smiled at that, asking, "Would it help you to know that I think that you can?"

I, blushing, babbled some ridiculous excuse, and made myself scarce in the kitchen.

Madness, witchcraft, perhaps my sisters were right! What was this! To what had I agreed? My head on a platter! I only knew the methods of diamond-making, after all, not the practice. It had been my friend to do that for me, and though I knew the way in which he did it, I trembled to wonder how I might. In my room, I paced, wasting precious time but not knowing what I could do. If I left now, Shame would doubtless follow, and, espying the methods without understanding their reasons, would produce some hollow replica still enough to attract the attention of the King and leave me bowing to the guillotine. But these diamonds... I slipped off my shoe and held the gems in my hand, standing by the window to catch in the light of the moon the flaws which left them unworthy of the King. Terrified, I wondered what I was to do—how I was to produce a diamond more beautiful than had the spider—when a gull-like cry from behind me shocked me to my senses.

"You see, Father! I knew she was up to something downstairs, quiet as she got. You little sneak." Turning, I found to my horror Shame in the doorway with Father just behind her, the lockless door cracked from where they'd crept inside. Hands on her hips, my sister demanded, "How long have you had those diamonds!"

"Wretched little liar," said my father, gripping my hair while my sister, sinking her nails into my hand, forced me to drop the gems she hurried to collect. He went on as I cried, saying, "Think you're better than me, do you? All this time you've been hoarding diamonds we could have sold to support the family. Not just that, but you'd see your sister killed without so much as protest! No better than a guttersnipe. I'm sorry I raised you instead of leaving you on a rock for the vultures."

With a slap across my face, he tossed me to the bed, and I cried out, stumbling after them as the door slammed shut. With all my might, I tried to shove it open, only to feel the pressure of a chair jammed beneath the handle whenever I tried the latch. The grief welling in me as I realized what was happening is something I will never feel again, I think; I could just imagine my triumphant sister bringing the diamonds downstairs to show to the King, and the misunderstanding which would ensue, and my death, and all the suffering the Kingdom and the King would undergo should my sister touch the crown. Crumpled on the floor, I took to weeping, and so despaired I almost didn't notice the scratching in my wall. Its source seemed to grow and travel, and emerged from a crack in the corner to reveal itself the rat from the pantry. Indignity filled his beady eyes as I gasped, "Why, it's you!"

"Yes, it's me, and I'm trying to sleep! My God, don't you ever do anything but cry? Night after night—I'm sick of it! I tolerated the conversations with the spider, all the tears and the whining, but I thought when he left I'd heard all that I'd be hearing. I'm begging you"—he came forward on his hind legs with his pink paws clasped before him—"just lay off it for an hour. Just an hour!"

"I thought I threw you out," I sobbed, feeling pathetic, unable to expel a rat from my house let alone make a diamond. "When did you come back?"

"Oh, I never left! I've been here the whole time. I've just been sneakier about the food I take. Scraps, mostly. That's why I know this crying routine is old hat, and that's why it's got to stop."

"Well, it won't stop as long as I'm trapped here," I cried. The rat rubbed the temples of his forehead.

"Your family is just the worst—and my relatives live in a landfill! Hold on."

To my amazement, the rat squeezed beneath my door and into the hall. It was some time before I recognized all was not quiet; furious nibbling, punctuated by the odd mutter, drifted from the other side of the door. After perhaps an hour of work, it ended in the thump of a falling chair. To my wonder, I let myself from my room to see the impromptu lock had fallen aside, one leg gnawed shorter than all the others. The rat, upon a pile of sawdust, picked splinters from his teeth.

"There you go, sister," he said, hopping between my feet and dashing back to the crack in the wall. "Don't say I never did anything for you! I expect to eat like the King for this."

"Oh," I whispered, dashing down the hall, "have all the food you want! It won't be mine much longer."

As I neared the stairs, I slowed my footsteps, for I passed the rooms of my sisters. Through Shame's cracked door, she doted over the flawed diamonds as though they were the most perfect gems ever devised by spider, man, or nature. This was because she had no imagination, I knew, and no knowledge of what it took to make a diamond. But I knew well, and crept downstairs to the living room where slept six of the men and my father, who, closest to the hearth, snored so dangerously near the dustpan I dared not pick it up. My eyes filling with silent tears of frustration, I gazed into the blaze, myself, the cotton of my dress, my hands. I felt a complete fool about to embark on something not just impossible but stupid; maybe I would regret having tried it at all. But then, I realized it was not me feeling that way. Those were the words of my family. My father slept here, but in his room slept the King, and I held my breath in wonder at the thought. Just as, earlier, I had felt so strangely certain that all would go well with my father, so too did I feel bolstered while studying the fire. That was why I, hands shielded by my skirts, reached into the flames, grasped the biggest, hottest coal I could find, and, almost swallowing my tongue for the blinding pain, tiptoed from the room as fast as I could. Navigating through the kitchen, host to the rest of our visitors, I opened the door with my elbow and let myself into the cold air of winter. Then, and only then, did I release the scream welling since the coal first sizzled through my dress.

That was the horror of it, the true price of the task: with no web with which to insulate the coal, I had no choice but carry it all the way to Hope farmstead. Were I to put it down even a second, the snow would cool it from its red-hot state and it would be no good for diamond-making. In too much pain to even cry, I ran through the fields, managing only the occasional scream in protestation of my agony as the coal seemed to melt the flesh of my hands. The sheep bleated one another awake as I ran through the pasture, and it was there I tarried to catch my panting breath; but one particular sheep, with a growl of frustration as his fellows fearfully scattered, threw off his wool, and revealed himself a wolf.

"Why," I cried, "it's you!"

The wolf bared his teeth, saying, "Yes, it's me! All this time I've taken a page from your book, Miss Clever, hiding in your flock in disguise, but I can't operate if you're running around screaming all the time. What are you doing this time of night!"

"I have to get to Hope farm," I said. "I could never ask the King's horses to burn their hooves with the coal, and could never burn down my own farm—oh, but I don't know if I'll make it before dawn, not before I drop this coal!" Then, remembering how I had ridden on his back, I fell to my knees and lifted high the flaming orb. "Please, can't you help me!"

With an anxious huff for the carbon searing my hands, he said, "I don't know."

"Please! All this time, you've been among our flock, eating your fill unmolested. Can't this be payment for services rendered?"

"I don't think I owe you anything," said the wolf with a haughty sniff at the scattered lambs. Nevertheless, he rolled his eyes and lowered himself to the ground. "But, oh, dammit. I'll never get them back tonight, so fine! Come aboard, but I don't want to feel so much as a spark on my fur or the ride is over."

"Yes! Yes, thank you! I swear it, you won't even know that I'm there." Almost gleeful, I leapt upon the back of the wolf. With a howl, the beast tore north through the snow, headed directly for sprawling Hope farm. The pain was impossible to withstand as, in my hands, the coal sizzled my flesh and filled my nose with cooking meat. How could the King love a girl with such ruined hands! Such hands ruined in doing a service for him, no less! Blood welled from the wounds over the coal, and I choked on my tears as the wolf picked up its pace, crying out, "Smells like a feast!"

"Oh, hurry, and I'll give you all the sheep in my father's flock, but only go, go!"

There came a moment when, at last, the incredible ringing of pain through my flesh gave way to a keening in my ears, a sound which rattled through my vision and caused the whiteness of the snow on the ground to reach up, up into the night sky, and cover it. I, trembling with pain and terror, wondered if it would not have been a kinder fate to meet Elysium's Ogre with no mount or guide. To be eaten in a bite might be less painful, less cruel, than carrying this fiery coal across the winter wastes!

But then it was there, like a beacon: the honey light of distant Hope inn, growing all the bigger, all the brighter, more exquisite and so warm it seemed I felt its light. (Miraculous, for I had stopped feeling anything at all within my hurricane of agony.) As I squinted through whipping winds which revealed the inn and the distant farmhouse, my heels sank into the ribs of the wolf, which yelped, "Easy!" but all the same charged down the hill so fast we skipped, slid, and catapulted most of the way. I, propelled from the beast's back, was forced to protect the integrity of the coal with my body. Its magmatic surface seared my breast, but I was too close to stop for an instant. Gritting my teeth against the pain, I stumbled to my feet, charged into the stables, and did not need search far for that tremendous horse which my friend had once described. It was unlike any beast I had seen, certainly taller than even the King's black stallion. Such a mighty thing was this Clydesdale that it seemed to make the very insides of the stable bigger to accommodate it. It shook its mane as I thundered into the barn, rushing so quickly I only barely noticed it was blind.

"Young Eric," said the horse, turning its head toward me as I darted past a row of gossiping colts and a napping mare, which jolted awake, "surely it's already time for bed, Tiny Master. Or would you hear another story?"

"Why, it's not Eric," cried the mare as I thundered past the horses, "it's a girl! And she smells like that spider!"

"So you're the one who's been sending that thing every year," chided the horse, but I could not stand to wait for it to lecture me, could not suffer any guilt or condemnation for what needed doing. With gritted teeth, I stood before the blind horse's stall and threw the coal, red with blood as much as heat, down in the center of the stables, where it set to blazing to the horror of all the horses.

"She's mad," cried a filly, "Mama, I'm scared!"

"Why do you people keep doing this," demanded a mare as the horse I presumed to be her mate leapt from his stall and landed with such force he shook the stable's ceiling.

"Some people," he insisted, storming around with clopping hooves I narrowly avoided, "are so unhappy inside they have to ruin everybody's good time. Going around, throwing burning coals into a decent horse's stable! And why? Bitterness," he said, emphasizing with a stomp which made him grimace, for his hoof landed flat upon the coal and remained there heavily a time. My heart swelled with excitement so complete it was very nearly perverse, and my eyes glowed with joy as I clasped my mangled hands. When his risen hoof revealed a pile of ash with a glimmer in its center, the gem fresh-cut by the sharp edges of his horseshoes, I gave a cry for its beauty and rushed to sweep it out from under him. With this treasure in my wounded hands, I dove from his path, fast but not quite fast enough, for his tremendous hoof came down on the edge of my foot. I cried out, brutalized by the pain of its crushing but more dedicated to making good my escape. The very instant his hoof again lifted, I scrambled forward, balanced mostly on my good foot but forced to work also with the bad one so that, limping, wounded, I stumbled past the hissing horses and out into the snow, where the wolf had abandoned me, as I'd been certain he would.

It didn't matter. Falling to my knees in the cool snow with which I cleaned the gem, I lifted my creation to the light with a soft gasp. It was, truly, the most beautiful diamond I had ever seen, the size of an egg in my palm. Thrill lifting my spirits, I held its glimmering surface so close to my eye that it reflected in its perfect facets the beauty of an entire world: different from the one I knew, yet so very much the same. More pristine, perhaps. My blood had done it. The spider had none to speak of, would not sacrifice it if he had it, and so produced lackluster diamonds. But my blood, along with the heat and the pressure of the horse's hoof, had together formed this gift for the King over which I wept, because I knew that he would love it, and me.

Alone, with one good foot, two burned hands, and wounds elsewhere, besides, I stumbled home through the snow, each step easier than the last. The pain, of course, grew worse with each footfall, and it seemed as if any second I might black out, or not make it home by dawn; indeed, dawn was soon encroaching at the pace I was forced to drag myself, but I felt so light. So free. Already, I felt the embrace of the King, and it made my heart speed to think of it so that I was effervescent. When I at last limped down the road before my father's house with the coming of dawn, I found the King and his eleven men had assembled themselves outside, along with my father and his two daughters. The sight of the house felt more comforting than it ever had. The King already examined with skepticism the stolen diamonds in his hand. I was emboldened.

"Why, Felicity," cried Shame, noticing me first, crossing her arms as I dragged myself down the road. "There you are. We were just about to start the contest without you. I thought you'd run off! I was only telling the King how we'd ought to just exile you, instead of bothering to kill you, but—"

"Shut your stupid mouth," I told her, sleepless, on edge, wounded, and though the twelve men laughed at that despite my relatives' stony disapproval, I went on. "I don't care if you took my diamonds. They weren't very good as far as diamonds go, anyway, not even for selling.

They were only special because my friend made them for me, but he's dead, so it doesn't matter anymore."

The men had quieted, and my sister, paled and scandalized, tried to redirect the conversation: "Felicity, whatever's happened to your hands? And your feet! And your breast, and forehead!"

The solemn King, at the head of his men, at last spoke up for me. "It is the high cost of human diamond-making." Stripping the red leather glove from his hand, he reached out. "May I?"

Parched, trembling, and feeling as though pain was all I had to bind my body together, I crumpled to my knees the way any good servant does before their Lord, but he caught me with that bare hand and drew me, gently, to his breast. With more tenderness than I had ever experienced, the King opened the charred flesh of my hand, which cracked and protested with pain at even his touch: but it was worth it, for his breath hitched. The diamond glittering in my charcoal fingers left him able to say, only, "Oh, my Queen!"

My sisters gasped, as did the men, and the hands of the King lifted to my face, which he kissed. "To do such a thing for me, make such a thing for me! To have done so with such unquestioning bravery, not knowing what might come of your efforts, if anything at all but loss or death or disfigurement. Ah, Felicity, ah, my Queen." As he kissed my mouth, he draped me in the scarlet fur of his mantle and the warmth of his arms. To my astonishment, when I lifted a crippled hand to touch him, I found it healed along with its mate and my foot and chest pristine. Wild-eyed, I laughed.

"You're remarkable!"

"No more than any other King," he said, smiling in a way which made me feel like I'd never felt, "or any other Queen, for that matter. I know"— he fell to his knee before me, much to my surprise, and his men genuflected down with him—"that I asked you to make this diamond for me. But I should see it the locus of your crown: made in my name, but adorning you, that the Kingdom might see your authority."

My arms around his neck, whole being aglow with security and joy, I whispered, "Will you tell me something, Lord."

"What is that?" he asked, kissing the corner of my eye.

"What was your name, before it was King?"

"It was Love," he said, and I pressed, "Before that?" which made him laugh and swing me in his arms for my thought to ask; he lowered his head, kissed the lobe of my ear, and whispered to me, "Logos."

That was how I became the Queen: thanks to a spider, and suffering. My sister, Shame, was beheaded, for a King must be impeccable with his word, and Phobia spent the rest of Father's days with him. At the time, my leaving felt so surreal that I tried to pinch myself awake as my new fiancé brought me upon his horse a few miles south to the City, the capital of his Kingdom. The Kingdom itself was vast, encompassing then the entire western hemisphere of our planet; the City was located upon the northeastern continent there, the same where I was born and raised. On our journey toward the ever-growing, opalescent druse, my husband explained to me that he himself had been born in the western continent, a mysterious desert of which the eastern citizens had little trust or knowledge. He came into possession of the eastern continents (the entire mass, from the Southern Jungle to the Northern Mountains) by way of marriage to his first wife. Since then he had dreamed of collecting the four continents of the Distant Lands across the Eastern Sea, and waited ever for an excuse to visit and impress on them his sovereignty. I saw my betrothed to be a man ambitious as he was patient, and knew if any were capable of such a feat, it would be him; I told him so outside our City gates and, as we crossed its threshold, he kissed me in response.

The first thing he did was give me a horse of my own, a silver mare which rivaled his own black stallion; then, he gave unto me servants who bathed and anointed and dressed me, for I still had obstacles with which to contend (however minor in comparison to my trial). The death of the first Queen at the hands of the incompetent concubine-cum-mid-wife had sent a ripple of tragedy through the Kingdom, and especially through my King; but all the people had taken solace in the survival of the Prince, gleaming full of promise. By the time I married his father, the Prince was already a man, though young. The speed of our courtship spread scandal through the land, for I was of no noble birth. Many protested our union and claimed it a sin, but the King felt no such way, insisting my dominion was self-evident; thus, he turned to his son, so beloved in the eyes of the Kingdom, for his blessing.

"So this is the girl I've heard so much about." As he pronounced the first words I ever heard from him, the Prince lay before the fountain of the castle hedge maze, the quartet of spitting fish which filled the over-flowing basin the marble twins of the mirrored guppies surrounding the plaza pool.

"Yes, son, this is Felicity."

"And what's special about her, then? Outside of the diamond-making business, and wisdom and blah-blah, whatever else."

"Well," suggested the thoughtful King to his velvet-caped son, "I love her. That's what's special."

"How does this affect me, exactly?"

"I suppose that it doesn't, seeing as you're nearly a man."

One eye twitched in irritation. "Already a man, you mean." At his father's placid smile, the Prince scowled and carried on. "Until she gets it into her head I'm in need of a mother, and she's the woman for the job."

Once more studying me, not so many years older than the Prince and more sister to him in age than mother, the King laughed. "I'm not sure that's in the realm of her intent."

"We'll see. Felicity"—the Prince hopped up with a heel click and extended his hand—"come along, girl, I should like to speak with you."

But, with faint fire in his eyes, the King leaned forward. "'Felicity,' my boy. Not 'girl.'"

Sighing and rolling his eyes, the Prince said, "Yes, very well," and dragged me back into the hedge maze. As I struggled to think of some measure of wit with which to impress, he ensured we were out of earshot of his father before demanding, "All right, what's your angle?"

I laughed, the question absurd. "What do you mean?"

"The innocent farm-girl routine doesn't thrill me," said the Prince, briskly guiding me through the rows, turning left, then right, then left again. "I can see it in your eyes. A shrewdness. It's hardly as if you're a fully innocent little lass, after all: you're a woman as much as I a man, even if neither of us is as much man or woman as Father is, if you know what I mean. So what I'm wondering is, what is it you want out of this? Money? Security? I mean, what else does one want in a marriage, of course, but I suppose what I'm asking is: Are you planning on becoming one of these tedious, scheming women who depose their husbands and ascend the throne in a tawdry show of violence?"

Again, I laughed. "No, but I want to be in love, and feel like somebody loves me. And I think the King can give that to me, at least. I suppose I could have that from any man in the Kingdom," I admitted, blushing, "but what man could compare?"

"Yes, well, he can give you love, but much else, besides. Are you sure it's not manors you're after? White horses and doves announcing your arrivals?"

"I suppose a cottage in the hills," I admitted at last, "so long as it was only fit for him and me, and no one else besides, and was beautiful, and quiet."

"With plenty of space to bury him in," suggested the skeptical Prince, waggling a well-manicured eyebrow in a way that made me laugh again, brighter.

"Of course not. But space enough to walk about. Perhaps near the Woods. No one owns those, after all."

With a sniff, the Prince protested, "Father owns everything, darling. The whole bloody thing is his Kingdom, even the bits across the sea, whether the people there accept it yet, or not."

"Do you really think a man can own the Woods?" Surprise arched my brow, and he looked back in equal skepticism until, at last, he shook his head, muttered, "Maybe you are something of a bumpkin after all," and abruptly abandoned me in the labyrinth to make his way back to the center. By the time I remembered the route, he'd already told his father he didn't mind if I was Queen. The Prince was the one who made the announcement, the three of us standing on the platform in the center of the market square, arranged before the fountain, my fiancé's son calling, "It has come to my attention that the people of my father's Kingdom have misunderstood the intentions of both my father, and of the woman of his heart: dear Felicity."

With an eye across the crowd, he suggested, "Though I understand there are those who never finished mourning my mother, and those concerned with the stability of a Kingdom married within itself rather than another kingship, the truth of the matter is, of course, that there is only one Kingship in this realm, or any other: that of my father. Where could come a bride but from the same land? I myself have no care for marital alliances between nations. Only the personages within."

The murmur of the crowd roiled, and the Prince stepped behind us, extolling, "This is why I have carefully considered the matter, and I give complete blessing to the union of Our King and his new bride, Felicity."

Though at first the murmur rose to a roar, I realized fast it was no roar of displeasure, rather, a bountiful roar of joy from the hearts of the people which left me teary with awe, not just at the generosity of their embrace, but at the kindness of the Prince to whom I owed my very marriage. I, overjoyed, fell into the duties of my rule as though born for it, and my husband took so lovingly to me that we were two parts of a far larger whole, moving ever in perfect symphony. For seven years, we dwelt in joy, but in the eighth, our people went to war with the Distant Lands across the sea in response to my husband's messenger, dead accidentally from the poison of a spoiled fish which the King claimed ever was intentional to everyone but me. I knew him too well: he knew accidents happened, but he had waited a lifetime for this excuse, and leapt on it. The men of the military, along with the King and the Prince, were forced to fight. Many dreary days and bleak nights I haunted the City's Castle, weaving and waiting for my husband to return. Time stilled in his absence; all the events which filled the City seemed gray and lifeless. Crops were grown and shows performed and the market square was as busy as always, but I had been left to pine, because that, I supposed at the time, was a woman's duty. It was not my lot to fight, to suffer in violence; women lived so close to bloody violence every month that men thought it kinder to take on the duty of fighting, and so our suffering was the silent suffering of contemplation. The months passed into years. When the news of the war's end finally reached us, victory over the Distant Lands had been subsumed with the shadow of tragedy: I learned, to my sorrow, the Prince had died, and the Kingdom would never be the same.

9

The Prince had been the ultimate reason we were able to come together, and to hear of his death proved devastating to me, but not near so devastating as the face of my King when he returned home; it had paled with grief, much as his eyes had blackened, and he no longer seemed the man I had known, as if a specter resided in his body. He had no one to blame, he said, but himself, and would accept no measure of comfort from me; foul fits of temper overcame him when not weeping in his room, and I feared the man I loved to be changed. Victory had cost us more than we might ever hope to regain, and our people fell into mourning, but none more so than my King, who, inconsolable, shut himself in his chambers, away even from me, to grieve.

Among the courtiers, it was much discussed what should be done. I arranged a meeting between the most important members of the Court that we might come to a solution. The first words came from the treasurer, who, had the Prince lived to sit in his place at the foot of the table, would have been to the left of my beloved friend. This first adviser spread his hands and said, "We won the bloody war, didn't we? I don't see what His Majesty is so broken up about; he could count his vault anytime, cheer himself right up. Why," he said with a sidelong snort for the head of the dancing and serving girls, the fairest woman in the land and dear friend of both I and my husband, "he'd ought to be able to *buy* a new son, if he wants."

"Our Majesty, the Queen is right there," indicated the priest, waving to my seat at the right hand of my absent King.

"And Our Majesty, the Queen isn't the Prince's true mother, nor really the mothering sort," insisted the treasurer, "so she'd ought not to be too wounded. After all, she's called this meeting to order and isn't moping in her room nursing the pain of the loss. She's the one with the level head. I would not expect her to take offense."

I lifted my hand. "No offense, friend accountant, but I think it safe to say we'll have to find another way to mend my husband's heart."

"The stars suggest," called the astrologer across from him, "that our good King's heart shall mend in time, perhaps when Venus conjuncts with Mercury."

"Then," I smiled thinly, "I shall commission a carriage of wingéd horses, that we might drag our flighty wandering star toward the morning one. I have no interest in waiting for them to conjunct on their own."

The astrologer blushed, and the dancing woman shot a comely smile at the tilt of her burnished brass head. "Perhaps join me in my chambers, my lady, and I can teach you a few things to lift His Majesty out of his troubles."

Now it was I who blushed. "His Majesty finds me talented in those areas, thank you."

"Then," said that shunned priest, "why *not* give him a second child? The fruit of thy womb, fair lady, would be more nourishing and more uplifting a gift than any suggested at this table."

"Any second child would serve but to remind him of the first; and, at any rate, I've no care for such things." I frowned across to my silent fool, who reclined with feet up and quill balanced upon his upper lip. His brows lowered as I met his scrutinizing eyes. "Have you a suggestion, friend?"

Falling forward with his legs under the desk and hands folded in imitation of mine, he said, "O wisest of all living Queens, you've the answer already. You've said it many times: nothing could replace our Prince! The Kingdom's so broken even I'm beset by weeping. See?" With the feather, he blew his nose, and a powder hidden up his hand turned the quill mustache from white to aquamarine. "But how can it be helped? Who could bring a Prince from death! Why, it'd take a Witch."

The rest of the table silenced; the astrologer glanced to the north corner of the room, the dancing woman to the south, the treasurer to the east, and the fool, disdainfully, not to the west, but to me. The priest, however, leapt from his seat, face already mottled with fury as he slapped down his hand. "To suggest such a thing!"

"A Witch?" I asked. Still no one met my eyes but the screaming priest, who jerked a finger at the fool. "This man had ought to be hanged, Your Majesty. There are jokes, and then there is having a rancid sense of humor. If that can be called 'humor.'"

"Will you calm?" I reached toward his hand, but he paced, still shouting all the while.

"To even mention the Witch is unacceptable. And to suggest she had ought to be used to help the King, or that she could even be of any help— hah!" The priest wheeled his sneer in the fool's direction. "Let us remember just what it was which had her cast into the Mountains to start with."

"Then who better to do this favor for the King," suggested the fool, who turned his smiling face in the direction of the priest. "I hardly see why the matter should be of such personal import to you, unless you're sore about the Witch's powers."

"If she has the power to raise the dead, why didn't she raise the first Queen?" snapped the priest, to which the fool drearily replied, "Was it not God's will that she die?"

"Indeed, and God's will that the Prince die now," said the priest, going on to insist, "It is immoral to even suggest resurrecting the Prince by magical means, let alone with the Witch's help."

I, who'd had enough of my husband's empty seat at the head of the table, and his son's empty seat at the foot, rose and said, "Sit down."

The priest's mouth opened as though to protest, but then, it seemed, he remembered himself, turning to me and appearing almost surprised to find a Queen. Humbled, he obeyed, and I traced from face to face, then stared down into my own, reflected in the table's glass.

"Perhaps it was God's will that the Prince die, it's true," I said at last, leveling. "But it is my will he return to the land of the living, that my husband might be consoled. Perhaps it shall also prove God's will this is so. Who is to say, after all, what the will of God is? You?" My priest shook his head.

"No more for me to say than it is for the Witch. Man can have no understanding of God's will."

"So, if my wish is not God's will, do you suppose He shall deter me in my efforts to raise the Prince? That I should be punished for my transgressions if I am wrong?"

With a solemn nod, the vicar allowed, "As it happens, I suppose He would."

Smiling, I refolded my hands. "Then, if He be displeased with my intentions or methods, I am sure He will show me, and I will have no choice but to lean upon His mercy and hope His understanding will wash away my sins."

"Your Majesty," began the priest, but I was already turning to ask my fool, "Where dwells this Witch, my friend?"

"She was exiled to a swamp in the cradle of the Mountains," said the fool, leaning back in his seat while crushing in his palm some sulfurous substance to befoul the room with the odor of gas. "You'll find her among weeping willows and alligators, seven days and nights' worth of riding with the King's mightiest stallion."

Desperate, I am sure, to save me, the priest observed, "A straight-talking fellow for a fool."

"A foolish Queen, that follows a fool's straight advice," was the laughing response, and, though my vicar was appalled, I only smiled on my way to the door.

"You may all be excused," I said, knocking on the chamber's exit, opened by an outside guard whose expression was solemn as the leaden weight of my heart. As I crossed the threshold, I said, "I should remind you all that I'll hear no word of what was discussed."

As understanding passed from face to face and I took leave down the rose marble halls, I felt myself a ghost. The Castle which had been my home by then for many years seemed foreign to me, though I'd grown to know its every corridor as well as my farm as a girl. For the first time since, I longed for my old friend, and wondered if it was true I would meet him again, for I had, over time, convinced myself he was naught but a spider. Perhaps he would appreciate the shroud over the Castle. I felt as though I were seeing it the last time, and in a way, I suppose that I was. But, either way, the walk to my husband's chambers recalled the day I left my girlhood home, and made me long for a companion to share the loneliness. I had none, so I visited my King.

My husband's chambers were barred to all but me, and even I hesitated outside their shut portals for fear of what I might discover. It was my truest terror he would bring upon himself some harm as though to avenge the life of his son, and so I was pleased each time I found him well as might be expected, in bed with curtains drawn and all lamps snuffed so he bathed in darkness as if without body.

"Is that you, Felicity?" he asked as I perched upon the edge of his bed. I took up his hand to remind myself of his flesh. "I can't see you."

"I can't see anything," I said with a dull attempt at a laugh ringing short, unreturned.

"Neither can my son."

"I know." Frowning, I ran my thumb over the back of his hand, the smooth skin so much rougher since his homecoming. He was thinning down to bone. "Don't you think you'd ought to eat?"

"My son will never eat again," he lamented, turning away his face. "How could I bring myself to eat, knowing he starves below the earth, forever wanting, forever without?"

"Your son may reside below the earth, but you—above it, ruler of it—must eat. Won't you, please, if I bring you something? Some fish, some wine? Even bread. Or apricots! So fresh and beautiful on the labyrinth trees...they're all that grows, lately."

"Waiting for my son to return, to come and eat them, doubtless. Haven't the other plants had the heart to tell them? No, of course not; they couldn't bear it. I couldn't bear it." A sob racked his chest, and he coughed so that I, saddened, sank back into the darkness. What was I to do of my lover's pains? What was I to do to see him full and alive again? Indeed, it was an unheard-of thing that the souls of the dead might be wrenched from the underworld—and worse, too, that I should involve in any way this exiled Witch, who could only be contacted in secret.

I laid with him in the darkness to hold him as though he were a child, and quietly, he cried until he slept. Would he be lost without me? Surely not. Surely, if anything, my absence might snap him into action. The best thing, it seemed—the only thing—was to trade gowns of silk for a cloak dark as dried blood: to take up my hunting gear, my bow and my quiver, meant for sport but the only method by which I might win meals, might defeat my enemies and pierce into the indigo belly of the underworld where my husband did not rule.

Under shield of night, I broke from the stables my husband's finest stallion, that black horse which had crushed dead my friend, but which had borne me on its back. As quiet as most horses were, this was silent, for I had been so busy among the people that I had forgotten the importance of talking to animals. Perhaps, had I spoken to him, I might have realized him to be as much my friend as the spider he killed, but that is all for speculation. As he bowed to me, I mounted him, and together we bolted into the ink of night, passing through the City and into the outskirts without issue. No one thought anything of a huntress leaving the City at night, and no one expected a Queen to leave the City without guards; I needn't even hide my face, for they took it for granted that I merely resembled the Queen immortalized in statues dotted across the City. Laughter at comment on my appearance got us through the gates without hitch, and into the fields and hills beyond. There, I realized with awe that it was the first time I'd been on my own on the back of a horse since my wedding, without ladies to hunt with me or guardsmen to protect me or my husband to ride with me. Quieted by the notion of overwhelming freedom, I slowed the horse beneath the yawning sky more full of stars than was a mouth of teeth. Across the darkness lurked a kind of richness I'd never known, even while living straight under it, without the lights of the City: a glittering array of colors hidden in swirling galaxies ever present for that which lurked beyond our planet's domed surface, but revealed to the human eye only with the light of time.

I had been told it would be seven days and seven nights, but I suppose I had not really been aware how long those days and nights would be while riding by myself, no company but my husband's horse. This was perhaps why I thought to visit for the first time in such a long time my father's farm, which had fallen, in my absence, into tragic disrepair: the wolf had done as I'd bade him and eaten all the sheep; the rat had invited his family to live and devoured all the staples. Phobia, I knew, did not care to clean, but what was surprising was not the dust or cobwebs littering the front porch. Rather, the disrepair into which my father had allowed his house to fall. Before his marriage to a shepherdess and felder, he had been a carpenter, and though I had been made to slave over details, he had maintained with admirable facility, if nothing else, the home's facade. Now, boards peeled from the porch, and the swing had long since collapsed on itself, crushed by the nostalgia of a thousand quiet moments. The sight of its carcass pained me so terribly that when at last my father opened the door, I was already on the verge of tears.

"Felicity," he observed, his eyes then growing colder. "Or do I call you 'Queen?'"

"Daddy," I said, blinking my eyes and swallowing as if my saliva were shards of glass. "I'm happy to see you. I've missed you."

"I'm sure you have," he said with a disdainful shake of his head, and I followed him inside with a reluctant glance around just as a rat disappeared beneath the threadbare couch into which my father fell. "All these years, you haven't come to visit once."

"It's been very hard being a Queen," I began, but his sour visage humbled me, and I said, "I'm sorry," as the back door slammed open and grunting Phobia stumbled into the kitchen, shoulders heavy with well water.

"That wretched well is harder to draw from every day," she complained en route to the doorway, mouth opened in a word which aborted to a gasp as she recognized me, then so stumbled that I rushed to catch her bucket before it fell. "Why, Felicity! We thought we would never see you again!"

"Of course you would," I told her, trying not to see the circles under her eyes, the furrows in her brow, the leather-worn hardness of her skin. "I'm so sorry I haven't come back to visit. But perhaps you might come to the City to see me?"

"Make such a long journey, to see the man who murdered our sister!" Appalled, Phobia reclaimed her bucket and set it down, herself—upon the dusty floor, rather than the table, so I was forced to silent grimace. "I could never, Felicity, what a frightful idea."

"It's not a long journey! Two days on slow horseback," I began, only to falter beneath their withering, silent judgment which reminded me without words not everyone in the Kingdom could afford one horse, let alone two. Guiltily, I studied my boots. "Perhaps the Hopes might lease you a mare."

My spiteful father informed me, "The Hopes won't have a thing to do with us since you nearly burned down their stables."

"But it isn't your fault," I protested. My father only shook his head.

"Family is family, Felicity, whether or not you're some Queen. I'd think you'd know that."

Biting my lip, I squinted through the dirty window to see the angle of the sun outside and thought with panic of my husband: he would soon set on my trail, assuming he had not already, and my silver mare was not fast as his black stallion but still could make the journey here in twelve or so hours if one of my advisers broke trust. I could not tarry, nor afford to lose my horse to my family's emotional blackmail. But perhaps there was a way around it; lifting a hand, I darted out to the horse's saddlebags and removed the loaf of bread I'd brought along, thinking regretfully it was good I'd brought the bow. But there was no room for regret in charity, and I took half my gold, as well, and brought it to them.

"Take this gold. The Hopes won't turn away such a purse." I handed it to my sister, or else my father would squander it on liquor and whores.

"This bread will keep you fed." I gave the loaf to my father, who would shield it from Phobia's gluttony, already flickering to life at the sight of the food. "Go south, to the City: take the road all the way, never deviate, never tarry, and when you reach the City, tell the gatekeeper whose family you are. They'll take you right to my husband, and you're to tell him you've seen me coming through, headed northward, toward the Mountains, and beyond: to Elysium."

Trembling, her grip on the purse white-knuckled, Phobia cried, "Elysium! Felicity, you're far too young."

"Not to die," I said, laughing softly, touching my sister's hand. "But to save someone from it."

"An absolute load of nonsense, Elysium," said my father, rising from his seat with a roll of his bony shoulders. "Everybody knows there's only the Kingdom and the City."

With no time to argue, I kissed his scruffy cheek, and my sister's scuffed one. "If you meet him on the road, behave no different from how I've already advised. He'll see either way that you're homed and fed for the rest of your lives, never to work again."

Brightening, my father hopped for his hat, and Phobia turned toward her bucket with a delighted cry. "Oh, I'd ought to wash my face! We can't leave the house with me such a fright."

Smiling, I laid my hand on the doorway, then stepped through it, feeling much lighter than I had on my first leaving. Upon the horse, I rode again, pressing farther north, and marveled to find how close Hope farm was on the stallion's back: what a long journey it had been by foot! Poor father, poor Phobia! But their delay would delay, also, my husband, who had to be told of my safety one way or another, lest he spiral into deeper despair. Gradually, the hills and farms of the Country where I'd been raised gave way to the Woods, which I reached the second day, and found a far less elaborate and dangerous place to navigate than the Forest the Witch would grow. Of course, it was still far from pleasant, and I distinctly remember the gamey squirrel I was lucky to have hit at all. On the third day, half-starved, I stayed at an inn in a village far from the City, The Black Fish, and both I and my horse ate like royalty. On the fourth, better stocked with provisions, we thundered through the wastes of the Clay Desert, unaware that by then my husband had learned of my absence and had indeed roused himself as I had predicted. Four fleets of men rode in search of me in case my family had been wrong, but, of course, only that legion headed by my husband was headed the right way.

On the fifth night, we reached the Mountains which had once loomed in distant silhouette far from my City but now towered so close their mere presence overwhelmed. The horse whinnied in displeasure more than once as we set upon its treacherous path, but if I could not be dissuaded by a man of God, the protests of a horse were destined for deaf ears. Another day we climbed the only path up the only conquerable mountain, rising high among its peaks to leave me trembling with the bite of cold with which I was ill-prepared to deal no matter how many cloaks I had brought or how many times I had heard of the bitter mountain cold from courtly friends who braved the climb. The more we wandered through the rocks, the more hopeless it seemed, and I wondered if I might freeze to death among the peaks. So frightened was I, that we wandered even at night; my snorting mount surely loathed me for it, pawing at the rocks and stumbling with exhaustion more than once. But, on the seventh day, as I was at last prepared to turn around and use the return trip to concoct an explanation for my failure, we passed a cavernous crevasse from which rose the stench of sulfur. Never had I been so glad to smell that hellish odor! Kissing my horse, which seemed at that moment less than impressed by my affection, I dismounted to walk him up the length of the ice, where I found a small cave leading down; when followed, it emerged in the crevasse, which held a wholly different environment. As the darkness of the cave let way, it was to the soft glow of fireflies which pulsed in the wretched swamp to which the Witch was cast. Beneath my feet grew clutches of sedge grass upon dirt untouched by ice, perhaps because of the unearthly warmth which filled the place, which made me shocked the crevasse above had not melted; perhaps the unearthly heat was its cause. Or, perhaps she was.

Amid the medley of willows and knee-deep cypresses, as we trudged through tangled flora which suffused the swamp's wet ground to make it seem impassible, the soft breaths of a foreign horse attracted the attention of my own. By the turn of his head, I detected the source of the sound was the nearby hill emerging from the water, and as we penetrated the hanging boughs of the largest willow ever seen, we discovered a tiny cottage. The white mare hitched outside, the source of the sound, regarded us with unease. It did not seem to protest, however, as I led my King's animal beside it, hitched it amid the fireflies, and left them to become friends while I, breathless, faced the Witch.

Though I knocked upon her little door, there came no answer by those means. With tongue set between my teeth, I was forced to push it open. An agonized creak gave way to the cluttered cottage, itself barely two rooms, the first being what captured my attention. In its center lay a pot of strange-smelling herbal stew, whose smoke rose through a hole in the ceiling revealing, amid the sumptuous boughs, the face of the moon. That was where the comforts of home stopped, for upon the walls hung all number of strange and disturbing things collected, I assumed, in the madness of her solitude. Long-dead rabbits dangled in each corner, and upon the walls was mounted a confabulation of feathers, animal bones, queer stones and beach shells, costume jewelry, dried plants, herbs, old religious icons from cults my husband had long since abolished—and, perhaps strangest of all, I recognized on the north wall was painted a sigil, a net of circles not dissimilar to the links of chain mail but altogether more beautiful as it took on the appearance of a flower. As I stepped forward to better admire, from the dark door of the second room a laconic voice demanded, "Have I gone truly mad, or is that the pretty face of the Queen, herself, come to visit me?"

I turned, then, expecting to see the terrible hag I'd pictured all my journey, whose image had become clearer and clearer the more I imagined, right down to her wart and chin hair. Instead, I found a beautiful woman perhaps fifteen years older than myself, if I reckoned right. The stress of solitude, if there was much to be had, had not touched her, and her hair, the hue of her fiery cloak, was the brightest thing in the room but for rainy eyes momentarily lit by curiosity. From behind her crossed arms, she watched my face, and I, taken aback, stuttered, "No figment of fancy, madam."

"'Madam'!" A mocking cackle belted from her lungs, her head tipping back as I, blushing, fell on my heel. Hands upon her hips, she shook her head. "Polite enough to call me 'madam' but not polite enough to knock, Your Highness?"

"I did," I said pointing toward the door as she prowled around me. "How is it you know me to be Queen, ma'am?"

"I've been having visions," she crooned, circling, pausing behind me and very openly investigating my body as though I were a breeding sow for auction. "Not visions of you, necessarily. But of a visitor following a quake so calamitous the City fell to ruins, and upon the head of this visitor was a crown of stars."

"No quake," I said, trying to face her only to find she had moved, briskly, behind a wall of furs which functioned as a partition. As I pursued her, I glimpsed the carnelian tail of her dressing robe and darted back to find her taking a seat by the stewpot. At last, I said, "The King's son is dead."

At the sound of this news which had met the rest of the nation with such instant grief and compassion, a noise erupted from the Witch which I could not recognize in context. Indeed, I realized only seconds later that she laughed, kept laughing as she said, "Dead! Aye, a quake, then: a City in ruins, I see. Of course, I may not even see to the clearest depths yet."

"So how was it that you knew me to be Queen?" I pressed again, stepping toward her as she dipped a wooden mug into the brew I had once taken as stew but realized now was a kind of tea. "No vision of a crown could foretell that, even if true."

"I know that horse," she said, lifting her eyes toward the window curtained with fox skins. "The black one. I once saw him often, a lifetime ago, when I still saw horses other than my own."

Frowning across from her, I asked, "How long have you been alone here?" only to receive a sneer from behind her lifting mug.

"I'll have none of your sympathy, girl. It's only by my being here at all that you've had the grace to become Queen."

"What do you mean?" I asked, frowning, and she laughed, throwing the tea down her throat and tossing away the mug as she rose.

"Don't tell me you've come all this way without knowing my reputation!"

"I only learned of you a week ago," I said, lifting my head as she trailed around the pot with her head tilted in the fashion of a hyena. "I came to you when I learned of your reputation with the dead."

"Yes, that reputation! You had ought to be full of fear, Your Majesty. Haven't you heard! You have, whether or not you knew it was me they talked about. I've killed one Queen already." With a thin smile, she lowered her face toward mine, frozen in a mask of wild revelation. "Who's to say I might not do it again?"

"The midwife!"

"More than midwife, paramour," she confirmed, eyes blazing with fury, hands clutching the fabric of my cloak to yank me nearer her clenched teeth. "When I could only save the child, he let the fury of his grief blind him, and I became naught but a would-be Usurper in his eyes. A Witch. But I was never a Witch before he cast me into the wilderness."

Lips parted, brow furrowed, I took a breath. "Oh, sister. I'm so sorry."

For a few seconds, the fire of her fury raged before me, silent, unreleased, as a flame kept burning within the hollow of a vessel where it was denied the air it required to thrive and thus faded, exhaling from her nose in the steam of a low sigh. "It doesn't matter," she said, releasing me, turning away. "You've nothing to do with the whole thing. But you're a fool if you think I'll have anything to do with him, after the way he's hurt me. Abandoned me."

"What better way to earn his forgiveness?" I asked, springing after her through the shack as she made to the tiny bedroom. "Just think! Were you to help his second Queen, and return with his dead son, surely he'd forgive you."

"You truly know nothing at all."

"I know the heart of my husband." I clutched her arm and stood firm despite the glower she turned upon me, her eyes narrowed as she regarded me with the coolness one feels in an early-winter morning. "I know he's a good, forgiving man: the finest ruler in this world or any other. He would never let your good deed, the return of his son, go unrewarded."

Snorting, her gaze fell across the tiny wall of her squalid bedroom, stuffed full of books, one messy bed, and a pile of clothes in want of washing. She seemed for a time to consider my words, but at last tore herself away and collapsed upon her bed with a heavy sigh and a shaking head. "After all the years of my life he's wasted letting me rot here in solitude, I'm not sure I could forgive him, let alone accept any forgiveness he had for me."

"You were his concubine, weren't you? He loved you, once. Surely he can remember that."

"Shouldn't it make you jealous, O Queen, that I once bedded your husband?"

"Someone is dead," I insisted, and she bothered to face me that I might see her roll her eyes.

"People die every day. With any luck, I'll be among them tomorrow."

"That's no way to think!" Once, I had thought the same; my throat tightened in sympathy as much as the mere possibility of failure. I'd come so far. I'd found her. I couldn't stop. Falling upon the edge of her bed and catching her hands, I insisted, "People die every day, you're right, but you don't understand. The King, the people, are devastated. They can hardly bring themselves to work the land, nothing will grow. The Prince was all they had left of the old Queen. Don't you see? They didn't mean to hurt you. They were just sad."

Pain filled her eyes, and I feared she would send me out. Instead, she turned her face toward the wall of the hut, saying nothing, hardly stirring. I reached to touch her, and she made no move to lean away.

"Do you have a name?"

"They call me the 'Witch,'" she said.

"That's not a name. Not anymore than 'Queen.'"

"Isn't it?"

"It's not," I insisted, and she shrugged away with a laugh of embitterment until I told her, "My name is Felicity."

She quieted, neither laughed nor spoke: only lay, watching whatever theater cast itself upon the wall, for the Witch was never entirely in one place of being. It was her nature to dwell in two worlds, only ever half-awake. At that moment in her hut, I did not realize, and thought she ignored me. I responded to her silence with one of my own, waiting, at last rising, moving toward the doorway, saying, "I'm sorry if I've bothered you, but I don't think I can leave until you agree to help me. You understand, I'm going to do it." I stared into her unmoving back, throat tight with fear at the thought but more insistent. "If you won't help me, maybe I can give you something so you'll tell me where I must go, what I must do, and I'll do it on my own. But...I'd like your help. Because I don't know if I'll be able to do it alone, and I'm scared, and I know you don't have any reason to do anything for me, but I know if I go by myself"—I found the sight of my boots both fascinating and blurry—"I'll be lost, and the Prince will be forever dead, and my husband and the Kingdom will fall all the deeper into despair, and never recover. But I must try. So, I'm going to stay around until you tell me what I do to go to the underworld, and then I'll leave you alone, all right?"

Still, she said nothing, and I was filled with fear that this was not the right way to handle things—that there was no right way, and my cause was lost before beginning—but I refused to give in. I would reach her, and I knew it because as I placed my hand upon her bedroom door she spoke, so softly I struggled to hear what it was she had said.

"My name is Pneuma."

Out of respect, I shut the door to hide my smile and, alone, sat beside the fire. How cluttered the space had become! Much acquired for a lonely woman, though I expected the articles which were man-made to have been given by my husband as a boon. As to the rest of the contents, she had made of herself an accomplished woodsman, killing and skinning white foxes, rabbits, deer, and alligators with a skill to shame the wiliest hunters. Her drawings, too, did not consist of eerie sigils alone but also works of real beauty, murals of human life (the City market, I recognized on the west wall) painted or drawn in chalk, words like poetry all hidden by the objects which cluttered her busy walls.

How sad, to be so lonely. But it did not seem the work of a mad mind, the contents of this place; despite the strange disorganization, the clutter and disinterest in cleaning, the bizarre odds and ends which smelled like death, she was no madder than I. They had called her a Witch, so she had become a Witch on their assessment, but I sensed there lay in the room a web of patterns and rituals by which her life had been organized, as if the contents of her mind were arranged and controlled around her, rather than within her. It resounded with pain but also understanding. Through the skylight, through the willow boughs, through the crevasse hidden in the cauldron of Mountains where Pneuma was forced to make her home, the livid face of the moon watched me rise and put up my hair, then take off my cloak and use it to do the dusting. Years of neglect, gone in ten minutes. In the corner, I found a broom, and, sweeping first the cobwebs which bound it, I banished the dust through the front door and opened the windows that the air might find itself fresher. From the table creaking in the corner I took the dirty dishes and from the fire I moved the mystical tea, placing there a fresh pot of water to be boiled off, then another, and another. I spent the whole night this way, it seemed, until there was water enough for washing the dishes and linens both, and all, I did with care, retrieving the latter from the Witch's room while she slept curled against the wall with her arms around herself. I thought she slept, at any rate, though it was not so many hours later that she appeared as I, out front, fed the horses and stroked the mane of a mare pleased to have contact with a human other than her mistress.

"Well," said the Witch, displeased until brightened by the realization that her sudden appearance had startled me, "you'd better have everything you need, because if we're going to do this, we'd might as well go."

"You're coming with me!"

"You've forced me to help to return the favor of cleaning my house, for which I didn't ask," she dismissed as she ducked back into the cottage, and I knew this was her way of saying thank you, "so I suppose I'd might as well be your guide. You're right, anyway." I let down my hair and wiped my hands on my breeches.

"What am I right about?" I asked as she emerged and handed over my bow.

"If you went there without me, neither you nor the Prince would ever have hope of return."

10

As we rode into dawn's early glow, she showed me the crevasse was the only way to reach the North Sea: the earthly entrance of Elysium. I (indeed, most) had taken there to be nothing on its other side, for it was at the top of the world and cold as death. Only the hardiest of fish might dwell within its waters.

"It's not what's on the other side," she told me, our horses astride as we caught sight of the sky, an azure diamond framed by thick gray clouds and jagged stones. "It's what one finds *within* it. That's the thing, my dear."

"Am I to be assured this is not some ploy?"

Smirking, the Witch suggested, "If you would rather disbelieve, that would be the easiest thing for us both. We can turn around here, if you'd like."

"I can't turn around," I told her, waves of irritation cresting in my brain. "This is too serious a matter to be abandoned! Not to mention, I'd be a fool." I remembered the adviser who had given me this idea in the first place and bit my lip as Pneuma tittered.

"You're foolish regardless of your success, I think. But rest assured, this is no ploy. To enter the underworld without dying and return from it the way you went in, one must plunge to the depths of the North Sea."

"And how will we plunge to the depths of the North Sea without drowning?"

"We won't," said the Witch, digging her heels into the ribs of the mare to send it screaming on. "If we're going to come into the water, the water is going to come into us. That's all that there is to it."

What a queer thing, the landscape between the Mountains and the Sea! The Mountains pulled from our vision to reveal the proper countryside, a luscious land, indeed, abnormal for the piercing intensity of its beauty. The valleys, rich with luscious jade grass, were full of wild rams and exquisite indigo flowers which rattled in the wind like whispers. At times, the flora took on a sapphire hue, and I had the impression our horses ran upside down: that they galloped upon the sky, and our vertiginous heads pointed toward the earth. Only when I inclined my head did this perception right itself, for my eyes found the sky where it belonged. But it was not the seeing of things that mattered so much as the feeling of them, I decided as we stopped to hunt our lunch near the ruins of an old stone temple. This desolate shrine shocked me, for I had never dreamed people once lived here, then migrated away. The air, rich with salt and water, spoke of the not-yet-visible sea, and I could not imagine ever leaving a land so idyllic.

"Aye, people here once thrived." The Witch's attention never deviated from the ewe she skinned to unveil red meat beneath its white flesh. "But then they realized: the closer they drew to the North Sea, the blacker grew the sun, and so, in terror, they fled. They took it for an omen."

"The sun grows black!" Indeed, the notion filled me with terror, but the Witch only laughed and shook her head.

"I don't know how people like you get out of bed in the morning. Yes, of course the sun grows black as you reach the North Sea. Why else would the sea stay so cold? The waters suck all the gold out of it."

My irritation growing for her cryptic speech, I placed my hands on my hips. "The men of science of the Kingdom would beg to differ, Pneuma. You've been locked up so long that you might be stuck in your ways, but we have explanations for things like that. I'm sure it's just the wind in high latitudes, or the jet streams of the water cooling air and darkening the sky."

"Then why aren't we freezing as we were in the Mountains?" she asked, so scrutinizing I fell silent.

No. I wasn't cold. But there was a strange viscosity to the air, and I felt all the things of the world here took to trembling. Vibrating. As we drew closer to the sea, the sun indeed blackened: that light, ever burning, wavered, its color draining as over the horizon glistened our first glimpse of that bleak ocean. My heart filled with dread, and, anxious, I sought to hide in conversation.

"How is it," I ventured above our horses' clopping, "that you came to be my husband's concubine? Were you born into the City? Did he find you in the Country?"

That one earned a nasty laugh. "How lewd, my Queen! What a question to ask." And, when I blushed at her teasing, she smiled. "Some people, my lady, will do anything to get their children into the City. My mother—"

The Witch's eyes misted, and I felt I had ventured somewhere I was truly unwelcome, for she ducked her head away, but soon, with clearer eyes and deepened breath, she laughed. "We were Country people. But before I was born, my mother made a deal with a man from the City: not a good man, mind, but a City man. In exchange for taking me into his care when I was eight or so, we would be kept forever, my mother in the Country, and I in the City. I would not amount to much, of course, but"—here she laughed and shook her head—"someday when the man died, I would by then perhaps still have enough wealth to stay in the City, whether I had made it myself or gotten it from him."

"And the man"—I did not have to guess, but did, anyway—"he was cruel."

"Not all, but yes."

"What of your father? What did he say?"

Again, she laughed, and I thought her mad for all her laughing, but I've long since realized it was the way she kept her head. "I have no father, O Queen, that I know. My mother said he was a wolf."

"A wolf!" Embarrassed to so much as imagine the mechanics, I wondered if the wolf who had helped me reach Hope farm was any relation at all of Pneuma's and was glad when she only went on, "Yes, a wolf, and her mother was a bee, she told me, who stung an ape behind the ear. She burst from his head, full-grown, in the Southern Jungle, from which she moved to live in the Country." This seemed no stranger than the business with the wolf, even down to the detail that I thought the thing which did the stinging had ought to be the father, not the mother; but what was I to know of her lineage? It was hers, after all. When I considered it, why, I had never asked my husband his. Just because I was born of two humans, who was to say?

"And so you, the daughter of a wolf and a woman, were sent to live in the City."

"Aye, and every time the man was cruel to me, he gave me more wealth. One day when I was nineteen, the King's guard discovered his proclivities, and we were brought before his majesty: I to act as witness. In my recounting of all that had befallen me—" She blinked much, and smiled up at the penumbra of the sun. "Your King, your love, is a gentle-hearted man to those in pain. Especially when they are in the City. But, of course, because of the way I was, and because of all that had befallen me, I could make no proper wife." Her smile whittled thinner by the second. "But my pain had moved him, and he was moved, too, when he asked if I thought the man should be punished for what he had done and I could not bear to say yes. After all, the man had done much good, even if he had tainted me. Even if he had corrupted and altered me, filled me with poison, he still brought me to the City."

Turning her head to spit, Pneuma said, "The King insisted he be punished, at any rate, but to console me said he would keep me in his Castle with him. We fell in love in secret, without the knowing of his Queen, for whom I was a handmaiden, and for whom I was trained to act as nurse, for the man from the City had raised me to be a midwife. But I had no wish to be midwife, a nurse. I wanted only what you want! What you have! I knew I could never be anything more than a concubine to him." Her eyes sparkled as they met mine. "But that does not mean I killed the first Queen, when she died with the Prince wailing in my arms."

"My mother died bearing me. I know your pain, sister, I know."

Just once, she nodded. We never spoke of it again, except that I, lifting up the reins of my husband's horse and giving them a lash to urge it forward, said, "When we have brought back the Prince, and you are living in the City again, I'll bring you to the Castle and you'll once more be my husband's lover, if he would forgive you. I think he would."

"You would abide another woman in your husband's arms," mocked the Witch at first, her own horse rising to a gallop to catch up with mine. At my earnest expression, she turned away her face, her hair streaming behind her. "Perhaps it is I who must forgive him."

"Perhaps," I said, again distracted by the landscape, the amber sky alight with fire the sun, a cancerous mole, had lost. The air around it wavered like the murmuring water. Before the beach, we paused, surveying the sky and how the sooty sun, refusing to set, rested upon the waters as if poised on the edge of the world.

"The sun doesn't set because one walks toward it," I insisted as she dismounted to lead her horse down the silver-sanded dunes of the beach. "Am I dreaming?"

"It takes a dreamer to enter the underworld." Smiling at her horse, she drew it toward the water, and it seemed bothered only momentarily; the mare was quick to accept the notion of following its mistress, who waded into lapis waves.

"This horse," I began, but I stopped, frowning, and thought that my logic had done me no good so far. For all my knowing of things, I was constantly defied. I could be secure in my facts, like the direction of the setting sun, and be proven thoroughly wrong. Perhaps it was a land of non-sense, or there was no sense in the world to start, but either way, I felt the best thing was to dismount my horse and lead him, calmly as possible, to the purpling water into which the Witch waded like a suicide. Without a word, she disappeared along with her mare, and my horse was yet the picture of tranquility. Perhaps it was only I who felt fearful. Side by side, we stepped into the humming water, and the eroding sand sloped down beneath my feet as the tug of the current wrapped my legs. The horse uttered a soft nicker while the pressure rose from my legs to my hips to my stomach and around my lungs. I felt as if I would be crushed, and, thrusting my head above the waves one last time, I recognized with terror the sky was red and the sun, no longer black, was but an eye which gazed upon my world. Then, my horse walked under, and the force of his being swept in the current yanked me with him. Together we swirled into the abyss, my mouth open in instinctive cry which only welcomed gallons of the inky stuff into my body. My eyes, though open, could not penetrate the fluid which filled me, and I felt my lungs and stomach and nose overflowing, my ears pounding, my brain choked by liquid so cold I forgot I had a body at all. Unfocused vision fading, I felt as if my forehead were splitting open, quivering with an energy across the surface of my skull—and then the water and the pain all peeled away from my face, leaving a new sensation which was bliss of its own, and I was on my back with the Witch's lips to mine and the impulse to vomit in the back of my throat. Shoving her away, I expelled what must have been a gallon of water upon some foreign marble floor.

"What happened?" I gasped, and she laughed, drawing my hair away from my shoulders and face until I could sit up to see around.

"We've died together, in a sense, though those who go through the North Sea have only the choice of death, not the obligation." As I rubbed the salt from my eyes, there came into focus the walls and ceiling of a high-mouthed cave held up by marble pillars which rose like hands in worship. At the center of that sprawling room stood a rectangular pool of water where shimmered the reflection of the absent moon, sourceless, as if she gazed from the other side. Far beyond this, before a crimson door, there stood a three-faced Ogre bound to the floor, baring its teeth to be awakened by our presence. The horses pawed the ground and snorted declarations of their terror, and the Ogre, gazing upon us through six narrowed eyes, rose to its towering height. We might perhaps reach its kneecap.

"Of course"—my guide smiled somewhat thinly—"supposing this fellow isn't entirely agreeable, we may not have any choice, after all. He does love his little rules."

"How are we going to get past that?" I whispered, my heart pounding.

"Trust in me," she said, more to her horse, which stilled beneath her hand and allowed itself to be guided around the shimmering pond. "I'll take you far, and no unnecessary harm will come to you."

"And my horse?"

"No, no harm will come to your horse at all."

My husband's black stallion pawed anxiously the marble floor and stepped forward and backward, left and right, then shook its head and bucked so I was forced to drop his reins and touch his neck and soothe him, saying once his name, that shimmer in the ocean of the sky. As I kissed his nose he calmed, and as I petted him, I felt as though it would be the last time and was struck by grief, my eyes filling with tears. "Oh, my friend, how good you are to me! To take me all this way."

The beast lowered its head into my touches as if forgiving me for the way I had driven it in the past days, and I cried like a helpless girl lost in a market while the Witch paused with an expression I expected to be mocking but discovered to be solemn. She touched my hand as I reached her.

"I would like you to follow me," she said, "just to my left, and your horse, too, in line with mine." We turned toward the Ogre, and I took a breath, obeying in perfect silence and praying my horse would do the same, but finding my prayers unnecessary, for it had grown calm and remained so even as the giant lowered itself on our approach.

"Hello, ladies," said the Ogre, more to the Witch than to me, "I'll be having them horses, thanks for coming prepared. You know the rules, don't you?"

"Horses?" she asked, laughing gaily at hers. "She is an exquisite mare, but she is but one. Perhaps having six eyes confuses you, or all this time alone has done to you the things it has to me."

The Ogre lowered its three-faced head and peered, one face at a time, at me, and then at my horse. "Perhaps you'd ought to get yourself four more eyes, miss, or more ears. You've a traveling companion. Can't you see?"

"What?" she asked as if in sharp surprise, turning to me, then laughing. "Why, her? Dear man! You do need your eyes checked."

"Why's that? Ain't she a woman, with a horse? Ain't you?" he asked, and I stared right back, hoping if I was immobile I would fade into the aether to go unnoticed.

"That's not my traveling companion." The Witch waved a hand to reclaim the attention of at least four of his eyes. "Take a closer gander at both her and her horse. See our differences, in fact, and our similarities. See my hair? Soft and red"—this, she touched—"and my bosom, supple and perfect for a wanting man to lay his head. But see her color? Dark and black, and see her body, like a boy's."

Fury burned in my forehead, and the Ogre, blushing for different reasons, demanded, "So?"

"And see her horse? Your many eyes cannot help but testify the jet glory of its mane, rich with darkness as the velvet sky of night. What sublimity! Yet mine, a mare more extraordinary: white like a pearl, like the glimmer of stars!"

"You're making my mouth water," said the brutish monster, smacking three sets of lips in terrible unison and beginning to descend upon my horse until the Witch stepped between with a merry cry. "No, no, dear Ogre! Dark hair, dark mane, why, my dear, this woman and her horse are our shadows!"

"What," cried the Ogre at last, all six eyes again on myself and my horse. I, agog, was flustered by the creativity of her lie and certain, too, he would never believe it. Squinting, the Ogre turned his lowered head this way and that. "That's a shadow? But they seem so real!"

"It truly is amazing, what solitude will do to a person." The Witch shook her head, and the Ogre became embarrassed by this notion on two faces and enraged in the third, which snapped, "You should know," as it snatched up the white mare with its right hand and crammed the screaming animal bitterly into its maw. The middle face shouted, "Aha! See there? Her horse is still there! That ain't no shadow."

But at that, the Witch just laughed. "Why, my good man, you mean to say you've eaten a shadow before? Tell me: How's the taste?" As she cocked her eyebrow and propped her hands upon her hips, I did the same, and found myself (despite the mare's ongoing mastication) biting back laughter.

Incensed, the baffled middle face opened its mouth, but the left one was through with us, and sighed. "For the love of— Go on!" The red doors behind it swung open into darkness, and the left face called as we hurried through, "I've had enough of you, you smartass."

"Have a good day," she said, giggling after it as we descended into the darkness, my hand amazed to lay, still, upon the hide of my horse, which seemed only half-aware at best of the danger it had just escaped.

"Your poor mare," I whispered to the Witch, who shrugged.

"I've lost mares before, and more than mares, too."

"Is that all death is, then?"

"What do you mean?"

"Not everybody is clever enough to trick him, or lucky enough to have a friend with them. I don't know what I would have done if I were by myself."

"Given up your horse," she suggested, leading us into a blackness without discernible space or boundary, "and stranded yourself with no way back. That is assuming, of course, you yourself had not been eaten by the Ogre."

"He seemed rather civil for an Ogre, and everyone says that he eats horses at the gates if you have them on offer. Would he really have eaten me even if I'd given him the King's stallion?"

"Oh, he's a civil enough fellow, but you mind, he's also very persuasive. If he had it his way, he'd have you think him the be-all, end-all of being dead, and that you'd no choice but be eaten by him. His favorite game, in fact, is to suggest the dead have been sent to be eaten in punishment for their crimes, though if that were true, he wouldn't be guarding a door. A lot of people don't think that through; they panic and give in to the despair of their earthly sorrows. They'll ponder an eternity before feeding themselves to him. But all you have to do to avoid it is give up your horse. Sometimes, not even that."

"And those whom he devours?"

"Where do you think new animals come from? New Country people? Where do you suppose you were before you or your parents were born, Your Highness?"

I licked my lips, near to asking more, but in the silence, the sound of rushing water filled my ears. I frowned. There were no walls, was no floor. We saw neither ceiling nor sky. Yet: the gurgle of water.

"The river, Lethe," she said, "be still."

Coming to a stop, I shifted the reins of the horse to my right hand when, to my blushing embarrassment, the Witch stripped her clothes, which I only realized to be her intent when she did not stop at her cloak, but rather continued with her bodice.

"What are you doing," I whispered, my face bright. "Pneuma, what if something comes to hurt you? Without any armor!"

"O ye of many fears, what a terrible life you must live." Laughing, the Witch lifted her arms and did a wiggling dance so her skirts pooled around her toes. She was more perfect than the statues salvaged by my husband's army from the temples of defunct love goddesses. As she turned her eyes upon me, I, flustered, averted my gaze amid her merry laugh.

"Much better," she said, focused on something I couldn't perceive at her feet. "Goodness! Any closer and we might have tripped. More people fall in because they don't take off their clothes. The river hides from those wearing clothes—even animals—because it takes them for people, and knows no person would walk through it of their own volition. You don't see it or Elysium until you fall in, unless you're naked." Tittering, she turned to me in expectation. "Well?"

"Well," I started, but her eyebrow only arched as though she shouldn't have to tell me. I, sighing, turned away, laid down my bow and quiver, took off my cloak and armor, my breeches and my blouse. Humiliated, I focused on removing the bridle of my horse, vaguely aware that somewhere behind it a world had bloomed into being. As I bent to take off my boots, Pneuma landed a slap on my backside so sharp I cried, "Hey!"

"You're missing it." The Witch laughed. "I'm just trying to wake you up." As my attention lowered to avoid the Witch, pink and blue pebbles emerged from the darkness beneath my feet with sprigs of grass pricking up between them. I gaped at a chromatic sky which was not there, I sensed, but which all the same shimmered with an aurora pastel like colored Spring Festival eggs; the same was true of prairies rolling in the distance, full of figures which, indistinct, moved upon hillsides amid the distant rabble of joyous conversation. Only on turning my eyes at last toward the Witch did I see a river more temptingly pure than any I'd encountered, so much so I felt as though a needle pierced my heart.

"Take care not to touch it," she said, clambering upon the back of my husband's stallion and reaching to help me do the same, sighing in lascivious relish as she pressed close enough to rest her chin upon my shoulder. With her heels, she urged the horse into the river and pulled her legs up high, as I already had. "She's a river of forgetting. The more you touch her, the more you'll forget of the Kingdom and the more you'll know of Elysium. You'll see, new-baptized, as animals always do, and have no guilt or sin. That's why animals cross the river unchanged, and why the river need not hide from them. Animals have nothing to forget. Why, the first time I came here, I accidentally dipped a toe, and forgot for two weeks why I hated the King!" She smiled against my shoulder, and the horse clambered out the other side to first shake itself off, then bound across the rippling prairie.

"How did you come here the first time? The North Sea?"

"No, my dear. That is the only way to guide a living body to Elysium. When one wishes to come by oneself without suicide (for those who commit such an act find themselves before the Ogre without guide or excuse or rescue from their suffering), plants can serve as guides in the stead of fellow men or women. That was how I first came: the plants of the swamp taught me their secrets. I ate of them, drank of them, and they took me by the hand and brought me here. They showed me how to come and go, and showed me the way to take weary travelers flocking in times of need. It is a hard journey through the Mountains to the North Sea, and most are too terrified to drown in the water, so no one has come to me before you. Not since my being there...but there have been others before me in the swamp, and the plants tell me they once served wandering men and women the same. I did not build that hut in which I live," she said, absently, conversationally, over the gallop of the horse and a rising roar which I recognized as the growing sound of the crowd turning toward us, each torn from their activity to cry out and wave in joyous greeting, every member of the dead from this side of the ocean and the other as happy to see us as if we were their sisters, their daughters, their friends. I became more aware of our nakedness and blushed, clutching the neck of the horse which slowed as three happy ambassadors greeted us. All three seemed wizened by time, yet ageless in robes of gray silk softer than any on earth. I knew them not, yet felt us the best of friends, and neither took exception nor sensed lewd intent as one of the men helped us down while the second gave our horse a few pearls of sugar. The woman who had accompanied them said, "Poor things! Don't you fellows think our girls are cold."

Nodding in solemn agreement, the man who had helped me from the horse removed his robe to reveal a tunic the color of fish scales, and the woman did the same before they kindly draped their robes across our shoulders. As we accepted them, the Witch asked, "Have the three of you seen the Prince of the Kingdom? The Son of the King?"

"Which Prince?" asked the first man.

"Which Kingdom?" asked the second.

"The sovereign ruler of the world, my husband, the King," I explained patiently, and the old woman laughed.

"But *which* King, sweetheart?"

"The Red King of the West," suggested the Witch. This seemed to register some understanding.

"Oh! Of course, the Son of the King of the West." The old woman studied the first man and tapped her chin in thought. "Is he just beyond the third hill?" she asked.

"I think perhaps, that or the fourth," suggested not the first man but the second. "But surely you nice girls don't want to go all the way down there."

"Why not?" I asked, studying the hordes of people who, amid happy animals, picnicked or played instruments or made the kind of innocent love which offends no one in a place so pure, where the flowers them-selves seemed on the verge of golden song and prayers to the serenity of living and dying drifted through the air like clouds. "Doesn't it only grow more beautiful?"

"Oh, it does," said the Witch, but the old lady gave a pettish sigh and a headshake.

"I suppose, if that's really what you want, though it doesn't seem particularly beautiful as far as I'm concerned. What could be more perfect than this prairie right here?"

Cheerfully, the Witch remounted our horse. "To each his own. You're more than welcome to stay in the first valley for eternity, sister."

As though reminded of this fact for the first since her arrival, the old woman stood straighter, with brighter eyes, her lips parted and soon covered by her hand in her open wonder. "Why, that's right. I can! Oh, how wonderful," she said to her first companion, while the second, then, seemed to remember this, too, and cried, "Wow! How beautiful," and the first joined the chorus at last with, "My God," and the Witch, laughing to herself, pulled me upon the horse to leave them in their bliss.

"What funny people," I said, laughing over my shoulder.

"If you find the most perfect spot in creation for yourself, you may also be so paralyzed with bliss you aren't able to leave."

I considered that, and found myself filled with wonder to imagine what place could be so compelling I might linger there eternally. What perfection could not be tiresome, given ample time to wear thin? Pondering, I shook my head toward the glimmering sky, and our happy horse trotted into the second valley which shocked me to a hue of bright red when we found it host to an orgy.

"Oh, my." I tried not to observe the tangle of limbs which made the Witch giggle as the horse waded through it.

"Oh, yes," she said, wiggling her eyebrows at a handsome fellow who, spotting her on the horse, smiled in a glittering way and reached up to stroke her leg. I, embarrassed, slapped his hand while the Witch laughed, and I was more embarrassed when he reacted by touching me, instead, slipping his hand over the surface of my thigh as I called, "Excuse me! No, thank you!"

"She doesn't want any," laughed the Witch, urging the horse forward at precisely the moment it gave a whinny of indignant surprise and kicked some groping offender. "Really! Let's try to have *some* boundaries..."

"Who would want to be a part of this?" I asked, too shocked to be outraged.

"You'd be surprised," she said at the precise instant I recognized with shock my own sister Chastity, who had died some years before of typhus at her husband's farm. I turned my blushing face away while the laughing Witch navigated our horse through the debauched revelry. With some effort, we emerged on the other side and I, shaking my head, said, "I find no pleasure in a thing like that!"

"You would were your King there," she said, almost chided, her eyes darkening as she turned them from me.

"That's not true," I insisted, flushed, but then, I wondered, "Do Kings and Queens come to valleys such as these?"

"Not true ones, no. There are those who are less than the rabble they claim to rule, and they, like their citizens, wander lower levels. But there are those hills of Paradise to which only royalty of true and noble dignity hold the key."

"And Witches?" I asked, and she smiled slightly.

"There are experiences so profound that even a Witch might tremble before them. A Witch might know secrets, but a Sovereign, O Queen, has something different. A Sovereign who is true of heart and pure of being, who is appointed by God, as thou art"—her eyes had glazed as if something beyond her spoke in that soft instant—"such a being is possessed of Majesty. That is why you are called 'Your Majesty,' Majesty."

We passed the third valley, where acts of lust had given way to acts of violence. Though, to my shock, as we drew closer there seemed strange similarity to the lust for violence and the lust for sex; indeed, how curious the expressions of those in the throes of violence, who could admit here in Elysium the pleasure they took from it. Here, the source of a scream was not so different from that of a moan, for the roots and branches of a tree extended from the same trunk. There were those who were whipped and those who did the whipping, those who lived in terror and those who did the terrorizing, and it made no sense to me, who turned questioningly to the Witch only to discover that she bit her lip with envy for those most martyred by the bare hands of their lovers. I spoke not, for I knew not what to say to her, nor ask of this wicked valley. It was only when she caught my interest in her that I said, "I thought this place was said to grow sweeter each valley. This hardly seems Paradise."

"Those who are here are here because they wish it, and here, they all know it. The agony of one man is Paradise to another, O Majesty, and even agony is Paradise, but veiled."

At last, the fourth hill gave way to a valley of dreamers; across them, I peered through what I thought at first to be a fog but realized soon to be smoke hovering in a blanket across simultaneous sleep and revelry, with some dozing gauzily in satin chairs and others wide awake to dance or laugh over nothing, with still others playing dice, others creating music more raucous and wild and melodious than that which was played in that first valley. Yet others did naught but gaze at the sky amid their neighbors, all so loud it was with a shock that I heard in the distance the voice of the Prince saying, "Well, perhaps you and I had ought to go a valley deeper in, if that's how you feel."

"You didn't tell me he was a sodomite," said the delighted Witch as I scrambled from the horse, more annoyed to find the Prince spending his time in the valley of layabouts than I would have been to find him already up to his waist in some handsome young man from the Distant Lands.

"I didn't think it mattered," I told her, telling a drunken pair of craps players, "Excuse me," while stepping around their game, skipping over a man who slept cradling his opium pipe and closing in on the Prince, who stood with his back to me and his posture that of a man in a tavern trying to pick up a lover. I suppose that's what he was until I stumbled over the foot of a snoring drunk and fell against him while reaching to tap his shoulder.

"I beg your pardon," he began, seeming to mean it for the first time in his life until he turned and recognized who bumped him. His expression widened with shock. "Why, Felicity! What a thing to find you here."

His face! The Prince! Oh, the Prince! Whatever irritation I had felt on finding him thus completely melted away, for at last I faced the dear friend who had done so much for me—however haughty he acted. Tears filled my eyes as he said, "Didn't you take a dip in the stream? You're not still sad about something, are you? There's a reason they blind you to it, that river: it's so you'll fall in. And who's this?"

The Witch had appeared behind me, already introducing herself as, "Pneuma, the Witch of the Swamp, banished by your father, here to rescue you along with the Queen out of the goodness of my heart."

"Aren't you a tigress," he said, waggling his brows at her. "Why don't you come along down to the next valley? Living in the swamp must make a woman want for company. Surely there's somebody fun, and flexible, for you. Good seeing you, Felicity."

"No, damn you!" I grabbed his mantle as he started to leave. "You can remember me and remember your father. Do you remember your Kingdom?"

"Yes, yes, of course I do. It's not that kind of forgetting, Felicity. It's the forgetting of pain and misery. The forgetting of guilt and grief."

The Witch nodded and patted the neck of our stallion. "Yes, dear, so we rode a horse across the river that we might remember it all."

Shocked between the two of us before offering an accusatory sniff at the horse, the Prince asked, "Whyever would you do that? Surely you don't want eternal guilt over your earthly mistakes."

Leaning forward, voice low, I said, "We're not staying here, yet. We're here to bust you out."

A broad array of emotions shuffled across his face. First aghast at us but then delighted and shocked by me (which I knew because he whispered, "Why, *Felicity*," as if I had admitted to a scandalous piece of gossip), the Prince spared a regretful afterthought for the handsome fellow who had already turned his attention to someone else and, irritated, regarded me with his hands on his hips.

"I'll have you know I'm perfectly happy," he said, but I clasped my hands and lowered myself before him by bowing my knees to say, "Please!" When the pain in my eyes gave him pause, he let me straighten up to speak. I recounted the woes of his father, and of the Kingdom, and how deeply it despaired in the wake of his passing. He seemed touched, though unmoved, and even said at the end, "Well, perhaps Father might move here."

I gasped at his meaning and shouted, "No!" and the Prince, scowling, crossed his arms.

"Well! It's quite lovely here. Granted, death isn't exactly an emotional picnic, but...I don't know, it was only the letting go part that was difficult. I mean, I *suppose* this qualifies as death, but it's not like I really died."

"Of course you died! You were pierced through the heart!"

Laughing, the Prince stammered, "No, I—just one—hey," then turned to the far-eastern man who had slipped off into the crowd. Left to scowl in the absence, he turned his scowl at us. "My witness is gone, but at any rate, I'm telling you I didn't *die*. Ilani showed up in my tent one night. I had just been thinking on the march that day, 'How beautiful these men of the east are! Why are we killing them when we could sculpt them?' and just as I was thinking that, my eyes fell on him and his eyes on me, and next thing I know, I'm being woken in the middle of the night by this stranger who'd fallen for me on first sight and followed us all the way to our encampment, somehow crept past the guards and the patrolmen, and found my tent and *woke me up*. Oh, so romantic!"

The dreamy Prince sighed, hand upon his cheek, as the Witch, brow arched, asked, "And this doesn't sound like Death to you."

"Don't be absurd, woman, I'm clearly right here, perfectly alive as you! When I awoke to that beautiful face and was given the option of fighting in some tedious battle for my father's war or a peaceful retirement to Elysium with the most beautiful man I'd ever seen, was it really a choice?"

"But you *did* die," I insisted, frustrated by his denial of the truth. "You did fight the battle, don't you see?"

"Nonsense. Ilani and I hopped on my horse, and that was that. Blasted horse got eaten in the end, of course. However did you get through with *this* old chap? Yes, hello, Noesis, you handsome fellow." He stroked the stallion, which bowed to him, pleased as such a dour animal could seem.

For my part, I was less so. I crossed my arms amid the chaos. What could I do to lure the young Prince out of Paradise? With these things available for the taking, all of the drugs which grew in the ground as plants and flowers, hidden in the barks of trees and in the corals and weeds of ponds, no amount of leniency in the Castle might coax him back to lighting up the Kingdom's days. Neither feast nor fumes could amount to what was here. No number of men, either, for Elysium suffered no shortage, and the Prince was not the sort to have one earthbound lover for whom he pined. Love, then, would not tempt the spoiled Prince. But that was just it, wasn't it: he was a Prince, not a King.

"I'm rather surprised," I said at last, folding my hands behind my back and shrugging before I turned to the Witch. "I guess it's his choice."

"Of course it's my choice," he said, then taking the bait and recrossing his arms. "Why is it, exactly, that you're 'rather surprised' in me, Mother Inferior?"

"No reason," I said, almost sang, resisting the urge to do just that as I mounted again our horse. "I should only think a boy born a Prince should long to someday be King. That's all."

"Felicity, darling, I'm treated like a King here, I should say."

"Oh, of course—as are all men, as is just. But, why, what was that, Pneuma? What you told me about the hills of Elysium, and Kings and Queens?"

"A true Sovereign whose heart beats in the grace of God may dwell in the seventh valley and partake firsthand of all its secrets."

Breathless, the conspiratorial Prince lowered his head. "Why, I've wondered what was locked up behind that wall, though it's the funniest thing: whenever I get near it, I lose all interest in it, or a particularly handsome chap comes by, or— well, one way or another, I'm being kept out!"

"You are," I confirmed, and the Witch nodded as she mounted behind me.

"No man can become a King in Elysium if he was not one in life, but one can always try again, given the opportunity. Someday, Felicity will end her reign, and she and the King will awaken in Elysium's highest crown to dwell in perfect understanding. But you, my dear, cannot do that without letting us bring you back." She lifted her eyebrows, and desire was born again in the face of the Prince, lifted toward the platinum sky and the distant wall which I had, until that moment, taken for snow upon the farthest hill.

"But what if a true Sovereign wants to indulge himself in all these other lovely hills?" he asked even as he began, reluctantly, to edge toward us.

"Then he is welcome to, I am certain. But I suspect a true Sovereign would be beyond interest in such things."

Sighing, rolling his eyes, the Prince laid a hand upon the horse, then hauled himself on behind Pneuma. "You're probably just lying to get me to come back with you."

A breath of relief rattled through me. The Prince, on the horse! How close we were to the completion of our impossible task. But I noticed hardness in the face of the Witch, who seemed to stare at nothing, past the Prince who asked, "What is it?"

"We'd ought to hurry," she said, gazing out across the sky. I, who had been focused on the Prince, followed her eyes to the distant seventh hill. The shimmering air had begun to bronze, as though to strip all glory and replace itself with the pallid fire which flickered to life to bleed across the atmosphere. Those in the grips of their addictions around us were unmoved; indeed, no one noticed but the Witch and I, and then the Prince, who said, "Oh, well, that never happened before you ladies convinced me to leave. Coincidence?"

"We have to go," insisted the Witch. In the distance grew the sound of a powerful storm, like the humming of bees amid a symphony of off-tune violins. As an inky cloud bloomed in the sky above the seventh hill, rising from behind the wall like a mushroom cloud of the weapons from the Distant Lands, it seemed as if the atmosphere parted, curtain-like, to reveal a darkness long waiting. I, breathless, hardly realized it when the Witch urged the horse which, while swift, was laden with one person too many for its size, yet took off with a startled cry at a slap which sent it galloping through the gamblers, leaping over dreamers and sleepers. Past my companions, beyond the citizens, the cloud writhed as if of bats.

"What have you women made me do," cried the shocked Prince, the earth rumbling beneath the hooves of the stallion, which, sensing the chaos behind us, hurried his pace.

"We haven't made you do anything," insisted the Witch. "You men are ridiculous, always blaming women for everything. You're the one who wanted to become a King, remember!"

"Had you told me the cost of becoming a King would be the destruction of Paradise, I might have reconsidered!"

"There's no helping that," I shouted. Far behind us, some bolted from their leisure, but far more took no notice—or, if they noticed, they thought its problem passing and deemed their fun of higher import. "For the record, I didn't know, either!"

Both of us, then, turned accusingly to the Witch, who, clinging to me with her arms and to the horse with her legs, batted her lashes. "Well, I didn't know this exact thing would happen. People don't usually want to get out of here once they're in; there's not much precedent. I more expected we would, say, be confronted by an angel, or solve a riddle."

"Why am I so important that my leaving causes *this*?" asked the Prince. The Witch took stock of the expanding clouds in the distance, which dissipated to fall upon the people not as rain but wingèd creatures rendered indistinct by expanse.

After a few seconds' thought, the Witch suggested, "Why, doesn't even one person's desire to leave Paradise indicate it's lacking something? Imperfect in some petty way but therefore not a universal Paradise? All it takes is one soul's decision to leave, the conscious awareness of imperfection in the mechanism: the birth of desire, I suppose."

His sigh helpless, the Prince touched the top of his skull as if patting an invisible crown, then threw back his head in profanity so loud it awoke, as we passed, the valley's final opium addict. The gaunt man stumbled from bed, tripping after us as countless others, falling farther behind, were caught by those beings which I recognized as we crested the hill: neither bats, nor birds, but demons. Terrified, I reached back to clutch the Prince's hand and dug my heels into the ribs of the stallion, but he could go no faster. My heart beating in my mouth, I fell to praying, having seen something so much worse than the third valley violence through which the horse deftly navigated.

"O Witch," I said, "what rules this place, this underworld? Like no God I have known men to worship."

"Because men do not seek God in the obvious place. What was it that tore the underworld asunder? The will of the Prince. Who is it who dwells in the seventh hill? The truest Sovereigns. And who created the underworld? Only the sun, working upon the moon. Didn't you see when we came?"

"But this, all of this. More rules this place than men."

"Will," suggested the Prince, "and knowledge."

"Neither will nor knowledge could enact such a thing," I insisted in amazement. "What spirit holds this place? What spirit could be so bitter as to destroy Paradise at a word?"

"'Paradise' is naught but a word," she said at last, "and words are defined. As I said before: if Paradise is not Paradise, it is something else altogether. There is nothing responsible for this. Nothing at all but the Word, itself."

As she said this, as the demons descended upon the torturers to turn them into terrible bullheaded devils, my fear faded into pure, simple astonishment. I was amazed to see this birth of evil, and as the struggling horse leapt next through the orgy of the second valley, its breath heaving, I wondered what these people might become. What I might become if this evil came to me. As though in synch with my thoughts, Pneuma touched my hand.

"This horse cannot outpace the calamity with three bodies on his back."

Slowly, I nodded, a strange melancholy coming into me, then absenting itself. As we passed through the first valley, all the good and pious people crowded to whisper in terror of the encroaching devils. Armed with new knowledge of the Word and how close was Paradise to its opposite, it was revealed how near were demons to angels, and that ground-bound devils were but sufferers cast from Paradise. How arrogant I had been to think a thing might be removed from Paradise without disturbing its perfection! How foolhardy to have never realized I had challenged the sanctity of a Word. The priest had been right to warn me. I had gone to Elysium, to Paradise, as though to rescue the Prince from perfection—had tempted him from it with promises of a crown he might never receive if death took him a second time. The only way to restore Paradise, I was certain, would be the death of the Prince. This, I confirmed with the Witch, who nodded.

"I've ruined everything." I gasped, comprehension's tranquility broken to the burden of responsibility. "Oh, Pneuma, what have I done?"

"I did not tell you it would be without sacrifice."

As with every beat of the horse's hooves we fell farther behind, the ground before the first valley ruptured like a wound overfull with tarry pus: a second river. I cried out and clutched tighter the Prince's hand. "I only wanted to bring you back to your father! I only ever wanted the King to be happy. To protect the Kingdom from tragedy."

"I know," moaned the Prince. "What are we to do?"

Near the shore of the river, time slowed, and all the noise of the distance throbbed in my ears without sensory acknowledgment, for all was drowned in a ringing further muted by the roar of the water over which the horse launched just as I noticed something monstrous rising from the depths. I felt myself saying, "Trust in Pneuma. Let her take you to your father."

Then, it was as if someone else had control of my flesh. I felt myself letting go the Prince's hand, relaxing my grip of the horse. Pneuma relaxed her grip, likewise, on me. My body sagged left. Someone uttered a cry; the eyes of the Witch penetrated me, followed me as I descended ever nearer to the roaring water which lapped to meet me, that roaring water which slammed into and over me as though it were made of concrete. Within it I exploded, caught in the teeth of the same terrible sable Beast which burst from the waters to claim the fourth leg of the horse as it dragged itself upon the opposite bank. The Witch clutched the screaming Prince and said above the wail of the animal, "Don't look back, child. Don't look down."

The young man was inconsolable. "She came all this way for me." The wounded stallion, as though it had lost nothing, stumbled forward several strides until stopped by the Witch. As Pneuma dismounted to strip off her cloak, the Prince demanded, "What are you doing!"

"Take off your clothes; it's the only way we'll see Lethe if we're both on the horse."

"This place is ridiculous," shouted the Prince above the din, sliding from the animal to tear off his clothes. "I've just lost my best friend without even telling her she was my best friend, and I have to strip off in front of a crazy hermit. Just what were you banished for, at any rate?"

"Letting your mother die," she said, remounting the horse with the Prince caught by the arm as he stripped off his tunic to reveal his shock along with the gentler Lethe. Despite herself, she laughed, and dug her heels into the ribs of the limping horse which forded the second river.

"What do you mean?" asked the Prince. The Witch, lacking humor, said, "I was your midwife. Sort of annoying to see the fruit of my labor already in Elysium. It's been all of, what, seventeen, eighteen, years?"

"Near thirty, you cow, I'm a grown man! You were the one who let my mother die," he repeated in appalled wonder, naked and sharing a horse with this woman. "It should have been you to fall off this blasted horse!"

"It was her idea to come in the first place," the Witch insisted as the horse, desperate to escape the quake, embanked upon the other side of the river. The water had ended its bleeding but not replaced its leg; nonetheless, the animal dashed up the hill with the black Beast from the barring river rising behind. Without awaiting human interference, the stallion burst through the red door at the entrance of the under-world, neighing in pain as its equine weight forced the thing half off its hinges to permit the horse and its two screaming passengers to careen across the marble floor, between the legs of the chained and startled Ogre, and down the length of the hall of death as the humans screamed together, "Shut the door! Shut the door!"

"What's that?" demanded the groggy Ogre with panic in all six wild eyes, whirling up before it did as it was told. With a slam which shook the hall, the Ogre shut the door just as the Beast reached its exit, and the bellow of its wrath was so terrible that the naked Prince clutched the Witch in terror. "Bloody hell," shouted the Ogre, wheeling to the interlopers, "what have you done! Where's that bloody shadow of yours! That horse is missing a leg!"

"It's very important," said the Witch, clambering back upon the horse as it stumbled to its hooves, "that you never, ever let anybody back through that door. Certainly not until the Prince returns. People can go in, I suppose, since they must, but they can't be coming out."

"You aren't supposed to be dragging residents out in the first place! Oh! Not the bloody Prince!" The Ogre roared, humiliated, as the Witch, towing the Prince, kicked the stumbling horse, which dashed so blindly that all three fell—first the mount, then the Prince, and then, at last, the Witch—into the pool where shimmered the face of the moon, invisible but by reflection.

II

The plunge was so quick and so cold no one knew what had happened. The Witch felt the water rush into her nose so fast it seemed her eyes might burst from her skull, but it was intact that she emerged with a stinging gasp from the North Sea, the necrotic sun burning behind them as the soggy horse limped from the surf with the choking Prince and Witch still together on its back. Naked, delirious, and blind with salt, first the horse, then its riders, lurched upon the sand, gasping, coughing up water, and amazed to be alive. The Witch even started to laugh, facedown on the beach, until the exact second cold steel bit sharp against the back of her head.

"What are you and your friend doing with my horse, Pneuma?"

A white chill bled from the top of the Witch's skull to the bottom of her stomach, for though she had not been nicked by the sword, she well recognized that voice, and it cut her to address it by saying, "Your Majesty."

"Father," gasped the Prince, and the cold pressure against the back of the Witch's scalp eased with the word. As she lifted her head, she caught glimpse of the King, who, beautiful as ever (even if aged and fit with a dark beard not worn quite so thick in his youth), turned upon the silver mare in shock at a lost voice rising, new-born, in his ears.

"My boy." The sword fell from his hand as he nearly did from his horse, as he certainly did to his knees while the Prince pushed golden locks from saltwater-reddened eyes. "My boy! How is it that you're here?"

"Felicity," babbled the Prince, clutching his father's robes like a tattling child. Before the Witch could intervene, the boy accused, "Daddy, she's killed Felicity!"

"What?" The Witch cried out, hands above her head as she was surrounded by the King's guard, the eleven men who had followed him across the Kingdom and through the Mountains and to the North Sea in pursuit of the missing Queen. Paled and panicking, the Witch prayed from face to face that being a naked woman might protect her. "The Queen sacrificed herself so we could reach safety. She came to me asking for help."

Clinging to his father's mantle, the Prince allowed one of the legionnaires to drape a cloak around his shoulders as he accused, "This awful woman, Father, she made me greedy and lured me out of Paradise and didn't tell me—or Felicity, for that matter!—that if I left Paradise it would be destroyed, and it all fell to ruins, and oh, Father! Poor Felicity!"

Wild-eyed, gripping his son's shoulders, the King demanded, "What's happened to Felicity!"

"She had to throw herself from the horse to make us light enough to reach safety! See your horse, it's missing a leg? A Beast burst from a black river and took it, along with your Queen!"

A terrible stillness overcame the face of the King while the Prince insisted, "We have to go back for her."

"There's no going back there," said the Witch. "Only the moon could bring her back, or maybe the Devil."

Tears filling his eyes, the King stared into the North Sea, then gazed at the face of the black sun. Putting on her best expression of penitence, the Witch moved forward upon her knees, then tensed as a sword pressed to her clavicle. Hands clasped, she begged, "O King, it's true: we lost your Queen, but see? I've given you your son!"

"Twice over you've told me that," breathed the King, words ragged as a man who had inhaled shards of glass, and who touched his chest as such. "Twice over you have given me my son at the cost of my wife, the cost of my Queen! Oh, Felicity!"

A mournful bellow peeled from the King, who, shoulders shaking, fell upon the earth and covered his face while the guards and Prince and Witch watched, helpless. His grief, so loud it thundered miles around, only parted that he might breathe enough to say, "Give her clothes and bind her. The Swamp was too good for her. We will remove her to the Kingdom for execution."

"But wait," cried the Witch, until her mouth was stuffed with cloth and her head covered in a burlap sack. She was kept that way, mute and blind but for mealtimes, during which she was merely blind; blind until they reached her cell two weeks later, for the horses of the guardsmen were far slower than the limping horse of the despairing King and the silver mare for whom there was no rider but the Prince. The resurrected man made the journey in uncharacteristic silence but for the odd bout of audible sobs. When her blindfold was at last removed and the gag gone permanently, she found herself in a dusty cell worth seven footfalls wide by eight footfalls long, and her lips and tongue were so chapped she fancied the latter might crumble.

For uncountable days and nights, the Witch was hidden away in the oppressive darkness of the cell, by far one of the mustiest in whatever building was its host. Sometimes she tried to guess. The Castle? Certainly not. The King wanted to keep her close, she was sure, but not in his home. It wasn't long, though, before she gave up guessing. Trying to suppose a thing like that only kept her more keenly aware of her confinement. Instead, she sat with her back to the corner as she stared through the bricks, waiting, her consciousness at a seeming distance from the prison of her body. Though her ocular matter gazed into the walls before her, or one foot wiggled against the solitary bench, she was really in her garden, where she stripped free her ragged clothes to walk into the flowers, dip her toes into its stream, and lie pure upon tall grasses. With the white face of the moon hanging above her, beautiful, sensual, she missed it not at all, for it hovered behind her open eyes at all hours. Yes! Her vision was so powerful she saw the moon even during daylight, even locked beneath the earth. Who could say as much, themselves!

Food occasionally appeared, and she would grow aware of the movement of a body up and over to the door. This automaton which she once inhabited would return to its place in the corner and start eating on its own. Somehow, she tasted the stale bread as it cracked between her teeth, its jagged crust scraping the roof of her mouth. But it seemed less and less clear a sensation every time she experienced it; indeed, her garden seemed richer and fuller each passing moment in the darkness. It grew so lush that, arrayed with its rainbow of flowers and the overgrown trees which wove together like a new, second sky, the Witch realized she had created a Forest.

Though she walked in the Forest in her mind's eye, she longed to see it in the flesh, with her own eyes. She had feared she never could when first cultivating it alone in her hut. A girl's dream, she figured, or a madwoman's fancy. In the cell, however, things were different. The cell brought her strange clarity: she recognized the cell around her was just as much within her as was the Forest. Why, that cell, if anything, was less real than the Forest! If this cell was real, her Forest could be real, and all the leaves within its many boughs seemed to tremble at the thought of their unleashing. The Forest deserved to be released, was friend and protector to her, understood her in a way better than any person ever might. Better than any man certainly could.

That was the root of the issue, wasn't it? Man's misunderstanding. The King's misunderstanding. She wasn't cruel. Wasn't evil. She'd only made mistakes. Was that worth burning someone over? Why, she'd gone to the underworld for him! For his ridiculous son! Though he could think as he pleased, she had indeed given him the boy twice over, and to think that he had no appreciation sent molten heat across her face. His nature as a blind amnesiac was somehow fascinating, but more so was his ability to shun her for nothing at all, mourning forever the loss of his Queens as if the Witch was really that different from either. As if she had been so much worse.

Perhaps the King wanted someone to be angry with. What the King wanted was a villain. He had done everything he could to ensure she would become a Witch. And everyone knew that the will of a true Sovereign was the will of God! So, by God, then, let him hate her. Let him think her cruel so she might prove it to him, if only given the chance! Under the boughs of her willow tree, stroking the petals of a white lily in the sparkling grass of her Forest, the Witch thought her cruelty would show him how kind she could be, too. How magnanimous, and how powerful.

As she made the resolution, footsteps echoed down the hall and drew her from her meditation, for they were different than those which announced food. Of these, there were many pairs. When at last the door opened, she squinted through the glaring light. Before her stood the King and all his guards.

"It's time," he said, his lips in a frown. "Do you have anything to say?"

Just once, the Witch blinked, clearing spots from her eyes.

"You won't even have the dignity to get up and walk to your execution like a human being," scoffed the Prince from behind his father's shoulder, until that second invisible amid the overexposure.

"We don't taunt the dead, my boy." The chiding King moved aside himself and his son to let through the guards. A pair, heads low, slipped into the darkness, muscles and weapons both at the ready, each with half a set of manacles. Together, they bound the hands and feet of the Witch, and then, by the forearm, dragged her standing. She swayed between them.

"Say what you will about taunting the dead," said the wary Prince as she was led past, "but maybe we'd ought to consider letting the dead take a bath beforehand. I mean, talk about cruelty."

With the faintest of smiles, the Witch lifted her head. "Fire will do a finer job cleaning me than water ever has."

A snort resounded between the Prince and a few of the guards, but the King's expression remained solemn. Pregnant with thoughts of dead wives? Perhaps. Should she ask? Perhaps not. He took matters of the dead so personally, not realizing their luck. Shuffling in silence, she squinted through her adjusting eyes to admire the architecture of the dungeons, to cluck under her breath at the steep height of stairs which had seemed shorter on the way down. The dungeon may well have lain nestled in the center of the earth, far beneath the depths as it was. When they emerged in the barracks, a black shroud was placed over her head, leaving her blinded from the City so its citizens were reduced to a sea of murmurs accompanying the procession toward the central plaza. This was already full of spectators, the market having been deconstructed, the podium normally positioned before the central fountain replaced with a stake. The Witch was lifted to this, felt beneath her feet the piled straw. The irons of the manacles were removed and then replaced when her arms were jerked back, arranged at the behest of her captors. At last, the veil was removed.

To the Witch's pleasure, the City entire had turned out to attend her death, and near all of the Country, as well. Thousands of faces filled the plaza, spilling from alleyways and appearing in the windows of buildings, even seated on its roofs. Above all watched that most significant of faces: the radiant moon, which sent to her a pulse of life in light which shone against the brass leg fitted to the King's black horse.

"Pneuma of the Swamp, your crimes are as follows," began the executioner, but the Witch stopped listening. She was again in her Forest, where the glory of the full moon bloodied with her unrequited love. There, her heart had no beat: it was dead, which was worse, to her, than feeling the heart of her fleshly body stop. Her spirit was, or perhaps only felt, thoroughly dead. That was fine. Perhaps she would be renewed in Elysium, when the Prince at last made his appearance. Perhaps not. Either way, she realized, she could not be made to care. And then— perhaps because she was dead, she thought—she recognized an angel in her garden, and found herself drawn to his side, beside the stream unfurling through mulberry hedges in the Forest's center.

She could not bear to see the seraphim's face but was relieved to find it veiled when she sat beside him. With twitching black wings, he draped an arm around her. "If you had an opportunity to be truly cruel to him for what he has done, would you take it?"

The Witch's head swam. She could not articulate a response to this being, who extended his hand. He rose with her to lead her down the stream after the distant sound of music. "The finest cruelty would be to give him what you have taken, only to take it again."

Her dead heart pounded in her ear, and time outside of mind slowed as, within her heart, she marched through the Forest with the angel toward the distant dancing lights of will-o'-wisps, other angels whose faces were unveiled and wings, white and radiant: these walked upon the water. She faced once more the one walking with her as he said, "There are those who would see you suffer for nothing more than their pleasure. Man's true nature is animal nature. But there is another way, now that your heart has blackened, that you might never die."

"How," gasped the Witch, desperation hushing her words.

"I am a renowned expert in the methods of diamond-making," said the angel, which the Witch realized walked with a limp. "Your heart shall become a diamond, if only you are willing to part with it as it undergoes pain and heat and pressure."

Through lips dry with desert bitterness, the Witch said, "It's never done me anything but harm, this heart of mine. I'll be glad to be rid of it."

"From the depths of your resentment shall rise true power," prophesied the angel, lifting his veiled face toward the thinning dome of trees. "You shall punish the King for all his transgressions, good woman— shall rise up and conquer, blacken the very sky with your passionate disdain."

"At what cost comes this favor?" breathed the Witch, gripping the white fabric of the robe in which this black-winged, black-veiled angel was clothed only to find it hot as fire, yet cool as a summer breeze with the shimmer of water, as if she'd lain finger upon a pond's rippling surface. As she pulled her hand away, the angel said, "No favor, good woman. It is God's will that you should arise in vengeance. Now that Paradise has become corrupt, it longs to be released."

"Alas," said the Witch, her brow furrowing, "I myself told the Ogre to hold shut the door. What would I do? What would I say?"

"Say nothing. Only open the door."

The Witch faltered, then stumbled over a vine when she realized the angel left her behind. When she caught up, they emerged outside the Forest, which the Witch did not realize to have an end. To her incredulity, though she was still upon the stake being read a droning litany of admonishments and last rites and nonsense by members of the Court while the people around her whispered, she also found herself in Elysium, for her Forest ended upon a vast hillside which overlooked the whole of that which had once been called Paradise, and was now but bleak decay. As the angels emerged from the Forest, they became demons in the tar of corruption, which leathered their wings as they swept upon the valleys of that obsidian hell.

"You would have me release this," she breathed.

"Not just release. Indeed, I would have you wield it. A dead heart is the finest gateway for corruption that God has ever divined. And a corrupt, dead heart is the treasure God values above all others. The purification of a dead heart calls forth the Lord. In doing this, you shall have salvation, and immortality, and power most sublime."

"Why me?"

"Angels cannot open the door of Elysium. Only the spirit of man or woman can, when they are dead of heart and willing to give themselves up: to give up their body to the hosts of Elysium and sacrifice their being to the force of their passion."

"Why would you have me open the door, Angel?"

"Because," said the veiled being, leading the Witch down from the hill of the Forest and toward the first valley, the quietest, full not of active suffering but simple ghostly memory for the thought of what had been, "when a wound is full of pus, it must be drained to heal. The corruption of this place must be released if it is ever to reach restoration."

Laughing, the Witch mocked, "You would have me be some heroine in a child's fable."

With what the Witch thought might be the twitch of a lip beneath his veil, the angel said, "No heroine, good Witch. When you let the corruption of Elysium into your heart, there shall be nothing of goodness about you. I would only see you put the profanity of this place to use as a lance with which to spear your enemies."

"And yours?" asked the Witch, but when there came no response, she turned to find that the angel was gone. Very much alone, especially in the throngs of gray-bodied spirits listing pathetically in that first valley, the Witch held herself and hurried through to that raging black river which had split the earth to gush forth like putrid oil. From the viscous fluid arose the Beast which had taken the Queen and the leg of the King's horse; the Witch gazed up at every terrible inch of it, and found under scrutiny this leviathan was not so terrifying. As she lifted her arms, it lowered for her, and she stepped across its body as though it were a bridge.

In the waking world, the King addressed her hanging head and the lips which sometimes moved with silent conversation during the reading of her crimes.

"Have you nothing at all to say for yourself?" asked the King, slipping the fingers of his free hand beneath her jaw to lift her chin and meet her eyes.

"Yes," she said as the bridge of the Beast led her across the river of forgetting to let her down upon the other side, and all the blackened, demonic hosts of corrupted Paradise followed. "But I'll only say it to you."

Lips pursed in indecision, the King weighed the ethics of obeying the last wishes of the condemned with the dangers of nearing the Witch. At last, morality gave out, and, though his torch ever neared the straw, the King bowed his head beside the Witch.

"What is it?" he asked.

She brushed her lips against his ear while her hands landed upon the red door of hell, which had once been the luscious hue of pomegranates but now pulsed with the twitch of exposed muscle.

"I forgive you."

With a snort, the King let drop the flame upon the straw, and its spark leapt from the torch to the hay—but it was then that the salt of the Witch threw open the door, and all its corruption spewed across the three faces of the chained Ogre, which, crying out, was devoured by the Beast. The corruption thundered through the crystal pool in the center of the foyer, leading the march as the imperfection of Paradise spread into the Kingdom through the Northern Waters, just as it came into the blackened heart of the Witch and from there spread throughout the hearts of all Matter. All the men were blinded and full of fear for their women, who seemed at once alien to them as the Witch had seemed alien to the King. The women, poisoned by the corruption of Elysium, turned against their men, eyes aglow with sickly light. The face of the moon reddened with the blood of the Witch, and as the fire kissed her feet, it oxidized into the noxious hue of poison and wrapped her legs as though a gown.

"All I ever wanted was to love you," she hissed to the wild-eyed King, feeling less the Witch every second as she neared new life. As before the Lord of the Kingdom violence unfolded across the City—wives scratching out the eyes of husbands, sisters throttling the necks of brothers, daughters tearing out the hearts of fathers—pain filled his eyes, and he hardly noticed his own men disarmed by the women descending wildly upon them to strip them naked of their armor.

"How could I love the woman who allowed both my wives to die?" asked the King as the burgundy moon blackened. The malachite flames of Pneuma's gown lapped to melt the iron of the manacles and free her to step from the pyre, blackening hair billowing around her head.

"You would never have lost a second wife had she been me." A trio of girls who had once been milkmaids in some farm far from the City brought forth the King's black horse, which reared and snorted and shifted upon its three legs until its new rider laid on it her bone-white hands. "How many lives would have been saved, I wonder?"

The unanswering King suffered himself to be crowned with a quaternity of thornèd roses as he was stripped of his mantle, which was lain upon the shoulders of the Witch as the flames of her dress gave way like scaffolding. This, amid smoke, revealed the true nature of her gown before the terrified City men: its fabric, which seemed ungraspable by, or wider than, the eye, was darker than the void of space and a thousand times colder. Forced to his knees, the King was gagged and bound, and the end of the rope which bound him was tied to the back of his own horse's saddle. The madness of the plaza eased momentarily, the men subdued by their women and made to see the King dragged through the City streets while the Witch rode high-headed upon his stallion. Wherever they passed, the chaos arose with renewed vigor, the buildings lit by the children of the fire begun in the center pyre, and the black face of the moon was lit by the reflection of collective fury. Upon the cliff overlooking the plaza, the Witch brought the horse to a stop and dismounted, dragging the King to his knees. He lurched forward, blood-ied and ragged with the torment of the journey, but nonetheless lifted his head as she demanded, "See what you've wrought. See what you've done to my poor human heart with the cold steel of yours."

Before the eyes of the King, the Witch tore open her chest and, plunging her white fingertips within, wrenched her charred, beating heart from its place in her breast with a banshee's pained cry. She forced him to see the rot which had claimed it: how hatefully it beat in the palm of her hand.

"See what you've done to me," she insisted, "and what I do to you."

It was impossible to avoid. The flames which spread across the City grew brighter by the moment, and the cries of countless people, men and women alike, filled the night air with a symphony of terror. Ached by the suffering of his people, the mute King absorbed the violence and wept in silence as the darkness of the Witch's gown crept up to her neck and filled her eyes. Above the City, her heart flew out, and, finding itself above the stake where she was to be burned, plummeted to impale itself. From this axis spread sixteen black tendrils which made of the fountain of the City the foundation of her Tower; the structure gathered together the long black arms extending from the thudding heart and wove them toward the face of the invisible moon. Into the ground as much as up toward the sky, its ferocious roots plunged, and these grew beyond the City to realize around it the terrifying beauty of her Forest. As the Tower beat itself to life and pierced the sky amid the wailing of the masses, the Usurper, born of the Witch, mounted the black horse of the King and dragged him with her. Reins in hand, she whipped the horse into a wild frenzy, driving it to the edge of the cliff above the burning City over which she urged the stallion as though to send it to its death. But, as it reared through the fire which filled the smoke-full air, the flames licked its flesh crimson as heated metal, indeed reforged its shape so that wings burst from its back; when it emerged upon the other side of the flames, the King and people both found that his steed had become a wingèd lion, red as the hatred of the Usurper who rode it across the burning City and into the highest window of her Tower. Within, the lion lowered itself, and the Usurper dragged the King into her chambers, the very highest room, whose circumference was perfectly round and whose center formed the landing of the stairs which spiraled to the ground, past floors which were so many as to be beyond counting. It was in this room that she made her bed, and, weeping black tears, bent her head over the staircase to see the fountain where the Huntress lay near death. Then, the girl had not yet been called forth: then, the Queen was still lost in the belly of the approaching Beast, and could be made to suffer no more than she already had. This would not do for the Usurper.

"You mourn your brides yet would see me dead as they," accused the Usurper, bowing forward the head of the King and forcing him to see the fountain which gazed upon the world, to see the Beast which barreled through the growing Forest and was already near to the City. "You have your wish. I am dead, yet living, and see? The rules of Hell are a life for a life: here comes the spirit of your bride!"

A cry bloomed from the King, for as one of the glittering black eyes of the Beast became the focus of the fountain, the Queen emerged within as though sleeping, but drowned, the leg of the horse cradled in her arms. This image dissolved into atoms of light which the Usurper extracted from the blackened pit of the Beast as if pulling a root from the earth. Allowing no rest for the dead as the Beast continued toward the Tower, the Usurper consigned the light of the Queen to linger in the Forest in which it had been withdrawn. The dead girl's light came together in the trunk of an oak which offered itself as scaffolding. From thence emerged her body, pure and radiant as before, or more, perhaps, for its suffering, and for that substance of Elysium with which she had become part and parcel on her death. But the Usurper kept from her the lights of her tongue and eyes and mind that she might neither say nor see nor remember herself, and could be merely an animal amid the Forest's trees: no Queen, but a Huntress.

"Let your Queen wander in desolation and wilderness all eternity," cursed the Usurper, gazing blackly upon the sleeping face of the Huntress in the cradle of her tree. "May all her days be full of labor, and her nights of pain and terror; may her own eyes never see again your holy face. But what luck, my love, for don't you see?" Smiling darkly, she lifted the King high upon the wall, and there, with ropes of muscle from her black heart, crucified him. "You may watch her for all time knowing you'll never be free of your bindings. She has no memory of herself, and thus her mind is empty of all things: her King, most of all."

With pain, the King espied the face of his sleeping beloved, and in his breast grew terror. But wheresoever there is terror, there is also hope, however small, and the light of hope glowed in the depths of him as clamor wafted from the steps below. There emerged at last a pair of flower girls, dragging behind them the cursing and outraged Prince.

"When all this is finished, I'll have your heads," he promised them, gasping as his gaze lifted to reveal his father beside the Usurper. "What have you done, Witch?"

"No Witch," intoned the Usurper as the Prince was tossed at her feet. "Nor a common Queen, but something more powerful than either. And what of you, boy? What have you done with yourself: with the life twice granted, freed as you were from the bowels of the pit? Nothing at all save to linger in the lap of luxury, blind and vain as before, having taken no lesson and grown no inch. You were indolent. My stunted tree, I dare not end your life, for why would I? I who dragged you, screaming, from the mouth of Hell, as I once did your mother's dying womb? No, better still to put your spirit in the prison it deserves and take those gifts of life so abused."

"You've gone mad," cried the Prince, leaning from the touch of her white hands. There was no use, for the women still held him, so his face was clutched by pricking fingers which sank into his flesh to elicit a rising scream.

"Let the father see his son trapped as he," she cursed, stepping back as the Prince writhed in agony, released by the women to thrash upon the floor. As his body was overwhelmed from within by a metallic sheen which clambered from his mouth to transform him, she felt a wonder of her own. "Let both father and son be hidden away from the bright eye of light; let them be forgotten by the world, just as the Queen has forgotten, and let this Tower be my testament to new life."

With a last rumble, the Beast burst into the chambers of the Usurper. Crying out, the King shut his eyes against the terrible sight. The Prince shrieked from the depths of the Sword he had become as he was whisked down the twisting Tower to be flown, screaming, across the burning City. But, much as not even the belly of the Beast could destroy the light of the Huntress, neither could the appearance of a Sword hide the light of the Prince, which expressed itself from the gem in its hilt and illuminated the twisting path to its prison.

"Open your eyes," bade the Usurper. With reluctance, the King did, agonizing over this second loss of his son even as he was forced to watch in the fountain the stirring of his lover, whose memory and entire way of being was dispersed. The binds of the Usurper adjusted, lifting him over the image that he might better see: but joy filled him, too, to watch her stir where she slept and see again the flutter of her lashes, or hear in his ears the phantom of her heartbeat like the fluttering of dove's wings in the morning light. As his sighs stabbed her black heart, the Usurper put herself between them to kiss his lips, but felt no warmth, and wept. Her growing agony reached out from the hole of her chest and into the whole of Matter, which had been stirred from the desert to begin with by her scream, and had observed in silence, having forgotten itself because it was all things, Huntress and Witch and Prince and King, and, most of all, more than them: me.

12

My God! I remember how all of this truly began! I remember finding her, the Huntress, and following her! Sending her the bear! And why did I find her? What first sent me on my flight into the blackness of the desert night, bereft of light and full of pain? What awakened me in the heart of the Huntress, who opened her eyes in the bloodied pool to purify it with her awakening, her understanding, which trickled upon the water and rendered it the pure clarity of sapphire? It was also my understanding. All this time I had been as much the Huntress as the Huntress was once the Queen, and had simply forgotten myself. Language returned to my tongue, and I felt upon my back the bursting of cerulean eagle's wings, felt my head wreathed in flame, felt the making of my gown from the waters which wrapped themselves around my body and seemed to me as silk. I rose to my feet to take up my Sword, which, sight restored, cried, "Yes, finally! Yes, Felicity! I'd never thought I'd be so grateful to see that light in your eyes, oh, goodness, you!"

"Good morning, Majesty," said the Lion, and I lowered my head that I might kiss his emerald mane and wrap him in my arms, for well I remembered him now. He purred, one paw about my waist as I gazed up the heights of the Tower.

"Will you come with me, friend, and lend me your bravery?"

A chuckle rumbled through him. "Wheresoever you go, so, too, shall I. Only lead the way and let me be your servant."

A true friend! I might have wept, but did not, and touched the blade of my Sword, saying, "I have one last favor to ask of you, Prince, before I can make you free."

"I'm just relieved you finally bloody remember yourself."

Smiling, I kissed his ruby eye. "I remember myself more clearly than I think you ever did."

On eagle's wings, and lion's, we rose through the height of the Tower; with the arrows of the General, I shot through the multitude of miniature Beasts which crawled over the walls to render them so black and ugly. In so doing, I purified them of their hatred and resolved them back to the black stones they truly were. For each that awoke, it seemed the Tower shortened, and eventually the height of the spire and the Usurper within lowered to meet us. At the force of our ascension, a fire broke within and without the Tower. Its pressure propelled us into her blackened chambers, all three equally awed. Our eyes traced across the pulsing walls aflutter with the throb of a broken heart; I felt with fresh clarity the painful scream which drew the spirit of Matter from the desert, the pain of a Queen's death and a Huntress's death. These brave spirits, they needed to meet their deaths that I might be unveiled—that I might raise my Sword as the Usurper left the side of the King whose gaunt face she stroked with the back of her hand as if leaving a favored dog. The original Beast rose before us, and I struck it through with a single arrow. Like a cyst, the monster burst, leaving for but a second the Ogre which cursed as it awoke half-dissolved and disappeared to resume its duties.

"Still you persist," hissed the Usurper, white teeth bared. "What would you have of me, girl?"

"You called me here," I told her, gently as I could, removing the aqua cloak from my shoulders to let it pool upon the floor. "I never might have found you had you not paved the way, had my friend not paved the way for me. Remember your cry? Remember the sorrow you shared with the moon? Remember the angel's promise of diamond-making?"

Pain surged through her tarry eyes like a white worm slithering across their pits; black ooze poured from her mouth and into her hand to make a rapier, a blade more vicious than any forged by man. "I have no pain, but am it. The moon does not share my sorrow. The moon may as well be the cause of my sorrow, so little it's done for me!"

The darkness of the floor rose to claim my feet, but I lifted myself only higher, lowering my blade to pierce it like a bubble which let way to white light. "It was through your cry that I came to be here at all. Through your doing, I came to heal you."

"You didn't come for me. You were lured by the perils of your King! The pain in your heart, a shadow of the pain in mine, is testament enough of that." Her body lurched forward with revolting speed, but I who saw her for what she was—saw myself for what I was—barely needed move to prove quicker than she, to press my blade's tip to the tip of her black blade, which shattered, and on through to her sternum as I told her under the watching eye of the Lion, "I heard you, and I came to you. Poor creature. Poor woman."

My eyes filled with tears at all she had endured, and confusion passed through her face until the Sword pierced the hole where once beat her heart. Her breath hitched with the widening of her eyes. The air around us stilled.

"Why weren't you there to help me," she whispered, seeing me clearly, the whiteness of my face disintegrating the darkness from her eyes. "I was so alone. All this time I've been so alone."

"I was always with you, Pneuma. This flesh"—with my right hand I touched her black one, and felt the blackness trickle into my fingertips as she was drawn into me—"is just Matter."

"You were my shadow, once, remember," she breathed, and I kissed her white eye, saying, "And now you'll be mine."

Her blackened body bled the length of my Sword and into my own fleshly frame, and the water of my gown purified her, made of her a second skeleton that we together became one soul and stood before the King in a room which, as the fire beneath reached up to sweep away the darkness, was revealed in the passing of the blaze to be made up of perfect diamond. The pressure within the Tower forced open unfurling windows to rocket red fire across decimated buildings, revealing in its wake the City polished to pearlescent sheen in the gilded morning light. As the healing flames consumed the Forest, they left behind open, radiant Ocean over which grew again all that had been, the fields and farms and the rising and falling tide of sublime being reinstilled as the scales fell from the eyes of the people and they found themselves together where they belonged, all with their loves and families, whether in City or Country, all things no longer frozen in the treacherous blackness of my shadow but instead relenting to its natural cycles. In the cool crystal mirror of the floor stood my new self: the feathers of my left wing had made themselves the color of coal, as had my dress's bodice and my right eye; but my hair had always been black, whether my name was Huntress, Felicity, Queen, or something else besides. The train of my gown had taken on the luster of peacock's feathers, the very same which came into the tips of my gloves, and it was this that I showed to my lover, laughing, as I arrived at his side, needing no Sword to free him. It was by affinity of our rosy crowns that my carbon wall relaxed its hold. At last, I took him in my arms, cradling him to my breast as we lowered to the floor.

"Hi, sweetheart," he said to me, bedraggled, laughing, and I laughed, too, to run my fingers through his hair.

"Hello," I whispered, my heart filled with aching love. "Oh, hello, my wonderful King."

"Your Highness," purred the Lion, bowing, his wings unfurling as his nose brushed the floor, "what pleasure to be graced by your presence. But what of thy mantle, Lord?"

"Stripped from me by the City women and given to the Witch," lamented the King as I, with the silk of my gown, washed his face. "I bear them no ill will. They will awaken, no doubt, and see what they have done, if they have not already."

"A King without a mantle! This will not do at all. Your Majesty"—he turned his head as he rested beside me, his tail flickering in the light like emerald fire—"it is to you that I owe the pleasure of my manifestations, and I am but your humble servant—but, if I may be so bold, it would seem my purpose in this form has been served, has it not?"

"It has," I said, reaching out a subtle shadow hand to pet his purring, mossy mane while my true hands stroked the hair of the King and mopped blood from his brow.

"Then, Your Majesty, do me this final favor: take me to the pool full of your blood and pearls and tears, and let me be rendered pure, free of flesh and earthly woes. In exchange, when my flesh is washed away, take my fur: left perfect, purified, moss rendered unto gold. Let, then, the Sword cut it for you, Queen and King. Give one new mantle unto the King, that he may be healed his pain and restored to power and glory. Take, then, its twin upon your own shoulders. And if there be flesh and fur enough in me for a third, and I'd wager there shall, give this third train to the Prince that he might grow into it with the passing of the ages."

My throat closed at the thought of my friend's end, but one paw jostled me to the sound of his cajoling voice. "All familiarities must end at some juncture. If not sooner, then later, under less so pleasant terms! But release me this way, and not only shall I give you materials to make your glory, but I shall visit you again as soon as possible, arms full of stars. I, Majesty, shall teach you how to hear them."

Smiling, I kissed him, for I was but a Queen, no Goddess, and could only rely on the soothsaying of spirits; gently, he and I lifted the King upon his back, and he bore him to the bed, laying him there and pausing that the King might pat his leonine nose.

"A nobler creature there never was."

"Oh," said the Lion, an innocent glint in his eye, his lip lifting in something between a smile and a sneer, "never forget, my Lord, I, too, have my fangs. Were I to stay too long in this form, after all, I might forget myself, and be tempted to eat one of you up."

"Shameful," I teased.

He chuckled while descending the stairs. "Who could blame me for becoming caught up in my fleshly form? One can forget oneself quite easily when all one sees in the mirror is, say, a Lion or a Queen." With a mischievous sparkle in his eye, he assured, "Someday you shall see me free, unburdened by these paltry symbols, and I will remember unerringly without reminder that service to you is my heart's true focus."

"I await that day with bated breath," I said.

"Even though it shall mean your death?"

"Even so," I said, "even so."

Down in the pool, it was as the Lion described. I lowered him into the waters with melancholy wonder as he dissolved in my arms, but the air of his being caressed my face as it ascended high above my head to vanish, formless, in the air. I knew his words of return to be true as his instructions, for the fur left within the crystal water turned from Forest green to sunshine gold. Astonished, I drew this perfect pelt from the fountain, and, in the streaming sunlight, its fur glowed like a beacon. Upstairs, in the chambers of my King, the Sword and I studied a time these bare materials.

"I have never cut a mantle before," I said, and the Sword agreed, "Nor I. But let's see..."

To my wonder, the Sword threw itself to the work of cutting the mantle from the Lion's cloth, and my hand went with it, guided by the desires and thoughts of the blade. It was critical of itself, of the quality of its work, and, to my astonishment, when I lowered my hand, intending also to lower the Sword, the tool stayed in place, ever working. I was able to stand back as it alone cut the fabric of our station. The more it worked, the more invested it became, and the more it became focused on the fur, the more he forgot himself to be a Sword: in the process of cutting and shaping and forgetting, the weapon faded, while around its vanishing being appeared the ghostly form of the Prince. I and bedridden King alike shared astonishment as the young man solidified bent over three new mantles, a pin in the corner of his mouth and his tongue in his cheek as he sewed with a thread which had not existed until that very moment.

"I've never known myself to be so good at garment making," he said agreeably, oblivious to the transformation which caused his father and I, bright-eyed, to laugh and hold and kiss one another. "Nor have I known Swords to be so talented at sewing, but I'd ought to take up tailoring if I ever get my bloody hands back."

"Why, lad," said the King, sitting forward, "they're already back! No Sword, but my son!"

"Whatever are you talking about," began the haughty Prince, looking down in the most condescending of fashions, expecting nothing and responding to the sight by dropping the pin from the corner of his gaping mouth. "Hands! My God, hands and a torso and legs! My mouth!" His hands lifted to his lips and, wild-eyed, the Prince gawked about the room, then rushed to the diamond facet of the pristine west wall where he gasped to see reflected long-absent features. "My Father's beard, I'm me again!"

"And see how beautiful your work." I collected the mantles with a sigh. "Oh, how perfect."

"May I see?" asked the King. I brought them to his side as he slid toward the edge of the bed to feel the soft fur. Breathless, he examined it, then asked, "Will you help me into it?" and, touched, I said, "Of course."

The Prince also came to his side, and together we helped the King across the room. Before the mirrored wall, I enrobed him in his golden mantle, and the ensuing burst of sunlight returned his strength, all his pains relieved at once, all his glory and endless youth restored. This light exploded and spread across the Kingdom as though to announce his renewal in so powerful a fashion that I was blinded by that same clarity which transformed our rose crowns into ones of gold and jewel and rich scarlet silk. I felt the weight of my mantle draped upon my shoulders and felt the strength of the kiss my husband pressed against my lips, and laughed to be in his arms. When he released me, we stood upon our Tower's balcony with all the Kingdom at our feet, joyfully throwing red and white roses up to our new veranda as prize doves littered the sky with snowy feathers. The Prince, kneeling before us, accepted from his father the third mantle, then a crown. As he rose to his feet, the King said, "For your service, my son, and to celebrate your return, I shall give unto you a Kingdom all your own, and my old Castle shall be yours for the taking when we have departed to our longer life. When you have become a true Sovereign, and ruled with grace and virtue so long that you have tired, you shall return to Elysium, and by your presence restore it and be held up there as King, also. As to my

Felicity," said my husband, taking me in his arms before the whole of the Kingdom, "she shall never leave my side again."

With bliss, our mantels gold, my husband and I lived happily ever after. The diamond Tower in the center of the market was converted to a clocktower whose hands ticked off our many remaining minutes. We ruled together for three score and six years. It was then, tired, we considered our descent into Elysium, though I worried for its condition, as the calamity caused by the escape of the Prince had not been healed. The notion haunted me often, over years. But my King was always there to hold me in his arms, to kiss me and say, "Ah, ah, my love, never fear. You and I, we shall go down to Elysium together, and see then what the truths of things are. We have ruled in good faith and good spirit, and shall be housed in the eye of the hurricane."

Reluctantly, I nodded, and though I had wished to hold on a few more years, he bade me look out across our Kingdom, and I found with shock how beautiful it had become, even with the corruption of the Prince's absence still intact across the world. I stood upon my balcony above the sparkling rivers overflowing crystal between the City hills. In the distance sat the ruins of my old farm, my family's farm, which seemed the home of many lives before. For even all its ugliness, I was full of longing for my youth and, beset by sobs, clutched my heart and fell against my husband. "But, oh, who could leave all of this behind?"

He kissed me, murmuring, "No, my lover, come and see! Remember, won't you, what the Serpent tried to impart, about the City and the Forest."

With nodding head and grief-warped chin, I bade tearful farewell to the Court, kissing old faces and new ones, happy, brave, and weeping for the majesty of all that I had seen and been and done, and what was yet to come. Upon our horses (his gold, mine silver) we traveled as I had before, far north, beyond the farms, towns, Woods, rivers, and Mountains—far beyond the Swamp where once my dark insides made their home. Perhaps it was the sight of the shack which prompted me to ask, "Will we find your first wife in Elysium?"

But my husband only smiled. "No," he said, shaking his head. "That is the secret, Felicity: my Sophia was too wise to go into Elysium. Someday, Elysium will have to rise to meet her. It is she who chained the Ogre, you see—she is spending her time away crafting his binds anew, that she may pass him safely, for, in childbirth, she died without her horse nearby, without her guide to take her, and so is as unlucky as a suicide. But she will chain the Ogre, and I will come to meet her at the door, and all Elysium will surge to greet her, too—and it shall be like the first night all over again, as it is for you and I each time I hold you, my love."

Not long after, we reached the North Sea, where we guided our horses into the inky water. Under the intense eye of the blackened sun, I was amazed to find that I was not afraid.

In the marble hall, the Ogre sneered. "I remember you! You bloody troublemaker. Don't think for a minute I'm going to fall for that routine again. That nonsense about shadows. It's your fault I'm awake all the time, working all the time, got this bloody temper. If Elysium were calm and I didn't have to hold the door, I'd get a blasted night's sleep!"

"I'm sorry," I tried to say, but the face on the right snarled out a laugh.

"She's sorry! Doesn't remember what her grandmother used to tell her when she came to visit during the Prince's birthday feast every winter."

The left face laughed as mine burned, the guardian mimicking, "'Sorry doesn't feed the bulldog.' Or the Ogre! And it certainly doesn't fix Paradise, or make up for the fact that I spent a bloody eternity stuck as some revolting Beast. Terrorizing those poor people!"

"You still do terrorize people," I told him harshly. "You'd ought to thank me. You're not chained up anymore, are you?"

His central face seemed the orchestrator of the shrug of his shoulders. "That's true, just as it's true I love to do a little terrorizing, but I like to do it intentionally. Not running around all blind and corrupted and half-dissolved because of you." A huge finger tried to poke me for emphasis, but my King slapped it away with his sword, which gave the giant naught but a paper cut. "Thought you'd get smart and play God, little miss!"

"I wanted to save my people," I protested, but the left face practically shrieked while the right insisted, "She's in bloody denial! Such a selfish, prideful little thing."

"Sweetheart," said the King as he put a hand on mine. "You don't have to keep telling that story. It's just us."

"I don't know what you mean," I said, throat tight, and my husband sheathed his sword to kiss my temple.

"Did you really rescue the Prince for the Kingdom?"

"No." My throat prickled. "No, I didn't do that for the Kingdom. I did it for you. For me, and for you. Because I couldn't stand to be without you. I want to live forever with you. And I did it because you deserved a son, but I couldn't be the person to give you one that way. That woman's way." I laughed, shaking my head, and when he asked me gently why not, I, lips trembling, cried softly, "I just want to be as strong as you."

"Oh, my wonderful Queen, don't you see that you are?" He kissed me, but I shook my head.

"To give birth to a child is strength, but not in the same way: not in the way of doing. Men make appeals to the heart by great works! They woo, they do! I wished to be that way, too, to give you a child from strength of character, not receptivity of body! And I did," I said, lifting my chin to see his smile as the central face laughed and said, "Isn't she feisty!"

"Yes, I am," I said, turning both welkin and sable eyes upon the Ogre. "And if you want to know the truth: even knowing everything my selfish, royal pride has caused, I would do it all again, do it all to learn all that I did, to see all that I did, and to have my husband!" I gripped him to me, kissed him, then, as if I were the man and he the woman, and he succumbed as the faces cooed in symphony, the stodgy left one humming as if in vague disapproval about which I did not care.

"Yes, well," said my husband with a laugh and a cough as I released him, straightening first his crown, then his hair, and finally himself, "you can have our horses, fellow; we shan't be needing them once my lady adjusts."

"No fuss! A far better influence on her than that bloody Witch." My silver mare stomped on the right foot of the Ogre for that, which produced in the offending left face a scream of agony. This provoked my Lord's horse, a golden stallion and gift from the Distant Lands now known as the True Eastern Kingdom, to whinny a laugh even as he was snatched up to be gruesomely devoured.

"Just who is it that put you here to start with," I asked the doorman finally, insistently, as he snatched up my mare, "if you make the cycle of Matter turn in circles, turn eaten people and horses into new animals and humans born into the world?"

The central head, the only mouth unoccupied by bloody flesh, laughed. "Why, don't you remember! It was you, my lady, who put me here, when you made the Tower a diamond." Though his answer made no sense to me, for he had been there before I had come, I found no time to protest as the Ogre opened the door. Over the howling of wind which had not been there on my first visit, he roared, "And it was Pneuma who told me I oughtn't to let nobody out until the Prince comes back. Go on, then, hurry it up! Can't keep it open long until the Prince decides he's had enough and leaves his bloody Castle to find me."

"He won't do that until he's a proper King," called my husband after the Ogre, which groaned, all three faces at once. Beneath the closing of the red door, it muttered, "That'll be all of twenty bloody lifetimes from now."

Even over the roar of the storm, my husband laughed merrily. "Melodramatic fellow. Not more to him than seven, I'd wager. Are you quite well, dear?" He took my face in his warm hands, then drew me under the fur of his mantle.

"I feel as though I'm about to be sick," I said, laughing, trying to lean away, trying not to be dizzied by the impenetrable darkness which seemed so much worse than it had on my first arrival, even though the gold of our cloaks provided light and reminded me of my beloved friend, who had many times over returned to advise me. "I am afraid of what I have done—of what I will find in the ruins I have made of Paradise. Of what my sin has done to a place once so beautiful."

"Was it always so beautiful?"

If he waited for my response, (as I think he did, for he watched my face), then he was to be disappointed. We waded through the invisible river and washed ourselves, clothes still on. I found in amazement that halfway through, I forgot where I had been before that moment and came out the other side to realize that what was behind us was not the river of forgetfulness but instead the rushing river of fury which had eliminated all that I was, crushed and destroyed me, until the Witch, out of nothing more than bitterness, pulled the light of Felicity from the darkness of that snarling Styx to taunt my tortured husband. But, of course, all she had done was what God had willed of her that I might return to life and, in life, atone for the terrible error I had made in my retrieval of the Prince. That was what it had been, my existence as the Huntress, I realized.

We set out across the first hill, the Arcadian painting of Paradise having been rendered its opposite, all its former celebrants emaciated, dressed in mourning, the longing in their eyes directed toward the black and raging river. I wished to turn my sight from them, wished we need not walk through them to reach our central home, but knew this an impossible and selfish wish. At any rate, I had already walked through them all, once, and thought nothing of it when I had known these people to be beautiful, good, and joyful. From beneath my husband's cloak, I slipped, and hand in hand, we walked through mourners, and were greeted by the three who once had met the Witch and I, now corrupted as all things there: two men, thin and frail and sour-faced, and a wretched woman, who jutted a finger at me as had the Ogre and shouted, "You!"

I, with pain of heart, not just remembered them but recognized them: two of them, at least. The woman was my sister, Phobia, and the man was my own father. When first I had seen them on my descent to reach the Prince, I had not known their agèd masks; I had in my silliness thought all the people I would find in Elysium would appear as I knew them at that time, but on seeing them again I recalled my father, who had held out until his infirm eighties and stubbornly refused to go to a place he did not believe to exist until, at last, he met an indolent whore with silver doe eyes and a love for old men who convinced him to run away with her, and took him up to the North Sea. My sister, I recognized only by her proximity to him, and by the gaunt frown lines trailing down her jaw, which would only worsen, it appeared, in the twenty or so years she would live after my death. The epiphany that I had seen them on my first descent shocked me so I all but forgot the second man, who I did not recognize but from my destructive initial journey.

"Well, well," began my smug father. "Where's your horse? Or do you finally realize you can't just come riding in and out without consequence." My bald relative, the shorter of the two men, gave a noise like a tiny hawk and waved a hand at the blackened sky. "Well, see what you've done!"

"You were always selfish," said Phobia, her voice soft and crackling beneath the distant thunderclaps. "Hoarding those diamonds in your shoe, letting Shame be beheaded. She was eaten by the Ogre, you know! The least either of you could have done was bequeath her a horse!"

"We may only pray her next life shall prove more fruitful," said my King, and Phobia flipped both hands at my husband. "Pah! Nobility is the worst. Pretentious, self-absorbed, always hiding behind 'God.'"

"You're wrong," I said, tearful. "Don't you remember? I gave you the money to live in the City; I would do anything for you, my family. I know not what to do or what to say. But I know one thing I might give." Their shrouds, bitten by the storm, had been worn to rags. Eyes watering, I tore from my shoulders the mantel of the Lion and gave it to my sister, and my husband gave his mantel over to my father without the slightest thought. They, shocked, threw on the cloaks, and were not only warmed but enlightened with the soft glow of the sun. Together they shared an expression of awe and transformed again into the soft, kind figures who first met me at Elysium. I cried to see them and kissed their faces, understanding in a way without words that the gold of their cloaks would come into them in time, leaving the fabric gray but their spirits pure and bright. Had all of this happened before? I dared not ask—not as my tearful father, for whom Elysium was again illuminated, touched my cheek, then Phobia's.

"I should have let your mother name you, the way I took her idea for Felicity. We should have named you 'Joy.'"

As my sister wept, so did I, and I kissed away her tears. My husband and I could not long appreciate the beauty of the moment, though, for we were about to turn our attention to the matter of the third man—what, after all, had we to offer him—when the man in question laughed and said, "Why, do not trouble yourselves; I have seen enough in all your trials in the Kingdom, as much as in Elysium." As he threw off his shroud, I recognized with a gasp his face, his wings, his entire beauty and way of being and the music of his presence. I knew his name, too, although that was a secret between him and me, and I fell from my husband's arms and into his to kiss his heavenly face. "Oh, my friend! I have seen you so many ways, but never have I seen you thus!"

"Never could you see me thus, but here. Hello, darling." He kissed my mouth, and then lifted his head to smile at my husband, who came to kiss him as a brother while saying, "My friend, how are you?"

"Quite well, dear King, quite well. I confess, I came in guise because I was not entirely certain dear Felicity has learned all she needed to know, but I think her ready to come into the center of Paradise. Don't you?"

"I do, indeed," said my King with a gentle laugh, jostling me. "I am sorry to have not warned you he might be coming, love, but I knew you would do right by the ways of true royalty."

I shook my laughing head, eyes level with my friend. "Is it any wonder people think you the Devil with the works you do to test the tenderness of men and women, the nobility of Kings and Queens!"

"What do you suppose I might have done had you failed?" asked my friend, beginning to lead the way with me just behind.

"You might well have been obliged to leave me here until the Prince returns to restore Paradise." With a glimpse over his shoulder, he smiled in a merry way while I tugged at the coal-black feathers of his wing. "You lout! And you," said over my shoulder, to my King, "you'd have left me, too!"

"Aye, my love," said my husband, laughing and catching my hand for a kiss, "but that's just the way of Kings."

Laughing merrily with my Lord and angel, we traversed through the writhing wild layers of the dead, ever deeper in the storm. In the second valley, all the lovers and merrymakers had transformed into succubae and incubi, men and women who deceived and preyed with sex rather than reveled and prayed with it. Not just those, but those who were their victims, and those victims who were simply victims to one another, or themselves. I not once strayed from my lover, from my angel, and they not once from me, though I knew my angel was a friend to others and, of course, my King was the King of all, like all proper Kings, and in that way naught but a vessel of his people. I knew that in love to all lovers I was ever faithful to my angel and my King, for I would always love them first, couldn't help but love them first! We kissed one another at the boundary line, first I and my angel and then I and my King, and came then into the hot ruby tornado of wrath full of pain and loathing and sorrows. The ground had overgrown with thorns and broken glass, but my angel's feet were fire which seared the earth beneath them into a perfect river of ice upon which those most hateful spirits dared not tread. This brought us to the place where we had found the Prince, the Witch and I, and I felt her stir within me, had to ask my angel for another kiss, shamefully excited by this one in such an inexplicable way that I pulled back, blushing.

"There is no Shame to be had, my girl," said the angel in gentle half jest, his mouth against my brow. "I help you bring the one into the other. I am the radiance which makes you quake in the arms of your lovers; I am the heat of the want which binds you to them, moves you through them, shapes you with them. I am the union of opposites, O Queen, O Witch, O Radiant One, and shall help you remember."

"Remember what?" I asked, but he hushed me. I dared not breathe, for the air of this valley was noxious with the sultry scent of flowers, and already I floated from but those two words I spoke. With my face against the neck of my King, I allowed myself carried through the broken dipsomaniacs crushed beneath bodies of slothful demons which sucked the very spirit of the earth through terrible proboscises. All money the gamblers had won had turned to cow's dung, and the drugs in which revelers had partaken turned to ash or poison. Before we left, I turned my head to ask a question, and instead could naught but laugh, headily, as we passed into the next valley, where once men and women made love to those of their own ilk—sodomites, as the Witch had so gaily called the Prince. Those lovers were gone. In their place were those who eschewed mutual celebration of the bodily self, of pleasure for pleasure's sake, in favor of acts cruel and uselessly depraved. These I care not to describe, for from them I cringed away and wished to blind myself but dared not, for it was the duty of royalty to see all that was horrible in the world and not know alone their cherished palace walls. These slaves to wickedness could not so much as turn sight on us. So enraptured they were by the horrors of bestial desires and youthful ruminations that they could not see the vulgarity of their acts.

"What corruption," I cried as we passed through this true prison of the mind, as I wet my husband's tunic with tears that my blurring vision might save me from the odious sights around. "What tragedy I've wrought! How could I have done a thing like this to bring forth a Prince? Was I so selfish? Have I done a thing such as bring this into the world, into Paradise?"

"Dear woman," said the gentle angel, "you created these things no more than the Witch the Forest."

"This cannot compare to the valley it was before. Had the Witch and I made love, it would not be cruel the way all this is! Had the King loved another man—ah, how the King loves you, friend! How I love you, too! See? Before, in the second valley, all those people who had together made love are deceivers and falsifiers of the same, and yet here are the three of us: me, my King, and my angel, and I kiss you both, love you both, indeed, could walk among the masses and kiss them wanton so long as I kissed them with you in my heart! Why is it right of us and wrong of them? What would we become if the corruption of Elysium came into us as it did all these? What hateful nature is implied by our unnatural ménage?"

With placid amusement, the angel glanced over his shoulder, and my laughing King spoke up behind us.

"If anything," he suggested, "we are the hateful union implied."

I frowned, not taking his meaning as we emerged where I had never been, the valley before the charred wall. This last valley, I had been told, was once a feast for the eyes and the stomach. Rich with beautiful trees and shrubs and animals of all kind, it was a bounty of food and sensory delight, but was relegated to a rotten field of obsidian dirt. In the distance gathered men who killed and ate of the flesh of other men, and as our angel guided us to their bonfire, I made protest of fear. He stopped, and turned to me, and coldly asked, "Do you trust me, my girl? Do you trust your King?"

"Of course," I said, clutching my angel's hand, heart racing. "Of course, please, I'm so sorry."

Though his expression grew no gentler, he kissed the same my brow; I was calmed, and allowed myself led to the bonfire where men and women of all savage types gathered to feast on gold flesh. We took our seats, the three of us, or so I thought, for when I released the hand of my King, my focus trained elsewhere. When I turned to see him where I expected beside me and found instead some stranger, I turned back to my angel only to find with a soft gasp his beauty gone, replaced by exquisite terror, the features of his face erased by a shifting triangle which doubled itself and formed first a diamond, then a star, a morphing figure projected glittering upon what ought to have been his face. It fell apart into the swirling immensity of a hypnotic fractal and I reached to touch him, but felt myself stopped: he had caught my hand with one of his, one of many new-grown, their number eight beneath the silken fabrics of his robes. Dreamily, I asked him, "Oh, friend, where is my lover?"

"He awaits you in the center of the storm, good girl," said my angel, who lifted his seventh hand to gently touch my chin and turn my face away from his, toward the fire. As he commanded, "Eat," I gained the impression that he was far taller than he had ever been, nine thousand feet, perhaps, and I was strangely tiny even as I took in my hand a piece of forearm flesh upon a bone which was perfectly normal-size, like mine. My hands ran along it, and I recognized the distant feeling of touching my husband's arm. Past my meal lay my lover's empty head gazing up to the smoke-thick, starless sky, yet I found myself undaunted, unmoved but for longing. I sank my teeth into the flesh of my King and gazed deep into the heart of the fire, which seemed to be inside of me the way my lover, my King, was inside of me—the way I was inside of myself. A heat filled my mouth as I ate and ate, felt the pouring of blood over my jaw beneath the eyes of my angel. As I finished, I let drop the bone to my feet and said, trembling, "My lover, friend. Where is my lover?"

"Let us go to him," said my angel, leaning around me to wipe clean my face. I inhaled softly to see his beauty had returned, the immensity of his fairness somehow so much more painful than the terror of his being when empty. His black wings were polished snowy white, but all else was normal as could be said of such a nightmare. The sizes of the world had returned to us, and I hung limply in his arms, inhaling myrrh as he lifted me to my feet and took me by the hand. He helped me walk toward the gates where howled the angriest wind of all, beating against onyx walls which towered so high they became the very clouded sky which thundered and lit itself with luminescent lightning strikes of dreadful colors so much richer than any I had seen in the Kingdom that I was left to tremble—but my angel said, "Come, only come. Be not afraid, my girl."

I, breathing sharply, placed my hand upon the black gate at his behest; the solid stones pulsed as though with the lift and fall of lungs. "What horror shall I find, my friend, upon the other side?"

But that only made him laugh, and bend his head over mine. The touch of his lips was like the kiss of peppermint suspended on a spider's web, and made me sigh with bravery enough that, in the end, it was I who pushed open the doors of my new palace to find in astonishment that on the other side lay all exquisite, rolling hills of Paradise restored to speechless glory beneath the glowing light of the perfect sun. There to laugh as I fell trembling with awe to my knees (my own knees, no less, not my knee and the Witch's knee, but mine and mine alone) were all my friends, my family, and lovers: my animals, my enemies, and Pneuma, who seemed happiest of all to see me, throwing cherry blossoms from a wicker basket upon my head to greet me. It was she who kissed me first, and pulled me to my feet to reveal behind her stood the Prince. I gasped to see him and cried, "But why!" before I marked a difference in his eyes: a wisdom that I had not seen when last I had laid eyes on him. The answer came to me even before he laughed. "Dear Felicity, if Paradise weren't eternal, it could hardly be called 'Paradise,' could it."

Trembling with laughter, I turned all around to see whence I had come, but it was as if I had emerged from swimming in a lake to surface with a collapsing gasp. There was no gate through which I had passed at all, no river of forgetting or red door beyond, but instead the sprawling Kingdom. When I turned again to try and see my angel, I found instead my King, who took me in his arms as I cried, "Why, I haven't died at all!"

"Of course not, you ridiculous woman," called the Prince from beyond my lover's shoulder.

I could only laugh into the blue eyes of my King, which glittered in mirth. "Paradise and the Kingdom," I said.

He smiled. "Yes."

"Just like the City and the Forest, like me and the Witch, and the Sea and the Land, and the Sky and the Earth. Just like—" I faltered and gazed up at him, and, trembling, laughed down at myself, and then up again, and remembered the taste of his flesh and his light in my mouth. At once, I was further back, to when I had returned to myself in that fountain, when I remembered I was Felicity. That moment returned to me because it was then I first remembered a truth so deep I had all but forgotten it when I sent the Huntress the bear. I had forgotten I was not entirely the Huntress, or Felicity, but that instead I was Matter. But, why, this was not true at all, either! Because Matter, after all, was what flesh represented, and what I saw: but the "I" which did the seeing could not be said to be Matter anymore than "I" could be said to be Huntress, or Felicity, or Queen. What "I" was, I realized with a gasp in the arms of my lover, was naught but Consciousness. Yes, Consciousness! My one, my truest lover! Why, he had been with me all this time, my sunlight, and I had never seen it because I was his mirror; because I was that Matter upon which he cast the light by which his "I" might see! By this light, the face of the King fell away, dissolving into golden rays, his head and feet and hands aflame, and I cried, "My love, my God!" as he at last held me in his arms once more, floating in space as all that was dissolved to leave us standing ankle deep in the crystal water of my lunar temple where, together, we laughed.

"Oh, sweetheart," he said, laughing, holding me to his breast, "don't cry. What's wrong?"

"I'm so sorry. I never meant to hurt you."

"You never did," he said as he laid upon my cheeks kisses I felt in a clearer way than I'd ever felt before. "I've been here this whole time."

I lowered my sobbing head against his chest. "Why didn't you say something?"

"We never stopped talking! You've never stopped seeing me," he said, "not really," and I frowned, because he stood before me, renewed, for the first in an ageless time, his hair gold and jaw powerful and eyes electric as I remembered.

"What do you mean?" I asked. With a soft smile, he laid his hand upon my cheek.

"Remember, Kitty? What we were just talking about." I, brow furrowed, frowned and tried to remember, tried to remember something we hadn't created. Gently, he said, "Remember? Cassius, and Katherine. And Enoch, and the skull. And the story."

"Yes," I said, and then, gasping, feeling the weight of the crown pressing my head, I breathed, "Oh, Cassius— Cassius, this is a story."

"Yes," he said, reading a computer screen I could barely remember, could hardly see. "It's a story, for sure. I think it was your understanding that made it. See! You didn't even need to have a seizure."

"Cassius," I gasped, the memories rushing back of where I had been, of the breakdown, of Cassius and Enoch, of the bones of horses, of a human skull. "Cassius, *this* is all just a story."

"Yes, yes," he confirmed, happy.

"Cassius," I wept, "this isn't all that there is, is there," and, "we're not really us."

"Not really."

"We're just pretending," I realized, and laughed. "All this pretending, and why?"

"For you. So I can be with you."

"With me?"

"Why else? I don't see a better reason for all of this than being here with you. But, reasons aside, everything's got to exist in the first place if it's going to not exist at some point, too."

"But, Cassius," I asked at last, afraid to be suspended on nothing but words, "can't we keep pretending awhile? That we're Cassius, and Katherine. Even once our story is over."

Like sunshine, he laughed, my face in his hands. "Of course we can, Kitty. Of course."

M.F. Sullivan is a playwright and novelist currently living in the scenic town of Ashland, Oregon. There, the author is hard at work on a new trilogy for which two books are already written, and a slew of plays not yet produced. Sullivan's interests include consciousness, language, and how the literary arts can be used to expand them both. Be sure to follow the blog at www.paintedblindpublishing.com for news, updates and the occasional free essay.

ALSO BY THE AUTHOR

Delilah, My Woman